ESTÂNCIA DEL
PÉREZ

ESTÂNCIA DEL PÉREZ

TONY BUNTS

ARPress
45 Dan Road Suite 5
Canton MA 02021

Hotline: 1(888) 821-0229
Fax: 1(508) 545-7580

Ordering Information:
Quantity sales. Special discounts are available on quantity purchases by corporations, associations, and others. For details, contact the publisher at the address above.

Printed in the United States of America.

ISBN-13:   Softcover   979-8-89389-996-2
            Hardcover   979-8-89389-997-9
            eBook   979-8-89389-995-5

Library of Congress Control Number: 2024919013

ACKNOWLEDGMENTS

I wish to extend my appreciation to Olga Pérez and the entire Pérez family, who lent me their names as characters in this book. This book in no way reflects the personalities of any person in the Pérez family, and there are additions to the family in this book that do not exist in reality. Also, there are persons in the family whose names do not appear in the book. I want them to know that I appreciate them all and am grateful to have been included in many of their family events.

I appreciated all Erica Frisby's efforts in explaining to the family my purpose in writing the book. In addition, she helped me by obtaining names and dates that were relevant to the narrative and could be joined with the storyline. In many cases, the same names are used for individuals in different generations—as occurs in many great families.

I extend my thanks to Carlos Chavez (aka Charlie Two Horse) for creating from my minimalist, articulated thoughts two drawings in the book and also the cover.

I especially want to recognize Ms. Jeanie Marie Schultz Ford (my best friend and mi amor). She tirelessly read this book and offered criticisms as well as encouragement. Her participation made this book possible. Whenever I slipped tenses, she would keep me in line. Her help was invaluable.

I extend my grateful thanks to Karen Husted for her encouragement and advice.

Thanks to Lynn Gray of Red Solar Serpent for editing this book and James O'Malley for proof reading.

Note: A list of characters can be found at the end of the book.

PROLOGUE

I t was May 1879, and Francisco Pérez Castro (Pancho to his family and friends) was facing the climax of a great achievement that started 16 years previous. He was about to walk across the stage and receive his degree at the College of New Jersey. Pancho was born and raised in Mexico during turbulent times, which made this particular day in his life even more remarkable.

His journey began when his mother, Doña María Elizabeth Baker Castro, the daughter of the British Envoy to Mexico, obtained an American tutor by the name of Benjamin Franklin White, a graduate of the College of New Jersey. Ben White was treated as part of the family, and he taught all the children on the Estancia.

The Estancia del Pérez was established in 1853 by Pancho's father, Gregorio Pérez Adame. Gregorio was the nephew of Manuela Pérez de Lebron who was the mother of Antonio López de Santa Anna, who was Presidente de Mexico at the time. He enjoyed the privileges of the Criollo class (people of primarily Spanish descent but born in the Americas) in Mexico and received a good education. At the age of 17, Gregorio joined the military as an aide to his cousin who was then President of Mexico. He quickly gained the rank of lieutenant and made himself essential to Santa Anna.

In 1835, Santa Anna abolished Congress and made himself dictator. Several states seceded, and three went as far as establishing themselves as the Republic of the Rio Grande, Republic of Yucatan, and the Republic of Texas. Santa Anna quickly put down the rebellions in the Yucatan and marched north, where he destroyed the Republic of the Rio Grande.

Gregorio, as a captain in the army of Santa Anna (known as "the Napoleon of Mexico"), was assigned as an aide to General José Urrea (whose family was from Durango and who was born at El Presidio San Augustine de Tucson). The Republic of the Rio Grande was quickly dispensed with, and the full attention of the army was directed toward the elimination of the Republic of Texas. True to his modus operandi when it came to rebellions, Santa Anna quickly took the Alamo and put everyone to the sword.

Colonel James Fannin was riding to the relief of the defenders of the Alamo when he was attacked by the army of Urrea. Gregorio was principal in leading a cavalry brigade that encircled Fannin and accepted his surrender. On Palm Sunday, Santa Anna personally ordered the massacre of Fannin and his 325 soldiers.

Gregorio was still with Urrea when Santa Anna—who attempted to keep Urrea and his army from grabbing more glory—led his depleted army into a trap at San Jacinto.

Urrea regaled the young captain with stories of the high valleys of Northern Sonora and Chihuahua. His stories of the majestic mountains, grassy plains, and the Sonoran desert made Gregorio yearn for the adventure and the establishment of his own small empire in that area.

Gregorio spent several years under the tutelage of Urrea and, by the time of the Mexican/American War and ascension of his cousin to control of the army and the government, he had become a colonel. As the war began, Gregorio was put in charge of the defense of a large area that spanned the present municipality of Janos west to the present municipality of Altar and to the south over the mountains and foothills of the northern portion of the Sierra Madre Occidental.

In 1852, for Gregorio's service, Santa Anna granted him the lands that started on the eastern side of the Portillo Mountains, which are located directly west of what is presently Mesilla in New Mexico and west to where the Santa Cruz River flows south out of the San Raphael Valley in Arizona. The land was bounded on the north by the United

States border on the Rio Bravo, which was established by the Treaty of Guadalupe Hidalgo as just south of the village of Doña Ana in what is present-day New Mexico. On the south, the border of the grant was established just north of Janos, Chihuahua. (The reader is referred to the map on the next page.)

Santa Anna began negotiating with the United States on the setting of the Northern boundary. The Americans felt the southern boundary of New Mexico should be just south of La Mesilla, and there were factions in the government that wanted to buy more of northern Mexico to establish a southern route for a continental railroad. In addition, private interests were pushing for the purchase of Baja California, where large American companies had mining interests.

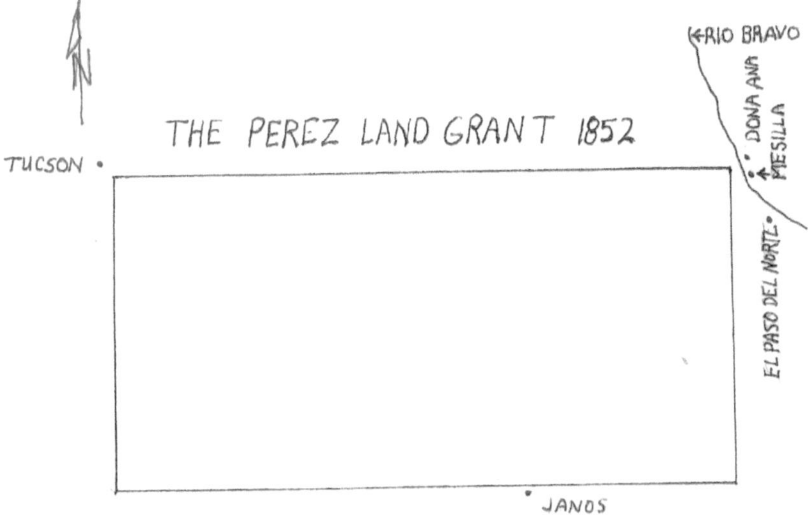

The Gadsden Purchase Treaty was signed by Santa Anna on June 8, 1854 and, as a result, the Pérez Land Grant was reduced in size, because the land grant would not be recognized by either government above the Mexican border.

THE PEREZ LAND GRANT 1854

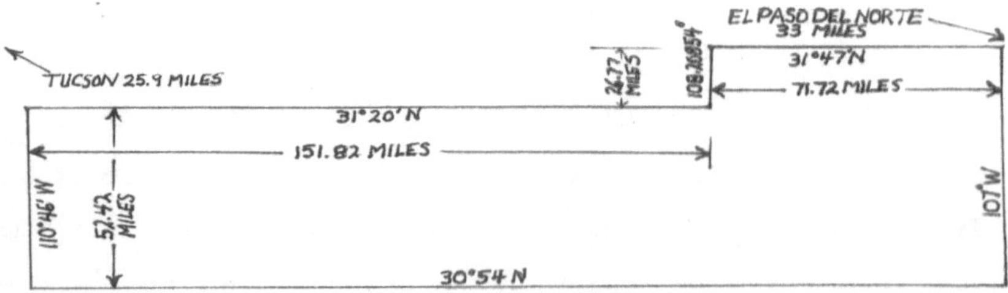

The Estância Del Pérez was the largest grant of land in Mexico at 13,648 square miles, but Santa Anna felt that Gregorio was a fool to gleefully accept a grant in such an arid land, certain that it was of very low value.

Gregorio moved to his Estancia in 1853. He built his first home northeast of Janos on the edge of the great grasslands, which still supported herds of buffalo that migrated south to the short grass prairie in the winter and north to the southern plains to sustain the Comanche, Kiowa, and Apache in the Spring. He stocked his ranch with breeding stock purchased from ranches in Mexico and from a Prussian drover by the name of Carlos Deus who was acquiring cattle in east Texas from the Prussian settlers in that area and driving them east to El Paso del Norte and then north to Taos and into the San Juan Valley of Colorado.

It became apparent to Gregorio that he could not manage such a vast ranch from a single headquarters on the eastern border, and he began to build a second headquarters on the western border of the ranch along the upper reaches of the San Pedro River.

The two divisions of the ranch came under the single name of Estancia del Pérez, and each division was distinguished by its location as Hacienda Oriental (the east branch) and Hacienda Occidental (the west branch).

Janos had been the northern military post that supported not only El Paso del Norte and Santa Fe but the entire northern domain of the Spanish empire in the Americas. The main problem for the Spanish was the depredations of the indigenous people during the first several hundred years of their occupation, so Janos became the main meeting place of the southern plains Indians and the mountain Indians of the Sierra Madre de Occidental. Many treaties were signed at Janos, and Janos became the gathering place for the tribes to deal with the Spanish and later the Mexicans.

The Spanish, through their treaties and the wise investment of soldiers, made it possible for both the settlers and the Indians to prosper. Janos became not only the military headquarters but a great trade center with the various tribes, just as Taos was in the north. The Spanish were also jealous of their domain and zealous in their defense of it against the intrusion by the Americans.

After the Mexican independence, Janos began to wane in importance. The Mexican government failed to maintain and stock its outposts. Military power was concentrated in the major cities and was used to control the populace and obtain power by both federal and state leaders. The protection for the towns and villages was moved to the cities, and all maintenance for the tribes was withdrawn. In the north, the Navajo began to commit depredations on whole communities by raiding their crops, animals, and children. The plains Indians, no longer sensing any strong government in the area, started helping themselves to horses. In the territories, first local and later federal leaders began to offer money for the scalps of Apaches. In the Piños Altos area of what is now New Mexico; some American trappers laid a trap and killed the wife and several children of Mangos Coloradans, the principle chief of the Mimbreño Apaches). Cochise, leader of the Chiricahua Apaches, and Victorio, leader of the Mescalero Apaches—who were both sons-in-law of Mangas Coloradas—along with most of the chiefs of the clans, declared war on the Mexicans. They were soon joined by the Utes and Comanche in raiding and hating the Mexicans.

At the beginning of the Mexican-American War, Kit Carson, Carlos Deus, and the Bent brothers negotiated with the Apaches a free and safe passage for as long as the United States was fighting the Mexicans. During this time, Gregorio was assigned the defense of the northwestern part of Chihuahua and northern Sonora, which was the heart of Apacheria (Apache lands). Although the governments of Chihuahua and Sonora continued to pay for scalps, Gregorio let it be known that if any of his patrols or solders caught individuals with scalps, they were to be hung where they were caught. This edict impressed the Apache, who never had a tradition of scalp-taking. Although the Apache and the state governments did not cease their warfare, both respected the authority and fair dealing of Gregorio and his troops.

When Gregorio left the army to create the Estancia del Pérez, many of the soldiers that he commanded went with him to live on the ranch. Chiefly among the men that joined Gregorio was Sargento Primero Roman Cesar Ochoa, who had been by Gregorio's side since his excursion into Texas with Urrea. Most of the soldiers in the army were mestizos (those of mixed white and indigenous blood) and many were Indios looking to achieve warrior status. These men represented many tribes including Mayan, Azteca, and Tarahumara. So, when Gregorio began to establish the Estancia del Pérez, he was well known to the Apache as a straight man and a friend of all people.

As was done by the leaders of Janos in the two preceding centuries, Gregorio welcomed all the tribes as peaceful compatriots to his Haciendas. He let it be known he wanted no one to cross or leave the ranch hungry and, if anyone needed to kill a beef to feed his family, all he requested was that they leave an arrow with a patch of hide in a tree so that all would know that a friend and not a thief had passed. Unlike the miners and villagers around the ranch, the people of the ranch lived at peace with the Apache and the Comanche.

The major threats to the ranch were its neighbors to the north. As the Americans moved into southern New Mexico and Arizona after the Gadsden Purchase, they began to stock their ranches with beef they had stolen from the Mexicans. It became a secret honorable trade to steal from the Mexicans—as though it was not really stealing.

By the year 1855, Gregorio had finished the building of his ranch and made a trip to Mexico City to court the woman that had attracted his fancy even as a young girl. At the age of 18 years old, María Elizabeth Baker Castro married Gregorio. Her father had passed away and, when Gregorio brought María home, they were accompanied by her mother, a niñera (nanny, Juanita García), and the household staff including the majordomo (butler, Edward Honeywell), and one mucama (maid, the wife of Edward, Juliana). The rest of the household staff included the chef—Gregorio's former mess sergeant, Pedro Gonzáles—and some of the wives of vaqueros who worked near the Haciendas.

On February 13, 1856, Consuela Angélica Pérez Castro was born to Gregorio and María, and her birth officially made the Hacienda a home. Angélica was followed by Francisco, Dulce, Roman, Roberto, Elizabeth, and Javier through the years.

Francisco Pérez Castro (Pancho) was born as the heir apparent on February 12, 1857. He was taught from the beginning that it was his job to take care of the family. He grew up knowing that he had special obligations, but that *he* was not special. His constant companions were Corporal, the son of Sargento Primero; Juan, the son of Pedro Gonzáles; Eduardo, the son of the butler, plus visitors of his own age, of which many were Apache boys. They had a kingdom to explore and were about their business.

By the time he was seven, Francisco had explored the ruins of Casas Grande and many of the mountains of northern Chihuahua and Sonora that were either on or bordered the ranch. He was given his first bow by the great chief Victorio, and he spent many a summer's night in the camps of the Chiricahua Apache. He lost riding contests to Comanche boys who seemed to be born to the horse and became part of one at birth. He also learned from both the Mexican and Indian men that he was nothing special—just a boy that could find his fair share of trouble and grief.

The boys' fall and winter explorations were restricted by the teachings and absolute discipline that were administered by Ben White. No child of the Estancia del Pérez could escape the tutelage and terrorizing gaze of Señor Blanco (Mister White). Their evenings were filled with learning the skills of a vaquero, which included not only the proper care of their mounts but the chores that came with the privilege of having the use of a horse. Plus, they had the duties of milking stock and gathering eggs. They all learned early that hoes seemed to naturally fit their hands, and the search for palos para la estufa (sticks for the stove) was their constant chore.

Sargento Primero began early giving them military instruction, which included discipline in the ranks and the proper care and use of weapons. They were all very sure that Sargento had spies that watched them constantly for infractions, and he was not sparing in his discipline.

In 1855, a revolt by Liberals resulted in the overthrow of the government of Santa Anna. Ignacio Comonfort became the President of Mexico, and his co-conspirator, Benito Juárez, became the President of the Supreme Court. The Constitution of 1857 was ratified and immediately became the source of conflict between the Liberals and the Conservatives. The Church was not allowed to own tax-free, economic land or to exact tithing as a tax. The Church's stranglehold on education was removed, and universal education was declared. For the first time, the illiterate were considered equal citizens of Mexico. Also, freedom of religion was declared, and the Catholic Church was no longer in charge of the souls of Mexico.

The Catholic Church, along with the Conservatives, fomented a revolt. General Zuloaga led the Conservative forces into Mexico City. On January 15, 1858, Ignacio Comonfort resigned. The Constitution of

1857 provided that the President of the Supreme Court was to complete the term of the President of Mexico if he was unable or unwilling to perform his duties, and Benito Juárez became the Liberal President of Mexico. On January 21, 1858, the Conservatives named General Zuloaga as the Conservative President of Mexico, and the civil war know as the Guerra de Reforma began. Juárez was re-elected President in 1867 and 1871. He died on July 18, 1872.

The Estancia del Pérez was greatly affected by the national upheaval. Many of the young men of the ranch joined Juárez in El Paso del Norte and at Chihuahua, just as their fathers had joined to defend their country earlier. Gregorio attempted to stay out of the politics of the time, but his help was needed, so he provided meat and grain to the government in exile.

Juárez, in a meeting with Gregorio, thanked him for his service to the revolution and then told him there was great pressure to nationalize the haciendas. He went on to explain that, in many cases, this was already being done. However, he believed this would not happen to the Estancia del Pérez, because it was situated in a rural area and had no conflict with the people or the government of Mexico. Yet, there was one problem that Gregorio needed to address to head off any conflict in the future, and that was the settlements of Ascención and Janos. At that time, they either were or soon would be encroaching on the ranch. He stated to Juárez, "So far, you have not addressed this encroachment by removing the settlers. In the minds of the settlers, there will always be a worry that you or your heirs may remove them after they have improved on the land. It would be best if you eased their minds." Gregorio took it upon himself to create the Ascención-Janos Ajuste (Ascención-Janos adjustment) on September 16, 1865, wherein he deeded the Ascención municipality an area of 36.6853 square miles, thus leaving it up to the government to give the settlers deed to their properties.

After Juárez's death, Mexico still suffered from political turmoil and, in November 1876, Porfirio Díaz seized power in a coup. For the next 35 years, an environment of political stability helped the Pérez family to succeed.

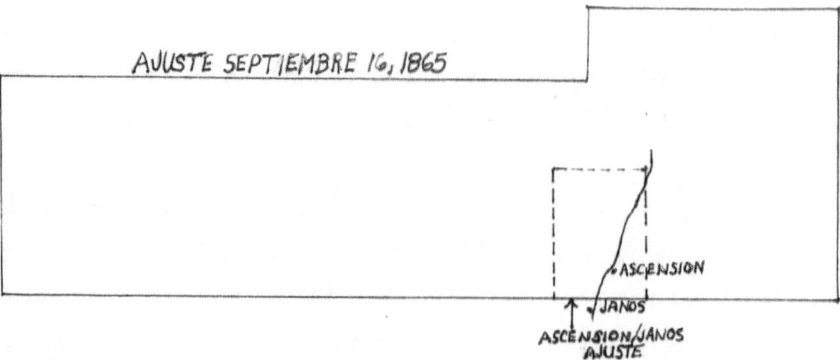

The following are the recollections of Don Francisco Pérez Castro as told to his children and family in the year 1901.

CHAPTER 1

I, Francisco, am the eldest son of Don Gregorio Pérez Adame and María Elizabeth Baker Castro. It was only 26 years ago that I showed up on the campus of The College of New Jersey in Princeton, New Jersey as a wild Mexican Indian, educated to be sure, but socially a wild man compared to my classmates.

Mother had made all her arrangements through agents in El Paso del Norte. By 1875, the postal service, through which mail was delivered by coach, was reliable, and Hacienda Oriental was within an easy, two-days' ride for a good dispatch rider.

Our trip to Princeton, New Jersey, was directly governed by Mother's and Dulce's comfort. Our entourage consisted of Mother (Doña María), Dulce, Panchita Honeywell (the daughter of the butler and his wife, Juliana); Corporal Juan Cortez (a fearsome man) was assigned as a bodyguard and driver for my mother and the company. We had a seven-day ride by coach from Hacienda Occidental to Guaymas. We stayed at haciendas along the way, enjoying the comforts of home on the great ranchos that rested against the western flanks of the Sierra de Madre Occidental. In Guaymas, we took a packet boat around Baja de California and up the coast of California to San Francisco. From San Francisco, we took the new intercontinental railroad to Omaha, Nebraska, and made connections on to New Jersey.

We arrived in Princeton on August 16, 1875 via the Penn Central Railroad. We had traveled for seven weeks and, in all that time, I had not been on a horse. I was going through shock, because I could not recall a single day in my life that I had not been on a horse.

My mother had hired agents to find me a place to live near the campus. I was anxious to be the master of my own home and was surprised to meet the staff of the house when we arrived. My mother, through her social contacts, had hired a middle-aged couple, the Ochoas, to manage the home and report to her. The plans I had envisioned were severely curtailed.

The property consisted of a large home with six bedrooms, a foyer, kitchen, dining room, library, and sitting room. This was the new headquarters of the Estancia del Pérez del Norte. Mother informed me which rooms would be hers and those of her traveling companions when she came to visit.

On September 7, 1875, Mother, Dulce, Panchita, and Juan left me to the tender mercies of the Ochoas. They headed for a shopping trip to New York City before they took a ship to Veracruz. From there, they proceeded to Mexico City, where Mother had planned stops and where Dulce and Panchita caused many broken hearts.

After my mother and the others left, the number of callers—mostly classmates—who'd sent me greetings from the University diminished to a trickle.

Classes began, and I threw myself into the business of being a student. My father's last words to me were, "For a Pérez, failure is not an option." Although I had learned English at the hands of Señor Blanco, it was not my first language. While at the University, it was to be my only language, and the Ochoas obeyed my mother's instructions, which were to converse with me only in English.

My being the heir apparent had many responsibilities, and one was to never show weakness. I so missed my family and the rancho. My father had given me an order to send news by letters at least once a month. I would send my father a packet by mail to El Paso del Norte, where the postmaster would hold it for pickup by someone from the rancho. From there, it would go to Hacienda Oriental, and each envelope would be forwarded to Hacienda Occidental as was required. The packet consisted of many letters. The letter to my father was first and foremost, as the packet was addressed to him. I also included letters for my mother, each of my siblings, a single letter to my compañeros (companions—Corporal, Juan, and Eduardo), a letter to Ben White, and a letter to Edward and Juliana Honeywell. Most of my letters were in Spanish. Writing in my native language was my escape into home.

The house in Princeton was large, but it was seldom empty. I received visitors from haciendas near ours in Mexico. Fellow students found our house to be a welcome respite from their cramped quarters, and many a lively study session was held there. Mother would make annual visits with Dulce or Elizabeth and Panchita. These young women would draw the immediate attention of my classmates, but their conduct was entirely proper under Juan's relentless glare.

On occasion, when the University had a function that drew the families of its students, the available accommodations were quickly taxed. Families of my classmates stayed with me, and I stayed in their homes on holidays and breaks. Often, when new students arrived, there was a time before they could find adequate accommodations, and they, too, were welcomed. There were many noteworthy classmates that availed themselves of the Pérez hospitality, and my life was greatly enriched by their friendships.

I single out one who remained my friend and confident throughout my life. He was Woodrow (Woody) Wilson. Woody transferred to the University in our sophomore year, and he stayed with me for about a month until he found adequate accommodations. By his senior year, Woody had become the class president.

My brother, Roman, started school in my junior year, and Roberto joined us in my senior year. My graduation ceremony was a Pérez party.

Mother had been joined by Elizabeth and María on her trip north, and the house was full of family and friends.

I received my degree on May 15, 1879 to great fanfare, and my mother gave Princeton, New Jersey, a taste of a Mexican fiesta. We had a pit-roasted steer plus all the delicious dishes of Mexico I had so yearned for. For the rest of my life, I never ceased to hear from my classmates about that unforgettable party. Many came to the Estancia del Pérez through the years to partake of the fiestas that were given in honor of their visits.

By the first of June, we all left for New York, where Mother and my sisters wanted to take in the opera and plays as well as shop for the latest styles. Juan stayed with the women. Roman (who had decided he'd had enough of higher education after two years) and I took in the nightclubs.

With Mother and the girls along, the trip home was slow, and we had so much to see. I only wanted to see two things—my father and the ranch. We sailed to Veracruz and then went by coach to Ciudad Mexico. We arrived in the city of Chihuahua on July 20, 1879, a day I will remember for the rest of my life. Once we got settled in the hotel, Roman and I went down to the bar.

CHAPTER 2

As we entered the bar, Roman and I spotted Juan Gonzáles sitting with a gentleman who looked official. As we rushed to embrace Juan, he rose up out of his chair, took his hat off, and said solemnly, "Don Francisco, I have news."

His news was already known. During our lives growing up, I had always been called Pancho, and now it was Don Francisco.

I held up my hand to stop him. I ordered beer for all of us, and then I asked, "How could this be? Papa is 62 years old, still in good health, and rides every day."

Juan shook his head in despair and introduced me to the gentleman sitting with him—Capitán Alfredo Carrillo of the Rurales (rural police)—and Juan begged permission to let the Capitán tell of the circumstances of my father's death.

The Capitán began with, "Don Francisco, it is with the greatest grief and shame that I must report to you the death of your father, Don Gregorio, and his companions. I was riding with Comandante Francisco Neri and a large detachment of Rurales to the east of Hacienda Occidental. Near the Campo San Bernardino, we encountered a rider from the Campo that was taking news to the Hacienda. There had been a raid on Campo San Bernardino by gringos and Mexicans. Many horses were stolen as well as a large herd of cattle. Don Gregorio had been at Campo Bonito when he got the news and had hurried to Campo

San Bernardino. He was preparing to ride and was calling in vaqueros (ranch hands) from Campo Guadalupe.

"Comandante Neri spoke to Don Gregorio and offered to put 10 Rurales and myself in the service of Don Gregorio. We were to leave immediately. Don Gregorio accepted the offer and told Sargento Primero to hold the vaqueros at the campo and await further orders."

Juan interrupted, "Con su permiso (With your permission), Capitán. Sargento Primero turned to Corporal and asked him if he had heard the orders. He indicated that he had, and Sargento told the patrón (the boss, Francisco's father) that his place was beside him. Eduardo also said, 'He goes with the patrón.' The patrón, Sargento, and Eduardo left with the Rurales."

Capitán Carrillo went on with his report. "We trailed the banditos to the border and, after consulting with Don Gregorio, we proceeded. The orders from Comandante Neri were to capture or kill the rustlers. We followed a clear trail straight through the Valle de San Bernardino to the headwaters of the Rio Batepito. We continued to follow the trail, which stayed to the west of the craters. It turned east just north of the craters and headed straight toward the Paseo Bonita (Pretty Way— also known as Skeleton Canyon, which extends from New Mexico to Arizona). As we were passing through the narrow canyon near the Camas Blancas (White Beds), suddenly shots rang out and tu padre (your father) fell immediately as did Eduardo and several Rurales. The rest of us ran for cover. We were under a lot of fire from higher ground. Sargento went immediately to the aide of the patrón, and he was shot. I and two Rurales were at the rear of the column. We escaped, but one of them was seriously wounded. I retreated down the valley and sent the unwounded Rurale for help while I attended the wounded one.

"The next morning, I was startled to see the Rurale coming back with eleven vaqueros. Evidently, Corporal had secured the Campo and had gathered some vaqueros together to follow at a distance to help if the herds were retrieved. Leaving the two Rurales, Corporal and I rode with the vaqueros for Paso Bonito. We found it deserted but for the dead. Two of the Rurales were hanging from a tree by their shoulders and their entrails had been pulled out of their bodies. I consulted with Corporal, and we decided we should immediately take the bodies to Hacienda Oriental. Corporal sent Pablo Yanez with another vaquero back to the two Rurales, and it was their task to help the healthy Rurale rig a litter between two horses so the wounded Rurale could be transported to the Campo San Bernardino where he could be cared for. Once this was done, Pablo was to ride to Campo San Luis, tell the jefe (chief, boss) of the campo what had occurred, and have fresh horses and supplies brought to us between the Hachitas Grandes and the Alamos Huecos Mountains.

"We buried the eight Rurales that were killed near the Camas Blancas and prepared the bodies of the patrón, Sargento, and Eduardo for their journey home. We continued through the canyon to the Animas Valley. We passed through a narrow valley near the Animas Mountains into the valley of the Laguna Playas and crossed between the Hachitas Grandes and the Alamos Huecos. Here we met Running Bear and 11 older vaqueros that had ridden with your father in the army. They had brought extra mounts and provisions. Running Bear immediately dismissed the vaqueros that were accompanying us, and he and his men joined Corporal and me on the final journey.

"Running Bear had been at the Campo San Luis when Pablo rode in. He sent fast messengers to Don José to give him the news and provide him with our route to the Hacienda. He ordered them to take two vaqueros and remounts and ride to help bring in the wounded vaquero. Then he gathered older vaqueros who had ridden with Don Gregorio, and they rode to join us in escorting Don Gregorio home. We had just rounded the southern end of the Hatchet Mountains and were approaching the great playa when we met Don José and Señor Honeywell, who were escorting the finest coach at the Estancia. Don Gregorio, Sargento, and Eduardo were transferred to the coach and we accompanied them to Estancia Oriental."

Carrillo paused. "Don Francisco, I admit to my shame in this tragedy. I should not have left the battle to go for help."

"Capitán, you must feel no shame," I replied. "You saved yourself and the lives of two of your men, you recovered the bodies, and you lived to report the deed so retribution can be accomplished."

I looked at Juan, and he continued the story. "Don Francisco, when we arrived at the Estancia, Señor Honeywell and Juliana took charge of the bodies of the patrón, Sargento Primero, and the butler's son, Eduardo, and they prepared them for burial. Señor Blanco demanded the story, which he wrote down and sent as a report to the Presidente de los Estados Unidos, Chester Arthur, with whom he had been acquainted when he was young.

Corporal immediately sent vaqueros to all the border towns and places where outlaws might gather. Their job was to find small jobs and listen for information about the herd and who stole it. Salvador, the brother of Eduardo, was sent to Tombstone, and he picked up a job cleaning at Big Nose Kate's saloon. The first night he was there, he listened while a drunk member of a gang called the Cowboys by the name of Johnny Ringo recited the ambush to the crowd and named all of the participants—Old Man Clanton, Ike Clanton, Billy Clanton, Curly Bill Brocius, Florentino Cruz, brothers Frank and Tom McLaury, Jim Hughes, Rattlesnake Bill, Joe Hill, Charlie Snow, Jake Gauge, and Charlie Thomas. He bragged that he got the old don with his first shot and then killed the old vaquero that came to his aid. He recited how Old Man Clayton told them to hang the Rurales by their shoulders in a tree and all watched as Florentino Cruz slit their bellies and pulled their intestines to the ground."

My heart was sick after hearing all this, but I gathered my thoughts and told the Capitán and Juan we knew who we wanted, and we knew enough to plan how to find them. "But, now is time for the living, and we must take care of that." Roman and I left to tell our mother and sisters the news.

Our lives had changed, but we were the family of Gregorio and we must show that we were in control. The hotel sent for dressmakers, and mourning clothes were ordered not only for the women here but those that waited at the Estancia. The carriage from the Estancia arrived that same day, and Juan was engaged in acquiring another so that some seamstresses could be transported to the Estancia to fit all the women who would be going into mourning.

As I went to bed that night, I began to reflect on my father. My whole life up to this moment had been guided by the preparation for this day. In my last visit with my father, he was reflective and gave me a vision as to the future of the Estancia. He stated, "My son, you will inherit an awesome responsibility. You will have the responsibility of caring for a large rancho and the family. You will find that your family is now all the people that live on the rancho. They will look to you to wisely guide the affairs of the rancho so their lives will be stable. That will not be a simple task. The environment that you must do this in is rife with political dangers. We still are a country of classes and, despite the revolution between the Conservatives and the Liberals, the conservatives did not learn a thing.

"I feel that Porfirio Díaz is going to weave a path through the classes. He is going to bring Mexico into the modern world, and both the Conservatives and the Liberals are going to resent the share the others will enjoy. The problem is that the Conservatives will resort to privilege and, as time goes by, they will subscribe to the theory that whatever is good for them will be good for the peons. The peons will feel that they should, by right, have the privileges of the Conservatives.

"On this rancho, the vaqueros and their families have always been partners in its success, and you must continue that. As always, we are receiving pressure from those who feel they have a right to take what is ours. I have followed a path that seeks to make it very costly for them. I want them to feel it is futile to try to take anything and to know that if they harm any person on the rancho, they will feel retribution swiftly and of like kind. The death of any vaquero or his family will be treated as the death of a family member, and retribution will be swift. The welfare of all the peoples of the rancho must always be primary, my son, but never seek retribution until you have overwhelming forces and there is minimal danger to the people of the rancho. Never allow the retribution to endanger the political wellbeing of the rancho."

Roman and I left for the Estancia immediately, and the women were to travel under the care of Juan Cortez and Juan Gonzáles. Capitán Carrillo followed with a squad of Rurales, so we had no fear for the women.

NORTE

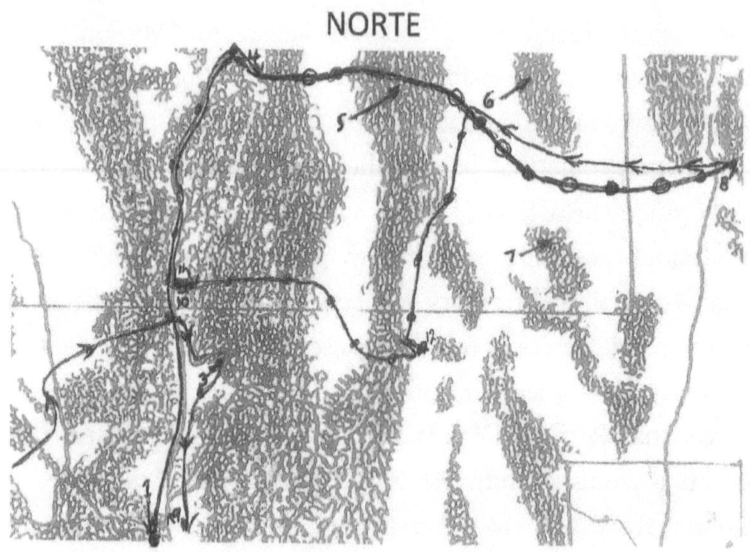

1. Campo Bonito
2. Campo San Bernardino
3. Campo Guadalupe
4. Paseo Bonita
5. Sierra Animas
6. Sierra Hachita
7. Alamo Hueco
8. Hacienda Oriental
9. Rio Batepito River & Valley
10. San Bernardino Valley
11. Guadalupe Canyon
12. Campo San Luis

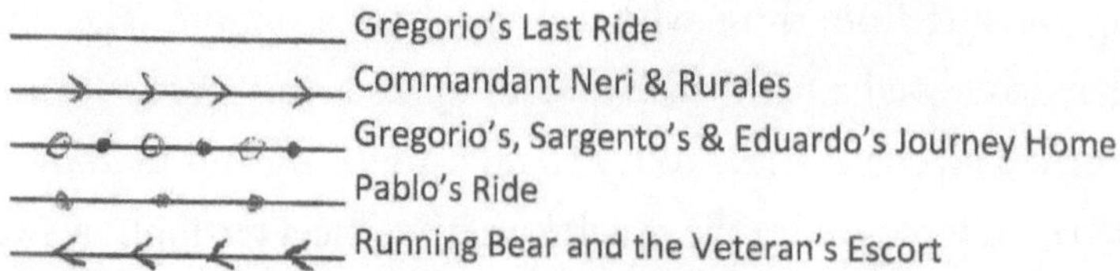

CHAPTER 3

It was August 1, 1879, and I was about the business of the ranchero. José Gallego, who married my sister, Angélica, had been put in care of the business of Hacienda Oriental by my father. I felt there was no need to disturb what had been working well. José agreed to stay on in that capacity and I felt free to move on to Hacienda Occidental.

That evening, Roman and I spent time in solitude with our mother and told her we must move on in the morning. Mother looked at us before we left and said, "Tu padre kept his family first and the rancho second in his mind at all times. It is your job to continue that, Francisco. After you have secured the family and the rancho, come to me. I would like to know your vision for the people of the Estancia after you know the people of this rancho are safe and we have the freedom of our own land."

We left before dawn. Trading horses at the campos along the way, we arrived at Hacienda Occidental late in the evening on August 4, 1879. In the morning, we met Corporal for breakfast and received a report from him as to the condition of the rancho and the disposition of the individuals he had sent out to gather information about Paseo Bonito. I thanked Corporal for his help and ordered him to go home to his mother and wife to properly mourn Sargento Primero, whom we would never be able to replace. I also informed him that Roman would be the manager of Hacienda Occidental and he, Corporal, would be replacing his father as the top vaquero on the rancho and would be answerable only to me.

During the next two weeks, I spent my time riding with Roman to all the outlying camps. The vaqueros saw with their own eyes that I was in charge and that Roman would be the one to whom they answered regarding the running of Hacienda Occidental. They were also apprised that Corporal would be the primero, and his words come from me. Juan Gonzáles arrived with horses and a herd of cows and bulls that José had sent from Oriental to help restock the range.

On their way back from delivering stock to one of the camps, Juan was hailed by He Who Hunts, a member of the Chihenne band of the Chiricahua Apache, which was led by Kas-tziden, often called by his Spanish name, Nana. He Who Hunts spent many nights at the Haciendas, and Juan, Corporal, and I spent many summers learning the skills of the mountains and desert from the elders of the Chihenne band when we were boys.

Juan and He Who Hunts showed up at our table that evening. In the true Apache fashion of never saying the name of the dead, He Who Hunts told of his grief over the loss of the noble one, and that the whole band grieved. He wondered what changes would be made in the relationship of the rancho to the People (his word for his band). I told He Who Hunts that I wanted to speak to the council of any gathering of bands that might happen in the near future.

He Who Hunts answered, "My brother, Kas-tziden, has sent me to request that you meet with Juh, Goyathlay (Geronimo), Bidu-ya (Victorio), Jlin-tay-i-tith (Loco), and himself at the rise of the river in the Patagonia, in two suns from this time." I immediately agreed to the council. The next morning, Juan and I happily joined He Who Hunts in what was a journey home.

We arrived at the gathering of the clans on the Patagonia. Our arrival was greeted with great fanfare by the camps. He Who Hunts took us directly to Nana, who greeted us and begged us to sit with him.

We told him it was our wish to do so, but we had responsibilities first to those who raised us.

We first paid our respects to the women who had fed us and disciplined us in the ways of the Apache those many years before. Our solicitations were greeted with giggles and the swish of a crop in our direction. We came back to sit with Nana, who had been joined by the other chiefs of the gathered clans. As is proper in these councils, no one spoke initially, and the women brought bowls and began to fill them with food. No Apache would think to hold council if he had not eaten with those he was in council with. Nana, as usual, held no expression that indicated his thoughts, but a slight smile appeared when he saw that the women had given us slightly larger bowls.

After proper burping and the smoking of the pipe, it was time to begin. Nana, who had requested we come and had been told by He Who Hunts that I wanted to talk to them, looked at me.

I rose and began. "My fathers, I come as the successor to he who has passed. It was he and you that made me the man I am. I could not in any way ever change anything that you had agreed to before with him and would never dishonor my fathers by suggesting that I am wiser than the wise councils that have gone before me.

"I am consumed with the desire to seek out the killers and to give them a proper answer to the deeds they have done. I know you would do this for me, because he was a brother to you, but I request of you that you leave that sweet deed in my hands. I would not turn down any help you could provide by letting me know of the passing of these dead ones or detaining them until I can meet them. This, I humbly request. If you would permit me, there are two vaqueros not far from here who are bringing 10 fat steers so we can have a celebration in honor of he who has passed and we who are still here."

Victorio rose as I sat down and said, "My son, the bow hunter, has turned into a warrior chief, and it is my wish that my brothers heed his request. My blood boils for revenge on those who caused our brother to pass, but our son's need is more than mine." He took his seat.

Nana rose and said, "I am glad the people need not hide or fight enemies on this land that we share with our son. I will heed his request."

There was assent around the circle, and the pipe was passed again before we departed.

As Geronimo walked by me, he said in Spanish, "Not a bad speech for a Mexican, my nephew."

Early the next evening, we sat in council again as Tiswin (Apache corn liquor) was passed around, and everyone took a sip or a full drink, however they felt. I found the liquor only suitable for sipping. At dark, the women brought great chunks of roasted beef that they placed before us. Each of us took out our knife and ate as the Tiswin continued to circle the council. After a proper time, Nana gave a loud burp and got up and left. Juan and I did the same, as we were leaving early in the morning.

CHAPTER 4

The weight of the Estancia was beginning to settle on my shoulders. For the first time in my life, my dreams were not of pleasant or unpleasant things. A dream catcher would not help. I slept with the problems of the rancho and my family. I needed to talk to my mother.

We rode from the council to Hacienda Occidental in the morning. He Who Hunts rode with us. As we approached the Hacienda, we embraced, wished each other good hunting, and parted.

I sat down with Roman the next day and received his report as to the disposition of the cattle. I gave him orders to chart all the springs on the lands of the Hacienda and look at the possibility of building dirt tanks so the cattle could be distributed evenly across the rancho. In this way, we could begin to rest certain areas by fencing them off from grazing so we would have reserves of grass. Roman had taken husbandry classes, and he understood that I would like to conserve the range and not have the marketing of our beef subject to the weather. This would also help us to know exactly where our stock was at any time and be able to detect rustling even on a small scale, whether it was by Americans or the inhabitants of the small villages that bordered the rancho.

Our father had always been interested in the exploitation of minerals found on the rancho or elsewhere, and I charged Roman with the task of directing the vaqueros to note any strange outcroppings so they could be charted and explored. The vaqueros were to share in any profit from their discoveries.

We discussed the experience of our meeting with the fathers and their assent to let us seek our revenge. Roman was to pass on to me any sightings of any of these individuals by either the Apaches or the vaqueros, who were tasked with observation in Tombstone or elsewhere. If the opportunity arose, it was his task to detain them on the rancho until I could arrive. I realized that detaining them while alive may not be possible, but I insisted that, with Johnny Ringo, alive was the only option.

Juan and I left the next morning for Hacienda Oriental. We rode the ranges looking at the stock and meeting with the vaqueros along the way. My father and Sargento Primero had schooled us to understand that the vaquero is the life of the ranch. His wise observations are what, in the end, a patrón must rely on, so it was always wise to let the vaquero know he was relied on. In this way, he gains ownership of his home and work.

Our trip back took us six days, and we arrived with a wealth of knowledge about the availability of graze and water. We learned a great deal about the small-time rustling that was going on in the south near Ascención and Janos. Gringos had been spotted coming down from the Mimbres Valley, where there was a gang of rustlers that had a ranch nestled in the valley between the Little Floridas and the Big Floridas. It appeared they were observing the conditions of the herds and the movements of the vaqueros.

It was autumn, which is the traditional time for roundup. We would be gathering steers for market, so we would not have to winter them. Small herds would be gathered all over the ranges and brought closer to the Haciendas and then on to market. Our markets in the past had been Tucson, El Paso, Chihuahua, and Sonora. On occasion, our friend, Carlos Deus, would take a herd north to Albuquerque, Santa Fe, or Denver as well as to the military outposts along the way. Nothing would change this time, but the Southern Pacific was building rail from

California to El Paso, and it was about six months out from reaching Tucson. The Texas Pacific was building rail from Marshall, Texas to San Diego, California. The Atchison Topeka and Santa Fe (AT&SF) had reached the middle of Raton Pass in 1878 and was building rail south in hopes of reaching El Paso before the Southern Pacific. Rails were being constructed to Nogales from Guaymas by the Sonoran Railway Company, a subsidiary of the Santa Fe. That rail would eventually meet up with the Southern Pacific track at a town on the San Pedro River called Benson.

We were being thrown into the modern world, and I was beginning to appreciate the foresight of my mother and father. They knew that to survive and guide the rancho into the 20th century, their children would need all the educational tools they could acquire. I must be vigilant and steadfast in seeing that my brothers, sisters, and the children of the rancho received all the education I could make available to them. I had much to discuss with my mother.

When I first saw my mother, sisters, and the other women on the rancho, I was shocked by the solemnity of full mourning. Custom was that the surviving spouse be in full mourning for a year and a day and half mourning for six months and a day. Children were to remain in mourning for six months and grandchildren for three months. When Juan and I arrived, we were surrounded by black. Mother had some black suits hanging in the closet, and I dressed in black. This was the first time I had ever seen my mother without her beautiful jewelry.

In the afternoon, I went into my mother's sitting room, and she greeted me with a hug and an order: "Tell me everything."

I began by reciting our encounter with Juan Gonzáles and Capitán Alfredo Carrillo. We discussed the actions of Corporal, who had come upon the bodies of my father and his father and still had the foresight to dispatch spies into the haunts of criminals. I told her of my meeting with the Apache chiefs and their wish to continue with life as it had been.

Mother interrupted with, "I wish to know how you plan to avenge your father and, at the same time, be the head of the family and guide the rancho through the perils your father knew were coming."

I answered, "It is hard for me not to just gather all of the vaqueros on the rancho and go attack the killers. My father taught me to use overwhelming force and attack when we have the advantage to succeed in our goal with minimal losses. Corporal learned the same thing from Sargento. He sent spies to assimilate into the society of Tombstone, so we would gain knowledge as to who the killers are and when would be the best time to seek our revenge. I will not rest until justice has been served on anyone who kills a member of my family—and that includes all the peoples of the rancho.

"My father taught me the business of the rancho must never be neglected, and that is the only way I can see to the welfare of the family and the peoples of the rancho. It is my intention to continue the modernization of the business of the rancho and, at the same time, offer the opportunity to my neighbors. In this way, we can best secure a future for all. I intend to do that by seeking diversified marketing not only in Mexico but the United States and the world. I want to incorporate a strategy of agriculture that incorporates innovation in both crops and machinery.

"I have already given orders that we are to start planning conservation in our grazing. We must have only the amount of cattle on any one area that the graze can support. I also plan to look at improving the stock in our herds and create a breeding system that will produce beef at different times, so we can guarantee a year-round market, not just in the fall.

"I am always aware of my father's warning that revolution is coming.

One of the lessons I learned at the University is that the United States is going to be a stable environment for business and raising families. It has had a terrible Civil War, and no one wants to experience anything like that again. I plan on taking advantage of that stability and ensuring the continuation of the existence of the Estancia del Pérez by purchasing both cattle and agricultural lands in the United States. The students we are sending to college in the States will be the vanguard of a secure future for all of us against revolution."

My mother and I discussed the rancho as to condition and prospects as well as some of the plans I had for it. Then it came time to discuss the family. She knew that José was continuing with the management of Hacienda Oriental, as he had consulted with her occasionally about staffing issues. I told her that Roman was now in control of Hacienda Occidental and, so far, he was doing a good job. It was as if he was born to it.

My mother looked at me and said, "He was. I never expected him to complete his education, because his heart was always in the rancho. He will make a fine patrón and will always remain a loyal son and brother."

That brought up the next subject, which I was somewhat hesitant to discuss with her, but I jumped into the breach with both feet. I felt we were selling my sisters short and they, like their mother, had contributions to make toward the welfare of the family.

My mother looked at me with a slight smile and said, "Angélica is contributing well; her two sons and daughter are, at this moment, running up and down the halls and breaking their mourning." We both laughed and had a drink of the wine that had sat untouched in the glasses before us.

That evening, we had an excellent meal of carne asada (grilled beef), papas (potatoes), and calabasza (squash) with stacks of flour and corn tortillas and sopapillas (flour popovers) from the kitchen of Sergeant Pedro Gonzáles. I asked my mother if we should look into getting Sergeant Gonzáles an aide.

My mother said, "I asked Pedro if he would like some help and he said, 'Go ahead and send someone into the kitchen, and I will make a fine chili con carne (a stew of beans and meat) out of them.' We decided not to broach that subject again until a lot more time had passed."

Mother had deftly turned the subject of my sister's education aside, and I decided it would be best to discuss one sister at a time. I told her I thought Juan Gonzáles had designs on Dulce, whom I knew had dandies in black lined up and offering their heartfelt condolences. Mother smiled and said that would be a far better match than the spoiled sons of rich men in their lace shirts that had been gracing our door. But, of course, Juan would have to wait until Dulce was in half-mourning to talk to her or us about his hopes and wishes along that line.

I confessed to my mother that Roberto had not been in my mind at all. I did not even know if he had been informed of our father's death.

Mother said, "I did not inform Roberto of his father's death. Since I am in mourning; it will be your job to get Javier settled at the college in January for the Spring semester and to inform Roberto of his father's death and what my wishes are for his further education."

I had no intention of leaving the rancho, and I informed her of that. Mother just looked at me and said, "I see. It is apparent you have more important things to do than to see to the education of your siblings, and you are not quite sure the people you have in place to run the rancho are capable. With your father, family came first and the rancho second."

I still had an ace up my sleeve. I mentioned the issue of my sister, Elizabeth's, education. "I feel she should have the chance to further her education to become a credit to herself and our family. We're quickly approaching the 20th century. The Estancia must enter the modern world or it will decay like an old log."

Mother gazed at me with pity and handed me a letter. The letter was from a school I had never heard of—Wellesley College—and it was from the president, Ada Howard. In it, she told my mother she had received the transcripts from Ben White as well as the family recommendations from the College of New Jersey and from Porfirio Díaz, Presidente of Mexico. She went on to state that María Elizabeth Pérez Castro and Dulce María Pérez Castro had been chosen to be admitted to Wellesley College for the Spring semester beginning on January 19th, 1880.

I had no more cards to play.

Mother explained that Wellesley College was a woman's college located in Wellesley, Massachusetts, west of Boston. She went on to inform me that since both Javier and Elizabeth had classes beginning on January 19th, I would need to have Elizabeth delivered to the college no later than the 14th. This would necessitate delivering Javier to Princeton, New Jersey, on or before January 1st. She had calculated that the time required taking the intercontinental train to New Jersey, the packet boat from Guaymas to San Francisco, and the trip from Hacienda Oriental to Guaymas would be 38 days, at the minimum. We really needed to leave no later than November 12th to be sure to make our connections. It was now September 7th.

I had only 67 days, at the most, to affect the roundup and transportation of the cattle to market and oversee putting the rancho to bed for the winter, which necessitated cutting large amounts of grass for supplemental winter feed. I summoned Corporal, Juan Gonzáles, and José Gallego to the Hacienda for a strategy session and explained the problem. We would need to conduct a roundup of all the cattle for market, starting tomorrow. This would require that all the vaqueros worked on gathering the cattle. In addition, we would need to cut all the grass hay as well as the alfalfa fields so we could store winter hay for both the Haciendas. These jobs would have to take place at the same time.

It would be the responsibility of Juan to ride to the Hacienda Occidental and inform Roman that he needed to start immediately on the roundup. I directed him to take three horses and deliver the news to Roman as quickly as possible.

José summoned his primero, whom he had stationed outside in case we needed him. I didn't know who José had picked as his primero, as I was in school when he became the patrón of Hacienda Occidental. The man who came walking through the door was Running Bear. Running Bear was a Tarahumara Indian who had joined the army under my father and moved to the rancho. He also was the first person to put me on a horse and pick me up every time I fell off until I stayed mounted.

I rushed to embrace him; it was so good to be in his presence. After a toast and pleasantries, we continued the meeting. José explained that we were going to have to push up the date of roundup, and he asked Running Bear if the grass that had been set aside for hay was ready for cutting and when he thought we could take our last cutting of alfalfa.

Running Bear answered, "Mi jefe, I have already ordered the movement of our cutting machinery to the grass pastures, as they are in ideal condition to be cut and, to do so now, would give them time to grow enough to withstand the winter. The alfalfa fields should be ready for their last cutting in 14 days."

José asked, "How many men will you need to cut the hay and move it to storage?"

Running Bear replied, "Emilio Vásquez has always been in charge of the harvests. It would be best to bring him here, because he can not only tell you how many men but for how long we'll need them."

José said, "By all means, bring Emilio. We need the best advice possible."

Running Bear left to get Emilio, and I turned to Corporal and said, "I am sure you have figured out what your first job will be."

He replied, "To see that we have the extra hands to get the haying done."

"Exactamente (exactly), Corporal," I said. "When Running Bear and Emilio arrive, we will have a drink together and then you, Running Bear, and Emilio will need to discuss the requirements. Emilio most likely knows the best people for haying in Ascención or elsewhere. If he feels it is necessary, get permission from Running Bear to take him along to help you with the hiring. It is imperative that both Running Bear and Emilio understand that we will need the vaqueros of the rancho for the roundup."

Corporal replied, "Sí, Patrón."

I held up my hand and said, "Corporal, we have shared many blankets together, and we both know the need to maintain proper decorum for the sake of the people of the rancho, but I do not want you to call me Patrón. 'Don Francisco' will suffice. When we are sharing a fire and blankets, I expect to be addressed as the friend and comrade I have always been."

"Sí, Don Francisco. It will be so," replied Corporal with a grin.

I turned to José and asked him when and how the hay was transported from here to Hacienda Occidental.

He replied, "Well, Don Francisco del Pancho…"

We all burst into laughter and took a sip of our drinks. José continued, "When all the hay is moved into the barns, large sacks are filled with it and loaded onto wagons for transport to Hacienda Occidental. It would be my suggestion that at least four wagons be sent with alfalfa hay for the horses immediately from what is already in the barn. The horses are going to be worked hard on the roundup, and it would be best that they have good feed and do not have to search for food while they are resting. I can send some older vaqueros, who no longer ride every day. They can deliver hay to the different roundups on Hacienda Occidental and accompany the herd back here. I also would do the same for our roundup."

I asked José how many men were on the rancho that did not work full time as vaqueros.

José replied, "Your father's soldiers were, for the most part, as old as or older than he was. They range from early to late sixties. Only Running Bear is still working. They would all welcome the chance to serve."

I replied that it was my wish that they accompany the roundup and ride assigned portions of the range to make sure no steers were missed. "Don't make their portions large," I suggested. "I believe four hours in the saddle will be enough. In addition, it would be best that you send old vaqueros to watch the valleys and the mountains to the north, and have a boy accompany each of them so he can be sent to report if danger is spotted. The vaquero will serve to protect the rancho, and the young boy will learn valuable lessons. Watching should be the most important task for them."

I then asked José for a rundown on the production of our fields and where we were in the marketing of the surpluses that the Haciendas would not need.

"The 80 hectares (about 2.8 acres) of maíz (corn) looks good, as we had ample rain before the planting. We needed to irrigate it only twice before the monsoon rains came. The cane is in the process of drying, and we will be pulling the dry ears by the middle of October.

"We had 60 hectares of sweet cane, which benefited from the same weather as the corn. It was cut for silage, and it has been chopped and put into the pits. We planted five hectares of tomate (tomatoes) and processed 55 liter barrels into pasta de tomate. From the five hectares of aji verde (a type of chili pepper), we picked enough to combine with our tomate and ajo (garlic), cebolla (onion), cilantro, and spices that were grown in the gardens to create 55 liter barrels of salsa. The remainder of any late tomate is to be picked by the families on the Estancia, and any remaining aji are being allowed to turn red so we can dry and grind them during the winter.

"We planted 100 hectares of algodón (cotton). The spring was cool, and the algodón got a slow start. It appears that if all the bolls set within the next two weeks, we will have a good crop. Of course, this is if we do not have a freeze until mid-November."

Running Bear returned with Emilio Vásquez. Emilio had always been in charge of assigning chores to the boys and girls of the Rancho, so they could properly understand where their food came from. I spent many a summer's day with an azada (hoe) in my hands, chopping weeds out of the campos (fields) of maíz, tomate, ajo, and algodón as well as the extensive gardens that supplied the Haciendas with fresh and canned vegetables for the rest of the year. In addition, he oversaw the milking of the cows, which was a twice-a-day chore for 10 boys and girls.

I embraced Emilio after he came through the door, and we all had a glass of wine while I explained to Emilio the time problem we had. He immediately saw the conflict with other harvests, which had become apparent to me after listening to José's report. I asked Emilio, Running Bear, and Corporal to discuss the problems amongst themselves and come up with a plan they could present to José and myself in the morning. I also told them of my plans for the retired vaqueros, so they and the vaqueros should not be included in their plans.

The sun was setting, which meant José and I needed to change clothes, so we would be presentable to the ladies for supper. We had a formal dinner that was lightened by the antics of José's and Angélica's daughter and sons.

At sunrise, I entered Pedro's kitchen. Sitting at a large table were José, Running Bear, Emilio, and Corporal. Pedro handed me a cup of coffee, and I joined them. The smells of salsa warming, tocino (bacon) frying, and tortillas cooking on the flat grill were overwhelming and my estómago (stomach) began to rumble.

At that moment, the door opened, and there stood my mother. She said to Pedro, "Con su permiso, me gustaría entrar su cocina (With your permission, I would like to enter your kitchen)." Pedro responded, "Sería un gran honor. Por favor, entre (It would be a great honor. Please enter)."

All of us were standing. My mother moved to the end of the table, and Corporal seated her before we again took out seats. Pedro set a china cup of steaming coffee in front of her. After a moment, she looked at us and said, "Por favor, sigan adelante, señores. Hevenido para aprender (Please, go ahead, gentlemen. I have come to learn)."

Running Bear stood, and I signaled to him to sit down to speak, which he did. He stated that he and his comrades thought 15 extra men would be sufficient to get the haying job done. He said they could switch to the other harvests until some of the vaqueros became available.

"If the vaqueros do not become available, when we start on the corn and chili rojo (red chili), we will need additional hands. Emilio knows enough competent men in Ascención that we would not need to go elsewhere to acquire help. But, he definitely will need to accompany Corporal to get the right men."

I glanced at José, who said to Emilio, "Time is important. Can you leave today?"

Emilio stood and said, "Sí, mi jefe," and prepared to leave.

I looked up at Emilio and asked him if Pedro would be angry because he was leaving before he ate the meal Pedro had prepared for him. Emilio looked at Pedro and replied, "Sí, mi jefe," and sat down.

We all smiled and dug into savory huevos rancheros (a spicy egg dish) and bacon swimming in a wonderful red salsa. After eating generous amounts of food, Running Bear, Emilio, and Corporal prepared to leave. I requested that Corporal remain for a while, and he turned to Emilio and asked him to saddle the horses, telling him he would meet him at his home when he was prepared to leave.

I told Corporal it was my understanding that telegraph lines had reached Ascención from El Paso del Norte. He indicated that they had. "However, your father felt our business was not private when we used it. There is a telegraph station at the old port of entry on the Mimbres to the north. If a message dealt with cattle movements, I would not send it from there. The only secure place for business messages is El Paso del Norte."

I went on to tell José, Corporal, and my mother of my plans and problems. I felt we needed to begin to market our cattle at the places of destination rather than through go-betweens that would profit from brokering the transaction. It was my hope that the family could become the brokers over time. "But, for this year, the bulk of the herds will be marketed in the old way. I will contact Señor Deus and ask him if he is interested in marketing cattle on a drive from El Paso del Norte to Denver. I need to contact him immediately and learn his answer as soon as possible. Therefore, I would like to draft a message to Señor Carlos Deus, which would inform him of the demise of our father and our need of his assistance." I turned to José and asked him to see this letter was delivered and the reply brought back.

I told Corporal he would be accompanying Señor Deus, and he was to take the proceeds from the sale of the herds—less expenses on the trail and a cut for Señor Deus—in the form of letters of credit that should be made out to me. He was to meet me back east, when I was delivering Elizabeth to Wellesley and Javier to the College of New Jersey. There would be a message sent to the Denver telegraph office giving him instructions as to where I was and how to get there. I released Corporal and then held a meeting with José and my mother.

I explained to José that my mother and I felt we needed to diversify to limit the repercussions if Presidente Díaz was deposed in the future. "Our father successfully navigated the wars of Liberals and Conservatives as well as the French attempts at empire. Our history is such that putting all our wealth back into the rancho is nearsighted. In the future, if we are unable to manage the Liberal desire for land reform, we will lose everything. Therefore, I feel it would be best if I encourage Roberto to tailor his last two years of school toward finance and the accumulation of financial contacts both at the College and with its sister schools—Yale, Harvard, and Brown."

I went on to state it was my hope that Javier would focus his education on engineering and geology. It would be of immense value to the family to have someone who could understand the geography of our lands and be able to consult or engineer the development of minerals both on our lands and in conjunction with our neighbors' lands. I also stated to Mother that Woody Wilson had gone to Harvard after graduating to obtain advance degrees, and I would like my brothers to consider the possibility of doing the same. I felt it would be a great benefit to the rancho and to them also to gain in knowledge and establish contacts.

Knowing my mother was not here just to listen, I asked her who she thought should accompany us on our trip.

Mother said, "I would prefer that you take Dulce and Juan Cortez. I would like her to make contacts again with young men there, so she can compare them with the useless sons of wealthy men that keep appearing at the door. I also want her to see the school that Elizabeth will be attending to see if she has any interest in continuing her education before she makes the decision to become a wife and mother. If she shows interest, I want you to get her enrolled. As you know, Dulce has been accepted to attend, also. I want her to attend, but it must be with her desire to do so and not out of obligation. I know you will be conducting business along the way, and you need not worry about the girls with Juan Cortez along. I have my family, and I will be secure.

"I will instruct your sisters that they are to end their full mourning and enter half mourning for the trip. I will further instruct Elizabeth that she is to end all mourning when she enters school. This might be an inducement for Dulce, who loves clothes and the chance to shop.

"José, I have no intention of ending my full mourning and I would like to have your permission to allow Angélica to take over one of my chores as the mistress of the Hacienda. I know my son would have problems asking me to get started with the meeting of the wives of the Hacienda, so we can determine what of the produce will need to be reserved for the rancho and what can be sold."

José replied," Sí, Madre, sería un gran honor que ella le asista en cualquier capacidad (Yes, Mother, it would be a great honor for her to be able to assist you in any capacity)."

Mother replied, "Good. I will ask her and tell her what she needs to do and how she needs to run the meeting."

Mother looked at me, and her look indicated I was to continue with my meeting. I brought up a security problem that had been nagging me.

I stated that when Juan Gonzáles and I made our visit to the camps of vaqueros on the trip from Oriental, we were advised that Cowboys from the Mimbres Valley had been observed watching the movement of vaqueros and, mostly likely, assessing the condition of the herds. I felt sure we were being observed by the Cowboys in the Animas, San Simon, and Sulphur Springs valleys. "I want our elders to serve as lookouts as soon as possible, because the observers will think it is an ideal time to take some small herds from scattered vaqueros before they are bunched at the Haciendas. José, please see that the lookouts are dispatched now with a boy of their choice as their runner. Please send a rider to find Comandante Neri, inform him that we anticipate trouble, and request that he station himself at Janos. Ask Running Bear to contact the Apaches and advise them of the lookouts and runners and the fact that the Rurales will be stationed at Janos so they can adjust their movements accordingly. Also, if they find someone suspicious and are unable to take any action, tell them to contact us or our watchers so we can respond."

CHAPTER 5

A large rancho is divided up into line camps (campos). Usually, a cabin is built, and several vaqueros work out of a campo. As time goes by, many of the vaqueros are joined by their families, and a small village may spring up. Each line campo is responsible for an area. At roundup, the most outlying campo is the point of beginning, and the vaqueros of the campo are joined by vaqueros from other campos. All the cattle are gathered and those that will be taken to market are branded with a road brand. This is applied in addition to the ranch brand that they should already have. The animals, which are headed for market, are then moved to the next line campo to be joined by the market animals from that campo. The cows and bulls are held near the campo for several days and, if any of them stray, they need to be driven back to where we want them on the range.

When a large roundup is started, the surrounding neighbors are notified so they can send representatives to make sure calves to be branded are not from their cows and that no road brand is applied to them. This is necessary, as most of the range is not fenced, and the cattle from the herds of neighbors sometimes mix with our herds.

Many of our neighbors were not large ranchos, and they had traditionally requested that we market their cattle along with our own. That request was usually delivered by the representative, and the brand of the owner was applied to the unbranded animals as well as the road brand. Once the tally had been made, each of the owners had to come to the rancho and fill out papers authorizing our marketing of their animals and the application of the road brand to the cattle. These papers were presented to the buyers as proof of ownership so they would not have anyone chasing them for payment.

Each rancho that sent cattle to market with us was obligated to provide riders for the herds during roundup and on the drive. The costs were determined by a tally at the beginning and at the point of sale.

Because we were doing a rush start, we needed to be extra careful in our branding. Each campo was notified that they should be observant, and questionable cows and calves were to be bunched together until all the representatives had arrived. It was imperative that there be no conflict.

Corporal and Emilio returned with 15 men from Ascención on September 16, 1879 (Independence Day). Normally, we would be having a grand fiesta, but the vaqueros were already out rounding up, and the rancho was still in mourning.

Emilio left the next morning with the hands to start the haying. Running Bear had taken most of the hands that lived at the rancho and dispersed them throughout the outlying campos. José, Corporal, and I rode out to observe the roundup at the same time that that Emilio left with the hands. We met with vaqueros along the way. As we were approaching the last campo near the border with the United States, we spotted a boy headed our way. José immediately identified him as Cachorro (cub), the grandson of El Tigre (the tiger), who was a Tarahumara and soldier under my father's command. José hailed Cachorro and asked him where he was going in such a hurry.

Cachorro answered, "Mi abuelo (my grandfather) has sent me to warn the campo they are being observed by four men who came down from the north."

I asked Cachorro if he could point out to us where his grandfather was and where the four men were. Cachorro pointed to an anvil-shaped peak and said, "Mi abuelo is watching from behind some rocks on the north side of the peak. The four men are on the mesa just north of him, and they have a camp in a bowl that hides it from eyes in the valley."

Corporal asked Cachorro how he was able to ride out without the four men from the north seeing him. Cachorro replied, "We had our horses in a small valley, about halfway down on the south side, where there was feed and water. Mi abuelo had pointed a way for me to ride south and around the long line of hills and then north toward the camp so it would appear I was approaching the campo from one of the campos to the south."

Corporal and I knew exactly where this valley was, as we had spent many a night camping there with He Who Hunts when we were boys. I told José to accompany Cachorro to the camp and alert the vaqueros. As soon as it got dark, he would send three vaqueros back with Cachorro, so the boy could guide them to the valley. Corporal would need to ride out to the north with 12 vaqueros until he reached the range of hills just north of the mesa that protruded out to the east. Once they were north of those hills, they would turn west and come to a steep valley that ran north. If the four men headed that way, they were to stop them until we arrived. If there was just one, they were to let him pass and follow him, as he was likely headed for the other rustlers, and we needed to catch all of them.

Corporal and I turned south. To the observers on the mesa, it would appear we had gotten some news from the boy that required us to turn south. One rider would accompany Cachorro to check out the camp and deliver orders to the vaqueros there. We traced Cachorro's path and arrived in the valley where we met El Tigre, who had observed our movements and knew we were coming.

El Tigre sported a full head of white hair and looked like he had been whittled out of a piece of ironwood. He had been toughened by the years and had not bowed to his age at all. I asked him what he knew about the men he was watching.

He said, "The stocky one is a man I have observed before when a camp was raided. He appears to be the leader. The other two men don't look like vaqueros. I think they are the jeffes of small ranchos. The fourth man left this morning toward the north. I suspect he has gone for more men that are waiting somewhere. I first spotted them crossing the border west of the Tres Hermanas Montañas (Three Sisters Mountains), and then they entered the long valley that cuts through the Colinas Carrizalillo (Carrizalillo Hills). From there, they went directly to the mesa, where they are now. They went straight. They knew how to stay hidden and arrive at the point where they could observe the roundup."

Cachorro and the three vaqueros arrived late in the night. We all bedded down to get some much-needed rest. A small fire was already going when I woke up, and the coffee and beans were hot. I wrapped some beans in a tortilla and downed some coffee. Once everyone had eaten, we discussed what we were going to do. I told Cachorro and the three vaqueros that there were three men on a mesa on the other side of the small peak above us. "These men are here to direct and participate in a raid on the roundup in the valley below. It is my wish that we capture these men without firing a shot. A shot might alert their companions, whom we believe the fourth man, went to bring in. El Tigre will be directing the capture of these men and he will be giving the orders."

El Tigre stood and described the terrain on the other side of the peak. "The mesa is bountiful with piñon (pine nut) and juniper trees. The oak brush has many acorns, and the cacti have ripe fruit. This means we have one big problem—to navigate the mesa without spooking all the deer, javelina, turkey, and other animals that have come to partake of the abundance as well as the predators that have been attracted to the game."

El Tigre went on to explain his strategy. "El jefe, one vaquero, and I will go out on the west side on foot. Cachorro, Corporal, and one vaquero will go down the east side, also on foot. One vaquero will stay back at the peak, so he can signal us if someone comes in behind us.

When we have captured the men, we will signal the vaquero, and he will bring the horses. Each side will have a mirror as will the vaquero who is watching. Three flashes meant 'stop.' One meant 'go.' Four meant 'bring the horses,' and five from the mountain means we have someone behind us. Both Cachorro and I will carry bows and arrows, if silent killing needs to be done. Mi jefe, I know Cachorro is just a boy, but he has had the training of a brave, and he already has made this trip twice to observe."

By daylight, we were at the head of the mesa. We had left the vaquero and the horses just behind the peak and, by now, I was sure he had found a perch from which to watch our progress as well as our backs.

We reached the west side without any hitches, and we signaled to Cachorro and the men on the east side to begin. We moved for about 15 minutes when some turkeys were startled ahead of us. We signaled a stop and waited to see if the turkeys would move behind us, but they remained in place. When we resumed, they moved in front of us. El Tigre signaled a stop and then disappeared. In about 30 minutes, we saw the turkeys moving south between us and Cachorro's group. As we waited, two does with yearling fawns silently moved south, followed by some javelina. About 10 minutes later, El Tigre appeared and signaled Cachorro to start moving.

In about an hour of slow moving—for about 30 minutes of which we could smell wood smoke—we arrived above the bowl where the three men were camped. We spread out in an arc and began moving. The men were not visible. We assumed they were inside their tents.

When we were about 50 feet away from the camp, El Tigre signaled that we were ready.

I addressed the camp in English. "You are surrounded. Do not reach for any weapons, and come out with your hands in the air."

A portly man, who El Tigre indicated by a nod to me was the leader, emerged from one of the tents lifting a rifle to aim, and two arrows suddenly sprouted from his chest before he fell. The other two men emerged from their tents with their hands in the air. Corporal and the vaqueros tied up the two men, and we signaled for the horses.

I knelt by the fire and helped myself to some of the coffee that was boiling. Corporal sat the two men down across from me, and I asked them who they were. Neither was inclined to talk, so I talked for them. I told them the cattle they were watching below were mine. The man they had sent back had been followed, and we had 20 men waiting for him and the men he was bringing back. When they reached the climb to the mesa, they would be captured or killed.

While I was talking, Corporal and the three vaqueros rounded up the men's horses and saddled them. Then they went about fashioning nooses from the saddle ropes and strung them from some strong tree limbs.

I set my cup down and said, "The two of you do not look like hired hands. You look like you do the hiring. You probably have families and, as things stand right now, they are never going to know what happened to you. It is your choice. You can start by telling me your names."

Bob Short and Simon Johnson chirped right up with that information and went on to answer my other questions about where they lived and ranched and the nature of the men coming to join them. As I suspected, these two men were from the area around the Florida Mountains, and the men that were coming were nine hands from three ranches plus the fourth man that had gone back to fetch them.

We put Short and Johnson on their horses with their hands tied, and we mounted up. We rode under the trees, where the nooses swayed in the breeze, and then all of us proceeded south up the mesa.

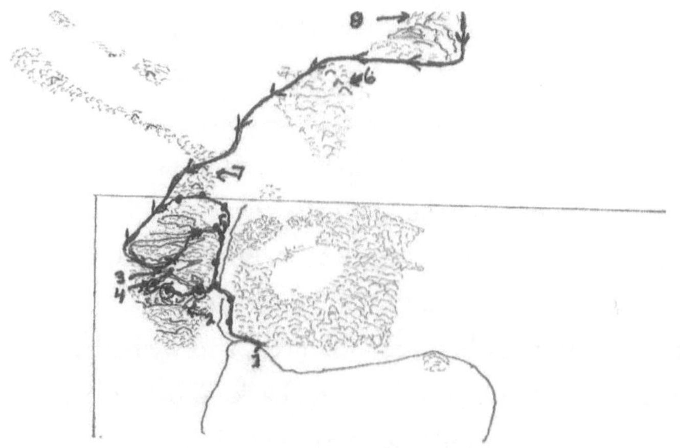

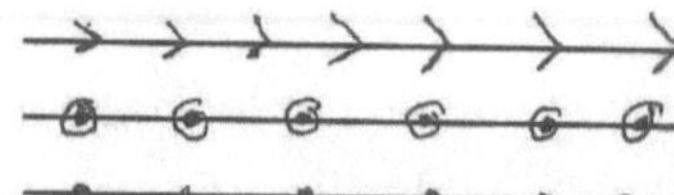

1. Hacienda Occidental
2. Cerro Grande
3. El Picacho
4. El Tigre's Camp
5. Campo Norte
6. Tres Hermanas
7. Carrizalillo Hills
8. Florida Mts.

Rustlers Route
Our Route
Jose's Route

El Tigre and Cachorro had left earlier and were well on their way to meet the men headed toward us. Just off the mesa, Running Bear met El Tigre and Cachorro, and they made plans to capture the 10 men that José, Running Bear, and the vaqueros from the roundup had been following. When we arrived, we were met by Cachorro, who directed us to a rocky outcrop. We could see the men riding toward us. They were right below us when Running Bear stepped out and hollered at them to stop, telling them they had 11 vaqueros sitting their horses with guns leveled at their backs.

The man who had gone back for the others yelled and started toward Running Bear. Two arrows thunked into his chest, and he toppled off his horse. The rest of the men sat their horses, not moving, and then Johnson yelled at them to drop their guns and quit. Reluctantly, guns were thrown to the ground under the horses. I addressed the men and told them they were to be escorted off the rancho at the American border. I told them they were not welcome on the rancho, because they had come to steal. If they were caught on the rancho, my vaqueros had orders to hang them where they were found. I told them they would take the bodies of their comrades with them, as I did not want them fouling the rancho.

José, Corporal, Running Bear, and I shared the camp with El Tigre and Cachorro that evening. El Tigre had killed a fat buck near the peak, and we all feasted on deer liver, heart, and ribs brushed with sage before they were roasted.

I informed the gathering that, after stopping by the Hacienda tomorrow, Corporal and I would be heading to Hacienda Occidental to see how the roundup was going and give my final orders to Roman before I headed out on my University journey. I told El Tigre that his work was done, but I would consider it a privilege if he would accompany Corporal and me on our trip to the oeste (west).

El Tigre immediately agreed to accompany us.

Cachorro said, "It would be a great honor if you would allow me to come also."

I replied to Cachorro, "Your service to me and the rancho reflects well upon you and your family. We would not have been able to complete our objective without you. But, you are a student of Mr. White, and I have no desire to raise his ire any more than we have already by keeping you away from your classes. You will be able to honor your family and the rancho by becoming educated not only in the crafts of a brave but in the ways of the coming world."

El Tigre then spoke to Cachorro. "My grandson, your deeds today will be spoken of over the fires of both family and friends, and I am bursting with pride. But, as Don Francisco has said, you must learn the crafts of the coming world as well as you have learned the crafts of a brave. You will lead and protect the family and the Estancia in the future. I am proud to be your grandfather."

I turned to José and Running Bear and let them know I had no idea what the circumstances were at Hacienda Occidental, but I must be back here in no less than 30 days. It would take six days just to travel back and forth, and I would take Juan Gonzáles with us. I knew they could handle the roundup. I requested that José check on a reply from Carlos Deus and, if it was in the affirmative, to ask him about market prices and how many head he could market on the way and as well as deliver a herd to the railhead. Also, I wanted him to tell Señor Carlos to bring whatever hands he wanted, and we'd supply him with enough vaqueros to make the drive. I asked José to contact buyers we had done business with before regarding cattle and surplus crops as well as any others that may be in El Paso del Norte, Juárez, and Chihuahua. I told them I felt that our best market would be in the north, but we must cultivate a Mexican market also.

I then came to the subject that had been working in my brain. "As you may know, the Southern Pacific Railroad reached Yuma, Arizona in 1877. The tracks have now been extended to an area eight miles south of the Maricopa stage station and will be in Tucson early next year. We can begin to ship cattle by train as early as next Spring. I put these questions to you gentlemen: Is it possible to hold back some cattle to ship in the Spring or even next Fall, or would it do harm to the pastures? In addition, can we begin to hold our surplus hay and use it as well as surplus grain to feed cattle directly for the market? If so, how many head could we hold back? I feel we should do a test run by keeping some head out of the market this year. I am not willing to get into the position of depending on the Southern Pacific; because word has come to me that they are gouging the agricultural areas they exclusively service for a large percentage of their production.

"Within a year, the Santa Fe Railroad will be serving this area, and that will give us an alternative. When I am in San Francisco, I will seek to get a commitment from the Southern Pacific Railroad on shipment costs, but I feel that talking directly to our buyers in Chicago and New

York, whom I already have a working relationship with, is the best way to go. I will discuss this with them when I am in the north. As I stated before, I need your input as to the feasibility of keeping steers back for delivery in the Spring or even next year as a marketing strategy and what we need to do differently to make this happen. I think the political climate is going to be such that we can grow and expand, but we always need to be aware that if Porfirio Díaz is overthrown by the Liberals, our way of life is in danger. We need to prepare for that for all the peoples of the Estancia."

We had a great feast on the deer, and a skin of good wine that Pedro had thought to bring along helped the feeling of comradeship that I hoped to foster.

Early the next morning, we departed for Hacienda Oriental. Running Bear left us once we gained the plain to check on the roundup and the movement of the steers and unwanted heifers toward the holding grounds near the Hacienda.

When we arrived at the Hacienda, I went to see my mother and report on the events that had occurred with the rustlers. I also shared with her the questions I had posed and what we might do with the answers. My mother listened to my thoughts and, in general, stated they were very good, especially the caution I expressed at the end. Porfirio Díaz would not remain in power forever.

Mother then gave me some news that was reported to her and Angélica in the absence of José and me. One of the men that Emilio had wanted to hire had declined to work, but he had followed the vaqueros after they had moved the cows and bulls back on the range and left to continue with the roundup. He captured a fat cow and started heading home with her. Two of the old vaqueros intercepted him. They knew the man, and they knew he was trying to feed his family. They also knew he had declined employment. The vaqueros decided it would be best if they brought him to the Hacienda for a decision by Don Francisco as to what should be done.

Unfortunately, the vaqueros ran into a troop of Rurales patrolling for Indians and cattle thieves. They asked the vaqueros why they were escorting the man. The vaqueros told them they had caught him with a stolen cow, and they were taking him to the Hacienda to face the patrón. The lieutenant in charge told the vaqueros that thieves were the concern of the Rurales, and they would take him to Janos.

The Rurales never made it to Janos with the thief. He died on the way trying to escape! I was very unhappy about the outcome, and I intended to speak to Comandante Neri about this. Of course, the news spread fast in Ascención and Janos that the free-meat market had been closed.

I knew that Mother was not through with this subject. She informed me that the man left a widow with six children. She said that Angélica had gone to Ascención and had brought the woman back to the Hacienda so she could have employment and her children would receive an education.

RANCH BRAND

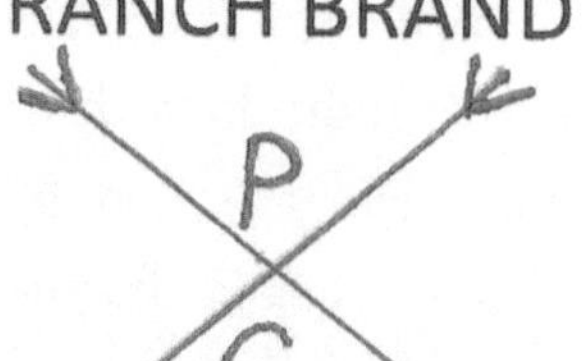

EATMARKS

ROAD BRAND

CHAPTER 6

I arose before daybreak and went down to the kitchen to see if I could find some coffee. As I walked through the door, I spied Pedro Gonzáles moving around and filling cups for his son, Juan, as well as José, Emilio, Running Bear, Corporal, El Tigre, and He Who Hunts. They were all sitting at the large kitchen table, which was laden with stacks of steaming tortillas, frijoles, huevos, and tocino. I went immediately to He Who Hunts and embraced him as a missing brother. I then shook all the hands and found my seat at the head of the table. I asked them, "If I sleep in this chair at night, would I be the first one to the table in the morning?"

They all looked at me and, in unison, replied, "No, Patrón." We all had a laugh and dug into Pedro's breakfast.

When we had done ample justice to Pedro's cooking, we settled back in our chairs with our coffee, and José asked Emilio to report on the harvest.

Emilio stated that all the grass hay had been cut and about half of it had dried enough to be transported to the hay barns. He said about half the alfalfa would be cut. I asked him how the grain and cotton fields were coming, and he said the grain fields were beginning to dry, and we should be harvesting at least the upper fields within two weeks. He thought we would have a good crop of cotton if we did not have an early freeze.

I thanked him and asked Running Bear if he had a report on the roundup. He said the outer camps had almost completed their portion of the roundup and, within three weeks, the steers and heifers at Hacienda Oriental would be at the gathering grounds near the Hacienda. He told Emilio he could release seven vaqueros to him if he needed them. Emilio eagerly assented.

José asked Standing Bear if he could spare any more vaqueros, and Running Bear agreed he could, in a pinch. José then said, "We are pushed for time. It is good that Emilio will have more help, and it is my wish that the hands that usually work the fields during the growing time and have families here on the rancho be the first that are released to Emilio. But, I would like to have even more young vaqueros to begin to bring in the gathered herds, so we can put them in the corrals and start with the road branding of those we intend to market. That way, we will be ahead and ready to move the herds out early to the various markets."

Running Bear said, "Mi jefe, I feel you have very good ideas, and it will be my pleasure to implement them as soon as I leave here. I will begin to move herds from the campos, so they arrive at different times, and put them into available corrals. That will eliminate us spending much time in the holding grounds trying to keep the unbranded cattle away from those that have been branded. Some of the vaqueros that bring herds will be able to stay and help wherever they are needed. I will tell those that stay where to report after they have delivered the herds to the corrals."

I looked at He Who Hunts and told him how much it pleased me to see him and that I was sad to be leaving that morning for Hacienda Occidental and would not have a chance to spend more time with him.

He Who Hunts replied, "My brother, it is my wish to accompany you to the west. The Rurales are patrolling the east very heavily, and I would need to ride with you as a vaquero. Would it be possible for me to accompany you in safety?"

I replied, "Any time I can ride with my brother is a time my heart sings. Go with Corporal, and he will help you to turn into a vaquero. Corporal, see that he has clothes and his appearance is made to be above suspicion."

I then turned to Juan and El Tigre and told them we should be leaving soon. "Please make sure we each have two horses to ride. Let He Who Hunts pick out some mounts from my personal horses, and make sure he has tack that makes him look like one of us. It would not do for him to ride an Apache saddle."

I turned to Pedro and asked him if he had any tortillas and meat that we could take along to sustain us on our trip.

He shot me a look and replied, "You would think that I had never cooked for an army. Your food is in the pack by the door."

I told Juan and El Tigre that I needed to talk for a minute with José and my mother, and then I would be ready to travel. I asked Pedro if my mother had sent for her coffee yet, and he replied that María was preparing a tray for her right now. I asked María if she would warn my mother that José and I were going to join her for coffee and to ask if Angélica would join us. To her amazement, I told her that José and I would carry the trays to my mother's rooms. She hurriedly prepared the trays as my mother would want them and left to give the warning.

José and I arrived at Mother's rooms burdened with trays of coffee and sweet rolls. María let us in, and we entered. Mother and Angélica were prepared to receive us. María poured the coffee and we all settled in. I began the conversation by asking Angélica if the produce had been apportioned and if there was any surplus. She replied that it had been taken care of and there were surpluses, which could be sold at market. I then reported to Mother the conversations we had with Standing Bear and Emilio and indicated I was satisfied with where we were at this time.

I then turned to José and asked him if he would contact the buyers we had done business with in the past and see what they had to offer.

I was interested in finding what prices I could expect for delivery to El Paso del Norte, Tucson, the nearest Santa Fe Railhead, and the nearest Southern Pacific Railhead, and when they would expect delivery and how many steers or heifers they were willing to buy. In addition, I wanted him to broach the subject of Spring deliveries to Deming and El Paso as well as Tucson. It would be wise to talk to slaughterhouses in both El Paso and Chihuahua regarding the market of fed beef. I asked that he send a messenger to me when he heard from Charles Deus.

I then turned to Mother and told her I would be in the west for 20 to 25 days, at the most. I would be taking Juan Gonzáles, Corporal, El Tigre, and He Who Hunts. When I returned, I hoped to have my plans finalized. "I know conditions here and in the west can change our final actions. I plan on leaving for the east in plenty of time to deliver Javier, Elizabeth, and possibly Dulce to school. The visit will be extended, so I can meet with people at the cattle exchanges in Chicago and New York to discuss selling directly to them, and they will be paying the freight from the time it is loaded onto the railroad. I may not return until mid-February. If I have the opportunity to meet Nana on my trip west, I am going to ask his permission to take He Who Hunts with me back east, if He Who Hunts will go with me. In any case, I would like Juan Cortez to go, and Juan Gonzáles will be accompanying me on the whole trip. We will pick up Corporal, wherever he ships out, and it will be up to him to let us know by wire where he is."

I then rose, hugged and kissed my mother and Angélica, and, with a handshake for José, I left to join my comrades who were waiting just outside.

The four of us, with our five extra horses and one pack horse, headed out on our trip west. Our plans were to make it a faster trip by exchanging fresh horses from the camps we encountered along the way. Standing Bear joined us on the way out, as he was going to the west to inspect the roundups at the camps and start moving cattle toward the Hacienda.

CHAPTER 7

We headed southwest, paralleling the southern remnants of the Colinas Carrizalillo. There were a few fields and irrigated pastures near the Hacienda, but the bulk of our farming was being done to the southeast. As we began to approach the fields, we turned west through a large valley that cut through the Colinas and toward the Alamo Huecos that stretched from the boot heel of the southern New Mexico Territory toward the heart of Chihuahua. On the eastern edge of the Huecos, five rivers converge on a large playa (lakebed) that spread out over a great area south of the Carrizalillo and drained into the valley of our farms and on south to Ascención.

Between the playa and the Huecos was Campo Playa del Rios. There were around 300 steers and heifers that could be sent to market in this one camp, as Campo Los Lamentos (Camp of Laments) to the North had already joined its herd with this one. Running Bear gave the jefe vaquero instructions to begin by moving 100 head to the Hacienda immediately and send eight men to deliver them. Four men were to remain at the Hacienda and report to Don José for orders. The other four were to return to the campo.

Running Bear told him that how many men were to remain or how many head should be delivered would be at his or Don José's orders. How many animals he could hold at his camp would be decided by el jefe del campo.

Running Bear then sent riders toward each camp to the south and southwest to begin moving their cattle to this campo. Running Bear went on to ask for four vaqueros to join us on our trip toward the oeste. He explained to the jefe vaquero that he was going to be the chief link in the chain for moving the herds to the Hacienda and soon he would be receiving cattle from Hacienda Occidental. He said it was very important that he instruct whoever got orders from Don José to be sure to ask him how many cattle he wanted in the next delivery.

We obtained fresh horses and continued on toward the west. The campo we had just visited was on the northeastern side of the eastern branch of the Alamo Huecos. Our next stop was at Campo Salado, which was situated midway down the east side of the eastern branch of the Huecos. Running Bear gave instructions to the jefe of the campo regarding the disposition of the market cattle and sent a rider west and north to Campo Las Palmas with instructions to move their market cattle to Campo Salado.

We proceeded west through a great rift that split the eastern branch and passed through a low valley in the western branch and came upon a large grassland. Running Bear had brought a vaquero from Campo Salado, and he sent him to Campo Las Palmas with instructions for the movement of the market cattle toward Campo Salado. They could move as many as 100 to Campo Salado in the first herd and more when the herds started coming in from the South. In addition, he was to instruct the jeffes at Campo San Basillo and Campo Janos that they should begin moving the market cattle north to the campo north of them on a daily basis and as vaqueros could be spared. He was to give those jeffes instructions to keep moving with the herds toward Campo Playa de Rios.

The valley between the Alamo Huecos was a great example of the short grass prairies of the southern plains, and this particular valley had served as a nursery for the southern herds of buffalo, which had disappeared during my lifetime.

We arrived at Campo Berrendo, a camp on the northwest side of the west branch of the Huecos. Each campo had a cabin for the jefe vaquero that lived there. When vaqueros had families with them, the cabins were expanded. Mother's edict about education stood for all school-age children, and those children would either move in with relatives at the Haciendas or their mothers would have to move back to the villages that were connected to the Haciendas. At roundup times, each camp was expanded by the amount of vaqueros that moved there from the Haciendas or the outlying campos that had completed the roundup.

I had a conversation with Running Bear after everyone had retired and complimented him on his organization of the movement of the cattle. Then I asked, "By continuing to send cattle to the gathering campo, are we going to overload the water and graze in that area, and would it not be a good idea to make this campo a holding area that could send smaller herds toward the gathering area?"

Running Bear replied, "It would indeed be a very good gathering area. I will give the orders."

Before we left the camp, Running Bear asked the jefe vaquero of this campo to join us and explained the reasons for the gathering camp at the Campo Playa de Rios and how we now needed him to make this a gathering camp that could filter herds toward the east. He instructed the jefe to begin by sending 150 head east every 24 hours. He should instruct one of his vaqueros to consult with the jefe at the Rios gathering camp and ask him how many he could take each day so that he was not overwhelmed.

As we left this campo, El Medio stood sentry over the valley to the south of us, appearing as a great ship on a prairie of grass. El Medio is one of many lonely mountains in Chihuahua, Sonora, Arizona, New Mexico, and the western parts of Texas. They stand as islands reaching for the skies and serve as guides and a haven for travelers, both human and animal.

To the west of us, blocking our view was the majestic on Sierra San Luis of the Sierras de Teras. San Luis ran to the southern boundary of the Rancho, where it was joined by the Sierra El Tigre on its west flank. El Tigre and San Luis were separated by the Rio Bavispe, which ran northwest between them and joined the Rio Batepito just south of our boundary. The Sierra de Teras is the northern terminus of the Sierra Madre Occidental, and it ends at the American border by splitting like a horseshoe to form the Sierras Animas as its western branch and the Sierras Peloncillo as its eastern branch. The lower center of the horseshoe is an ancient great lake, north of which is the Valle de Animas.

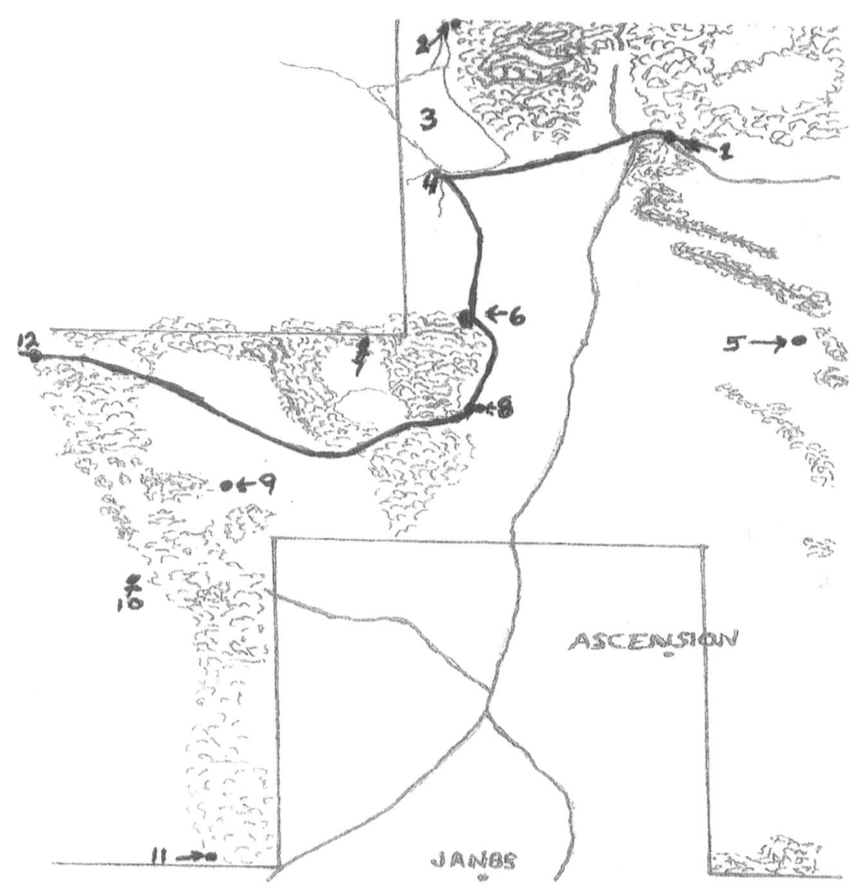

1. Hacienda Occidental	2. Campo Los Lamentos
3. Playa de Rios	4. Campo Playa de Rios
5. Campo de Las Lilas	6. Campo Monumento
7. Campo Las Palmas	8. Campo Salado
9. Campo Palmar	10. Campo San Basillo
11. Campo Janos	12. Campo Berrendo

Our Roundup Trip

Lilas – Lilac Lamentos – Laments Palmas – Palms Palmar – Palm Grove Berrendo – Pronghorn

The border between Estados de Chihuahua and Sonora meanders down the length of the Sierra San Luis into the Sierra Madre Occidental proper. The borders of the Estados de Nuevo Mexico and Arizona began by being split by the Sierra Peloncillo, which eventually wandered into Nuevo Mexico and moved northwestward into Arizona, forming the western boundary of the Valle de San Simon that terminates at the Rio Gila.

Just after we had cleared Campo Berrendo, we were met by a rider hailing us. He had been sent by the jefe de Campo San Luis, which had been hit by rustlers earlier in the night. The rustlers had gotten away with 50 head—a mixed herd of cows, bulls, and calves—and had crossed the border into Nuevo Mexico between the Sierras Animas and the Hachitas. One of our vaqueros was killed and another badly wounded. The jefe of the Campo San Luis was confident there were no more than four rustlers.

I instructed Corporal to return to Compo Berrendo with the rider, where he was to ask the jefe de campo to send a rider to us with four extra horses. The rider needed to be capable of explaining to the jeffes of Campos Nogales, Medio, and María on El Medio the need to send the market cattle to Campo Berrendo. He was then to take four riders and pursue the rustlers and, at all times, be on the alert for an ambush.

He Who Hunts swung his horse around and rode off with Corporal. I knew I would be unable to hold him back, and I had my hands full keeping El Tigre with me, so we could converse with the watchers.

I dismounted and asked Juan and El Tigre if they could build a small campfire and get some coffee going. Once we all had a cup of coffee in our hands and had settled down, I told them my plan. When the rider got there, Running Bear was to give him his instructions. Juan Gonzáles was to take one of the extra horses and ride to Campo Angélica, where he would inform the jefe of the raid on Campo San Luis and have him prepare to receive all the cattle gathered there. He was also to see that a rider was sent from Campo Angélica to the camps south of him along the Sierra San Luis and tell them about the raid and the need to move their market cattle in small bunches toward the campos to the north and on to Campo Berrendo. Once he had taken care of the business at Campo Angélica, he was to join us at Campo San Luis.

Running Bear, El Tigre, and I were each going to take an extra horse and make a forced ride toward Campo San Luis. Some distance from Campo San Luis, we were met by the watcher that had been assigned to the area. He was a primo (cousin) of El Tigre, and they conversed in the Tarahumara language as to how this could have happened and where the raiders had gone. El Tigre told us that his primo had detected some movement to the northwest of Campo San Luis and observed three men headed in the direction of Campo El Lobo. He was continuing to observe and follow them when he saw signal fires from Campo San Luis. He sent his grandson to warn the vaqueros at Campo El Lobo and turned back to Campo San Luis. When he arrived, the raiders were well on their way toward the border. He immediately started following them with several vaqueros. When they reached the border, he turned back, but he sent Mario Cortez, who could speak English, to observe where the raiders went.

We continued to ride toward the campo, and I was dealing with men ready to avenge the raid. Chief among those eager to head out now was El Tigre. My immediate concern was to talk with the jefe vaquero of the campo and determine the condition of the wounded vaquero and the herd.

The jefe vaquero at San Luis indicated that the herd had been scattered but was easily regathered, and there was a double guard on it as we spoke. He also said the market cattle had not yet been separated. The wounded vaquero was in serious condition and was going to need better care than could be provided at the campo. He told the jefe that the rustlers had spoken Spanish.

El Tigre interrupted to say that the summer village of his people at Sierra El Tigre was in a large, open valley in San Luis, and it was an easy day's ride. There would be someone to care for the wounded vaquero there. His suggestion met with immediate approval, as it would be at least four days' ride to either of the Haciendas with an injured man.

It was decided that Tall Runner (El Tigre's primo) would guide the vaqueros to the village and ride with the wounded man on a litter between their two horses. This would be much more comfortable for the wounded man than being dragged behind a horse as they climbed the mountain. They decided to grab a nap and leave in two hours.

I gave permission for El Tigre to take three men of his choosing and trail the rustlers, keeping an eye out for Mario Cortez and the men from Campo Berrendo. Juan Gonzáles rode in and reported to Running Bear and myself that the rider to the campos south of Campo Angélica had left prior to his departure. He also said there was plenty of feed and water, and there would be no problem adding the herd from Campo San Luis.

In the morning, I asked Running Bear to bring in all the vaqueros so we could have a talk. I told them that I understood their desire to seek revenge on the raiders. "The problem is that there are still strangers moving around and looking at the herds. Vaqueros that work for the rancho are in danger, and we must see that the Rancho is secured. I am ordering that all your cattle be moved to the camp south of here. I want this done today. In addition, I will be ordering the vaqueros at Campo El Lobo to begin moving all the cattle in their district toward Campo San Luis and south to Campo Angélica."

I had one more chore to do, and that was the burial of the vaquero that had died. We buried him on a point overlooking the camp. I ordered the jefe vaquero to tell Running Bear that I wanted a stone made for the grave. I told him to send the order to Hacienda Oriental, with the provision that if there was any of the vaquero's family that wanted to come see the grave and the placing of the stone, we would provide for them to do that.

Juan and I spent the next two days riding with the vaqueros, making sure there were no strays in any of the small canyons, because I wanted all the cattle moved out. On the evening of the second day, Corporal, El Tigre, Mario Cortez, and He Who Hunts returned, accompanied by two gringos. After they had been well fed, I asked Corporal, El Tigre, and Mario to report to me what had occurred.

Corporal, said, "Mi jefe, I know it is my place to report, but since Mario Cortez started the pursuit, I think the story should be his to report and I will fill in the rest afterwards."

Mario said, "Don Francisco, Tall Runner gave me instructions to only observe the rustlers. I caught up to them within several hours, as they did not go far before they stopped to eat and rest. I slipped up on their camp to observe and listen. There were four of them, and they were Mexicans from around Janos. They discussed that they were taking the cattle north of the Mogollon Rim where a group of Mormon settlers had established settlements and were in need of cattle. They were to receive 50 dollars for good bulls and 20 dollars for good cows with standing calves. They were gleefully talking about what they'd do with their money.

"I returned to my horse and was about to mount when I was ordered in English to keep my hands on my saddle and not move. Two gringos stepped out from behind a tree and walked up to me. The older one asked me if I spoke English, and I told him I could, but poorly. He asked me why I was following the men in camp. I was extremely worried that these men were companions of those men, but I felt the best I could do was answer them truthfully. So, I told them that the cattle were rustled from your rancho, and they had killed one vaquero and wounded another. I went on to explain that I had been sent to observe them.

"The gringo then indicated I need not keep my hands on my saddle, as what I told them was what they assumed after watching me for several hours. The older one asked me why I had come alone, and I told him that word had been sent for help, and I believed that help was already on its way.

"The younger of the gringos left to observe the rustlers, and I stayed with the older one. He explained that the two of them had moved into this valley from Tejas (Texas) and were seeking to establish a rancho so they could bring their families out. He asked me about you, and I told him you were the son of Gregorio Pérez. He knew the name from his father's stories. His father had fought in the guerra (war) de Tejas independence. They knew in Tejas that Don Gregorio had captured a Coronal Fannin and that, when Santa Anna ordered the massacre of Fannin and his army, Don Gregorio had declined to participate and had moved out in protest. His father had told him that the name of Gregorio Pérez was the name of an honorable man.

"I told him that Don Gregorio had been murdered by gringo rustlers from the Tombstone area earlier that year, and he expressed outrage and sympathy. He went on to say he was from the family of Baker. The younger man came back and said the rustlers were on the move again. We followed them at a distance after they went over a rise.

"We saw Corporal riding toward us. I explained to the Bakers that he was your man and was most likely in charge of the group of men that were watching the rustlers."

Corporal then gave his report. "Mi jefe, Mario introduced me to the Bakers and told me they had befriended him and accompanied him soon after he had caught up to the rustlers. I told the Bakers I had five men waiting along a stream in a line in front of the rustlers, and they would be stopping them very shortly. I did not expect they would surrender willingly. Señor Baker said he and his brother would like to lend a hand if we would not be offended by their intrusion in our affairs. I told him I would appreciate the help, as it was my job to guard the back door. We moved up behind the rustlers just when He Who Hunts and the vaqueros challenged them. The rustlers immediately showed fight. He Who Hunts killed the lead rustler, and the other three scattered. Two of them came toward us. I killed the rustler that was quartering to my right, and Señor Baker killed the other that was headed straight at us. He Who Hunts followed the fourth rustler and came back shortly saying he was no more. Just as the fight was over, El Tigre and three vaqueros rode up to us from the south. I ordered four vaqueros to gather up the cattle and start back to the campo. I ordered three vaqueros to bury the rustlers and then help with the herd.

"I then asked El Tigre if he had any provisions he could whip up for one of his famous camp meals, and he said he would be happy to take care of that chore. I then sat down with the Señores Baker to properly thank them for their assistance. The first Señor Baker told me about the rancho they were going to establish in the valley and asked if we might be able to sell him the cattle the rustlers took. I told him I did not have the right to sell him cattle from the Rancho but that you were here at Campo San Luis, and I felt sure you would be happy to sell them some seed stock. I persuaded them to accompany us back here".

I asked Mario to introduce me to the Bakers. The older of the Bakers said his name was Robert and his brother's name was Mike. I told them my name was Francisco, and I was in charge of the rancho. I then opened the business discussion by stating that Corporal had indicated they were interested in buying cattle.

Robert said, "Yes, we need some seed cattle to start our own herd, and we think we have enough funds to at least buy that small herd."

I replied, "Please do not think of me as forward, but I have some ideas and would like to know what kind of future you are looking forward to on your rancho."

Robert answered that he was not offended by the question and explained that they had two more brothers back in east Texas and, now that they had a location staked out for their ranch, they would send word to their brothers to bring their families out.

I told them 50 head were not going to be enough cattle to support four families.

Robert agreed but said they were going to have to start small.

I then offered them a proposition: I would be willing to advance them a herd of 150 mother cows, seven bulls, and 50 one-year-old heifers under conditions that I went on to explain. "I am leaving in a short time for New Jersey and New York and, while I am there, I want to make deals with large meat companies. I propose to sell them cattle on a yearly, contracted basis for a price of two dollars a head less than market price if they will accept delivery at the nearest railhead. The cost of freight would be on the buyer at that point. I will assure them a steady supply in the thousands, which we will negotiate annually." I paused, and then continued with my proposition. "If you agree, I would provide you the seed stock, and you will market your cattle through my contracts and pay me back for the seed stock at 20 percent of your proceeds. Twelve percent will go to the purchase of the cattle and eight percent will go to the rancho to cover our marketing costs and a small profit. You can choose the cattle you want from a herd that is being gathered just south of here at our Campo Angélica. You can discuss my proposal and give me an answer in the morning." I also said that if they did not want to go with my proposal, I would still sell them 50 head.

The next morning, as I was sitting down with my first cup of coffee, I saw the Baker brothers headed my way. They told me they agreed to my proposal with one slight adjustment: The 20 percent was fine, but they would like the 20 percent to be 13 percent toward purchase and seven percent toward the marketing costs. I immediately agreed to the change, and we had a deal. They then made another request: "Do you have any way to post mail to the States?"

I said, "Yes. Mail goes out weekly from Hacienda Oriental to El Paso del Norte, where it is posted on the U.S. Mail." I called for Running Bear and told him, "When the gentlemen are ready, go with them to Campo Angélica, where they will pick out 150 cows, seven bulls, and 50 one-year-old heifers. They will give you a letter, so see that it gets to the Hacienda so it can go out with the mail to El Paso."

I then turned to Robert and Mike and told them to direct their brothers to Hacienda Oriental on the Estancia del Pérez. "They will be accompanied to your ranch with no danger of an attack by the Apaches. If they send a letter or telegram to the Hacienda letting us know when they are to arrive in El Paso, someone from the Hacienda will be there to accompany them to the Hacienda. I will be most likely gone, but my brother-in-law, José Gallego, is the manager of Hacienda Oriental and I will inform him about you. In addition, the man before you is Running Bear, and he is the foreman of Hacienda Oriental."

The Sierra San Luis is not only the border between Chihuahua and Sonora; it is the border between the management of Hacienda Oriental and Hacienda Occidental. The drainage to the east is in the management of the Hacienda Este (Oriental) and the drainage to the west is under the management of Hacienda Oeste (Occidental). Corporal, Juan Gonzáles, El Tigre, He Who Hunts, and I left immediately after breakfast for Campo El Lobo, which was on a northern drainage toward the ancient lake in the Valle de Animas.

We arrived at the campo around noon. The vaqueros were all out on roundup except for three that were keeping a large herd bunched up. I asked Corporal if he would check with the vaqueros about where the jefe of the campo was located and ask him to come in so I could converse with him.

When the jefe arrived, I asked him if Tall Runner's grandson had warned him of the three men that were riding through. He answered in the affirmative and said that Felipe Gonzáles, who was the watcher in this area, followed them north to where they turned into the Canyon de Guadalupe and moved into the San Simon Valley. I told the jefe I was concerned about the large herd of cattle there that was being contained by only three vaqueros. I went on to explain to him that I never thought the campo was in great danger from three men riding through, but I felt they were looking at the roundup and for vulnerabilities in preparation of a raid. If that was so, all they had to do was look at this campo. I then informed him that four men had raided Campo San Luis and had killed one vaquero and wounded another.

I also informed we were moving cattle to gathering spots, and he was to immediately begin to move all stock to Campo San Luis to be moved on to Campo Angélica. He was to move the cattle in small herds of 50 to 100 head. Once these cattle were moved out, he would have time to complete the roundup, and the cattle would be secure. I also mentioned that from here on out, I did not want more than 50 head held here for more than one day.

I then asked him if he had seen any of the Apache bands coming through. He replied that a large band had just come through, and Nana was with them. He went on to explain that Felipe Gonzáles had reported they made camp in a valley south of his location.

I told the jefe I hoped he had not relayed this information to anyone else including his vaqueros, as the Rurales were out on patrol. He replied that as far as he knew, this information was limited to Felipe and himself.

I thanked him for that, asked for Felipe's location, and said my goodbyes. I immediately started off with He Who Hunts, Corporal, Juan Gonzáles, and El Tigre.

Felipe, as a watcher, caught our movement in his direction, and he and his grandson met us before we had gotten halfway to his camp. I was interested in finding out if Felipe had noticed any movement from the north. He had seen the three men the same day he was given the warning from Running Bear. He said, "The travelers observed the camp and the herd and then turned north. I followed them, and they continued in a straight line north toward the Animas Valley and then turned west and went into a small canyon that headed toward Guadalupe Canyon on the east side."

I took this as a clear indication they were most likely part of the Cowboy group of the Clantons, and they were checking on prey. I then told him that the jefe had informed me that Nana and a large group of Apache had moved in close to him. He replied that Nana went into camp about three hours' ride down the ridge to the south. I knew the location, because Corporal, Juan, Roman and I had spent a lot of time camping at that location.

I asked Felipe if they had cleaned out the cattle in that area, and he said, "There are still many cattle in the valleys on both sides of the ridge, as the jefe is not sending vaqueros in this direction."

I turned toward Corporal, and he asked, "How many"?

I looked at Felipe and he replied, "60 to 70."

I replied to Corporal, "Ten head should do, and He Who Hunts, El Tigre, and I will warn them that you and Juan are coming, so they can lock up the girls."

We rode into Nana's camp mid-afternoon to much celebration. It was good to be among my friends. There were many remarks about the appearance of He Who Hunts, because, to strangers, he looked like another vaquero, but, to his family, he looked like a shorn brave.

I told Nana that Corporal and Juan were bringing meat for a feast. He replied that two steers had appeared near his camp the previous day and had been moved there. I made a note to thank the jefe vaquero when I next saw him.

We talked about the pressure on the Apache to move to San Carlos as well as the increased threat to the people by the Rurales.

Nana said, "I and some of the braves are leaving the people here before they move on to El Tigre. We are joining Victorio, who is at war with the American army, which has moved the Warm Springs People to San Carlos even after a treaty was signed by Victorio and myself with a general who spoke for the Great Father. In this treaty, the People could live on their traditional grounds if they remained at peace. Victorio and the Warm Springs people had remained at peace for two years and had not raided the Jornada del Muerto (Journey of Death) the entire time." The Jornada del Muerto is a 100-mile portion of the El Camino Real de Tierra Adentro (the royal road inland) that stretches from Ciudad Chihuahua in Mexico to Santa Fe and on to Española and Taos in New Mexico. It lies on the east side of the Rio Bravo (Rio Grande) river, between the Oscura Mountains and the San Andres Mountains on the east side and the Fra Cristobal Range and Caballo Mountains on the west. The Jornada begins at Paraje Fra Cristobal in the north and runs to the Point of Rocks at the south end, which is near Ft. Selden, north of Las Cruces. The closed and flat Jornada basin is completely devoid of water and firewood in places. The journey was truly a death trip of four to seven days for those unprepared and strangers to the area.

Nana continued, "A large group of soldiers rode into Victorio's and Loco's combined camp freely, as friends, and informed Victorio that the treaty with the Great Father had been rejected by a group of people named Congress, and it was ordered that they were to be forcibly moved to San Carlos. This move was being made to punish the Warm Springs band for acts of war committed prior to the treaty and was made even though there was a reservation (Ojo Caliente) on their traditional hunting grounds.

"Victorio had no knowledge of what Congress was and why they were not at the treaty signing. The people offered no resistance, and they were immediately moved to San Carlos with no time to prepare for food or water. Many of the elderly and children died on the way. This was in July of 1879 and, within one month, Victorio escaped with his band back to the Jornada and their home in the San Andres Mountains. Victorio and the Warm Springs band were at war with the United States."

Loco, who had been advocating peace as the only way for the Apache to survive, remained with his band at the San Carlos Reservation.

As Nana and I were talking, I heard someone approaching from behind me and felt a hand on the back of my neck—something no man would do to another brave. I knew from that touch it could only be from our boyhood friend, who tended to get us all into trouble. Naiche, the mischief maker, could find a way to create excitement in a camp or on the rancho with the ease of water flowing over a rock. Naiche was the youngest son of Cochise and the hereditary chief of the Chihuicahui band of the Tsokanende (Chiricahua) people. His father had been the principal chief of the Tsokanende, but, at his death, the chiefs of certain bands chose not to recognize the sons of Cochise as the principal chiefs, which caused strife between some bands. This had always been the case prior to Mangas Coloradas' and Cochise's efforts to unite the bands as one force.

Naiche, He Who Hunts, Corporal, Juan Gonzáles, and I had spent as much time together growing up as we had with our siblings. Naiche had kept the Chihuicahui band out of raiding and had honored the peace that Cochise had made, but the betrayal of the peace with Victorio had taught all the remaining Apache chiefs that there could never be a peace of equals with the Americans as had been the case with the Mexicans for the past 59 years. Naiche left the hated San Carlos Reservation, led many of the people back to their traditional lands, and sent the elderly and young to the Mescalero Apaches, who gave them shelter on their reservation. War was coming.

I was elated to see Naiche, and the request I was going to make to Nana would now be to Naiche—with Nana's wise counsel. I explained to the chiefs that I would deliver my brother and sister to schools in the eastern United States, and I had a request for them to consider. "As you can see, He Who Hunts has the image of a fine vaquero, and I would like to be able to take him along not only as a companion but as an additional protector of my family. It would give He Who Hunts an opportunity to observe the people in the east and be able to bring back this information to his people. I have not brought this up to He Who Hunts, because I know he is going to want to go with Nana to fight alongside Victorio."

Naiche turned to Nana, who was a war chief, and said, "It would be good for the people to know more of their enemy, and He Who Hunts is a quick learner."

Nana said, "I will send him with my son, so he can observe the enemy in their home and report back to me upon his return. This way, you and I will know more about how and where to fight them. It will be his duty as a protector of the Tsokanende. It will be your duty, my son, to make him understand his position and bring him back to us."

I replied, "It shall be done, my father. I will honor and protect him as the brother he is to me."

Nana called He Who Hunts to the council fire and told him how he was to serve the people. We spent the rest of the night eating beef, drinking Tiswin, and speaking of good times in moons past.

We stayed in camp one more night, so I could pay homage to those who had fed me and disciplined me when I was a lieutenant in Naiche's troop of mischief-makers. We are sons of our mothers before we can be anything else.

Felipe Gonzáles and his grandson met us about halfway back to El Lobo. I knew nothing was going to surprise the camps as long as Felipe was on guard. Felipe informed me that a herd had been leaving the camp every day. I thanked him and told him that I was going to need to go back to the camp before we headed toward Campo Central. I also informed him that when we arrived at the camp, I would be sending him a vaquero as a companion and that it might be best that we get his grandson back to the Hacienda, because none of us had the power to withstand the wrath of Señor White when his students were kept away from school. Felipe told his grandson to get his things, as he was going to be leaving with the patrón.

When we arrived back at Campo El Lobo, I talked to the jefe and asked him to send a young vaquero to be Felipe's aide. I also told him to send a young vaquero to be Tall Runner's aide and let him know I wished not to incur Mr. White's ire by keeping these boys from their studies. He could send his grandson to Campo San Luis, where he would meet Felipe's grandson and they could accompany the cattle as they moved toward the Hacienda from campo to campo.

I told him I realized he was becoming shorthanded. It would be best that he send a request to Campo San Luis with the next herd for extra hands, as Running Bear was either there or at Campo Angélica. I then told him he would be receiving cattle to forward on to Campo San Luis from the campos in the central mountains. He would need to be mindful to not have more than 50 head in camp when he made up a herd to send to Campo San Luis. In addition, he would be receiving only the market cattle, and I wanted him to keep a count of what he moved on from the central camps. He should not combine his mixed herds with their market herds, so he might be sending more than one herd a day. It would be up to him to pass on the order not to mix market herds with mixed herds down the line. The five of us got fresh mounts and took an extra horse for the ride to Campo Central, which was a long climb from where we were.

We stopped short of Campo Central and camped along a stream. To push on would have us entering the camp during the night and disturbing the sleep of tired men. In the morning, we rolled out of our beds and saddled our horses, forsaking coffee, as we would be in camp in an hour.

When we arrived the smell of breakfast was still in the air and, upon seeing us, the cook put some more coals under the grill and started frying eggs and making more tortillas.

I asked for the jefe vaquero and, when he arrived, I told him what had transpired at Campo San Luis. I then told him what we were doing regarding the movement of cattle on the east side. I asked him if he had seen Don Roman, and he indicated he had, but it had been well over a week that he came through heading south. As Roman was not there, I decided I would go ahead and give some operational orders to get things moving. I asked the jefe if they were capable of separating the market cattle from the cows, bulls, and heifers that we would keep from the cattle they had gathered plus the cattle from the campos Cañon Bonito and Ciervo.

He said, "As far as the terrain goes, yes, but I may be short some hands."

I told him he would definitely need some hands, and he should ask for them first from the jeffes of Cañon Bonito and Ciervo or keep a few hands that came in with the herds brought to him. I said, "We will arrange it with the jeffes to leave you some vaqueros at the beginning. If you need more, you are going to have to ask for them. It will be your job to move the market cattle in 50-head bunches to Campo El Lobo as well as move much larger herds of cows and bulls to Valle Batepito for the winter. As soon as I find Roman, I am sure he will send you some fine-tuned orders that will tell you where they are to go."

We visited several more campos and, when we arrived at Campo Central, I told Corporal and Juan that He Who Hunts, El Tigre, and I were going to proceed on to Campo Guadalupe and then Campo San Bernardino. I told them I would like for them to head south to Campo Cañon Bonito and tell the jefe what we were doing and get him started as well as let him know he would be receiving cattle from Campo Ciervo. It would be their job to find Don Roman and accompany him to our meeting at Campo San Bernardino. I added, "Depending on what you find out about where Roman might be; one or both of you will need to continue on south to Campo Ciervo and tell them what we are doing regarding the movement of the cattle. If either camp has finished up and has already separated the market cattle from the stock, they need only move the market cattle toward Campo Central and move the stock off into the Valle Batepito. I will look forward to seeing you both at Campo San Bernardino in a few days."

We rode west toward Campo Guadalupe and stopped mid-afternoon. He Who Hunts went out to see what he could scare up for our supper, and El Tigre went about making camp. We were camped by a stream, and I went over and sat down on a rock and gazed into the water. I saw a trout about nine inches long with a bright red mark under its throat rise to the surface after a fly and, at that moment, I was drawn back to those lazy summer days when we would try to catch trout in the streams above Hacienda Oeste.

I asked El Tigre if he had anything I could make a hook out of. He reached into a leather pouch and pulled out a hook and string. I found a limber, green, willow stem and tied the string to the end of it.

Remembering my boyhood, I then began turning over flat rocks and gathered some yellow grubs. I impaled a grub on the hook, cast the string upstream and let it float down toward a small hole below some low rapids. The line went instantly taut, and my willow stick started gyrating wildly. I pulled the fish in, took it off the hook, ran a forked stick through its gills on one side, and placed it into the water. I did this three times before He Who Hunts entered camp with a venado (deer) draped across his shoulders. I knew we would not be eating fish tonight, but trout is a delicacy for breakfast.

He Who Hunts and El Tigre dressed out the venado and left the hide on, as we were to dine on heart and liver. He Who Hunts tied a rope to the deer that he swung over a high tree limb and pulled the venado out of the reach of any oso (bear) that happened by. El Tigre had dug up some wild onions that he sprinkled with a little dry sage from one of his pouches, and we ate like kings.

The next morning, I went down to stream early to fetch the fish for breakfast. When I got there, I found the stick with three fish heads on it. A mapache (raccoon) had already had its breakfast. We had to settle for venison steak, which El Tigre had already cut from the carcass.

We reached Campo Guadalupe by mid-morning. Campo Guadalupe was the largest Campo on the rancho, and many of the vaqueros had homes there as well as the jefe vaquero. After having been in rather austere camps for a while, it was a shock to see women and children about. The jefe invited us in, and we sat down to coffee and pan dulce (sweet bread) that his wife had prepared. I told the jefe about the gathering camps and said he could start moving his market cattle toward Campo San Luis right away. This camp had the largest area to cover on the ranch and was in mountainous territory, so I was concerned about how far they had gotten with the roundup. He told me they had built corrals in valles to the west, and most of the cattle had been branded, separated, and were ready to be moved. I asked him if he was ready to ship from the east side of his area, and he indicated he could, so I suggested that he begin soon and then move cattle from the west side to those empty corrals to discourage cows coming back looking for their calves.

I told him about the three men and that I was concerned about being raided from a ranch near Tombstone and was looking at moving the market cattle as safely as I could from the west to the east. I asked him if it would be possible to have Campo Guadalupe be the shipping point for Hacienda Occidental for all stock shipped to Hacienda Oriental. He believed the corrals and water as well as graze were sufficient, but it might be wise to have those that were bringing market cattle here to take back stock for the range toward the Valle Batepito. I agree that he had a good plan and I would discuss it with Don Ramón. In the meantime, he should begin shipping to Campo San Luis. I complimented him on his industry and said there was no reason for me to linger. I would move on toward Camp San Bernardino.

We arrived at Campo San Bernardino in the evening and were there in ample time to partake of beans and tortillas. He Who Hunts had left the carcass of the venado with the Jeffe's wife at Campo Guadalupe.

The next morning, we rode out with the vaqueros and helped with the roundup. I had the opportunity to use a riata (rope for lassoing cattle) for the first time in a long time. Mexican saddles have a front-rigging called a dee located under the pommel of the saddle on both sides. The dee is a D-shaped ring to which a cinch strap that goes under the horse is attached. The breast strap is hooked to the D ring on the other side as well. When a vaquero ropes an animal, his horse has been trained to switch ends (turn away) from the roped animal before it completely extends the rope, so the breast strap takes up the force of the animal when it hits the end of the rope. In addition, most Western horses are trained to "set up" when the animal hits the rope. This means their front legs are set straight and their back legs are bent, which puts the horse into a slide and stops the animal.

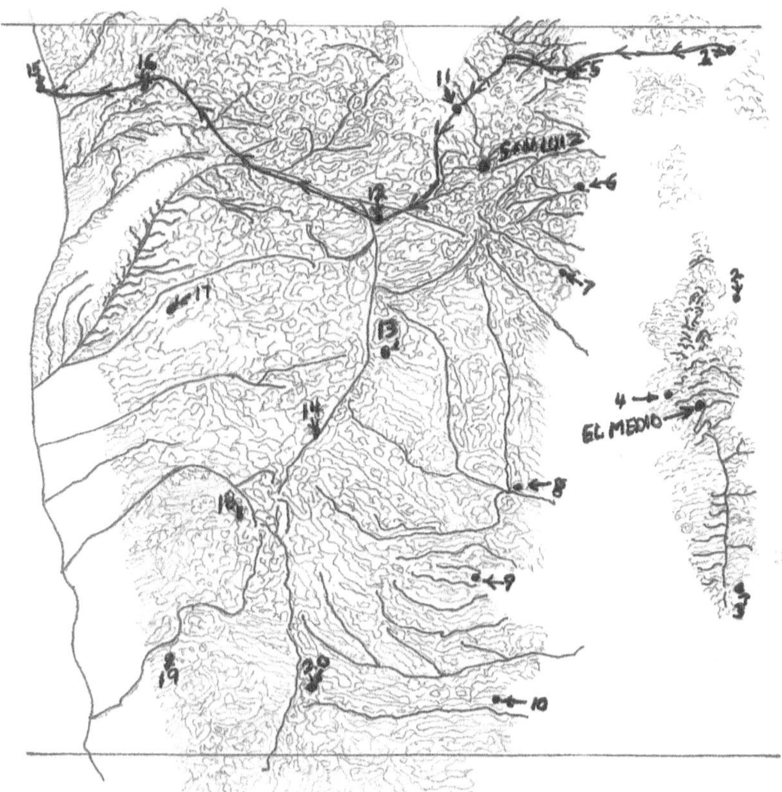

1. Campo Berrendo	11. Campo El Lobo
2. Campo Nogales	12. Campo Central
3. Campo Medio	13. Campo Canjon Bonito
4. Campo Maria	14. Campo Ciervo
5. Campo San Luis	15. Campo San Bernardino
6. Campo Angelica	16. Campo Guadalupe
7. Campo Dulce	17. Campo Jaguar
8. Campo Elizabeth	18. Campo San Fernando
9. Campo Abudante	19. Campo Pinones
10. Campo Azul	20. Campo Ocelote

 Francisco's Route

Azul – blue Canjon – canyon Ocelote - Ocelot

The Western or Texas-style saddle is good for roping calves and is necessary for heeling (catching the animal by its back heels), but, without a Mexican-style breast strap, the rider can be in big trouble if they rope a big animal. On our rancho, the horses were trained to switch ends with a jerk to the left when the loop at the end of the rope settled on an animal, and our saddles always had a breast strap with a double cinch.

It had been four years since I had roped anything. Fate had it that I was roping a 1,500-pound bull. I was still a good roper, and my loop settled over his horns. I snapped the rope taut so it cinched around his neck. The problem was I was slow about that little jerk to the left, and my horse was broadside to the bull when he hit the end of the rope. My fall was not elegant. It gave the vaqueros something to laugh about once it was decided I was not killed. El Tigre had a grin on his face the rest of the day.

At dusk, three riders were spotted coming from the south and, long before I could ascertain who they were, both He Who Hunts and El Tigre announced the arrival of Don Roman with Juan and Corporal. It was so good to see Roman. I did not know how much I missed him until I saw him. We had always been competitive, but, at the same time, we had always covered each other's back. I knew Roman was there for me, and his judgment was sound. That did not keep Roman from mentioning he was sure that Running Bear was still teaching roping, if I might be interested. After supper was over and we had a couple of toasts, Corporal and Juan made their excuses of chores needing to be done, and the others followed their lead. Roman and I were left alone.

I asked how the roundup was proceeding, and he replied that we had a good crop of steers and heifers, and the southernmost camps had moved to their northern neighbors. He said that, before long, we would have some large herds. He mentioned that some buyers from Tucson and Hermosillo had approached him for local market beef, and one rancher from the States had approached him with a proposal to buy 500 steers to winter in his pastures and sell in the Spring market when the trains were expected to be here. The man said he could only afford to buy 500, but he would like to work out a partnership on a larger herd if we were willing. I told Roman that I would indeed be willing to look at this proposition, but time was short and I explained to him how our mother had backed me into a corner with my own words and that I would shortly be taking Javier and Elizabeth east to continue their education.

Roman looked astounded. "Are they letting girls attend the College?" he blurted.

I laughed and said, "No, she has been accepted to a college in Massachusetts." I then went on to explain that Dulce had also been accepted, and she was going with us to be a companion to Elizabeth on the trip. "It is Mother's hope that she will see the place and want to attend also. Mother has not told Robert about the loss of Father, and it will be my job to tell him and convince him of the value of his completing his education and of my hope that he will direct his next two years to studying finance, because the family will need this skill in the future. It is also my hope that Javier look into geology, as I know there is mineral wealth on the rancho worth exploiting, and I am afraid that another revolution will come along and the Haciendas, as they are, will not survive the social upheaval. Our father walked a fine line between the Juaristas and the Conservatives who had joined with the Royals."

I then asked Roman if this rancher would be amenable to meeting me at the Hacienda as soon as possible, so we could discuss the possibility of going into business together. Roman thought he might be able to do that, because his ranch was east of the Sierras de Santa Rita in the Valle de Las Cienegas.

I asked the cook if he would send his boy to ask Corporal to come when he could.

I then went on to explain to Roman what we were doing with the herds as they were being moved toward the Hacienda Este. I said it would be a good idea for him to start moving herds of 300 to 350 head toward the gathering places. If he could begin by moving his eastern herds first, that would give us time to adjust to the demands that may come up after our negotiations with the rancher.

We went on to discuss the danger I perceived from the Cowboys to our herds and that we were going to need twice as many vaqueros as normal to move each herd. I also asked Roman if he was in a position to release some of the watchers in the south so we could send some up into the States to watch the approaches to the border and forewarn us of any large movement of Cowboys in our direction.

Roman brought up that this would be a fine time to lure the Cowboys into an ambush. I agreed, but I wanted to be there for that and could not devote the time needed now and be on the road to the colleges by mid-November. "Our best path is prevention," I said. "We will have our time of revenge soon enough."

Roman replied, "I look forward to that time, as my heart burns."

I replied, "As does mine, my brother."

Corporal and the boy arrived. I told the boy that I appreciated his help. I told Corporal we had an arduous task for him that Roman could explain. Roman told him where he could find this gringo rancher and why we needed him to go. I then told Corporal I hoped to see him in four or five days at the Hacienda and mentioned to Roman that El Tigre would be a good man to put on the job of establishing the watchers in the north. After that task was done, I told him I would like him to join us at the Hacienda. I said my goodnights and headed for my bedroll.

When a vaquero notices the aroma of tortillas cooking in the morning, it transports him to his mother's kitchen and all the associated warmth. He opens his eyes to the reality of his current place and time, but he yearns to be in that place of his memory for a few more seconds.

Besides tortillas, the cooks had red chili and beans with eggs frying on another flatiron. One only needed to grab a cup of coffee and a tortilla onto which he could heap chili and eggs. He had his coffee and breakfast in his two hands, and nothing else was required.

As I sat down, Roman and Juan Gonzáles joined me, carrying their breakfasts. After a few gulps of coffee, Roman said, "El Tigre has left for the southern camps to summon five watchers for an early warning system. In addition, I have sent three vaqueros along with El Tigre to notify Campos San Fernando, Piones, Ocelote, Juanita, Conejos, and Cierro Prieto to move their market cattle to Campo Bonito. I instructed El Tigre that he is to tell the jefe of Campo Bonito to hold 500 head of market cattle and move the rest to Campo Guadalupe to be taken to Hacienda Oriental.

El Tigre indicated he did not think he could set up the watchers in a short time, but, as soon as he had set them up with communications, he would be along. His idea was to make Felipe the hub of communications and use mirrors and lights to signal between the mountains.

Corporal had left last night to get a jump on the trip, as the gringo might need a little time before he could leave once Corporal reached him. I would send one vaquero to Campo Contenido with instructions to begin moving their market cattle in herds of no more than 50 head to Campo Guadalupe. There were more than enough cattle to start the first move to Hacienda Oriental and, because there was good graze and water there, it could serve as the western gathering camp for the campos south of Hacienda Occidental. I would give instructions at Campo Aguas Frescas to start moving their market cattle toward Campo San Juan. In addition, I would give instructions to two vaqueros to alert Campos Malcate and Alta to move their market cattle to Campo Cananea, where they were to be held until we could establish how we were to market the western herds. Once we arrived at the Hacienda, I would send vaqueros to Campos Huachucas, Santa Cruz, San Lazaro, San Rafael, and Aquas Abundantes and let them know they needed to move their market cattle to the Hacienda. I would tell the northern campos to move their cattle in as large a herd as they could manage, and move the breeding herds toward the south for the winter in a separate move.

I informed Roman what was happening and how the cattle were to be moved. He made it the Jeffe's responsibility to inform the campos on both sides of the Rio Batepito.

All cattle were to be moved through Campo Guadalupe as soon as he was through with the roundup. He was to move the stock to the Valle Batepito and help the jefe of Campo Guadalupe coordinate the moving of the cattle east. Roman emphasized that the rustlers were professionals and ruthless, and would take advantage of any weakness. He insisted that there always be twice as many vaqueros as needed when moving the herds or guarding the northernmost herds.

As we headed west, we stopped at Campo Aguas Frescas and warned them of the danger of rustlers. We asked the jefe to send a rider to consult with the watchers in their area and, if they had seen any movement, even if it was just one rider, he was to send a rider to inform us. In addition, we would place some watchers on traveled routes in the Estados Unidos, and they would communicate with the watchers here. Roman gave them instructions as to what they were to do with the market cattle and the breeding herds. They were to continue to work the areas around their camp but move the gathered cattle as soon as they could make up herds so as not to make it easy for rustlers. Roman informed the jefe as to the method we were using to move the cattle eastward. The jefe in the camp from the east would inform him about how many cattle he could handle, but he should not keep herds of over 50 head. It would be his responsibility to inform the jeffes to his south and west as to when to begin to move their stock.

Cananea – Canaanite   Aguas Abundantes – abundant waters

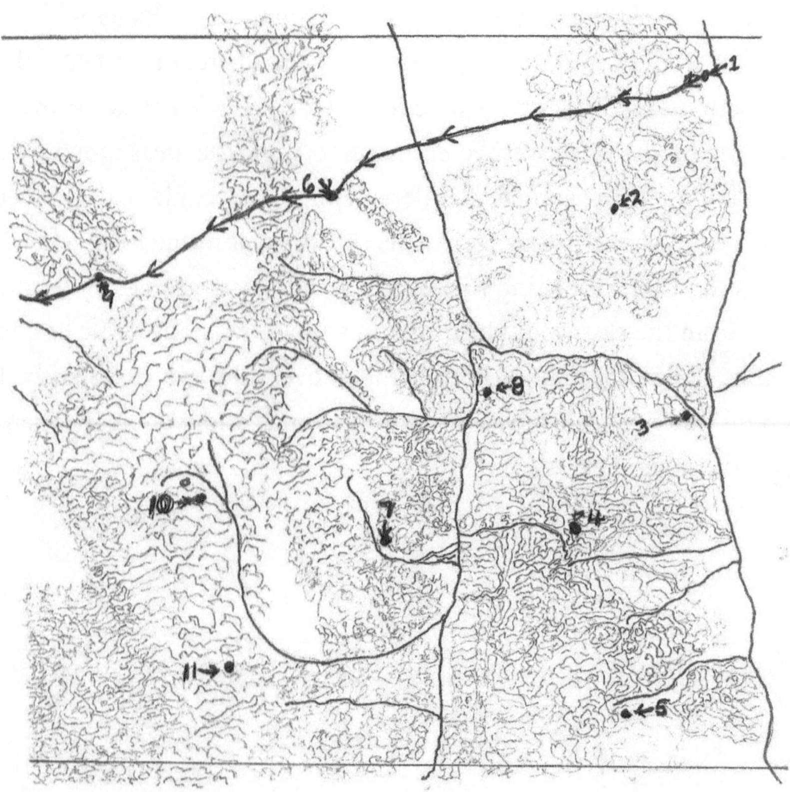

1. Campo San Bernardino
2. Campo Contenido
3. Campo Bonito
4. Campo Solo
5. Campo Juanita
6. Campo Aguas Frescas

7. Campo Conejos
8. Campo Cerro Prieto
9. Campo San Juan
10. Campo Malacate
11. Campo Alta

Francisco's Route

Contenido – Content   Prieto – Tight   Malacate – Winch   Aguas Frescas – Fresh Waters

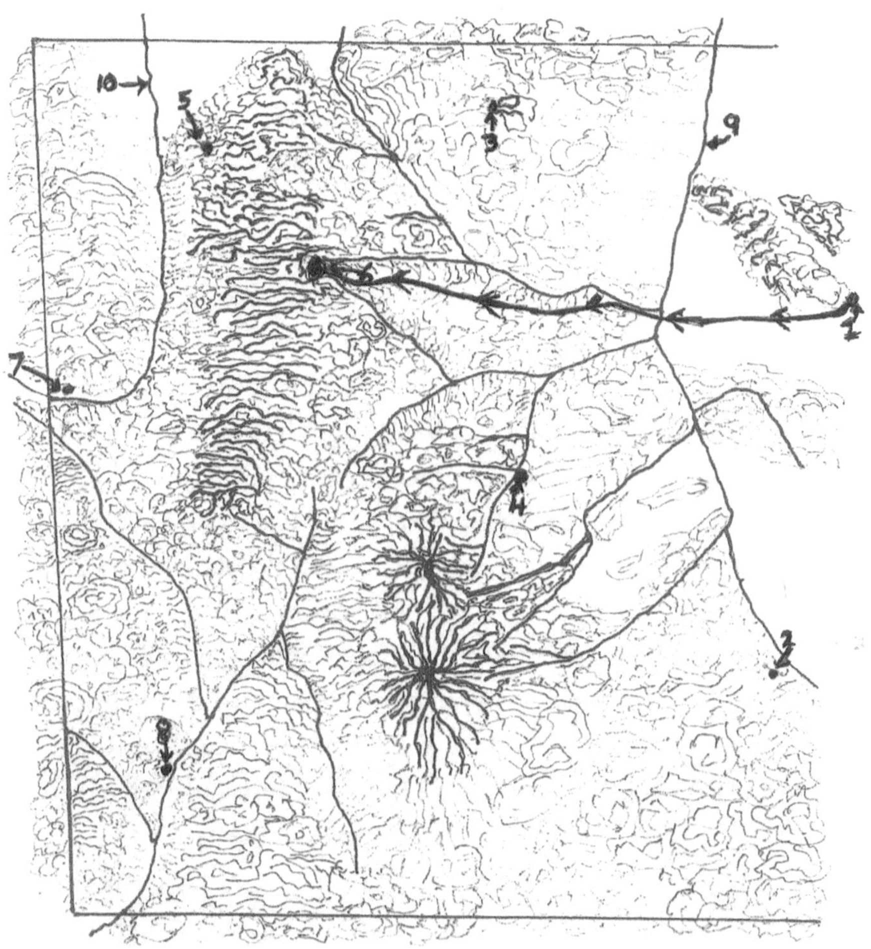

1. Campo San Juan
2. Campo Cananea
3. Campo Huachucas
4. Campo Aguas Abundantes
5. Campo Santa Cruz
6. Hacienda de Oeste
7. Campo San Lazaro
8. Campo San Rafael
9. Rio de San Pedro
10. Rio Santa Cruz

_________________________ Francisco's Route

It was late afternoon when we reached Campo San José. Roman told the jefe of the camp that we were moving the stock toward Hacienda Occidental, but that we might have a market for some cattle here. In the meantime, it would be best that he move his herds to Campo Cananea, where it would be much harder for the rustlers to get at them. It was not necessary to separate the herd, as they could separate the market cattle at Campo Cananea.

We had several riders catch up to us with news that riders had been spotted watching but moving on fairly rapidly. They could be travelers, or they could be lookouts posing as travelers. I tended to err on the side of caution and told them to keep alert. It would be nice to have watchers watching the watchers in case they were other than travelers.

As we came over a rise, we could see Hacienda Occidental. I got the old feeling of arriving home again that I had felt so many times before in my youth. The Hacienda sat on a hill that was the blunt end of a long ridge flanked by two valleys that tumbled down from the mountains. Each valley had bubbling springs that were home to cutthroat trout that I and my companions spent many a lazy summer day attempting to capture for the frying pans of the Hacienda. The streams swirled into some wonderful pools where we had learned to swim and tried to catch the big yellow catfish that had burrowed holes in the banks.

Hacienda Occidental was not as grand as Hacienda Oriental. It had no fields, and the workshops were much smaller, but it had been a place where the family could escape our responsibilities and where I really got to know my parents.

As I rode toward the Hacienda and looked at the veranda that ran around both sides and the front of the house, I missed seeing my father and mother rise from their chairs and wave to us as we came home from our adventures. I needed the ease of sitting in front of the fireplace that evening with my compañeros and letting the cares slip from my shoulders, if only just for an evening.

Roman went off to give instructions to the vaqueros and inquired as to the location of his primero, Antonio de Oso. He Who Hunts stated he was in need of some meat of the venado or pavo (turkey), and Juan thought it would be a great idea if they brought one or the other to the cook. They took off on their errands.

I could not think of a thing I needed to do. When Manuel, the cook at the Hacienda, came in with a tray of pan dulce, I thanked him and told him I was going to take it to the veranda. I told him that if he could find some cigars and mescal, I would appreciate it if he could join me while we waited to see what our intrepid hunters brought in.

It was a time to reflect. News had come that Victorio's War was heating up. Victorio—with the warriors that had joined him not only from the Warm Springs band but also some Mescalero and some southern-plains Comanche and their families—were approaching Ojo Caliente when they detected a small patrol from the Ninth Cavalry (Buffalo Soldiers). In the ensuing battle, eight soldiers under Captain Ambrose Hooker were killed, and their bodies were mutilated. There were no reported Apache casualties.

News of the Battle of Ojo Caliente spread rapidly through the Southwest, and the army dispatched thousands of soldiers to hunt down Victorio and his warriors.

The news reached the reservations, and other Apache bands left the reservations to join in the fights. American settlers were being killed, and militias were being formed to protect the settlements and enact the settlers' revenge. The Southwest was at war.

CHAPTER 8

He Who Hunts and Juan Gonzáles returned with two pavos and a venado. Because the hour was late, Manuel declared that we would be having the venado liver, heart, and ribs for supper and that he would prepare us a grand feast of the two pavos tomorrow evening.

At nightfall, El Tigre rode in with his primo, Tall Runner. I asked Tall Runner about the health of the vaquero that he had delivered to the Tarahumara summer camp on El Tigre.

He replied, "The women of the village are taking care of him, and they are confident he will make a full recovery."

I thanked him and stated that we would need to send the village 10 fat steers as payment for their help and generosity. He said the jefe of Campo Juanita anticipated your orders and had seen that this was done.

I asked El Tigre if he had gotten the watchers established on the American side. El Tigre answered, "Sí, mi jefe. I assessed the problem and felt we needed more than five watchers. I sent older men such as myself and mi primo who knew the country from before. Therefore, I did not need to take them to where they needed to go but only needed to tell them where they should establish themselves. I also wanted men who scouted for your father in the army, as they had learned to talk with mirrors. I took the liberty to send out nine watchers and arranged that Tall Runner would be their contact. It is already working, as I received a message coming here that Señor Corporal and two riders are camped near the frontera (border) and will be here before midday tomorrow. They could have ridden in tonight, but they would have disturbed the house, so they elected to stop early."

Manuel came to the door and said something about throwing supper out the back door, so we rushed in to dinner.

After supper, we retired to the veranda, where Manuel had set up a table with coffee, brandy, and cigars. After everyone had selected their poison, I opened a strategy session by asking everyone in the room what they might do if we got notice that a group of men were headed toward one of the campos or had staked themselves out along the trail on which we were moving cattle. Corporal, Juan, and He Who Hunts spoke up immediately, each saying we should attack them and wipe them out. Roman held his tongue as did Tall Runner, El Tigre, and Manuel. I then addressed El Tigre and asked him what he would do.

El Tigre responded, "Don Francisco, when I was a young man, I was angry and quick to violence. The elders of my tribe felt that because the Mexicans seem to be always fighting each other, it may be a good idea for me and Tall Runner as well as others to see how the rest of the people in Mexico were coping with the wars and violence. They suggested that we join up with the army and learn how the Mexicans fought.

"As people of the mountains, we were somewhat isolated from the rest of the world, so we went down and talked to our friends, the Pima, who lived in the valleys and tilled the soil. They said a young colonel, who was born and lived his early years at the presidio in Tucson where his father, José de Urrea, was an officer, had learned the language of the O'Otham. Urrea had sent recruiters among the O'Otham and Yaqui to join his army in a city called Durango, where they were fighting the Comanche.

"It was 1835 when we left our village in the Sierras and traveled to Durango. We were all young braves, around the age of 15, and we needed to prove to the world that we were fierce. Being Tarahumara, we distained the use of horses, as we could easily outdistance a horse in a run. When we arrived in Durango, there were people there to join the army to fight the Comanche who lived on the plains of Texas, Chihuahua, and Durango and seemed to hate all people. Each of us held up our hand and swore by our ancestors that we were freely joining this great band of warriors.

"We were placed in bands where there was a war chief called a Sargento and a segundo called Corporal. They took away our war clubs and taught us how to use a rifle and to kill with a bayonet. The main thing they taught us was discipline. We were no longer braves looking for our personal glory. We were soldiers, fighting for the warriors in our band and, thereby, the entire army. I say this because I want to emphasize the rest of what I will now say.

"Our first engagements were not with the Comanche. The citizens of Zacatecas had revolted against the rule of General Santa Anna who, after having been elected Presidente, took over the government of Mexico as a dictator. We got used to the life of a soldier in the army under Colonel de Urrea. Our army was ordered on the expedition that was being led by General Santa Anna wherein he viciously put down the revolt by slaughtering all that opposed him. Because of our success in these battles, Colonel Urrea was made a General.

"Our regiment was taken over by your father, who had been sent by Santa Anna to report on General de Urrea. Most everyone in Urrea's army held your father in high suspicion, because we felt he was a spy for Santa Anna. Colonel Gregorio de Pérez quickly proved himself as a loyal and able officer under General Urrea. We fought many skirmishes, and what I learned from Colonel Gregorio de Pérez was that strength wins wars and saves lives.

"Tu padre ordered his regiment to surround the Tejans at the Battle of Coleto. When they were totally surrounded, he went forward toward the Tejan lines with a white flag, exposing the entire regiment to the Tejans, who realized the hopelessness of their cause and surrendered. Tu papá accepted their surrender and ordered that they be fed and treated as noble prisoners of war.

"After our regiment had moved on with General de Urrea's army down the coast of Tejas, with the object of keeping the British and the Americanos from supplying the Tejanos from the sea, General de Santa Anna sent a regiment to overwhelm the squads that were left holding the prisoners and slaughtered every last prisoner. All the goodwill that we had created while defeating the Tejanos but not killing them and treating them as noble prisoners of war was wiped out. Along with the slaughter at the Alamo, our nobility had been erased.

"I say you should best show the raiders you are much stronger than they and that their cause is hopeless. I further propose that you never slaughter. If it is necessary to execute leaders, do so, but never lose the moral ground. This suggestion humbly goes for those who raid. If they surrender, do not kill the soldiers. Mi patrón, I hope you will forgive my boldness."

I looked at the other men on the veranda and said, "It would be a good idea for us all to sleep on what we have heard here, and we will set up a strategy after breakfast and before Corporal arrives with our guests."

As always, when I opened the door into Manuel's kitchen the next morning, all the men were eating heartily and drinking coffee. I sat down, and Manuel set an empty plate in front of me. I started filling it with eggs, chili con carne, and frijoles. I gathered some tortillas and began to eat.

No one had said a word, as all were busy with the job at hand. When all had finished, Manuel stated, "I will prepare some burritos and tacos for lunch for those that are hungry. It will be on a table on the veranda, because the kitchen will be closed in preparation of the grand meal for our visitors. This will be a formal meal, and any dirty cowboys that show up will be thrown out, so I suggest you dress for dinner."

Manuel had his boys set up a table with coffee and pan dulce on the veranda, and we retired to discuss our plans.

I opened the discussion by asking the question, "Does anybody have anything to say about what we heard?"

None of the men were anxious to speak first, and just as I was about to take the floor, He Who Hunts said, "I have learned much from my brother of the Tarahumara. One should not fight just to win the raid, battle, or war. He should fight to win the peace."

I looked at my friend with new-found admiration.

Roman spoke up and said, "I greatly appreciate how El Tigre put all of this in perspective. I believe Tall Runner and I can set up a strategy of action based upon our warning system and sending orders to campos to dispatch riders to meet us at a point we designate, so we will always present an impressive force."

I thanked Roman and said I thought they had a good plan going. I added the following: "I do not want any vaquero to kill unless he fears he is threatened. I want our forces to always look like they cannot be overcome. I further do not want the leaders executed. What I do want is that all leaders be detained and turned over to the Rurales for whatever they deem is proper justice. I want to make sure that a rider takes back the news to the Estados Unidos that the government of Mexico is dealing with the rustlers—not the vaqueros of this rancho.

"However, if you capture one of the men that had a hand in the killing of my father, you are not to harm him or to turn him over to the Rurales; they shall be reserved for the justice of the rancho. If I am not here, it will be up to Don Roman to determine what that will be. It is to be done with as few witnesses as possible, and the body is to be left on the northern side of the border with no indication of how it arrived there. I hope that each of them meets a painfully bad death, and I want them to know why they are receiving the justice of the Estancia del Pérez."

I asked for comments, but there were none. I looked toward He Who Hunts and said, "You are on my team, so find three more vaqueros to side us, and we will meet Roman and Juan with their teammates on the stickball court in thirty minutes. I would appreciate it if El Tigre and Tall Runner would officiate. Their word is the law. I feel sorry for Roman, Juan, and whomever they choose."

Most of the vaqueros on the rancho were soldiers that served with my father or their descendants. Urrea had recruited heavily amongst the Indios of Durango, Chihuahua, and Sonora. Stickball was the main game of teenagers and young men throughout the Americas, and all tribes participated. The game was like war and, at times, it was used to settle differences rather than going to war.

My father had set aside areas at each of the Haciendas for the purpose of stickball games. There were games quite often between neighboring ranchos and, when we were being visited by bands; there would often be a game.

Our little game of five on five quickly became a game of ten on ten with many willing substitutes. We were still hotly in the game when Corporal and the two North Americans arrived. Corporal introduced me and Roman to Walter and Edward Vail. Corporal took my place in the game and, within a few minutes, all the substitutes had picked a side. The game looked much like a mob riot under the direction of El Tigre and Tall Runner.

We settled down to cool drinks and tacos on the veranda, where we could watch the riot and get acquainted. Walter Vail explained that he and his brother were partners with an Englishman named John Harvey, who stayed at their ranch to watch over things. I explained to them that I was the eldest son of Gregorio Pérez, who was the recipient of a land grant and established this Estancia del Pérez. I told them there were two divisions, each of which had a hacienda. This Hacienda, which we called Hacienda Occidental, was managed by my brother, Roman.

We kept our conversation light while we were eating and relaxing. Walter Vail said he had seen a game like this once in Princeton, New Jersey at the college. He said, "Isn't it like lacrosse?"

Roman and I looked at him with surprise, and Roman asked, "When were you in Princeton?"

Walter answered, "I believe it was in the Spring of 1876. My partner at the time and I stopped in Princeton on our way to California."

I replied that he had shocked Roman and myself, because if he had seen a lacrosse game at the College of New Jersey in the spring of 1876, I was most assuredly in it, having attended school there from the fall of 1875 through the spring of 1879. Roman attended school there from 1877 through 1879.

It was the Vails' turn to be a little astounded, as they had grown up in Plainfield, New Jersey and had been to Princeton many times. I went on to explain that I would be going back in a few weeks to take a brother who was to enroll and see a brother that had already been there two years. I also explained I would be going to Massachusetts to install one sister in Wellesley College and possibly another. "I mention this so you will know that what we agree to will have to be managed by Roman, as I will be away."

I mentioned to them that our cook was preparing a grand dinner for that evening and, if they needed to take a siesta or rest up from their trip, I would understand. "If not, we can begin our business now."

Walter replied he would rather get started right away. I asked the cook's helper attending us if he could bring us out a large pitcher of tea, and then I said, "Let us get at it. Please tell me what is on your mind."

Walter said, "We are interested in purchasing 500 head of stock cattle. Since we acquired our original land, we have been buying adjoining properties when we could persuade the owners to sell to us. Many of those properties have some stock, and some have none. We can only afford to purchase at this time about 500 head at 10 dollars a head for heifers and 30 dollars a head for 20 range bulls."

I told them I would be happy to sell them heifers and bulls at that price, but, at that price, we would select the cattle they could choose from. If they wished to pay 13 dollars ahead for heifers and 40 dollars a head for range bulls, they could pick from the herds what they wanted with two provisos—the heifers must be two years or younger and the bulls must be three years or younger. We haggled back and forth and settled on heifers at 12 dollars a head and bulls at 35 dollars a head. They would be able to choose the animals based on the conditions that I had stated with the proviso that the bulls could be four years or younger.

I then went on to ask if they had any other business they wanted to discuss, and Walter spoke up and asked me about my market strategy for such a large operation. I told them I would be attempting to set up a steady, year-round market that would be freight on buyer.

Walter said, "I would really like to discuss with you sometime in the future the possibility of joint marketing."

I asked Walter whether this purchase of 500 head would stock his range.

He answered, "No, but that is all we are able to purchase at this time."

I then stated I was considering withholding cattle from the Fall market with an eye toward shipping cattle on the railroads the following year, and I would welcome a proposal from him to put some of those cattle on his range for fattening next Spring. At that moment, El Tigre stepped up onto the veranda and told me a large force of Rurales was approaching.

CHAPTER 9

I sent the cook's helper to let Manuel know there would be at least four more guests for supper. I then turned to Roman and asked him to see that the Rurales were well provisioned with food and drink.

El Tigre spoke up. "Mi patrón, con su permiso, seria un honor ver que la carne se brasa (My boss, with your permission, it would be an honor to prepare the barbeque)."

Roman replied, "No habría manos más capaces a quien yo podía dejar esa tarea. Muchas gracias (There could be no more capable hands to leave that chore to. Thank you)."

Roman sent vaqueros to prepare a campsite and see to the comforts of the Rurales and their stock. I told Walter and Edward that Rurales were approaching, we would ask the Rurale officers to dine with us, and our people were preparing a barbecue for them.

Walter replied, "Since all our hands are vaqueros, I have learned their language enough to get along, so I did catch the flow of what was happening. Do you get these visits often?"

I replied that it was exceedingly rare to see such a large contingent of Rurales.

Corporal, who knew the officers of the Rurales, went out to meet and escort them to the Hacienda. He explained to the officer in command that both Don Roman and Don Francisco were here at the Hacienda and begged the officers to join them for refreshments. He told them the comfort of their men would be attended to, and we would be honored if they would join us for dinner at the Hacienda this evening.

It was not long before many of the Rurales were choosing sides in the stickball game, and the madness ensued. I turned to Walter and Edward and said, "You have never seen such a riot at the lacrosse games in Princeton, I'm sure," and they laughed.

As the officers arrived, both Roman and I went down to meet them. Capitán Carrillo introduced me to Comandante Francisco Neri and the two lieutenants. We received Comandante Neri's regrets on the loss of our father, and we extended our condolences on the loss of the Rurales.

I introduced Comandante Neri and his officers to Walter and Edward Vail and told everyone I would introduce them to the other guests at dinner. After we had all settled down and watched the stickball game for a few minutes, Comandante Neri told us the reason for his visit.

"Don Francisco," he began, "as you know, Presidente Porfirio Díaz formed the Rurales as a Federal Police Force to protect the border from rustling and hostile Indian incursions. Our job is to prevent rustling of Mexican cattle and the bringing into the country of stolen goods from the United States. Last year, we were informed by the government of the United States that they would set up an outpost on the east side of the Huachuca Mountains and move two companies of the Sixth Cavalry to address the threat of the Chiricahua Apache and secure the border with Mexico. This is much the same mission that we are charged with.

"Presidente Díaz has received three complaints from the United States Government about problems near this rancho. The first complaint was that ranchers in the Deming area and south to the border are being harassed by Mexican bandits that are in collusion with Apaches and are keeping the ranchers from lawful business on their land. In addition, two men were killed. The rest heroically escaped certain death while carrying off the bodies of their fallen companions. A second complaint is that vaqueros hired by some ranchers along the Gila and the Mogollon

Rim were ambushed by Apaches and bandits. Their herd was stolen and moved into Mexico. This complaint was made to the commander at Camp Huachuca. The third complaint, which also came from Camp Huachuca, is that lawful ranchers are being harassed and followed by Mexican bandits originating from this rancho."

He saw the look on my face and quickly added, "I know these are not legitimate complaints, and so does Presidente Díaz, but Presidente Díaz is trying to attract funds from the United States for investments in industry in Mexico, and he has charged me to talk to you about settling these problems."

I related my version of these events, and Comandante Neri replied, "That is exactly what Presidente Díaz thought occurred, but it is our duty to set up a working relationship with the officers in command at Camp Huachuca. The commander at Camp Huachuca is a Captain Whiteside. Presidente Díaz sent a message to Presidente Hayes of the United States that he was sending a message that emissaries would be arriving to meet with Captain Whiteside in the near future. By now, Capitán Whiteside has that message and is awaiting our meeting.

"I am really squeezed for time," I told Comandante Neri. "I had planned on leaving here tomorrow, as I need to set up the marketing of our herds, and I am making a trip to the eastern United States. If necessary, I can delay my leaving here by one or two days to give a messenger time to go to Camp Huachuca and set up a meeting here at Hacienda Occidental as soon as possible. Would it be possible for a couple of your officers to accompany Corporal to Camp Huachuca to invite Captain Whiteside and whomever he would like to accompany him to this meeting?"

Comandante Neri replied, "I am quite sure that Capitán Carrillo would prefer that he be the one to ride with Corporal again. Captain, will you be ready to ride in the next hour?"

Capitán Carrillo answered, "I am ready now but for a fresh horse."

Corporal said, "We can pick up a couple each at the stables, and we will be off."

I replied, "Then go, but stop by here, as I am sure that Manuel will not want you to go with empty bellies." Out of the side of my eye, I saw one of the kitchen hands slip away to report to Manuel.

I turned to Comandante Neri and the Vail brothers and told them I was going to have to beg off awhile. "I need a short siesta, and I am going to need to send some correspondence to Hacienda Oriental." I told the Comandante that a room had been prepared for him, and one of the boys here could show it to him.

I retreated to my rooms and quickly wrote out a request to José for an update on Señor Deus and what he had found out from our traditional buyers. "Also, I would like to know how we are proceeding on the road branding. I think we should hold off doing any more road brands if we have reached 5,000 head." I sent the note to Roman to be dispatched immediately. I also told him to let the Vails and the Comandante know that dispatches were leaving and, if they had any mail to post, it would be in El Paso in four days.

We had a grand supper. Manuel really outdid himself. He had prepared the turkeys in the same manner as those I'd enjoyed as a guest in the homes of students at the time of Thanksgiving—roasted turkey with piñón (pine nut) and pear dressing, mashed potatoes, calabacitas (chopped squash with onions and peppers), taquitos de carne seca (rolled tacos made with beef jerky), pan (bread), and gravy. There were all kinds of relishes and, to finish it off, we had flan (custard) and cactus candy. José, He Who Hunts, Roman, and Antonio joined me in representing the rancho.

Comandante Neri was not fooled by He Who Hunts' presence at the meal. After dinner, he told me that Presidente Díaz had told him about Gregorio's concession to the tribes, and that there had been no one that broke the peace on the rancho. It was made his duty by the Presidente not to break the peace on the rancho.

I told him I was raised among the Apache as well as the Comanche, and the peace of the Estancia del Pérez would remain as long as I lived. After cigars and drinks on the veranda, the lieutenants begged off to their duties, and the rest of us engaged in light conversation. I told the Vailes that both Roman and I were going to be busy the next day, but Juan, He Who Hunts, and Antonio would be at their disposal if they wanted to start choosing their stock here and at the camps to the south and southeast. I told them I would see them at breakfast at Manuel's kitchen table, and we would have a good dinner tomorrow evening—hopefully with the commander of Camp Huachuca.

Walter said they had met him before and would be glad to see him again and possibly do some business.

Roman and I were finally left by ourselves. We invited Manuel to join us, and we lit up some more cigars, opened a bottle of mescal, and chatted about old times.

The next morning, I joined the Vails as we walked into Manuel's kitchen to be greeted by Juan, He Who Hunts, El Tigre, Antonio, and Roman, who were busy working on their breakfasts. We found some chairs and began ladling our choice of eggs, tocino, steaks, patatas (another name for potatoes), and salsa de pimento rojo (red chili sauce).

Manuel was pouring our coffee when Comandante Neri came through the door followed by his two lieutenants. He said, "I see that sleeping in is not the custom here."

We all laughed and begged them to join in. Having had a goodly supply of Manuel's pan dulce, Juan, He Who Hunts, and Antonio requested permission to leave and asked the Vails if some horses could be saddled for them. The Vails thanked them and said they would be right behind them.

I told El Tigre that we were expecting company, and he said that he and Tall Runner would look out for them.

A short while later, the Comandante, Roman, and I were in the stables, where he was admiring the horses, when El Tigre found us and said Corporal and Capitán Carrillo had just crossed the frontera and were accompanied by four soldiers de Los Estados Unidos. I thanked him, and Roman immediately instructed one of the stable hands to warn Manuel there would be four more for supper and they would need to be given accommodations.

It was mid-afternoon when Corporal, Capitán Carrillo, and the four soldiers arrived. Comandante Neri, Roman, and I stepped off the veranda to meet them. Capitán Carrillo did the honors by introducing Captain Whiteside, his lieutenant, a sergeant, and a corporal. Comandante Neri and the officers saluted, and we all shook hands.

Roman addressed the Captain and said, "Accommodations have been made available for you and your men at the Hacienda. If you care to, you can remove what you need from your horses. The stable hands will care for the horses, and these young men are here to put your goods in your rooms. Would you be so kind as to join us on the veranda? We have refreshments and tacos, and we will be expecting you for supper this evening."

We all sat down on the veranda and refreshed ourselves with coffee, tacos, and brandy. Manuel set out cigars and we lit up and watched yet another stickball game. The sergeant and corporal left us on an errand to check the horses and get closer to the game.

Comandante Neri turned to Capitán Whiteside and said, "With permission from Don Francisco and Don Roman, I would like to address the concerns that were relayed to my government by your government. Presidente Díaz is very concerned and wants me to investigate the complaints. I told Don Francisco and Don Roman about the complaints, and Don Francisco has firsthand knowledge of all of them. With his permission, I would like to relay them to you".

Comandante Neri told the story of the intruders near Hacienda Este and the Mexican bandits at Campo San Luis who murdered one vaquero and wounded another. He told him about the pursuit of the bandits and the help of the Baker brothers in the death of the bandits and the recovery of the herd. The Comandante also told the captain about the loss of our father to rustlers from the Estados Unidos at Canyon Bonito. He then went on to say there had been many riders observing our roundup, and we had kept tabs on them—even following them back to their homes. He stated that he felt this was not harassment but prudent action to prevent further rustlings.

Captain Whiteside turned to me and said, "I would like to express my condolences to you on the loss of your father. His and General Urrea's tactical movements during the Texas War of Independence and the Mexican-American War have been studied with admiration. Your father was well known in military circles as an honorable man."

Both Roman and I thanked him for his condolences and the words about our father.

He went on to say, "My orders are to check the raiding by the Chiricahuas and to secure the border. It has come to my attention that the Apaches are using your rancho as a base of operations."

Comandante Neri asked the captain to let him address the issue of the Apaches, and he agreed. "Historically, Janos was the Spanish military outpost for the territories of Spain's northern frontier. The Spanish had come to an accommodation with the Apache and the Comanche wherein they paid tribute to the tribes and there was peace for 200 years between the Spanish and those tribes. Much later, the government of the United States followed that example with the Arapahoe, who were making the early use of the Santa Fe Trail a very expensive proposition. When the Mexicans won their independence from Spain, they chose to cease those payments, and the tribes went back to raiding.

"During the Mexican-American War, Don Gregorio, who was a student of history, was in charge of protecting an area from the Gila River south to Guaymas and all of the northern Sierra Occidental from a line starting at Guaymas. As you know, this area includes what both you and we know as the homelands of the Apache. He had an impossible task—to ward off any intrusion from the Estados Unidos and keep the Apache in check. He also had the problem of the Mexican government paying for Apache scalps. As you can imagine, there were many hunters of Apache scalps, and they did not quibble as to what Indian tribes the scalps came from.

"General Gregorio charged his men with the duty of hanging all scalp-hunters in his area of influence, and he let the Apache know that his army would protect them as long as they did not raid in his territory. You may recall that the United States had made peace with the Apache at the same time and made it known to them they would take it very favorably if the Apache attacked Mexicans.

"After the Treaty of Guadalupe Hidalgo, Presidente Santa Anna, who was a cousin of Gregorio's, was jealous of Gregorio's fame in Mexico and felt he could best be rid of him by giving him a large land grant in Apacheria. Gregorio gladly accepted the land grant and established the Estancia del Pérez.

"Gregorio knew the rancho would never be viable if he did not make peace with the Apache. He called the Apache and Comanche chiefs to a peace conference, where he established the Peace of the Estancia del Pérez. In this peace, he promised to be brothers to the tribes and to share the wealth of the rancho with them. In return, they were to treat the people of the rancho as brothers and not to use the rancho as a base for raiding, either into Mexico or the United States.

"When Don Gregorio was killed, Don Francisco met with the chiefs and assured them that the peace of the Estancia del Pérez would always be there. Both Don Francisco and Don Roman are brothers to the Apache and were raised with them. I, too, am charged with stopping the raiding of the Apache on Mexican citizens, but Presidente Díaz has also invested me with honoring the peace on the rancho, so I am not allowed by my Presidente to harass the Apache on the rancho. I will pledge to you with my honor and the honor of the Presidente that the Apache do not use the rancho as a base of operations. It is a place where their women and children can live without fear. As a representative of the National Police, I am in charge of this district, and it is also my duty to protect the people from thieves, whether they come from Mexico or the United States."

Captain Whiteside replied, "I was not aware of the peace between the Estancia del Pérez and the Apache, and I do understand the necessity of it. Nevertheless, the citizens of the United States are going to look on the situation as the rancho harboring and enabling the Apache."

I replied, "Captain, I understand what you are saying. To the ignorant, it would look that way, but to us it has been a way of life. Long before the United States became our neighbor, the Apaches were my neighbors. I learned the way of a brave in their wickiups. I was taught as a son by their chiefs. I was disciplined and fed by their women. I honor them as brothers, sisters, fathers, and mothers. They do not demand of me that their enemies be my enemies. I do not demand of them that my friends be their friends. I hope we can be friends."

Captain Whiteside responded with, "I am a Canadian by birth. I started in this man's army as a private and became an officer from the enlisted rank of Sergeant Major. I did this by following orders and doing my duty. I did not come to this position by privilege and, therefore, I learned to think for myself. Whom I choose for my friends is dictated by myself, alone, and not custom or class. I think we can be friends. As an officer of the United States, I cannot follow the Apache into Mexico, as that would be an act of war, and my orders are very firm on that.

"I mentioned that the second objective of my appointment here is to secure the border. On June 18, 1878, the United States Congress passed the Posse Comitatus Act, which was signed by President Hayes. This act came about due to the excesses of martial law by the military in the southern states after the Civil War. It is a good law. Because we are soldiers and not policemen, we are now prohibited from enforcing civil law. The same congressmen that made this law have constituents that are complaining about the situation at the border. They do not want to hear these complaints, so they want the army to secure the border. My orders are to secure the border and prevent the Mexican Army from crossing it. Do I make myself clear as to what I will do?"

Comandante Neri replied, "Yes, very clear. Regarding bandits moving across the border in either direction, you have no police powers."

"You are absolutely correct," replied Captain Whiteside. "I also am charged with feeding my men, and I have to purchase goods in the area at the best possible price for that purpose. I am aware that the cattle I am purchasing are most likely stolen cattle. I also know that the people I am purchasing them from are disreputable. My orders are to get the best price possible. Therefore, I cannot arrest the rustlers of your cattle, and I am required by my orders to enable them. This is also true for the cattle of ranchers in the United States. The brands on the cattle I purchase are irrelevant to the bargain of purchase." He paused, and then said to Neri, "You are a comandante of the National Police of Mexico. Is it not your duty to police the borders of the nation of Mexico?"

"It is," replied the Comandante.

"Then, sir, I request you do that, regardless of the origin of the miscreants. My men will not stand in your way when you are doing your duty. We have no national police, and the territory of Arizona has no police. The only policing being done is in the local villages and towns by county sheriffs. They do their duty as they see fit, and the custom is that they have no duty to prevent raiding in Mexico by citizens of the United States. They do see their duty as preventing Mexicans from retrieving stolen property from the citizens of the United States, whether their ownership is lawful or unlawful. I can promise you that I will attempt to scare the hell out of the bandits, regardless of their origin, but I will not arrest them."

I thanked the Capitán for his frankness about his problems and orders. I went on to say that I was putting in place as much protection for the rancho and my vaqueros as humanly possible. "I am not looking for confrontation. I am looking for security. There are Mexican bandits who look at our cattle as a way to enrich themselves, but I assure you they are not on the frontier. They are on our southern borders, and we are addressing that issue with vigor. Comandante Neri's effective efforts are greatly appreciated.

"Our main concern is that, on the border with the United States, there is a pervasive belief that stealing from the Mexicans is a national right that should not be abridged. I was educated in the United States, and I know this is not the belief of a high percentage of Americans, but I know they, as well as many congressmen, are being fed the belief that Mexicans are crossing the border with impunity to steal. In most cases, they are seeking to recover their own property, not steal another's. I do believe we have exhausted this subject, and we all are in agreement about what can and cannot be done." I took a breath. "Capitán, your enlisted men are invited to dinner with us, but there will be a barbecue and music on the field if they are of a mind to attend that. I would like to be able to tell Manuel how many guests will be at dinner. By the way, the Vail brothers, whom I believe you are acquainted with, will be at dinner tonight also. I am ready for a glass of mescal and a cigar. I hope you will join me."

We had no more than lit up when the Vails were riding up with Juan, He Who Hunts, and Antonio. Antonio and He Who Hunts took the horses to the stables, and the Vails and Juan joined our happy company. The riot was still in full swing on the stickball court, and it was a good respite to watch after our heavy conversation. I informed all that I would be leaving in the morning for Hacienda Oriental. I invited the Captain and the Vails to come in the Spring for a visit and a fiesta. I also told them I would be visiting Chicago, Princeton, New York, and Massachusetts while I was back east and, if they wanted me to carry anything to their loved ones in these cities, I would be happy to do it. All they need to do was bring it to the Hacienda, and it would be forwarded to me.

Walter Vail stated that he and his brother had picked out a 100 head and were planning to go to some of the southeast and eastern camps in the morning. I told them Juan and He Who Hunts would be going with me, but I was sure Antonio would be able to provide them with capable help. Roman advised them that some vaqueros were bringing the cattle they had chosen here and would keep them in the corrals at the Hacienda until they had gotten their herd together.

Manuel's dinner was again outstanding, and we all met in his kitchen for breakfast. We were gathered around the table when El Tigre came through the door with one of the Rurales. I knew by the look on his face that we had trouble, and I got up to meet him. He had just received a message that 16 riders had left the Clanton Ranch on the San Pedro and were headed south. I informed the gathering of what we knew and that I would be leaving shortly to meet them before they did any mischief.

CHAPTER 10

Capitán Carrillo ordered the lieutenants to get the troops ready to ride. Roman told Antonio to have 10 vaqueros ready to ride with the Rurales and send fast riders to warn Campo Huachuca, Campo Santa Cruz, and Campo San Pedro. Their orders were not to put up a fight if they were attacked before we got there. They were to retreat and abandon the herd they had gathered and alert the watchers for signals telling them where the rustlers were heading. At the moment, they were coming down the San Pedro and were north of the frontera. Once the jefe de campo knew the raiders had turned away from them, they needed to send half of their vaqueros in the direction the raiders had gone.

Everyone needed to know that our objective was prevention of a raid not conflict. Groups of men must ride in a wide line, so they did not leave a dust cloud that would warn the raiders of their approach.

I said to Comandante Neri, "I know you are much more skilled in this than I am, and we will need your help. I hope it would not be presumptuous of me to suggest that the Rurales go in four, single-line waves. We always know when you are coming and how many men there are by the cloud of dust your horses make when they travel as a troop. Presently, those of us stationed at the Hacienda will move toward the San Pedro just north of Campo San Pedro."

Then I addressed Antonio. "Whoever you send to Campo San José needs to relay these orders to other riders, and he and they need to see that Campo Aguas Frescas, Campo Contenido, and Campo San Bernardino are warned and the orders are passed on. Tell everyone to watch for the signals."

Captain Whiteside as well as Walter and Edward Vail requested permission to go as observers. I told them I would welcome the observers, as they may be able to counter the lies that would come of the action today. "Please get ready to ride. The stable has ample fresh mounts for you to pick from."

Roman, Corporal, Juan, He Who Hunts, El Tigre, Tall Runner, Antonio, five vaqueros, and the Vails were in the first wave with me, and we were spread out and moving in less than 30 minutes. All our goods were on our horses, as we would not be returning to the Hacienda.

El Tigre, accompanied by Tall Runner, rode up next to me and Roman and said, "The signals say that the raiders have turned east just north of the Montañas Mulas (Mule Mountains), indicating that their objective was most likely Campo Aguas Frescas or Campo Contenido. Roman and I discussed it and agreed this was most likely the objective. Antonio and Corporal rode back to tell the other waves and let them know the raiders were not going to be able to see any dust we raised for the next six hours at the least. We would be stopping at Campo San José, and those that needed to get a fresh mount should do so.

As we were approaching Campo Aguas Frescas, El Tigre and Tall Runner, who had been joined by their four Rurale students at Campo San José, came forward. El Tigre said, "The raiders have cleared the Mule Mountains and will soon be able to see our dust. They are still headed toward the southeast, which indicates Campo Contenido or the big prize at Campo Guadalupe. I feel it is Contenido. They will have observed cattle at both campos and, if their observers are good, they know that Guadalupe is a large camp with many vaqueros, and this would put them at a disadvantage. Contenido has ample cattle and much less defense."

Antonio and Corporal, who had gotten fresh mounts at San José, were sent again to appraise Comandante Neri and the other riders of what we knew and suspected. If anyone needed a remount, there would be mounts at Campo Aguas Frescas. The early-warning system had worked well. They signaled that the raiders were headed straight toward Contenido.

We had all reached Contenido while the raiders were still two hours out. I met with Comandante Neri and explained that the large hill to the north presented two ways for the raiders to approach. I suggested that, from my experience studying our raiders, they would split up and approach from both directions. I proposed that we place some men on the hill and the rest in the shape of horseshoes on both sides of the camp. The raiders would see a vulnerable camp with cattle and horses and proceed down the mouth of the horseshoe. "When we feel they are where we need them to be, we will signal the hidden men on the hill and in the horseshoe to make themselves known and shoot into the air. I believe the raiders will turn and flee on tired horses, and we make sure our bullets fly near them to hasten them along. I will want the men in the horseshoe and on the hill to hotly pursue them to the frontera. At the frontera, Antonio will continue the pursuit with 25 men on fresh horses. When they get within sight of the San Pedro, they are to halt the pursuit, head to Campo San José, and report to Roman.

Captain Whiteside said, "My men and I will ride with the pursuit and, when they break off at the San Pedro, we will cross it and return to Camp Huachuca. I will be sending an eyewitness report of this engagement to my superiors, and it will be interesting what complaints will be forwarded to us by our congressmen. I would like to be in the room when they are apprised of the true circumstances. By the way, your vaquero, He Who Hunts, is a very impressive man."

I replied that he had been my friend and companion my whole life. "I look forward to showing him Chicago and New York. I think it will be a good education."

Captain Whiteside laughed and said, "Indeed it will, indeed it will. I remember my first time seeing New York. The city is a wonderment to a country boy."

A dispatch rider came in and brought us the news that Victorio's War had resulted in another battle. After the battle of Ojo Caliente, Victorio continued to move south toward Silver City in the New Mexico Territory. As the band moved along the Animas River in the Black Range, they raided some ranches to obtain food and ammunition. The band was attacked by a militia made up of miners. The battle resulted in the death of 10 miners and a loss of 50 head of horses, which were added to the 68 that Victorio had captured at Ojo Caliente. Victorio's band suffered no casualties.

Two Navajo scouts that had been attached to the Sixth Cavalry and detached to the Ninth Cavalry had picked up the trail of Victorio's band. On September the 18th, the First Battalion was in pursuit of the band, and they spotted an Indian woman in a clearing and moved to capture her. They were engaged by two Apache warriors, who fired shots at them. The Battalion, under the command of Captain Byron Dawson, pursued the warriors across a large clearing and into the Animas Canyon. The Navajo scouts tried in vain to stop the charge. The 75 troopers and officers were well into the canyon—which was 30 yards wide at its entrance but narrowed to 16 yards wide as it meandered in an S curve—when they were engaged by the 61 warriors and one woman (Nana's wife) that Victorio had lining the rim of the canyon. On the first volley fired by the Apaches, 32 horses were killed, and the troopers were trapped.

The Second Battalion, under the command of Captain Charles Beyer, heard the gunfire and came down the Animas. As they approached the canyon, Victorio's band held their fire and let them in. As they got close to the First Battalion, the Apaches opened fire again, killing their horses. Four companies were now trapped, and the troopers could be killed from their concealed positions. It was a classic ambush. There were several attempts by different small detachments of troopers to climb to the ridge and turn the Apaches' flanks. In each case, the Apache would let them climb to an exposed place and then trap them. By late afternoon, the troopers began to withdraw by laying down withering volleys and moving back out of the canyon. After the engagement, there were 15 graves in the clearing, which included the two graves of the Navajo scouts.

This news was distressing to Captain Whiteside, who needed to get back to Camp Huachuca. Our ambush worked, and the cowboys left in a complete riot on tired horses. There were no casualties on either side, although I do suspect they may have ruined some of their horses in their escape.

The next morning, Walter and Edward thought they would look over the cattle here at Campo Contenido. Roman gave instructions to the jefe de campo and told the Vails that Antonio would be back by the next evening to arrange for the movement of the cattle they had picked. I bade them all goodbye and headed east with Corporal, Juan Gonzáles, El Tigre, and He Who Hunts.

CHAPTER 11

On September 24, 1879, two long, hard days and six horses each got us back to Hacienda Este. I met the post rider between Campo San Bernardino and Campo El Lobo. José's message was that we had 3,000 market cattle branded with the road brand, and he was stopping until further notice. In addition, he had received a telegram from Señor Deus, which stated he was in Pueblo, Colorado and was negotiating by wire with buyers in Denver for a local market for feeder calves. He would be leaving Pueblo by train and then taking a stage from Lamy, New Mexico. He should be in El Paso by September 28th. I sent a note to Roman with the post rider stating we needed to reverse the flow of the market cattle to Hacienda Oriental and proceed to gather them at Hacienda Occidental. We would be sending him hands to assist with road branding if necessary. I also told him I would tell the jefe at El Lobo about the change in plans.

We arrived late, and everyone went off to their respective homes. He Who Hunts went to share Corporal's quarters. A young boy had taken our horses. As I approached the door, I was greeted by Edward and Juliana Honeywell. Edward bade me leave my gear at the door and asked me if I had eaten.

"I am starved," I replied, "but I dare not bother Pedro, as I am sure he has retired."

Edward said, "Juliana can fix you something to tide you over till tomorrow."

I thought that was not a good idea and I cautioned, "I don't want to get Juliana in trouble with Pedro."

Edward replied, "It is Pedro that will not want to be in trouble with Juliana. There will be no problem."

My hunger forced me to give in, and I followed them to the kitchen. When we arrived, Edward begged off for duties and left me to watch Juliana stoke up the stove, put on some coffee, and begin to warm up some food. It was just a few minutes before José, Angélica, and Mother came through the kitchen door. Juliana set out pan dulce and coffee cups, and I gave them a report on Roman. They stayed with me until I had eaten, and then Mother said, "I think it is time we all went to bed."

When I arrived in my room, I found that Edward had stowed my gear, drawn a bath, and turned down my bed. It was nice to be home.

The next morning, I arose and rushed down to the kitchen to find it was empty. Pedro said, "They have all eaten and are down at the branding. Your mother ordered your breakfast sent to her sitting room." He looked at me and added, "I believe you should change for breakfast. I will send the meals up in 30 minutes."

I was beginning to feel like a young boy instead of Don Francisco.

I knocked on Mother's door, and she bade me to enter. I entered and closed the door. My eyes immediately fell on a vision in bright blue that was sitting next to my mother. As I stared at her, I heard my mother say, "Do you remember Olga Celaya, the daughter of my friend Juanita and her husband Manuel from La Reforma?"

I looked at my mother incredulously and thought, *How could she ask such a question?* I had never seen this angel in my whole life. I stammered that I knew Juanita and Manuel Celaya, and we had stopped by their rancho when I went off to college, but I definitely did not recall this young lady.

"Do you recall any children of the Celayas?" Mother inquired. I replied that there was a little girl, and I remembered Roman raving about a Celaya girl when he enrolled in school.

A sound came out of the vision and said, "I am one and the same on both counts."

Mother looked at me and said, "Little girls grow up."

I was thinking, *Not like this. This is a direct product of God.*

I had forgotten all about Don Francisco and his duties. It was mid-morning when my mother said, "Your breakfast is long finished. You may leave now."

A horse was stationed in front of the house. I walked out, grabbed a hunk of mane, and swung on. I had never done that before, and I rode down to the branding corrals. Running Bear, José, Corporal, Juan Gonzáles, and He Who Hunts were all watching as Javier, with rope in hand, directed the completion of the branding. Running Bear proudly said, "Javier ran the branding corrals and did a great job. He never forgot to turn his horse once his loop was settling over the horns." He said this with a great smile, and there were guffaws from Corporal, Juan, and José.

That evening, we had a formal supper, and I was sitting at one end of the table and Mother was at the other. Mother struck her wine glass with a spoon and asked me if I was completely recovered from falling off my horse—referring to my embarrassing tumble at Campo Bernardino during the roundup a few months' previous. I was sitting next to Olga, and even she had a big grin on her face. I tried to recover some dignity by saying to José that, after breakfast in the morning, I would like a full report on the herd.

José replied, "Sí, Don Francisco."

I then attended to my food with great concentration.

I was greeted by grinning faces at the breakfast table the next day and salutations of, "Good morning, Don Francisco." I had decided to just ride this one out, so, after everyone had eaten, we retired to the veranda where cigars were lit up and José handed me the tally sheets. After a proper time, I asked José if he could join me in the library to discuss the crops and cattle.

In the library, José gave me a verbal on the tally. There were 2,600 three-year-old steers, 3,100 two year-old-steers, 3,800 yearling steers, and 1,800 heifers. In addition, there were nearly 1,400 cull cows and bulls that were still bunched up and on the range awaiting decisions. He stated that the culls and the heifers had not been road branded.

I asked him what he had come up with on prices for cattle. José replied, "The prices, which are based on hundred weights in Chicago or Cincinnati, are based on the size of the cattle. An 850-pound animal at the slaughterhouse is bringing five dollars per hundred weight. We have received offers for a minimum of 2,000 to a maximum of 3,000 animals to be delivered to Lamy, New Mexico—which the Santa Fe has just reached—for a price of three dollars and 60 cents FOB (freight-on-buyer). The cattle are to be delivered no later than November 15th, and the animals must average at least 850 pounds."

I asked if there was any distinction as to steers, heifers or older animals. He replied, "There is none."

I asked if many of the cows were being culled because of age or not having calves.

He answered, "Most of the cows failed to produce a calf and are in good condition. Many weigh 1,000 pounds. In addition, some of the two-year-olds would make the average weight of 850 pounds. I think we can meet or beat the 3,000-pound threshold even with an average trail loss of 50 pounds per animal."

José went on to report on the farms. "The grass hay has been harvested and the high alfalfa fields are being harvested. The lower fields are several weeks away from being ready to cut. About 50 hectares of corn are close to dried out and ready to be combined. When we can begin using the combine depends on a break in the annual rains, which have been heavy. The other fields have a time to go. We did have some grass hay that was damaged by the rain after it was cut, but, overall, we have escaped much harm. The red-pepper fields are being harvested as we speak, and the drying ovens are running 24 hours a day. We have planted almost 1,000 hectares in winter wheat, which is benefiting from the rains. We have close to 100 hectares of cotton, of which 15 percent was lost to hail, in the lower valley as well as 20 hectares of red chili peppers that were completely destroyed by hail. Overall, the losses were minimal, and it appears the farms are going to bring in a very good profit."

I asked José if he had been able to get some offers on cotton. He said, "I am sorry that we did not have the opportunity to discuss an offer that I received from English buyers for cotton delivered to the docks at Veracruz. The reputation of our high-altitude cotton and its fiber length has earned us a premium. The average price for cotton at the wharf in Alabama is 8.6 cents per pound. I was able to obtain a price for us and our neighbors, who contract with the gin, of 12.6 cents per pound for up to 7,000 bales delivered to their warehouse at Veracruz no later than April 1st, 1880. We must deliver, at a minimum, 4,000 bales or we will suffer a penalty of one cent per pound. Last year, we produced, with our neighbors, 4,600 bales. As you know, your father purchased two more gins last year, and they were added to the three we were already running. We built an additional steam plant for the extra power, and we now have the power to run seven gins, if we should choose to add more in the future. On the basis of the increase of gin capacity, we added 550 hectares of cotton to our farm. The farmers in Ascención have added an extra 150 hectares. At our average production of 3.2 bales per hectare, we should exceed the 7,000. In addition, I have negotiated with the neighbors we have contracted with to gin their cotton a price of two cents per pound produced and 25 percent of the seed produced. It has also been agreed upon that the price for shipment to Veracruz will be two cents per pound, and anyone under contract can join in transporting the cotton to Veracruz and will be paid that fee."

As always, Edward Honeywell had a young man stationed on the outside of our door, and I asked him if he would be so good as to ask my mother when I could have a private talk with her. The kitchen had sent up some coffee, and José waited with me for the answer. I told José that after my private talk with Mother, I would like for him and Angélica to join us so we could discuss some further family business, as I would be going to El Paso in the morning to meet Señor Deus and work out the movement of the cattle. I also told José to draft his reply to the offer to purchase the 3,000 head and request a formal contract, which I would sign and send back while I was in El Paso.

José replied, "We will be eager to join you, but I will take the break to tell Running Bear to start branding the cull cows that are in good shape. You will have the draft in the morning before you leave."

When I arrived at Mother's room, she was waiting for me alone. I asked her about the circumstances of Olga Celaya's visit to the Hacienda.

Mother answered, "Juanita and Manuel sent Olga to be a companion to me, because two of my daughters are leaving and Angélica has her hands full with the children as well as the added duties of running the Hacienda. I told them this was very satisfactory to me." Mother smiled and said, "And it is."

I told her I had asked for José and Angélica to join us after our private conversation, and she thought that would be a good idea, but she wanted to include Olga. I assented but tried to not appear too eager.

Mother went on to inquire how Roman was doing in his job as manager. I told her he was doing a great job managing the Occidental division of the rancho. Mother then informed me she planned to spend next summer at Hacienda Occidental, while she was in half mourning. She had discussed this with Edward and Juliana, and they agreed to send Panchita and her sister Rosa to the Hacienda in November along with Juliana's widowed sister, Imelda, to domesticate the place. She was sure it had become uncivilized due to the absence of women. She also said that Edward, Juliana, and Olga would be accompanying her in the spring.

I looked at mother and asked, "Do I detect a plan for domestication of Roman here?"

Mother replied, "We will let Nature take her course. It is time to summon the others and ask for some refreshments to be sent up." She rang the bell, gave the orders, and we waited for the others to show up. In the meantime, I told mother I had asked for Angélica and José to join us, as I would be leaving the next day to meet Señor Deus in El Paso, and I had some business to discuss with him that I felt would affect the future of the rancho.

Mother gave me her "wake up, boy!" glance and said, "Then we need to have this meeting in the parlor, and I insist that Elizabeth, Dulce, and Javier be present also, as this is their future, too."

I immediately agreed, and Mother asked Edward Honeywell to prepare the parlor for a family meeting and to tell Angélica, Olga, and José the change in plans as well as request that Elizabeth, Dulce, and Javier attend. I then asked mother if Javier had suits to take to college. She indicated she had seen to his wardrobe. I told her that Corporal, Juan Gonzáles, and He Who Hunts would be accompanying me to El Paso so I could see they had proper clothing for the trip.

I went to my room to freshen myself up and told my mother I would be back in 30 minutes to escort her to the parlor. When we arrived at the parlor, all were in attendance, and Mother informed me she had asked Edward and Mr. White to attend the meeting also.

I began the meeting by stating I had watched our father negotiate during the revolution and keep the rancho alive. "Now we are in a period of progress under Presidente Díaz that Mexico has never experienced before. But, not all are participating, and the ideals put forward by Presidente Juárez—that the land must be for all—is still very strong and will most likely come up again. Most of the owners of the haciendas do not live on their land but rather leave the management to others while they enjoy the luxury of society living in Mexico City or travel the world. It makes no difference that we are the exception. When the revolution comes, we will be painted with the same brush.

"Therefore, I want to continue to build on our success here as well as look to a future when we may no longer have the rancho. In the future, we will have to part with land, just as our parents did when they deeded land to Ascención and Janos. Towns will grow up and, to stave off political pressure, we will need to preemptively stay ahead of the hunger that others will have for our land. I have come to understand that the vastness of our holdings was an asset in the beginning, but it will increasingly become a liability. As our neighbors multiply to the north and south, they will look to our cattle and prosperity as a source of income, and we will not be able to sustain that pressure.

"Thanks to Mother and Mr. White, we have been afforded the opportunity of education, and we are continuing that education so we can compete in the world. We are just beginning to see the potential of controlling the variances of the market by direct marketing and future contracting. This already is being done in our farm products, and we are looking forward to it in our cattle operations. Many of our neighbors are cooperatively marketing their farm crops and cattle with us now and that can be a great source of revenue for the family in the future world.

"As the railroads expand, our ability to market our products both in Mexico and the United States will expand as well. Right now, we are contracting with the British textile industry to provide them with cotton. I understand there have been attempts to ship meat to the northeastern cities of the United States in iced box cars from the large stockyards in Chicago and Cincinnati. The first attempts in the early 1870s met with mixed results, but now it is becoming quite commonplace. There has even been some shipping of meat to the British Isles, which is way more efficient than shipping live animals. There is no reason we cannot be in the vanguard of setting up a market we can use to ship directly from Mexico—say Veracruz, for example. The British are looking forward to this right now and are purchasing large portions of land in Wyoming and Montana and setting up ranchos to produce their own beef for market around the world. Because of the history of the United States, the freedoms enjoyed by the people there, and the stability of the government, which became assured with the end of their Civil War, ownership of the means of production will not be constantly challenged by revolution brought on by the rise of an entitled nobility and class system that is so prevalent here.

"Therefore, I am going to propose some long-term goals that I have been working on. I plan on talking with Señor Deus about the purchase of grazing land in the San Luis Valley of Colorado. He has negotiated grazing rights for our younger cattle that we will be taking up the trail. We will be able to market them at all times of the year rather just when we drive them up in the Fall. I propose we do as the British are doing and look at purchasing ranchos in Wyoming and Montana as well as California and the northwestern United States. There is no reason we should not follow our calves from birth to the dinner table.

"I am going to be talking to Roberto about continuing his education with an emphasis on economics and marketing. We will need a strong voice and someone who will be able to negotiate within the halls of money in the United States.

"It is my hope that Javier will focus on geology and mining in his education. The family and the rancho could benefit largely from the minerals we already know exist here on the rancho as well as investments in mineralization elsewhere.

"We have benefited greatly from the social contacts that Señor White developed during his higher education, and I am hoping to benefit more, because I am going to rely on him to find out what kind of legal mechanisms we will need to have in place so we can be ensured right of title to our purchases in the future as well as our investments. Our sisters will have the opportunity to expand our social contacts by enriching themselves with a continued education, and I know they will, in the future, contribute to the growth of the family's security.

"The last thing I would like to address here is education not only of the family but all of the students that go to Señor White's schools. Many of our classmates in Señor White's classes are as adept at learning as we in the family. We need to cash in on that potential. I propose we offer the opportunity to anyone who graduates from Señor White's school and who wants to continue their education in a college or whatever vocational training they may want to pursue. They will be a credit to the rancho and their family.

"We will need an educated army if we are to move into the 20th century and prosper. As an example, who do we have to run a rancho in the San Luis Valley? I have my man picked out, but I will not reveal him until I have spoken to him. I am aware that people ready to step into managerial positions are in short supply, and we need to have people loyal to the rancho or what it may evolve into in the near future, and time is short.

"In closing, I have already made the case that the rancho, in its present form, will not endure. We have many families that have been with us from the beginning. We owe a debt to the men that fought beside our father, as they made it possible for us to have this rancho, and they know it is theirs as well as ours. One way we can preserve this rancho is to contract with these families to begin to take over portions of the rancho. They will gain title by paying us a portion of their production, and they will be allowed to market their products along with ours. This will stave off confiscation by the government in the next revolution and give them an even larger stake in the accomplishment of a future. We will work cooperatively to attain a secure future for all."

Mother asked me, "When do you plan to start breaking up the Estancia?"

"Not immediately. We have already done this in many ways by establishing the campos, so all we need to do is establish more over time as we improve both the herd and our husbandry through fencing and resting of pastures. We will have our natural division, and the vaqueros will establish a loyalty to the division their family lives in. We need only discover those that have the skills of entrepreneurship and encourage them through education. The divisions are already happening. We need only recognize them and manage them. It might even be that our influence will go beyond the present boundaries of the rancho as families grow."

Señor White injected, "You will need lawyers to create the mechanisms by which you can incorporate the family business as well as the cooperative businesses. You will need this in the United States so that, in future economic downturns, laws are not made that prevent foreigners to own land. Foreigners are always branded as problems if they appear to be successful when natives are unsuccessful, regardless of what country you are in. You will see that here when the next revolution comes. Nationalization will naturally follow, and it is necessary that the ownership appears to be national within the country."

José asked, "How do you envision these coming changes affecting our farming enterprises?"

I replied, "It could affect them greatly if we have not made ourselves essential to the success of our neighbors. Our only protection is that we have been instrumental in making our neighbors successful by establishing essential businesses that all benefit from, such as the gins. Our neighbors' success is the only thing that will make us continually successful and give us political protection."

Javier said, "I have no idea whether I would want to make minerals my life's work."

I replied, "I am not asking you to make it your life's work. Your first love may be cattle, but we need someone who understands what the people we hire are saying. We will need to make judgments as to what action to take when we receive recommendations about properties we own or are invested in. We can only make those judgments if we are informed."

Elizabeth said, "I am not sure what you expect of me. I will not be studying minerals or marketing."

I explained, "My most valuable confidante and the one I constantly rely on to be aware of problems is Mother. Mother grew up in a world of power. She knows how to listen and, when she talks, she should be heeded. You will be attending Wellesley College. Your fellow students will be the daughters of forward-thinking people of power who see value in their daughters continuing their education. Not only will you be getting a general education from the faculty, you will be receiving a wealth of education from your fellow students. You are going to learn to navigate the halls of power and learn how to wield it. I am absolutely sure you will be a strong influence on the future of this family.

"I know I have given you all much to think about. I did this so you know what I am planning for the benefit of the family. The rancho is in good hands with José and Roman. I will not only be taking my siblings to college, I will be looking into the marketing of our cattle in the future and the present. I hope to meet with people that Señor White contacts, so I can safely purchase properties in the United States. I hope to find a source of blooded Hereford cattle, so we can purchase bulls to begin to improve our cattle. In addition, I am eager to find someone knowledgeable in the creating of pastures and the rotation of stock, so we can begin to maximize our use of the land and, at the same time, take care of it for the future.

"Tomorrow morning, I will be leaving with Corporal, He Who Hunts, and Juan Gonzáles, so I will be in El Paso when Señor Charles arrives. I want to be able to plan the movement of the herds toward the north. Hopefully, I will be back in four or five days with a plan. Once the herds are moving, I will want to leave earlier than planned, so I can make observations along the way.

"Señor White and José, if you have any messages, I will be happy to send them when I reach El Paso. Señorita Celaya, it would be a great honor if you would allow me to escort you to dinner tonight."

I didn't sleep well, as Olga kept floating through my mind. The vision of her enhanced my hunger for her presence. I was becoming aware of how lonely I was, and the desire to have her in my arms was growing stronger. I knew I could not stand to be separated from her, as she had quickly become my confidante and friend as well as the object of my love.

We left just before daybreak in one of the coaches. We began our journey traveling east along the north bank of the Casas Grande River. The first 17 miles were easy traveling, and I drove the four-in-hand (four horses with one driver controlling the reins) while He Who Hunts rode shotgun. We arrived at Campo Nava and had coffee and pan dulce while the teams were changed. We left there with a six-in-hand with Corporal driving and Juan riding shotgun.

We turned southeast and crossed the hills to Campo Alamos. He Who Hunts persuaded Juan that it would be best if they changed places and he rode shotgun. Corporal picked up the pace, as it was nine miles to Campo Alamos, and we would be changing teams again there for the next long leg.

We had covered 26 miles and, by mid-morning, María, the wife of the jefe de campo, loaded us down with burritos for our next leg. When we got back into the coach, a new six-in-hand team was hitched up, and two barrels of water were tied in the boot. In addition, a small barrel of water wrapped in wet cloth was placed in a holder in the middle of the floor in the coach. Our trip would go more slowly from here on.

Juan took the reins, and Corporal rode shotgun. We stopped every two hours and let the horses rest for about 30 minutes before giving them some water. We switched drivers each time we stopped, and we arrived at Campo El Ahorro de Agua (Camp of Saving Water), which was about 27 miles from Campo Alamos, in the late afternoon. The teams were changed, and water was added to the barrels. In this last leg, we left the Estancia within a mile, and we had another 36 miles to go to reach El Paso. I took the reins, and He Who Hunts joined me up front. I started the horses out on a quick walk and then put them into a light, easy gait that would slowly eat up the miles.

We continued the routine of two-hour stops and changing drivers. He Who Hunts joined me as shotgun for the last leg into El Paso. After a 90-mile trip, we crossed the bridge into El Paso and drove up to a seven-room adobe building on El Paso Street at Little Plaza. Father had built this establishment in the 1860s, as there had been no lodging in El Paso save Mrs. Rohman's Boarding House, which was always full of new arrivals eager to take advantage of the West's opportunities.

We unloaded our gear, took the coach and team down to the livery on San Antonio Street, and rubbed the team down before we turned them over to the livery hands to give them special care. It was still several hours before dawn, when the town would begin to stir, and we were ready for our beds.

When I awoke the next morning, I gave José, the caretaker of the place, messages to be delivered to the telegraph office. I also asked him to check on the stagecoach schedule from the north. Salomé, his wife, soon had breakfast on the table for four hungry men. The coffee and food energized us. José returned and reported that a stage from Mesilla with connections to Albuquerque would arrive in an hour, and there would be another this evening.

I escorted my three men down to Samuel Schutz's Mercantile Store. I had met Señor Schutz early in my life, when I visited with my father. He always greeted me as if he looked forward to seeing me. I told him my problem. These three young men would be accompanying me on a trip back east, and they had no clothes that were suitable for anywhere but on a horse. I told him two suits each and two changes of leisure clothes would be necessary. He called in a seamstress, and she began taking measurements. It was comical watching her measure He Who Hunts. No woman had placed her hands on him since he was a young child. He would flinch like he was being stabbed with a needle.

I left them in the care of Señor Schutz and his seamstress and went back to the stage depot to watch the arrivals. The coach came in, and the first man off was Señor Deus. I was so glad to see that old Alemán (German). We had shared many adventures.

Señor Deus and I quickly went to the nearest cantina, as his thirst was vast, and I had no problem indulging. We checked his luggage with the bartender and found a table, each of us carrying a large mug of beer. While we were drinking, Señor Deus told me about a companion on the coach who was returning from delivering some cattle to a ranch near Cimarron in the New Mexico Territory. According to his story, these cattle had been bought in Mexico in the early summer by his employer—a man by the name of Clanton—who had sent them up to the Mogollon Rim to summer and fatten out. He had then moved them north to the Cimarron, and he was coming to El Paso to look at opportunities.

I asked Señor Deus if the man had dropped his name.

"He called himself Charlie Thomas."

"A man by that name had been involved in the rustling of a herd of cattle along with the Clantons and the Cowboys, and he participated in the killing of my father."

Señor Carlos pushed back his chair and said, "Let's go have a talk with Mr. Thomas."

"It would be better to keep an eye on him and have a talk with him this evening.

"I have eyes on him right now. He is the man standing at the bar with another Cowboy."

I stood up, strode over to the bar, and asked the bar boy if he would run over to Schutz's Mercantile and tell Juan Gonzáles to come to the cantina alone with him. "When you both arrive here, ask him to remain outside and let me know he is there," I said to the boy.

The bar boy was back shortly and told me the man was waiting outside. I handed him a dollar and told him this was between him and me. He shook his head and went back to work. I went out and told Juan that one of the men we were looking for was in the cantina. I described him and asked Juan to keep an eye on him. "I will send Corporal to relieve you. It is important to remember that revenge belongs to all of us, and I want to save him for the trip home. Do not go in until Señor Carlos and I leave. I do not want anyone to know we are together."

I went back inside and asked Señor Carlos to accompany me to Señor Schutz's Mercantile.

When we entered the Mercantile, there was an immediate shout of "Deus!" and Señor Schutz rushed over and hugged Señor Carlos. They started speaking in a language I had never heard before, but I assumed it was Alemán. When I could get a word in edgewise, I asked if Señor Schutz was through with my men.

He replied, "I am, and we will send the clothes out next week with your order.

I then handed him a list and asked if we could have the goods itemized thereon by that evening.

"They will be ready," he said.

I turned to Señor Deus and begged off due to tiredness and the need for a siesta. I inquired if he would be able to make his way to the house.

"I know the way and will be along once Señor Schutz and I have caught up over a few steins of beer."

I motioned to the men, and we left.

Once we got back to the house, I told Corporal and He Who Hunts about Charlie Thomas. I went on to further explain I would like to leave early the next morning for the rancho, and I wanted Charlie Thomas to accompany us part way. "We need not invite him until we are ready to leave in the morning."

I asked Corporal to check on the horses and make sure they were able to make the return trip. If not, we would need to stay an extra day. It would be his and Juan's duty to watch Charlie during the day, and we would leave him in the capable hands of He Who Hunts in the evening.

The long trip and the beer resulted in a long siesta. I woke up to the smell of food and men talking. I walked into the kitchen. Salomé pointed toward a chair and started filling up a plate. When I was finished, José handed me several telegrams, and Corporal said, "The horses are not ready to go. They will need an extra day."

I asked for suggestions about our guest, which Juan was watching, and he said, "We can risk watching him for another day, but he could figure out he is being watched. I think we should take him tonight and deposit him in a room in the house."

I agreed and called José to inform him that Señor Carlos was here and would be coming to the house later. We would be entertaining an unwilling guest—one who had a hand in the death of Don Gregorio— and he would be staying with us from later on that night until the following evening, when we would all leave. I asked if there was an adequate place for him to stay until we left.

José replied, "We have a root cellar that can only be accessed from the kitchen."

I thought to myself That *would be an appropriate space to keep such a dog.* I thanked José and told him to make any preparations necessary and inform Salomé about our guests, but she need not bother herself about the one in the cellar.

Corporal informed me that Juan had made friends with Charlie Thomas and was buying rounds of drinks. He would be leaving to join the party in a couple of hours. He went on to say, "Señors Carlos and Schutz are at the same cantina. Would it be better if you joined them and invited them to some other location?"

I asked José to run over to Mrs. Rohman's and ask her if I could bring two guests to supper tonight and that one of them would be Señor Schutz. José was back in 15 minutes and said, "Mrs. Rohman is delighted that you and your guests would like to share her table. Dinner will be served at seven."

I looked at Corporal and He Who Hunts and said, "I leave it in your capable hands. Do not kill him tonight."

I went over to the cantina and had a stein. I told the señores they were to be my guests for supper and, in the meantime, I thought we needed to move to a more upscale establishment. They readily agreed when they found out I was buying, and we left before Corporal went in to join the party.

As we left, I asked Señor Carlos if there were any awkward moments with Juan being in the same bar with Charlie Thomas.

He replied, "No. I explained the situation with Herr Schutz in German, and he was all for the intrigue. He held your father in high regard. I told Señor Schutz we would not be leaving this evening, and I will pick up the order tomorrow evening. Now it is time to paint the town."

Señor Carlos and I returned home about midnight. José took Señor Carlos in hand and directed him to his room. When he came back, he told me our guest was in the cellar. He Who Hunts had efficiently questioned him, and all were satisfied with the answers and had gone to bed. I thanked him and took to my bed.

In the morning, I arose early to read the telegrams and compose answers. The buyers had increased their upper limit to 4,000 head, and I replied that we would meet that figure. There were telegrams for José and Señor White as well as a couple for my mother.

I met with Señor Carlos, and he told me he had Fall and winter grazing set up for 600 head, and he had found a local market for 50 head. I then asked him if he knew of any ranches for sale.

He answered, "I had hoped to get more additional grazing, but two ranchers did not want to participate. They were selling off their cattle and putting their ranches up for sale. Between the two, there is enough winter grazing for 1,500 head, and they have summer grazing in the mountains for the same number."

I asked him to contact them about the prices they wanted for the ranches.

He replied, "I will send the messages right now."

I told him that if we did not get the answers that day to warn them they might not hear from us until the next week.

He replied, "They have both moved their families into San Luis, which has a telegraph extension from Fort Garland where the Denver and Northwestern Railroad passes through on its way to Alamosa. The railroad crosses La Veta pass to Walsenburg and then on to Pueblo—which is served by the Santa Fe—and on to Denver with connections all the way to Cheyenne, Wyoming and a connection to the Union Pacific Railroad."

I asked, "How do you rate the stagecoach ride to Albuquerque from El Paso?"

He answered, "The ride through the Jornada del Muerto was somewhat bleak, but there are adequate way stations and, overall the trip was much better than going around to California."

I then let the bomb drop. I told him I had signed a contract for the delivery of 4,000 head to the Santa Fe yards at Lamy, New Mexico to be delivered no later than November 15th. Señor Carlos was ready for a drink, and José presented us with a bottle of tequila. We both asked for a glass.

He said, "I have 20 hands following the trail from Taos south down the Rio Grande Valley. I have mapped out a trail that will take us to Lamy."

I asked Senor Carlos if he would be using the trail I had accompanied him on 10 years previous.

He replied, "Yes, it is the trail that Indian traders have used since ancient times to bring goods from the Mayans and Aztecs to Taos and the Pueblos of northern New Mexico on north to the plains Indians and into Canada. It is a trail that follows the waterways and avoids the hardships of the Jornada del Muerto."

I told Señor Carlos that about 20 percent of the market cattle were owned by my neighbors, and they would provide 30 of the vaqueros needed. "I still have cattle to protect on the range from rustlers and cannot send all my vaqueros on the drive. I can send about 70 experienced vaqueros from the rancho and can make up the other 30 with older boys who will need to learn on the trail. We can accomplish that by pairing them with experienced vaqueros and, with the 20 that you will bring, we should have adequate hands."

Señor Carlos said, "A trail drive is a great school, and I have started out with many boys who returned home as young men. Francisco, we need to address the problem of logistics. All these men need to be fed, and you will have as many as 12 herds moving separately at one time along the trail. That will require 12 chuck wagons as well as a supply wagon and equipment wagon. Our meat will be walking along with us, but everything else is going to need to come along with us as well as having pre-positioned supplies along the trail."

I informed Señor Charlie that my neighbors were supplying five chuck wagons and we had another six ready to go. "I have another two being outfitted, so we will be in good shape with spares. We will have adequate supplies to start with as well as enough equipment wagons to hold spare parts and all the vaqueros' gear. I had thought to pre-position supplies, but I need direction as to where to have them positioned. Would four wagons starting from Piños Altos north to the beginning of the narrows on the San Francisco River be adequate?"

Senor Carlos said, "I think six would be better, and we will only take seven with us to begin with. That way, they can join us through the narrows, and we will have a couple of spare wagons along for any problems."

I asked him where else he would need pre-positioned supplies.

"When we reach the plains of Saint Augustine, there should be four supply wagons at a waterhole south of Mangas Mountain."

I told him I could contract in Albuquerque for a freighter to meet them there with four wagons.

Señor Charlie went on to say there should be two wagons waiting for the herds at Santa Domingo Pueblo. In addition, he felt any additional supplies that might be needed could be purchased in Taos on the way through.

I said we would send older men to drive the wagons as well as have wheelwrights and carpenters to pull extra duty driving supply and equipment wagons. I asked him how big a remuda (a group of ride able horses) would be needed.

His reply was quick. "We will need three horses for each vaquero and six mules per wagon. According to my calculations, that would be 450 horses as well as 216 mules. Of course, the remuda for each group will be dictated by how many vaqueros and wagons are with each herd. When the vaqueros return to help herds following, they will need to take their extra horses with them. The question is whether to take the horses back to the rancho or sell them at the end."

"In most cases, the vaqueros are going to want to bring the horses they use back with them when they return and, of course, the mules will be used to pull the wagons on the return south, as they will be needed to move farm goods during the winter."

I stated that if I was successful in purchasing a ranch in the San Luis Valley, I would want to leave a few wagons as well as vaqueros at the ranch. I also would be looking to hire local vaqueros, and they would need extra mounts, so the question would remain in the air for a while.

Señor Deus injected, "I sent telegrams to the owners, and I have high hopes that they respond to me today."

I apprised Señor Deus of our guest in the cellar and asked him if he had any qualms about riding back with us knowing we would be taking this man along in the boot. He had none and was happy to hear that retribution was forthcoming.

I looked at Corporal and He Who Hunts and requested a report on their interrogation of Charlie Thomas.

Corporal said, "Once Señor Thomas saw that his interrogator was an Apache brave with knife in hand, he began to sing like a lonely male dove. He confirmed what we already knew about the participants in the ambush and Johnny Ringo's drunken account of the event. He did this without any coaching from us. He also added the names of two other men—Jesus "Ojos de Serpiente" (Eyes of the Serpent) Valenzuela and his primo, Angel Rojas. Thomas said Valenzuela held the legs of the two Rurales while Florentino Cruz disemboweled them as they lived."

I asked Corporal if he needed to see this man die to satisfy his thirst for revenge.

He replied, "I only need to see Johnny Ringo die. It will be enough for me to know that Thomas will die."

I replied, "It might serve our purposes better if he dies at the hands of the Rurales." I then requested that Corporal go to the Rurale headquarters and use my name to inquire as to whether Comandante Neri or Capitán Carrillo were in the area. "If they are, tell them I may have some information they would be interested in." I asked Corporal to go immediately, and I instructed He Who Hunts to find Juan Gonzáles and tell him to come see me.

When Juan arrived, I asked him to go to a smithy shop and request they make a small branding iron with the brand of the rancho. "Ask them to do it immediately, as we are leaving town this evening, and we would like to take it with us."

I found Señor Deus and inquired as to whether this would be a good time to acquire a few steins of beer. He wholeheartedly agreed, and I told José and Salomé we would be at the cantina if anybody was looking for us. I asked José if he could check at the telegraph office for anything that had arrived for the rancho or Señor Deus and bring it by the cantina.

We had finished our first stein when José came in with some wires. One of them was addressed to Señor Deus. He opened it and reported to me the ranchers were indeed willing to sell their ranches for a sum of $3,000 each with no cattle included.

"Señor Deus, how many cattle would these ranches support?" I asked.

He replied, "Year round, in the vicinity of 1,500 head of mother cows, but I would be much more comfortable if you would not buy these ranches sight unseen."

I wrote a reply to the ranchers that I would purchase the properties at their price once I had verified their condition and size. I told them I would be able to close prior to November 15th, and my lawyers would contact them in the next few days as to any particulars that would be needed in the deeds and agreements.

I then sent a telegram to one of my classmates by the name of Mahlon Pitney, who was practicing law at his father's law firm. I requested that his firm oversee the purchase of the property, which I would want in my name. I told him I understood it was too small a transaction for them to travel to Colorado to oversee, but I was sure they had contacts they could hire in Colorado to do the work on the ground. I told him I would be very appreciative if they would oversee the transaction. I included the names of the sellers and the particulars as I knew them and told them the sale was conditional upon my inspection. In addition, I would wire them about when I would do the inspection, and I would like to close immediately if the inspection proved the ranches were as advertised. I apprised him of the fact I would be leaving El Paso that evening, and any wires I received or sent would be subject to as much as a seven-day delay. I also told him the payment for the ranches would be in a draft or a letter of credit from Drexel, Morgan, and Company of New York.

I asked José to check for any other wires prior to the closing of the telegraph office. Señor Deus was on his third stein, and I had some catching up to do. I had just gotten started when Corporal came through the door with Capitán Carrillo, who was wearing the clothes of a common vaquero. I ordered them a stein each and told Carrillo about our guest in the cellar. I told him I was willing to turn Thomas over to the Rurales, but we needed to give him a little attention prior to that. I asked his permission to leave Thomas on the side of a large arroyo about 15 miles to the west on the road to the rancho. I assured him he could pick him up at daybreak.

Capitán Carrillo asked what condition the man would be in, and I replied he would need some clothes and would not be able to walk, but he would be alive. Capitán Carrillo agreed to this on the condition we pick up a Rurale waiting for us at the border and let him accompany us to the site where we would leave Thomas. I immediately agreed and told him about Ojos de Serpinte Valenzuela and Angel Rojas.

CHAPTER 12

We left El Paso two hours after dark and picked up the Rurale at the border. Once we cleared Juárez, the prisoner was liberated from the boot and was put in the coach. We did not stop until we reached the large arroyo. I stopped the coach on the road and directed Juan to start a small branding fire and put the iron in it.

Corporal and the Rurale unloaded the prisoner and took him to the vicinity of the fire, where I directed them to remove his clothes. He became combative, as was expected, and I directed He Who Hunts to disable him but to do so in such a way that he would not bleed to death. He Who Hunts deftly cut both of Charlie Thomas's Achilles tendons.

I then told Thomas I was the son of Don Gregorio Pérez—one of the men he and his cronies killed during the ambush at Cañon Bonita. I then pointed to Corporal and said, "This is the son of the man that went to my father's aid and was also killed. We seek revenge for the death of our fathers."

Señor Thomas wailed like a baby and insisted he was not the one that killed them. I replied that he was there, participated with the killers, and, therefore, he was one of the killers. As he did not kill them outright, I told him I was not going to kill him, but I would leave him with a reminder of that deed and turn him over to the Rurales.

I asked Juan for the hot iron, burned the brand of the rancho on his right hip, and asked Corporal to earmark the beast.

After watering the horses, we left the arroyo. When I looked back, the Rurale had built up the fire as a signal for Capitán Carrillo to move in. I smiled, pulled my hat over my face, and slept to the sway of the coach.

We arrived at the Hacienda in the late afternoon. Pedro Gonzáles had been alerted by Señor Honeywell and, by the time we reached the veranda, there was a selection of beer and other drinks as well as dried meats to slake our thirst and munch on. José and Javier soon joined us and, after they and Señor Deus had exchanged greetings, I told him the contract had been changed to 4,000 head. "In addition, we will need to send 680 head of two-year-old steers to the Valley of San Luis in Colorado, and an additional 500 head of two-year-old heifers will need to be gathered to be placed on one of two ranches I am entering into a contract to purchase in the San Luis Valley or be sold by Señor Deus if we do not come to agreement. Also, we will need to send at least 100 head of older cows with the heifers and 24 bulls. Make sure all but four of the bulls are three- or four-year-olds, if the cows are pregnant, they are not far along. Roman still has many three-year-olds that he can send immediately."

José smiled and said, "You have just given me a great task to oversee, and I am sure Javier is up to it."

Javier looked up, surprised, and muttered, "I better get at it." He downed his beer and left to find Running Bear.

José said, "Javier is going to get a lesson in management when he tries to pass most of this on to Running Bear. Running Bear will divide the responsibility with him, and then he will assign men to see to the responsibilities he has assumed. I will watch over Javier and help him to delegate his portions also."

I went on to apprise José of what we would need as far as a remuda, wagons, chuck wagons, vaqueros, and skilled hands such as carpenters and smithys who could double as supply- and repair-wagon drivers.

I then broached the subject of the extra cattle from Hacienda Occidental. "Would it not be better if the road brand was applied at Hacienda Occidental and the cattle driven from the Hacienda or wherever you have the cattle gathered to Campo El Lobo and then north through the Valle de Animas? Just north of the Montañas de Animas (Animas Mountains), you could turn northeast on a line just south of the Montañas de Burros (Burro Mountains) and intersect with the trail we will be following north. This would save driving the cattle from Hacienda Oeste to Hacienda Este and then back northwest to that point on the trail. In addition, the vaqueros and horses we will need from the Oeste could travel with the herd. If that is a workable solution, we could get the cows and bulls needed from the Oeste also."

Señor Deus stated he thought that could be a workable solution, but he did see that integrating the herds would be a small but solvable problem. The three-year-olds would have to be moved into the front herd and the cows and bulls into the herd with the two-year-olds. It would also help to stabilize the younger herd to have them in the front of the herd. He felt there could be some problems with the bulls, and it might be better to wagon them instead of driving them, as they could be a disrupting influence.

I thought about that for a minute and said, "We have at least two weeks before we need to decide on the bulls. It may be best to purchase some bulls and bring them in by train."

José interrupted to say, "Pedro will be ringing the bell for dinner soon, and we all will need to dress. I will apprise Javier and Running Bear of our discussion, and we can take up further matters tomorrow. Let's get ready for the ladies."

When I reached my room, my bath had been drawn and my clothes were laid out. Edward had left a note stating he would not presume to decide what clothes I should wear, but he was under orders to choose them. I went to dinner in the casual clothes of a don. It was not my style, but I had my orders. I also had a note stating I was to escort my mother and her companion to dinner.

When I was admitted to Mother's waiting room, I was greeted by a beautiful girl dressed for a fandango (a fast, Spanish dance). *I can't stand much more of this,* I thought to myself. *She already dances in my dreams and crowds my thoughts during the day.*

It was a wonderful evening, and my weariness flew away when I was in the presence of my lovely companion. I told her I was dreading leaving her for months while I went off to the United States. She confessed that she, too, felt a deep dread at the thought of me leaving for such a long time. I told her I was in great despair and needed to talk to her father to ask permission to marry her, but it was not possible for me to go to La Reforma and also tend to the duties of the rancho before my departure.

She said, "There is no need for despair. My parents are due to arrive tomorrow. Your mother has sent a coach for them."

I was so grateful that my mother had arranged all of this, but, at the same time, I was beginning to feel like a puppet on a string. Yet, for now, I was quite content to be a puppet. That night, I slept on a cloud surrounded by angels who looked like Olga and sang to me.

When I burst through the kitchen doors the next morning feeling ready to take on the world, I was faced with the sight of my friends all gathered around their plates and planning the day. It seemed strange to me that they did not know this was no ordinary day. I sat down, took a plate from Pedro, and ate slowly, trying to bring myself back to the here and now.

After I had eaten, I sat back with my coffee in hand. José started the conversation. "If we could get 900 three-year-old steers from Roman, it would necessitate including only 500 cull cows to meet our goal of 4,000 for the contract. In addition, that would make it possible to have more long two-year-olds (cattle over two years old but less than three) that will be good market cattle in the Spring."

I immediately agreed and requested the long two-year-olds be included with the two-year-olds we were sending to the San Luis Valley, and an additional 50 head would be a good idea in case we had some losses. Then I said, "Friends, I have a lot on my mind, but I think I have given you some direction, and I am sure you will feel the need to change some details. After consulting with José and Señor Deus, I believe things will turn out well for the drive. I need to take care of some other matters. Juan, could you stay for a while? I need to discuss something with you."

I stepped out of the kitchen and asked one of the maids to go up and tell my mother I would like to talk to her privately. The maid came back immediately and said I could go up right away. She then went into see Pedro about some coffee and pan dulce that my mother would like taken to her room. I told Juan I would talk with my mother, and I would call him up there shortly.

Mother greeted me with a kiss and hug, and we sat down. She was fully aware of my conversation with Olga, and she indicated she highly approved. I told her I was concerned about my conversation with Olga's parents, but she just laughed and said, "When would you like to get married?" I answered, "Tomorrow!"

She smiled knowingly and said, "That would be a little bit soon. I will work it out with Juanita. Will you want Olga to accompany you on your trip east?"

I indicated that was exactly why, for me, tomorrow would be perfect.

Mother's retort was, "Juanita and I will work it out so you can take her with you on your trip."

I then told her about purchasing the two ranches in the San Luis Valley and that I wanted to ask Juan Gonzáles to manage them. "I would like to have a small meeting with Juan and his parents and include Edward and Juliana in on the meeting as well, as I intend to recall Salvador from Tombstone and send him up as a segundo (second) to Juan. Roman can set someone else up in Tombstone. Juan is waiting for me downstairs. Would you like to be in on the meeting?" I asked.

She replied, "I would. I want to meet in the parlor, and you can pick me and Angélica up in 45 minutes." I left to arrange the meeting.

I went back to the kitchen and told Pedro we would have a family meeting in the parlor, and it would be nice to have some coffee, pan dulce, and treats for 10 people. I then told him we wanted him and María in on the meeting.

I turned to Juan and said, "Will you please bring your mother? The meeting will be in 40 minutes."

He left to get his mother, and I went to find Edward and Juliana. I told them about the meeting and asked that they attend. I sent a young vaquero to tell José, Javier, and Corporal about the meeting in the parlor in 30 minutes. I then sat down on the veranda and sought some solitude with a cigar.

I escorted Mother and Angélica to the parlor. We walked in, and Mother and Angélica went over and hugged María and Juliana. Mother poured coffee and put everyone at ease. When we were all settled, I told them I was in the process of purchasing two small ranches in the San Luis Valley of Colorado, and I was going to need someone I trusted to manage them. I then turned to Juan and said, "Juan, I would be honored if you would accept the job of managing the ranches. The purchase is not final, but I need to get everything set for the possibility of it happening."

Juan regarded me with a stunned look and said, "I only hope I can live up to your trust."

I replied, "I have no doubt that you will."

I then turned to Edward and Juliana and told them the reason I had asked them to this meeting was because I would be recalling Salvador from Tombstone, and I would like for him to act as the segundo for Juan. "I will have him come here and, if he agrees, he will accompany me on the trip north. We will work out the details as we need to, but I expect to leave in two weeks to examine the ranches and finalize the purchase. I will work out the details with Juan and Salvador in the future."

Mother rose and said, "I know we are sending your sons far from the rancho, but I want you to know you all are part of this family. When you feel the need to visit your sons in Colorado, do not let your responsibilities to the rancho keep you from going. Remember, in our eyes, they are still on the rancho, and those ranchos in Colorado will become part of the business of the Estancia del Pérez."

There were hugs and congratulations all around, and I asked Juan and Corporal to stay after all the others had left.

I said to Juan and Corporal, "This is just the beginning. The only thing holding up the purchase is my inspection of the property. I am going to have to rely on the two of you more and more. I will be looking for additional properties in the San Luis Valley as well as the San Juan Valley, and it will be up to you, Juan, to manage them. You, Corporal, as my primero, will have to assume more responsibility in overseeing what I am not able to. In this case, I am going to send you with Juan to do the inspection of the properties. Together, these ranches are to support 1,500 head. We will own the land in the valley and have grazing rights in the mountains. It will be your duty to see where the boundaries are and make sure there is adequate graze for that many head. I will be sending 500 head of two-year-old heifers and 100 head of older cows to the valley to stock the ranches. I will need to purchase bulls to be shipped in by railroad. On Señor Deus's advice, I will not send bulls from here, as they would be disruptive to the drive. I am looking forward to this being a mother-calf operation, but, for the near future, it will also receive Spring drives of two- and three-year-old steers that can be fattened up and sold in the Fall. You both need to be ready to leave in a week or before. I will give you an exact time by the end of the day."

I went out and found He Who Hunts and Standing Bear. I asked Standing Bear if he could send two vaqueros with He Who Hunts to meet a carriage coming from the west and due to arrive today. He hailed two vaqueros, and they all left in about 10 minutes. I knew Roman would not have let them come without an escort, but He Who Hunts was my extra caution.

Señor Deus and I rode down to the gathering grounds to look over the herds. We found José, Standing Bear, and Javier in a discussion. The concern was that the herds had been gathered here for some time, and we were supplementing the graze with hay. They had come to the conclusion it would be best to move the two-year-olds to north of Campo Nava and the three-year-olds to a location between here and Campo Nava. Señor Deus told them this was a good solution to keep them grazing in the line of travel. The 500 cows that were going to market were being road branded and, when we hit the trail, we would want them in the lead.

José said, "Our dispatch rider has come in from El Paso, and he has some wires for you. He also brought the clearance papers to take up to 6,000 head for market or stock purposes into the United States. There is a blanket visa for the vaqueros taking the cattle into the country. Señor Deus, you will need to turn in a list of the vaqueros going on the drive to the port on the Mimbres River just east of the Montañas de Floridas."

I was dumbfounded that I had not thought of permits and visas. I needed to tighten that up and make sure a bureaucratic misstep could not derail business in the future. I made a note to myself to discuss this with Señor White today. I took the messages that were for me and went back to the Hacienda. It was hard to concentrate on business, so eager was I to see the coach come in.

I caught up with Señor White, gave him his letters and telegrams, and asked him if he had the time to meet with me. He answered in the affirmative, but it would be about an hour before he could get free from the school and read his mail. I knew what I would be doing in an hour, but, for now, I just sat on the veranda with tea and a cigar. Mother and Olga joined me after a few minutes. My day was looking up.

Señor White arrived, and Mother said to Olga, "It looks like my son is going to be busy for a while, so I think we can leave him."

I was still in a glow, but the dark cloud of the unknown hovered close. What if Olga's father said no?

Señor White started out by saying, "At this time in the United States, there are two methods of recognized ownership of real property—fee simple and through a trust. The major problem with a trust is that a trust cannot own a trust, so you would have to establish a trust with each form of business. The same is true in Mexico, but here the trust is even worse in that you must have a financial institution as your trustee. That means putting someone else in charge of your money or business.

"In England, they have established corporations wherein individuals of common interest in business or property incorporate into a form of ownership in which a board or manager runs the business for the benefit of all. Just this year, British law went even further to state that the board members or managers could not be sued for harm done by the corporation as long as they were personally not breaking any laws. By treaty, the United States recognizes British corporations, and they can and do hold vast expanses of real estate in the United States. At this point, I do not know if you, as a Mexican citizen, can incorporate a company in Britain. However, New Jersey is, as we speak, working on setting up laws that will allow for corporations. It has not happened there yet, but my sources say it can be done by hiring a New Jersey Law firm to set up a corporation, and they would transfer the stock over to you—or you and whoever else—and that would make it perfectly legal for you to own such a corporation. Every state must recognize a business from another state or territory as long as it is a business in good standing in the state of incorporation. It is anticipated that, in the future, all states will allow incorporation of companies within their borders and will require that outside corporations register before they do business within the state.

"As there is no state that presently disallows foreign ownership of land—and the railroads would fight tooth and nail against any attempt to make such a law given that most of their income is from bringing foreign immigrants over and selling the land along their right of way—I would not let a lack of mechanism hold me back. You should continue to purchase in your name and create a mechanism by will for transfer of the title were you to die."

I thanked Señor White and asked him to keep an eye out on the New Jersey legislation. I told him I had studied a little about the British corporations and that I hoped New Jersey's corporations would be as good as or better than the British version.

Switching topics, I told him I was relying on him to alert me to children that would benefit from continued education. I also confessed I was somewhat ignorant as to higher education and technical schools in Mexico.

Once the meeting was over, I grabbed a horse tied to the rail in front of the house and took off west. I directed my mount up the mountain and, when we were high enough to see into the distance, I turned him south and followed the contour of the hill until I could see off to the west. Out in the distance, I could see a large cloud of dust. I sat there watching it for some time with the question running in my head. *What if he says no?*

I watched the dust cloud for an hour until a coach and riders appeared in front of the dust. I turned my horse down the mountain toward the Hacienda. I would have my answer soon.

I was standing in front of the house when the coach pulled up. He Who Hunts and the riders left for the stables, and I opened the coach door. Juanita stuck her head out and handed me a valise. I gave her my hand and helped her down. Two young ladies followed and then Manuel. We walked up to the veranda.

Edward had young men headed to the boot to get the luggage, and Elizabeth came out of the house to hug Juanita and her daughters. She told her that mother had refreshments in her sitting room and was waiting for them.

Pedro had sent two young men with plates of sandwiches and beer, and we men sat down. I was still unable to eat, but the beer felt good, and I waited until Manuel had settled in. Manuel asked me how the roundup was going, and I told him we would be shipping next week.

I knew exactly what I intended to say, but the words would not emerge. I took another swallow of beer, gave up, and stammered to Manuel, "Olga and I want to get married and right away."

God, that did not come out right at all!

Manuel said, "Do you love her?"

I replied, "With my whole heart."

He said, "Then you have my blessing."

He did not say no!

I excused myself, went up to Mother's rooms, and entered without knocking. My eyes found Olga, and I reached out to her.

She came into my arms, and I whispered, "He said yes!"

Mother, Juanita, and my sisters were all smiling. My mother said, "Remember this when young men come to talk to you about your sisters and daughters. When do you want to set the date?"

I told her, "My plans have changed. I need Juan and Corporal to leave in no more than seven days for Colorado. Our herds should be on their way no later than seven days from now, as we are going to run out of graze for such a concentrated herd, and cold weather is approaching. Today is October 2nd. October 8th sounds like a lucky day. Juan and Corporal can be my best men and leave for Colorado on the 9th. Olga, He Who Hunts, Salvador, and I should leave by the 11th. We will take a stage out of El Paso to Lamy, in the New Mexico Territory, where we will board a Santa Fe train that will eventually drop us off in Pueblo, Colorado. From Pueblo, we will take a train on the Denver and Rio

Grande Western Railroad to Walsenburg and over La Veta Pass to see the two ranches we are purchasing, following the route taken by Juan and Corporal. If all goes well, we will backtrack with Juan and Corporal to Walsenburg, where all the papers will be signed, and then Olga, Salvador, and I will continue on to Denver. Corporal, He Who Hunts, and Juan will go back to Lamy. At Lamy, Juan will head back to the Estancia, and Corporal will ride with He Who Hunts to meet the herds coming up. All of these plans are subject to change, of course, but, at this moment, these are my thoughts.

"Mother," I continued, "I need some guidance from you as to the route my sisters and Javier will take on their trip back East for the period of time that I will not be with them. They can either take the Guaymas-San Francisco route or they can take the El Paso-Lamy route. If they are to take the San Francisco route, I will meet them in San Francisco. If they take the Lamy route, I will meet them at Lamy."

Mother replied, "I will talk with them and give you an answer this afternoon."

I replied, "Bien (good). Now I must make an announcement. There will be a fiesta at this rancho tonight!" I kissed Olga and left on a cloud.

As I floated out the door, I hailed a passing vaquero and told him I needed José, Señor Deus, Juan Gonzáles, Corporal, El Tigre, Javier, and He Who Hunts to meet me on the veranda. I then went and located Señor Honeycutt and told him I was calling a meeting on the veranda. I asked him, "Would you please attend and ask Señor White and Manuel Celaya to be there as well? Also, would you ask Pedro to break out our finest tequila and join us?"

I found myself a seat on the veranda and lit a cigar. Life was good.

It took about 30 minutes for everyone to gather on the veranda. I then opened the meeting by stating I had decided the cattle drive must start as of October 9th. I then went on to say, "José, we will need someone to be the jefe of the vaqueros that are going on the drive. He will be subject to the orders of Señor Deus, so he should be able to speak

English. He will serve as the foreman on the drive. In addition, you will need to pick three young, unmarried vaqueros that have attended Señor White's school and speak English. They need to be willing to live in Colorado on the new ranches. They will not know if they are to stay until Corporal and He Who Hunts meet the herds. I will send a letter today to Roman to pick a man to be the top hand for the drive, and he will answer to the jefe and Señor Deus. I must emphasize that Señor Deus is the law on this drive, and he has brought 20 men to help him. How he manages those men is his business. He will give the jefe orders, and the jefe will give orders to the top hand. Roman will also need to pick three vaqueros to live in Colorado under the same conditions. I will be giving Juan the authority to hire local hands as needed—and I am sure they will be needed by Spring.

"While in Denver, I will begin the search for bulls. We will need 24 to begin with and, once we have located and bought them, I will be sending them to the new ranches with Salvador. Salvador will take charge of the ranches until Juan returns from back East."

I then said, "Señores, I would appreciate it if you would all pour yourselves a glass of tequila, as I have a few more announcements to make."

After everyone had a drink in one hand and a cigar in the other, I got out of my chair and requested everyone to remain seated. I announced, "Mi amigos (My friends), this morning I asked Señor Manuel Celaya for the hand of his daughter, and he said yes. Señorita Olga Celaya and I are to be married on the 8th of October. Señor El Tigre, is it possible for you to see that two fat steers are butchered and cooked for a fiesta for this evening?"

El Tigre came over, gave me an abrazo (hug), and said, "It will be an honor."

We drank a toast to Manuel Celaya, which would be one of many. Señor Honeywell and Pedro excused themselves to stir everyone up to prepare a fiesta, and I received many abrazos.

It was a grand fiesta, and I had my moment to howl.

I have no idea when it got done, but the news of the drive and all the preparations for it were sent to Roman as well as the announcement of the wedding. Mother and Juanita had all the ladies busy making preparations. Mother had sent for a priest. I had lost all sense of time and place, as I was guided through everything I needed to get done by Señor Honeywell and Mother. After a couple of days, I took hold of the reins of the rancho and started seeing the preparations for the drive and our trip north.

A few days before the wedding, Mother sent me a note requesting I join her for lunch in her drawing room. When I arrived, Mother was sitting and having a conversation with Juan Gonzáles. She looked at me and said, "Juan has a question he needs an answer to."

I had no idea what was going on, but it got real serious when Juan said, "Don Francisco, I would like permission to marry your sister, Dulce."

I sat down, poured a glass of wine, collected myself, and started with, "Juan, I thought this was a possibility, but I hope you will forgive me. I need to gather my thoughts. You are like a brother to me, and I am happy to have you as a brother-in-law. I would love to throw you a grand wedding, but could you and Dulce wait until Spring to get married? At the moment, your life is in turmoil with escorting the ladies back east, and I really need Dulce to accompany Elizabeth on her journey. Also, we have no idea what kind of accommodations there are at the ranchos in Colorado, so it may be your duty to see that these are adequate before you take her to your new home. Could you and Dulce discuss this and come up with a wedding date in the Spring? I am very excited for the both of you, and I would like to announce your betrothal at our wedding dinner."

Juan said, "I will discuss it with Dulce and your mother, and we will set a date in the Spring. I regret this complicates your life at this time, but things are moving so fast, and we are so much in love."

We sent for Dulce, and I gave both Juan and Dulce hugs and said, "Get back to me about a date."

Roman came riding in on the evening of the 7th, and we needed to do some more celebrating. I told him that Juan and Dulce were betrothed and would be getting married in the Spring. We shared a large family dinner that included the Pérez, Celaya, Gonzáles, Gallego, Honeywell, and White families as well as Corporal, He Who Hunts, Señor Deus, and the four surprises that rode in that afternoon in the persons of Victorio, Loco, Nana, and Naiche. It was truly a family gathering. Olga sat with me at the head of the table, and everyone reminded us that we should enjoy our time together, because we were forbidden to see one another again until we met at the altar the next day.

CHAPTER 13

The priest wrote in the church records that at mid-morning on October 8th, 1879, he presided over the exchange of wedding vows between Francisco Pérez Castro and Olga Celaya Osuna. That is the way history will look at it, but, for me, it was not that simple.

Roman had insisted on celebrating after dinner the night before, and it was very late before they poured me into bed. I woke up the next morning and looked out my window to see the ball field looking like an iglesia jardin (garden church). My mother, Juanita Celaya, the Celaya sisters, and my sisters were working with the men and women of the rancho to prepare the setting.

I had been thinking the affair would be simple, with just a few friends and family attending, but that was not to be. The priest was directing the placement of an altar on a flower-festooned stage that was not there before. I could see that Olga and I were to be actors in a jugada (play)—a jugada in which our mothers and the priest were the directors and this was the ritual we must perform.

I had been anticipating this moment, but I had no idea about the ritual involved for me to get where I wanted to be. I felt I was entering the lion's den.

I did not want to go down to breakfast and, shortly, there was a knock at the door. I opened it to Señor Deus and Victorio, who were standing there with a plate of food and a pot of coffee.

Señor Deus said, "Your mother thought we should have a talk with you, as she says you are not acquainted with how a formal wedding is conducted. As I have had several, I want you to know if your legs are shaking and your stomach feels hollow, this is a normal reaction. The wedding is not for the groom. It is for the bride, families, and friends. It is the price you pay, and you will live through it with your dignity intact."

Victorio came over, put his hand on my shoulder, and said, "You remind me of a young man that was asked to speak to the council. It appeared likely to us that he would run away, but I knew he would not. He stood his ground with his head held high and proved himself a brave. I am proud to call him my son."

They sat down with me and drank some coffee while I ate. We smoked cigars and talked of the time when we rescued Señor Deus's niece in Durango.

In what seemed like a very short time, Roman and Corporal appeared, and Corporal said, "It's time to get dressed."

Señor Deus and Victorio left, and my brothers and I got ready for the jugada.

Corporal, Roman, and I arrived early and greeted our guests. My family was sitting on the right side of the aisle. My fathers, Victorio and Nana, and my brothers, Naiche and He Who Hunts, sat in the third row and were joined by José. José's three children were seated in the first row and had been joined by some of the other children of the Hacienda. Señor White, Señor Honeycutt, Pedro Gonzáles, and their families took up the next four rows. On the left side, the space for the bride's family was empty at the moment. The rest of the chairs were taken up by neighbors and friends mixed in with the vaqueros and their families, who took up all the other rows except for the first two rows on the left side, which were reserved for the Celaya family. Everyone seemed to be relaxed and engaged in light conversation.

Father Salvador came over, took my elbow, and led me up to the right side of the altar. He then arranged Corporal and Roman to my left, and we stood looking down the aisle. I was beginning to feel uneasy. Elizabeth sat down at the organ, which had been moved out of the house, and began to play a song that sounded like a march. I felt myself going into a trance.

The first person I saw was Señor Deus and, walking beside him on each arm, was mother and niñera Juanita. He escorted Mother and niñera Juanita to the second row and sat between them. They were followed by Javier, who escorted Olga's mother, Juanita. She sat opposite Mother on the bride's side.

Following Juanita were Olga's sisters followed by Angélica and Dulce. They went to the left side of the altar and the priest arranged them. The music became louder, and my legs began to feel weak. I was beginning to dread that everyone would see how they were shaking.

Manuel appeared with an angel on his arm. She floated down the aisle and, when she reached me, she held out her right hand and placed it on my arm as we turned to face the priest. It was a miracle how her appearance took the rubber out of my legs. We said our vows, took communion, and exchanged rings as if in a dream. The priest pronounced us married, I raised the veil that was over Olga's face, and we kissed. I was flying on golden wings. We walked out to smiles and good wishes followed by the bridesmaids and my best men. I realized I was still breathing.

Then I became aware of the smell of meat cooking on a mesquite fire. I wondered why I hadn't smelled it before. Olga and I stepped up onto the veranda and sat in two large chairs that had been placed there for us. Our friends, families, and guests joined us while the wedding chapel was cleared away. Large tables were set up where people were to sit, and food was placed on the tables. In less than an hour, our ball field became a grand ballroom, and we all went to the tables to enjoy a wonderful feast.

To start the proceedings, two glasses of wine were brought to us. Olga took hers and held it up for me to drink from, and then I held mine so she could drink from it. Many toasts were made, starting with Roman and Manuel. In the background, we could hear the songs of the Maríachis (traditional Mexican musicians). A gran pastel de boda (wedding cake) was sitting on its own table, and soon it was time for Olga and me to cut it. I cut the first slice, and Olga held it while I took a bite. I did the same for her.

We were then released from the festivities and went up to my quarters. When I ushered Olga into my rooms, I was shocked. My rooms no longer looked like a bachelor's quarters. They had been transformed and looked much more like Mother's rooms. They were now Olga's rooms.

When all had left our door, we came into each other's arms. Over the next several hours, we became one.

CHAPTER 14

It was Sunday, October 12, 1879. We were in the grand coach, on the last leg of our trip to El Paso and were to be in Juárez within an hour. Olga was asleep against my shoulder. He Who Hunts had spent the entire trip on top of the coach. We picked up new drivers along the way, and Salvador alternated between riding inside the coach and on the top. I had begun to think of the business of the Estancia.

The morning after the wedding, I woke up to the sun. A horse had been tied in front of the Hacienda for me, and I rode out to bid good journey to the men that had started the drive. The point rider had already passed the Hacienda and was headed west, closely followed by a large steer that acted as the Judas goat. I caught up to Señor Deus to wish him a good journey and rode with him until noon, when I turned back.

When I reached the Hacienda, the last of the herd of two-year-olds had just passed, and I waved to the men riding drag.

Corporal and Juan had left for El Paso before I rose. They had my instructions and funds. At the camps along the way, people had turned out to meet Doña Olga. She smiled and conversed with all and admired the kids and babies.

The coach that would be taking us on our journey up the ancient trail known as the Camino Real de Tierra Adentro between El Paso and Santa Fe would be leaving early on Monday the 13th. It was my fond hope that we could rest and make the late Sunday morning mass at the Mission of Our Lady of Guadalupe of the Meek in Paso del Norte. This church was established by Franciscans in 1659, completed by 1671, and had been in continuous use since then.

We made the mass, and Olga was appropriately amazed at the ancient, simple church with the carved wooden ceiling. The devotion that went into building the church over 200 years previous by priests and Indians could still be felt when one entered it.

The coach out of El Paso was not as nice as the grand coach of the Hacienda, but it was comfortable. We stopped in Mesilla for lunch and at way stations to change teams and take on refreshments. The passage on the Jornada was hot, dry, and bleak and would have been deadly if not for the way stations, where either a well had been dug or water was hauled in. He Who Hunts insisted on riding on top of this coach as well.

Victorio was still raiding. He knew of our passage, and we knew we would be safe, but He Who Hunts felt riding on top guaranteed safe passage.

We arrived at Lamy in just over three days, and we were all worse for wear. After the passage, I was glad that Dulce and Elizabeth were going by the San Francisco route. It would not be pleasant if they had been forced to endure the ride. Olga made the trip with a smile, but she seemed to be extraordinarily happy that I had ordered a railroad car with a wardroom and bath for our next leg of the trip on the Santa Fe Railroad.

We rode the Santa Fe until just outside of Bent's Fort, where our car was detached from the train and connected to a train going to Pueblo, Colorado. We spent the night of the 16th of October in Pueblo and headed south on the Denver and Rio Grande Railroad at Walsenburg. We took the San Juan Extension over La Veta pass to Fort Garland.

When the train arrived, we saw Juan and Corporal waiting for us with big smiles on their faces. They announced that the ranches were as advertised, and they would indeed be able to sustain 1,500 head on a year-round basis by wintering the cattle on the lowlands and moving them up into the mountains in the Spring.

Juan said, "The housing is adequate for my and Salvador's needs, and there's adequate housing for at least 16 vaqueros."

Corporal added that he had arranged for good lodging for us at Fort Garland for two nights. "We can be at the ranchos in about three hours' ride from here, and it might be good if Olga and you set foot on the ranchos to check out whether the lodging that Juan has picked out might be adequate for all of the family's needs."

I understood his meaning. It should be Olga that determined whether it was adequate for Dulce. We agreed that Corporal should wire Señores Hertshaw and McCleen (the current owners) to advise them we would be at the ranches the next day and that the inspection of the ranches revealed they were as advertised. We would wire the lawyer in Walsenburg that we would like to close on the sale after the train delivered us to Walsenburg. He went on to tell them it would be good to meet them at the ranches tomorrow and, if they accompanied us to Walsenburg, we could finalize the transaction and they could leave with the funds.

I took Olga up to our rooms at the hotel, so she could freshen up and take a siesta. Once she was secure, I went down to the cantina to meet with Corporal and my companions. After drinks had been ordered and received, Corporal began his report by stating the two ranches were a division of a single ranch. The señores Hertshaw and McCleen were brothers-in-law, and they were moving their families to California to be nearer the rest of their family, which had settled there. They had treated the land well, and there was no sign of overgrazing or depletion of the soil, which was so prevalent in the West.

He went on to explain there were two older hands staying at the ranches now as caretakers, and they had been living on the ranches before Hertshaw and McCleen bought them. Corporal voiced the opinion that we should keep them, as they knew every rock and arroyo on the ranches and would prove invaluable.

Such luck was unexpected, and I immediately agreed. I turned to Juan and Salvador and said, "I hope you two will treat these men as we treat the honored elders on the Estancia del Pérez. They are valuable assets that all the hands in our employ are to honor and respect. They will be elders of the ranches and will have valuable information about other properties we may be interested in."

Corporal pointed out the restaurant attached to the cantina and said it had good food. I informed my friends that I would join Olga in a siesta, and then it would be my honor to host them to dinner at dark.

Before I went upstairs, I asked Juan to accompany me to the restaurant, where he introduced me to the owner/cook, who appeared to be an Alemán. I told her I would like a table for six at about dark and asked her what she had on the menu.

She stated she was preparing beef stroganoff over buttered noodles.

I said, "That would be great, as I have not had that dish since I was a student in New Jersey." I then asked, "Fraülein, will you be having Black Forest cake for dessert?"

She replied, "Regretfully, no, but I have strudel and éclair."

I looked at her and said, "I can see I am going to have to visit the San Luis Valley often."

I took Juan to the side and told him I did not doubt his opinion of the adequacy of the home for Dulce was sincere. "I just want to pass on some information my father told me: Never declare that something is outright good or that you like it just as it is. Have reservations, because if you declare it good, the women in your life know that a man has no concept of what is good, and they will want to change it. I would suggest you always have reservations when it comes to matters in which women are involved. If you leave those matters to the women, they will find fewer objections, and life will be much smoother."

At supper, I was a little concerned about how my companions would enjoy what, to them, was strange fare. He Who Hunts dug in and, when it came to dessert, he had a strudel *and* an éclair. While he was drinking coffee afterwards, he had more dessert. The dinner was a success.

We left early in the morning. I was driving a spring carriage with Olga by my side, and the four men rode horses. We met Abe and Jake, the two older hands, when we arrived at the first of the ranches and were soon joined by Señores Hertshaw and McCleen. Olga proceeded to inspect the house with Juan in tow while the men got acquainted with each other and the ranch buildings. It was apparent that care had been taken with everything, and I was happy with our first acquisition in the United States.

Juan caught up to us and said, "Doña Olga has done her inspection and is ready to go." We decided we had best adjourn to Fort Garland.

At Fort Garland, I accompanied Olga to our room, where she took ink, pen, and paper and began to write lists of things that needed to be done at the ranch. I was hanging around, and she looked up and said, "Go on and join the men. I am going to be busy for a while. Just call for me for dinner."

I had been dismissed, so I rushed down to join the men in the cantina.

We had dinner for eight and the beef rouladen followed by desert, which was Black Forest Cake that was beyond compare. My companions were now totally appreciative of the Alemán. We all went to bed contented.

The next morning, we boarded the train to Walsenburg at 8:00 am. The Pitney law firm had contacted a lawyer in Walsenburg by the name of Silas Leven. When we arrived at his office, he had all the papers prepared. Señores Hertshaw and McCleen signed as the sellers, and I signed as the purchaser. When all the documents were signed, Señor Leven gave each of them a draft for $3,000 on the Drexel, Morgan, and Company account. He explained to them he had pre-cleared the drafts with the local bank and they could either deposit them or draw some or all the funds on them immediately.

Señores Hertshaw and McCleen left, and Señor Leven told us he would file the papers in Denver the next day so there would be proper notice. We could pick up certified copies the following day.

I asked him about his fees, and he said, "The fees are through a contract with the Pitney Law Firm, and you owe nothing at this time." I asked Señor Leven to keep his eye out for more ranches that may be available in the San Luis or San Juan Valleys. "I would even be interested in looking at land elsewhere in Colorado," I added.

We caught the afternoon train to Pueblo, where we all acquired rooms for the night. That evening, I informed Juan that he would be escorting Elizabeth and Dulce on their trip to Guaymas and San Francisco and that Javier and Juan Cortez would be with him. "You will be in charge of the arrangements, and Juan Cortez will be in charge of the security of my sisters. Please keep me informed as to the day of your departure and your progress by telegraph. You will be able to reach me at the Palace Hotel in San Francisco. I will have rooms waiting there for you."

I confirmed with Corporal that he and He Who Hunts were to accompany Juan to Lamy, where they were to purchase some good horses and ride down to meet the herds coming up. It was imperative that we deliver the market cattle to Lamy on or before November 15th. "It will be up to Señor Deus' judgment, but I would suggest that once you have cleared the narrows with the market herd, it might be best to continue on with them and not wait for the other herd to join you. You two will have to make that decision. Once you have delivered the herd and received the funds in the form of a draft, you and He Who Hunts will need to proceed with haste back here, where you will take the Denver and Rio Grande Railroad to Denver and make connections on to Cheyenne, Wyoming. Wire me at the Palace Hotel when you leave Lamy. It is possible—in fact, probable—that it would be best for you to proceed on to San Francisco. I will have instructions for you at Cheyenne."

Corporal checked the train schedule and found there was a train heading east in four hours that had an hour layover at Bent's Fort before the train arrived that went to Lamy. We reserved two rooms, and the men joined Salvador in one while they waited for the train. Olga and I ordered a tray from the restaurant at the depot hotel and retired for the evening.

On the evening of October 21st, Olga and I found ourselves on the third floor of the Grand Central Hotel in Denver. Salvador had a room on the first floor with orders to fend for himself. I would meet him for breakfast in the dining room in the morning. I was still in business mode, but Olga and I had the evening to ourselves. We ordered trays and did not leave the room.

Salvador and I met for breakfast and walked to the Colorado Cattlemen's Association offices, where I went through the process of joining the Association. I told them I had bought two ranches in the San Luis Valley and had a small herd coming up from New Mexico. My immediate concerns were the purchase of some bulls to transport there. Several of the local ranchers were in the offices enjoying the amenities of coffee and cigars, and I was quickly engaged with questions. I informed them I was looking for 24 bulls, three to four years old, and I would be happy to consider any that were available.

I soon had offers, and we made arrangements to travel to four different ranches to look at bulls. I still had some business to take care of, and I delegated Salvador to begin looking at bulls. I agreed to meet a rancher at the Cattlemen's Association after I completed my other business, and we would travel out to his ranch. His ranch was not far from town, and I had no intention of leaving Olga alone overnight. I had received a draft on Drexel Morgan for $5,000, which I had ordered forwarded to me through Señor Leven. I took my draft into the Colorado National Bank and set up a bank account.

By October the 26th, Salvador and I had identified the bulls we wanted to purchase, and I had made a deal with the ranchers to bring them into the shipping corrals at the Denver and Rio Grande Railroad. I had made arrangements for their shipment to Fort Garland. One of the ranchers had offered Salvador the use of two of his hands to help get the bulls to the ranch, and all was set for the next phase of our trip.

Olga and I checked out of the Grand Central and were delivered to the depot of the Denver Pacific Railway and Telegraph Company for our ride to Cheyenne, Wyoming. In Cheyenne, we had a four-hour wait before we could board our train to San Francisco. The depot was a bare-bones building, but it did have a women's waiting room, and Olga retired there. I sent telegrams to Hacienda Oriental to inquire as to news of the drive and harvest. I also wanted to know when Juan and the girls were going to depart for San Francisco. I sent a wire to the Palace Hotel in San Francisco requesting a suite, gave them the train number and time of arrival, and requested transportation to the hotel.

We arrived in San Francisco on October the 29th in the evening and were instantly whisked away to the Palace Hotel. We were finally on our honeymoon. Our suite was on the seventh floor, and we reached there with the assistance of a rising room (later to be called an elevator). Our suite had a large drawing room, which was entered from the hallway, and, adjacent to the drawing room, was our bedroom, which had its own bathroom. There were extra doors, which were closed and locked, that led to other bedrooms with their own baths. Those rooms had hall entrances. This provided for inclusion of a larger group if necessary and I anticipated that might happen later. For now, this was our world, and we did not leave the suite for four days. We ordered our food delivered to our room and spent the time exploring each other.

On November 3rd, we received a wire informing us that Javier, the girls, Juan, and company had left Hacienda Este headed west on their journey to San Francisco on November 1st. I computed they should arrive around November 19th and alerted the hotel that we should need at least three more rooms starting on the 16th and an additional room by the 18th. It was my hope that these rooms would adjoin our suite or be very near.

Olga announced she wanted to explore San Francisco to discover places that would be interesting for my sisters. I stated I would rather stay in the room and explore Olga. That night, we had a reservation for dinner in The American Room, which was the beginning of our discoveries of the city.

The next night, we dined at the Baldwin Hotel and watched a performance from our proscenium box. We enjoyed other performances from our French boxes at the Egyptian Hall, California Theater, and Metropolitan Theater. We attended mass at St Mary's Cathedral and continued to enjoy exploring one another.

On November the 15th, I received a wire from Lamy stating we had fulfilled our contract and had delivered 4,000 head to the satisfaction of the buyers from Chicago. Corporal had taken care of all the business and was awaiting orders. I sent him a wire instructing him and He Who Hunts to come to San Francisco and join us at the Palace Hotel, where I had accommodations waiting for them. "I will be looking for you around the 18th or 19th." I received a wire later that day from Juan informing me their packet boat had stopped at Los Angeles and was departing for San Francisco.

Olga was working hard making plans for the girls, and she was interested in seeing He Who Hunt's reactions to some of the plays as well as the view of the wharfs. I was still interested in a little more exploration of my wife, but I had rivals for her attention in our upcoming guests.

Among its many amenities besides The American Room, the Palace Hotel had great dining in two grills named the Ladies' Grill and the Men's Grill. Many of San Francisco's businessmen as well as visiting businessmen gathered at the Men's Grill for breakfast. Once all our guests had arrived, we began to separate ourselves by dining at the respective gender of grill.

I was interested in expansion into California as well as Colorado and had heard there was ample opportunity for both farming and ranching in the central valley and mountains of California. It was not long before we connected with people who professed to have knowledge of good land. I wired the Pitney Law Firm and asked them to contact a reputable attorney in Sacramento for the purpose of representing the Estancia del Pérez in the possible purchase of ranches in California.

Later that day I received a wire from Mahlon Pitney stating his cousin, Gerald Pitney, who had worked at the Pitney Law Firm, had set up an office in Sacramento, and Mahlon would have no qualms about contracting with his cousin to represent the Estancia in California. He would get in touch with him immediately and have him contact me for a meeting. I acknowledged and thanked him for his promptness and informed him I would be seeing him in mid-December.

I received a wire from Gerald Pitney asking for confirmation of a meeting at the Men's Grill at the Palace Hotel on the morning of November 29th. I sent him a confirmation.

As I had guessed, my sisters, Juan, Javier, and their entourage arrived on the evening of November 19th.

Another of the pluses of the Palace Hotel was its large billiards room and well-appointed bar. As children, we had all learned billiards, and He Who Hunts mastered the game the first time he played. His hand was steady, and his eye was sharp. It was as if he was sending an arrow on its way when he looked down the stick. Corporal, Juan, He Who Hunts, and I had some lively games in the billiards room with regular stops for refreshments at the bar.

Juan, Corporal, and I met Gerald Pitney on the 21st, and I gave him my wish list of ranches and the possibility of the purchase of arable land with water. I introduced him to Corporal and stated that, in most cases, it would be Corporal who would accompany him to examine possible purchases. I introduced him to Juan as my friend, future brother-in-law, and the manager of our Colorado holdings.

Olga had done some shopping with my sisters, and they had taken in a play at the Egyptian Hall with He Who Hunts as an escort. She said He Who Hunts sat through the performance in stunned stoicism and, when it was all over, he smiled at her and said, "I would appreciate it if you request me as an escort again if you attend more plays."

One day, Olga handed me several sheets of paper that had been written in Elizabeth's fine hand. She explained that, rather than discuss her findings on the ranch house's adequacy with me, she had discussed it at the Women's Grill with Dulce and Elizabeth. On these sheets were the modifications and changes that would need to be made so Dulce would be comfortable being the mistress of the Estancia's Colorado headquarters.

I glanced at the list and saw immediately that Juan had his work cut out for him. The ranch house would need to be more than double in size. There would be indoor plumbing and a much larger kitchen.

I asked Olga if provision had been made for Mother's lodging when she visited as well as ours when we visited.

She said, "I informed Dulce that no one shares space with Mother. Her rooms await her arrival." She said they would make the adjustments at the Grill tomorrow and present a final copy.

I then told her such extensive modifications would mean Juan must leave our company at Cheyenne and head south to the ranch to have everything in order for his bride's arrival in Colorado in April.

Olga said, "Dulce has already come to that conclusion and is prepared to console him and send him on his way with his appointed errands." I then asked her if she would be ready to leave on November 26th.

She said she would, but added, "It has been such a sweet time. I will miss our honeymoon hotel."

CHAPTER 15

We began our journey east on the 26th of November. Juan was stunned by how much of what he thought was adequate housing needed to be changed to accommodate his future wife and her family. He readily agreed that his journey east must end at Cheyenne.

I had informed our party we would have to make a detour to Denver, as I had made arrangements to meet Señor Deus there. I had made reservations for the 29th and 30th of November at the Grand Central Hotel and provided for a car to be waiting for us in Cheyenne on the first of December.

Thanksgiving Day has been a national holiday in the United States since 1863. The first Thanksgiving celebration in what is now the United States was celebrated in 1598 in Paso del Norte (El Paso), where a Thanksgiving Mass was celebrated and a great feast was prepared to celebrate a good harvest and God's plenty. Most people in the United States learned that the first celebration of this holiday was in a Virginia colony in 1619.

President Hayes made a declaration that this year's celebration was to be on November the 27th, and we celebrated with our fellow passengers as we moved out of the Sierra Nevada mountains and began crossing the Territory of Utah.

The afternoon of December 1ˢᵗ found us leaving Cheyenne for the east. Señor Deus was paid for his services and expenses for running the cattle drive. He would be helping Juan get acquainted with suppliers in the area and providing expertise in the renovation of the ranch house, which would become the headquarters of the Colorado operations and would be named Hacienda Pérez de Colorado. I was hesitant to name the ranches until we could incorporate. My last act at Cheyenne was to wire Roberto to let him know how many of us were coming and that I would keep him informed of our progress.

We arrived at the train depot in Princeton, New Jersey on December 8ᵗʰ. It had been exactly six months and seven days since I had left there as a carefree graduate. I had been ready to take on the world, but now it seemed the world had taken me on. I arrived this time as Don Francisco with my bride and entourage, and the weight of my world was sitting firmly on my shoulders.

Roberto and the Ochoas were at the station to meet us. Javier and I had purposely gotten off the train as soon as it stopped. I gave the Ochoas abrazos and told Roberto we would go on to the house while the Ochoas helped the rest of the party get their baggage. I had specifically asked Dulce and Elizabeth to not leave the train until I had departed with Roberto, as they were still wearing half-mourning gray.

We caught a hired carriage and started toward Hacienda Norte. On our way, I professed a great desire to stop at a favorite German watering hole for a draught. When we were seated with beers in hand, I related to Roberto our meeting with Juan Gonzáles and Capitán Alfredo Carrillo. Over two more draughts, I gave him the story of the family and the Estancia up to the moment—including our father's death.

Roberto related to me that he had felt a dread, but Mother's cheerful letters kept him questioning himself. He immediately said, "Of course, I will leave the school and go back to the Estancia to help pull my weight."

I replied, "It is our mother's and my wish that you remain in school, so you will be equipped to help lead this family into the 20th century. We have plenty of vaqueros on the Estancia. What the family will need are leaders to guide it. It is our mother's and my hope that you specialize in finance, so you can represent the Estancia in the places of power both here in the United States and in Mexico. Mother, Roman, José, and I will keep the Estancia going and growing until you have gained the skills to take on your responsibilities. I will be contacting J. P. Morgan at Drexel and Morgan with a request that he take you on as an intern next summer, so you can gain some practical knowledge by observation. Our mother and I have also discussed the need for you to become our authority on American law, and I will be talking to my classmate, Mahlon Pitney, about the possibility of you reading law and studying for the bar. You will be most valuable to the family by being proficient in finance and as an abogado (lawyer). We are moving into ranching in the United States to expand and protect the family from the ravages of revolution. We are in great need of family expertise in this field as well as the willingness of a family member to consider the possibility of becoming a citizen of this great country to help anchor our family into the future."

I then turned to more personal matters. "I have brought Dulce and Elizabeth as well as He Who Hunts and Corporal on this trip. I know your sisters are anxious to hold you in their arms. You have another sister. I married Olga Celaya, and she is also here. It is with great pride that I tell you that Dulce and Juan Gonzáles are to be married in the Spring, and they will be moving to the ranches we have purchased in Colorado. Juan is there now, as we have stocked the range. He is also creating Hacienda Pérez de Colorado, so he will have a proper home for his bride."

We continued to Hacienda Norte, where the girls had gotten settled and Roberto was surrounded by the love of his family. Everything I had told him began to find its place in his mind and heart.

On the 10th, Roberto, Javier, and I went to the college to formally enroll Javier for the Spring semester of 1880. We indicated that his main interest was mineralogy.

I sent a wire to Mahlon Pitney to inquire if it would be possible to meet with him and his father on December 12th and also asked him if he would make arrangements for two rooms at an adequate hotel, as I would be bringing my wife and brother with me on my trip. I received a wire later that afternoon stating that two o'clock had been set aside on his father's calendar to meet with me. He stated that he had a large house and would be insulted if we stayed elsewhere. I sent a wire confirming the times and asked Corporal to pick up train tickets for Olga, Roberto, and myself that would allow us to arrive in Morristown, New Jersey no later than noon on the 12th.

Our meeting with Henry and Mahlon Pitney was extremely helpful. I asked them to represent the Estancia in our efforts to incorporate a business in the state of New Jersey once New Jersey had gotten its incorporation laws established. I told them they should communicate with Ben White at Hacienda Oriental on the Estancia del Pérez, informing them I had utmost confidence in Señor White.

Señor Henry asked me if the Ben White I referred could be the same Benjamin White that graduated from the College of New Jersey in the class of 1858. I said, "It is indeed the same man, and he has operated the schools on the Estancia since that time."

Henry Pitney was happy to be able to renew a friendship with an old school acquaintance, and I issued him an invitation to visit the Estancia and Señor White. I then asked the two men if it would be a breach of protocol to contact Señor Leven in Walsenburg directly to engage him in handling the business of the rancho in Colorado. Señor Henry stated he appreciated the question, and he would not consider it to be a breach in protocol. He said he would communicate with Señor Leven that he should, from now on, handle our Colorado legal needs without going through the Pitney firm.

I then discussed with them my desire that Roberto spend the last two years at the College of New Jersey focusing on finance and then read law in preparation of joining the bar.

Señor Henry stated, "I believe the coursework at the College will be adequate, but he will need to spend his summers in an internship. I feel certain I can persuade Tony Drexel and J. P. Morgan to take him on in that capacity, especially since the Estancia del Pérez is a large client. I will look into where it would be best for him to read law. I assume you would want to emphasize a legal learning in finance—particularly agriculture and minerals?"

Both Roberto and I agreed to that.

Señor Henry went on to say, "Reading for the law is something I feel Roberto will have no problem with, but, to practice law in most states, he will have to pass the bar there and be a citizen."

Roberto said, "I knew that would most likely be a condition and, although I am proud of my Mexican heritage, I know the rancho would best be served if I become an American citizen. Could you guide me through the naturalization process, and can that be done soon?"

Señor Henry replied, "I will see that you are helped by the College to get that done during your next semester."

When we had arrived at the office, Mahlon had a clerk and female employee of the firm escort Olga to his home. I thanked Mahlon for his courtesy and requested he make reservations at the best place in town for dinner—which would be on me—and invite Señor Henry and any of his family that would like to join us. Henry thanked me for the invitation but stated this would be a time for classmates to catch up, and he had other engagements.

On December 14th, we all left Princeton for the big lights of New York. I had made arrangements at the Gilsey Hotel for a three-bedroom and a two-bedroom suite, which were adjoining. My sisters joined Olga and myself in our suite with the ever-watchful Juan Cortez. The four young men were left to their pursuits in their own suite.

I had long thought of improving our herds and, in my conversations with the Vails, they had mentioned that John Chisum of Lincoln county, New Mexico had a herd of crossbred Herefords. I had contacted John Chisum about purchasing some of his crossbred Herefords and possibly some purebred stock, also. I mentioned I would be traveling in the east and would like to visit his ranch in February on my return. Señor Chisum had wired me back that he would be glad to host me in February.

He also mentioned that, as long as I was back east, I should look in on some acquaintances of his who raised purebred Herefords in the state of Maine. I had contacted the two breeders, located in Augusta and Searsport, Maine, and told them I would be arriving on December 17th. I asked them if they could arrange for accommodations of two separate rooms for four people. I received a wire back stating the rooms were arranged, and they eagerly awaited our arrival. I then told Olga my plans were to leave on the 16th for Maine and left it to her to decide to stay with the girls or travel with me. She instantly replied, "I'll go with you."

Olga, He Who Hunts, Corporal, and I boarded a train bound for Maine on December 16th. Our trip through New England was like a passage through a winter wonderland. We took the New York and Northeast line from New York to Boston. From Boston, we took the Boston and Maine Railroad to Portland, Maine and connected with the Maine Central. We arrived in Augusta mid-morning on the 17th.

Over two days, we bought four bulls and 16 cows. I made arrangements for Corporal and He Who Hunts to pick up the cattle in Augusta on Monday, January 12th.

We celebrated the Christmas holidays in the Gilsey and departed for Boston on Monday, December 29th. I had made reservations for us at the Parker House Hotel. We spent the next week exploring Boston and celebrating the arrival of the new year at the Parker Bar. Our evenings were greatly anticipated, wondering what delicacies we would encounter at the Parker Restaurant, where we got our first taste of a Boston cream pie and Parker House rolls.

On Tuesday, January 6th of the new decade, Elizabeth, Dulce, Olga, Juan Cortez, Roberto, and I took the Boston and Albany Railroad for a day excursion to Wellesley. While her sister and brother toured the town and campus, Elizabeth, accompanied by Olga and myself, met with Ada Howard. I was concerned that Elizabeth would be here by herself and wanted reassurances that she would be secure and happy. After meeting with Señora Howard and touring the campus, some of my fears were calmed. Señora Howard was well versed in family concerns and, by the time we left, I had made all the financial arrangements for Elizabeth's schooling and living arrangements including setting up a fund for her to draw on from the College to provide her with necessities and spending money. We arrived back at the Parker House that evening.

Over the next few days, Olga, Elizabeth, and Dulce, accompanied by Juan Cortez, spent their time combing the Boston shops for clothes that Señora Howard felt would be necessary for a student at Wellesley.

On Thursday, Roberto and Javier left for Princeton. I made arrangements for two cattle cars to be in Augusta, Maine on January 12th and set up the transportation of our bulls and cows from Augusta to Fort Garland. I set up passage for Corporal and He Who Hunts to accompany them and see to their needs on the trip.

On Sunday, January 11th, Corporal and He Who Hunts left for Augusta, and we all bade each other farewell until we would meet at Hacienda Colorado. The next morning, Elizabeth, Dulce, Juan Cortez, and I took a train to deliver Elizabeth and her baggage to Wellesley College.

The following day Olga, Dulce, Juan Cortez, and I started our trip from Boston to Chicago, where I was to meet with our cattle buyers and set up a contract for delivery of cattle in the future. Due to the ongoing construction of the railroads, it was impossible to set a location of delivery. Our first contract was the delivery of 2,000 head of cattle to a Santa Fe depot in Lamy no later than April 30th and Pueblo, Colorado. The contracted price at Lamy was $5.25 per hundred weight, and the price at Pueblo was $5.60 per hundred weight. I also had contracted a herd of 4,000 head to be delivered to Albuquerque, New Mexico no later than October 30th for the price of $5.40 per hundred weight.

We left Chicago on January 20th bound for Fort Garland, Colorado. We reached Fort Garland on January 26th, and Corporal met us at the station. He reported that the bulls and cows had made the journey well. He also reported that the building of Hacienda Colorado was well on its way with the help of local builders and 10 skilled men that were sent north by José from Hacienda Este. He had obtained our old lodging at Fort Garland and had taken the liberty of making reservations for dinner at eight. Olga and I retired for a long-needed siesta, and we took over the restaurant for the evening.

The following morning, I drove Olga and Dulce to the ranch to see the progress on the new hacienda. I spent three more days with Corporal, Juan Gonzáles, He Who Hunts, and Salvador, riding the range and making plans for the ranch. We would be importing barbed wire to fence our lower pastures, and I was anxious to keep our Hereford cows away from any of our range bulls. It was my plan to move the Hereford cattle to Hacienda Oriental when we could move them south by railroad and leave the male calves at Hacienda Colorado to begin to build a herd of Hereford crossbreeds on our Colorado holdings.

I wired John Chisum that I would be leaving El Paso on or near February 6th and requested he give me directions to his ranch. I also told him it was my desire to purchase six, four-year-old, purebred Hereford bulls and 50 cows plus as many as 80 half-breed cows. I received a wire back from him on the day we were leaving stating he could meet that purchase, and I should find him at his ranch on the Bosque Grande (big woods), which was about 40 miles south of Fort Sumner. I wired José to send me 15 vaqueros from Hacienda Este to meet me in El Paso on the

5th of February. I also asked him to send the grand coach to transport Olga and Dulce back to the Hacienda.

On February 6th, Olga and Dulce were safely on their way back to Hacienda Oriental, and the vaqueros, Corporal, and He Who Hunts were riding with me. My heart was heavy, as I already missed Olga. We had not slept apart since our marriage. Las Sierras de los Manos (Hand Mountains, now known as the Franklin Mountains) were to our backs as we rode toward the Sierras de Huecos (Mountains of Hollows). It was early afternoon when we stopped at Hueco Venado (Deer Hollow) to rest our horses and enjoy the cool waters. It was difficult to leave the shade of the árboles (trees) and continue our journey across the Huecos.

We made a dry camp on the east side of the Huecos and, in the morning, we headed east using the Sierra El Capitán as our guide. We had brought an extra horse for each rider and 10 mules to pack supplies and water. Our journey to the Guadalupe Mountains was a long trip, and we changed our horses twice. He Who Hunts directed us to waterholes along the way. The last part of our trip was across an ancient lakebed covered with salt. It was night before we made our camp on the west side of the Guadalupes near a small stream.

In the morning, we passed south of El Capitán and headed northeast along the east side of the Guadalupes. There were many streams, and we no longer needed to pack water. On the fourth day, we followed the Rio Negro eastward and finally left it and arrived at the Rio Pecos. We followed the Pecos north and, on the seventh day, we arrived at Señor Chisum's ranch in Bosque Grande.

CHAPTER 16

Throughout our journeys, we were being kept up on the American view of Victorio's War. All the military outposts had one job, and that was to apprehend Victorio. Both the Ninth and Tenth Cavalries were out in force, following and attempting to ambush Victorio and Nana, but they were never successful. At every engagement, the Apaches were the victors and had minimal losses.

On our journey to Chisum's ranch, we received visitors during the night who recited different versions of events. One was that, as part of the government's war on Victorio, the food supplies were being withheld to both the Mescalero and San Carlos reservations—which, of course, forced people to leave the reservations due to starvation.

John Chisum greeted us as long-lost friends and was a grand host. After three days of riding the range and picking out stock, we were ready to begin our journey back. In addition to the stock I had requested to purchase, I had asked Mr. Chisum if he had an extra 15 large steers he might be able to part with.

He replied, "Of course I do, and I would be happy to sell them, but it occurs to me that you must be steer-poor as it is. Why would you want to purchase only 15 steers?"

I explained to him that my family had always had a relationship with the Apache and Comanche, and I knew they were starving on the Mescalero reservation. "I would like to bring them some meat."

Mr. Chisum said, "I will give you 30 head for each reservation and four riders to help deliver the steers. You can tell them the cattle are a gift from John Chisum."

I reached out, grabbed his hand, and said, "Thank you. We will deliver the steers to the Mescalero first."

The following morning, we headed south down the Pecos River valley. He Who Hunts and the four vaqueros that John Chisum had sent were herding the 30 steers, and Corporal was managing moving the Hereford herd. When we reached the confluence of the Rio Hondo and the Pecos, we turned our small herd to the west and parted ways with Corporal and the Hereford herd.

We met several army patrols, and they saw nothing suspicious or out of the ordinary, as John Chisum had several ranches, and cattle were always being moved. He Who Hunts said the soldiers were not the only ones watching us and, one moonless night, we had visitors. We explained what we were doing, and they suggested we follow the river up until we reached the Rio Ruidoso. When we got to the head of the valley, they told us to camp there, and they would contact us.

Two nights later, I was visited by Nana, who had been raiding along the west side of the mountains and was headed back to join Victorio. He took He Who Hunts, and they rode off to the southwest. A few hours later, He Who Hunts came back and said Nana had showed him where to take the steers. He said Nana wanted him to relay the message to me that I was a true son and a brother to all Apaches as was John Chisum. He Who Hunts also told me he had asked to accompany Nana, and Nana refused him. Nana told him he was the future of the people, and he should no longer wage war but should look for ways to help the tribe when war is no more. He was to meet with Naiche when he was called for, and Naiche would give him his direction.

We delivered the cattle to a small hidden valley that Nana had directed us to. There were many women there with knives to prepare the meat. He Who Hunts and I parted ways with the vaqueros, who rode east toward the Pecos. We rode west to Tularosa. In Tularosa, we picked up two extra horses and headed south down the east side of the white sand dunes. By the next evening, we were in El Paso. The next morning, we were on our way to Hacienda Oriental.

The morning after I returned, I met José, Running Bear, He Who Hunts, and El Tigre in Pedro's kitchen before daylight. They reported we were being raided constantly from both the south and the north. The one bright spot was that a lesson had been learned in the Mimbres Valley. There were no raids at this time, but the Cowboys had become emboldened, and the Rurales were not much help, because they had been tasked to track Victorio along the border.

José said, "Roman is virtually in a war with the Cowboys, because the soldiers at Camp Huachuca are off chasing Victorio, and no one is patrolling the border on either side. Roman sent word that they were constantly outgunned. Many of the vaqueros have no guns, and those that do have poor weapons.

I drafted a letter to Corporal, in which I told him to meet with Señor Schutz in El Paso. "We are going to need at least 60 repeating rifles," I wrote. "If there are any in El Paso, buy them up. If not, get Señor Schutz to order the Winchester model 76, 45/60 caliber. In addition, we need at least 20, 50-caliber Sharps rifles. Make sure the Sharps are all the same caliber."

I apprised José as to what was in the letter and told him the guns would have to be smuggled into the country. I would leave that to whoever he sent to help Corporal. "I don't want them running into either Rurales or American military patrols. If they are caught, the implication would be that they are trading in guns with the Apache."

José sent a rider to catch up to Corporal with the letter as close to El Paso as possible. In addition, he sent orders for four pack mules and two more men to meet Corporal in El Paso.

José told me that, between the two Haciendas and 200 head from our neighbors, we had 1,400 head of steers in the holding grounds, and they would be ready to move at any time. All the wagons were on standby, and the vaqueros were ready.

I asked him who was going to be the trail boss, and he said, "Running Bear has asked for that honor, and I could not deny him the right."

I replied, "You could not have a better man, but you need to be aware that you will not have him until at least the 20th of May. Running Bear has not been on that drive before, so do you have others that know the way?"

He replied, "All the hands were on the Fall drive."

"I will be sending Corporal to meet them at Albuquerque. The railroad will be there, and I have been assured there will be corrals built to receive cattle for shipping. I will want Running Bear to accompany Corporal to the Colorado ranches. Hopefully, they can make it to Pueblo to meet the other 600 head. Our contract is for at least 2,000, so I will want at least 800 head to be delivered to Pueblo from the cattle we have contract-grazing on the other ranches and, if need be, from our own herds."

Mother called me into her rooms that evening to have a talk. When I got there, she was flanked by Dulce, Angélica, and Olga. My first thought was, *What did I do?*

Mother poured me a tequila and asked me to sit. Directly, she told me I was to be a father.

The first words that came to my mind were, *How did that happen?* But, I bit my tongue. After a moment of shock, I spilled my drink as I jumped up and went toward Olga, who was waiting with open arms.

I'm going to be a father! I thought as I held my wife. *How am I supposed to do that while I am fighting a war with rustlers and steering the Estancias? Oh God, thank you for Mother!*

After my heart had calmed down, I sat next to Olga. Angélica handed me another drink, and I asked Dulce when her wedding was to happen.

Dulce replied, "Because we need to move the cattle to the railhead at Pueblo by April 30th, Juan and I decided we should have the wedding no later than April 1st, here at the Hacienda."

"What are your plans for a honeymoon?" I asked.

Dulce said, "We have not discussed it. By the time we get through delivering the cattle to Pueblo, we will be into Spring branding and moving the cattle to the mountains. I just don't see a good time."

I then asked, "What are your plans for the winter after you deliver your Fall steers to market?"

She said, "We have made no plans."

"If you would permit me, the Estancia would like to send you on a honeymoon over the winter. I would like you two to decide where you want to go. You can go back to San Francisco or to New York, Ciudad Mexico, or even Europe—or a combination of them. I want both of you to know the rancho is yours as well as ours, and you will have earned your way."

Dulce replied, "I would like to discuss this with Juan when he comes." She hesitated a moment and then added, "You may have to make the same offer to others before next winter."

It was February 25th when the Hereford cattle arrived with great fanfare. Running Bear had sent out vaqueros to relieve the vaqueros on the drive. When the replacements found them, they were near the Huecos. Corporal had received his letter, and the relieved vaqueros had been back for five days.

On the 26th, Corporal came in with the pack animals loaded with guns and ammunition. Corporal said Señor Schutz had worked miracles and filled the order. That evening, Pedro set out plates of tacos, tamales, and many other dishes, and there was a well-stocked bar. I had invited everyone to join us, as I was ready to howl. I announced to all gathered that Olga was expecting, and then I got roaring drunk. It was time to let the wolf loose.

On February 27th, our Spring drive headed toward Albuquerque. On Sunday, the 29th, Roman, El Tigre, José, Corporal, and I met to discuss how we were going to protect the Spring roundup and set up a permanent, protective shield around the Estancia. El Tigre reported the watchers were still on the job, and the old hands were eager to have the assignment.

I indicated we needed to get very active in discouraging susurro (rustling), and that was why I purchased the guns and ammunition. I felt that what we needed to do first was make an assessment of the susurro activities.

José began his report by saying, "The susurro on the area controlled by Hacienda Oriental is minor on the far east, which consists mostly of meat hunters that butcher an animal and carry off the meat. Most of that pressure is coming from La Ascención, with some instances from Juárez. There has been little activity so far from the Mimbres Valley, but we are beginning to have a constant problem in the Animas Valley on the east side of San Luis, where the Clantons have established a ranch."

Roman began his report with, "Mi compañeros, Hacienda Occidental is under siege. Our vaqueros are running off cuatreros (rustlers) on a daily basis. We have carniceros (butchers) from the south, east, and Cananea areas. When we scare them off, they just find a different way to return. Our methods are good at catching them, but we are not discouraging the susurro negocio (rustling business) at all. They are simply not afraid. In addition, we are receiving a lot of pressure from the pandilla (gang) known as the Cowboys that are coming from the Clanton ranch on the San Pedro. We are outgunned, and I won't let my vaqueros engage them unless we have overwhelming numbers and surprise."

I then addressed them. "I hesitate to order our vaqueros into peligro (danger). I do not doubt that, if asked, they would immediately engage the cuatreros, regardless of the conditions. I do want to arm them well, but I prefer that well-armed vaqueros serve as a disuasivo (deterrent).

"I have purchased both repeating arms and long-range guns. El Tigre, I would like to arm many of the watchers with the long-range guns. Do you think that most of the watchers are good marksman?"

"Sí, Don Francisco. All of the watchers were scouts for your father's forces. They are all Indios who are both competentes (competent) with guns and bows," answered El Tigre.

I then addressed all my compañeros by saying, "The reason for the long-range guns is not to kill at a distance but to deter. I do not want the carniceros to even see who is shooting at them, and I do not want the watchers to shoot them. I just want them to miss closely if they are stalking our cattle. If that does not frighten them away, I want their animals killed, so they have to walk home. If the watchers or the vaqueros come upon a carnicero that has killed an animal, I want the animals that they are riding and the pack animals killed also. I want our beef to become very expensive.

"For the pandillas susurrantes (gangs of rustlers), I have a different plan. If the pandillas are spotted by the watchers when they are headed south, I want the warning to go out that every vaquero in the vicinity is to ride to confront them. I want the vaqueros to block their paths with a large force. I do not want them to start shooting or ambush them. I want to run them off and discourage them. Once they turn around, I want them followed to the American border and sent on their way. It is imperative they see you following them. It is all imperative that our vaqueros are wary of an ambush.

"If we are raided, and they get off with a herd or injure our vaqueros, I do not want them to see they are being pursued. It will be necessary for the jefe on scene to order the stalking of the cuatreros. Only the people that are in this room and Running Bear and Antonio can order an ambush. El Tigre, if a watcher is hurt, do not wait for permission."

We retired to the front veranda, where Pedro had set out some pan dulce and beer. I asked José if he had any ideas as to how we were going to set up a breeding program with the Herefords.

He replied, "Pancho, I am concerned about how we are to best use the bulls and cows. I have put the question to Running Bear, and he has been consulting with his sons, Bull Tamer and Hungry Fox, and they have come up with a plan as to how to integrate them into the herd. Con su permiso, I would like to send for them and have them make this presentation to you and the family now. As you know, Running Bear is leaving tomorrow."

I spoke up and said, "By all means, we want to hear from them."

Running Bear sent a boy to bring his sons, and I turned to Roman and asked how the Spring branding was going. Roman stated, "As you know, we are fighting susurro, and that has held us up, because we have had to combine the campos to create a defensive force. It appears we do have a very good Spring calf crop, and the branding, cutting, and earmarking is coming along well but much slower than normal."

José injected, "On the east side, we are having the same problems along the San Luis, but, south of the Laguna de Guzmán, we have completed the branding and have been moving vaqueros over to help along the San Luis."

Bull Tamer and Hungry Fox arrived and, after getting a beer, sat down with us. Running Bear then addressed us. "Don Francisco, Don Roman, and Don José, it is a great honor you have given us to ask us to come up with a breeding plan. As you all know, Hungry Fox has never had a problem with his words, so we have asked him to make this presentation."

Hungry Fox stood up and started with, "Mi patróns y compañeros, we feel that, for the present, we need to set up breeding pens where we bring the heifers to the bulls. It is the stated objective, as we understand it, for the rancho to improve the breed of our stock and move our herd toward a Hereford breed.

"To do this properly, we will need to change the way we keep records. We are going to have to mark our stock so we can keep track of its linage. We need to begin to remove the bulls from the herds and keep them in bull pins, so we can direct when the cows and heifers are bred and by which bull. We should look toward a late Spring or early summer breeding season. This will help us to control what cows are bred to what bulls, and it will give us the added information about the strength of the seed from the bulls and the fertility of the cows and heifers. This will lead to better production from our stock.

"It is our suggestion that we keep the 50 purebred cows with two purebred bulls in a safe range near Hacienda Oriental. We need to pull all other stock off that range, which we should fence. For the half-breed cows, we recommend they be paired with three of the best bulls we have on the range. I would look for those bulls on San Luis, as we feel the best place for them would be about mid-range on the oeste side of the San Luis, and that area should be fenced.

"We further recommend there be an immediate building of bull pins at both Haciendas and at our large campos, so we can begin to understand which bulls are fertile and control when our calves are born. This should not only help us control our stock but also its marketability. The additional four purebred bulls should be paired with 25 of our best heifers in individual fenced pastures in handpicked locations for the same obvious reasons."

I jumped up and exclaimed, "That is the best I could hope for and exactly what I want done! Roman, I would like you and José to sit with these young men and create a plan of implementation to make this happen. I want them to work with you to get it going and assure the vaqueros of the Estancia they have my and your full backing in making it happen. As of now, we begin to take control of our cattle."

José interrupted to say he had just received a telegram from Silas Leven stating that a neighbor to the south of our Estancia had passed away, and his widow was willing to sell. "He states that the place is essentially the same size as what we own now, and she wants to move back East to live with her daughter. She is willing to sell it stocked with about a 1,000 head of cows, bulls, heifers, and steers at the price we paid for the other properties."

I told José to wire Mr. Leven and tell him we were interested. "It would be faster if he would wire Juan, and he can inspect the property.

Once he has done this, I will want him to wire both you and me. If it is a go, all he needs to send is, "Go." If his inspection is not favorable, he will send us the word, "Bust." If I see "Go," I will have the funds sent to Señor Leven's office, and Corporal and I will contact him from Albuquerque when we arrive there. Corporal, please tell He Who Hunts we all will be leaving on the morning of the 3rd. Until then, find some women to chase."

I looked at Roman and José and said, "I am so happy I was born into a family of fine, upstanding men I can count on." I then turned and walked out the door.

I went up to my room to inform Olga I would need to go to Colorado and may be gone for a week. Olga asked why I needed to go and then informed me she would be going along. I immediately protested that she should not travel while pregnant.

She replied, "I am pregnant, but I am not an invalid. I will decide whether I go or not."

I knew I was not going to prevail in this discussion, but I did have an ace in the hole—Mother. I told Olga I was going to Mother's rooms to inform her of what was happening and would be back for a short siesta.

I arrived at Mother's rooms and, after I had sipped tea with her, Angélica, and Dulce, I brought her up to speed on the new security arrangements for the rancho. I told her about the presentation by Hungry Fox. She was not surprised at all. Señor Blanco had mentioned Hungry Fox's name to her many times as an exceptionally bright boy. She went on to say that she would have Señor Blanco make some inquiries about a top agricultural school immediately. I asked her to have him look into the new school of mines in Colorado for Javier. She looked at me somewhat amazed, but she agreed.

I then told her about the opportunity to double our holdings in Colorado, which would mean a hacienda that could manage 3,000 head year-round. I told her it would be necessary for me to leave here in three days and that Olga had insisted on going along.

Mother looked at me and said, "Good for her."

I knew how a duck felt rising off a pond when the gun went off. Then I heard another shot from Dulce.

"I will be accompanying you also," she said, "as I will be good companionship for Olga, and I want to see both the hacienda and Juan."

I did not even attempt to protest. Looking at my sisters and my mother, I realized I was not all-powerful. I started to back toward the door when Mother said, "Have you talked to your brother?"

"Yes," I replied. "He was at all the meetings today."

Mother said, "I know he was at the meetings. My question is did you and Roman have a personal conversation?"

"There was no time to shoot the breeze."

Mother told Angélica to summon Roman to her room at once. Mother had a stiff drink poured for me, and I sat there waiting for the next ax to fall.

When Roman arrived, Mother directed him to sit in the chair next to me and told him to tell his brother what was going on in his life. I handed Roman my drink. He downed it and then said to me, "This morning, I asked Edward and Juliana for Panchita's hand in marriage, and they gave their permission. We are planning to have a double wedding with Juan and Dulce on April 1st. Would you stand with me at the wedding?"

I jumped up, grabbed him in an abrazo, and announced, "Tonight we will have a fiesta!"

Mother said, "The food is already being prepared. What you need to do is make the announcement and get the party started."

At that moment, Angélica and José came in and stated that the entire Hacienda Oriental had been notified there would be a fiesta tonight. No one knew why, but they were always ready for a fiesta.

Mother gave me that look and said, "I am sure Olga is waiting for you. You need to go to her and leave me alone, as this is siesta time."

I walked into our rooms and into Olga's arms.

That evening, with all the people of the Haciendas gathered in front of the veranda, I stood with Olga on my right and Mother on my left, raised my glass, and made the announcement that Roman Pérez Castro would be wedding Francesca Honeycutt on April 1, 1880.

CHAPTER 17

In El Paso on March 4th, I received a one-word telegram: "Go." I sent a telegram to Drexel, Morgan, and Company to wire $1,200 to our bank account in Denver. I then wired our bank in Denver to wire $9,000 to Silas Leven in Walsenburg, Colorado.

The evening of March 7th found us in Albuquerque, and we were at the Lamy station the next day. We boarded a train that would get us to Pueblo on March 9th. By the morning of March 10th, we were standing at the depot at Fort Garland. We had our regular rooms and reservations for an Alemán feast that evening. Silas Leven had wired he had the money and had made an appointment for 10:00 am on March 12th for the closing with the seller. I wired him I would be there for the closing.

Dulce rode with Corporal and He Who Hunts, as she had no intention of waiting for Olga and me. The two men were going on to inspect the new place. It was our hope they could pick up Abe and Jake as guides. I wanted both of them to assess the ranch and the cattle as well as come up with a quick count of stock.

When Olga and I reached Hacienda Pérez de Colorado, we were greeted by Dulce, Juan, and Salvador. Juan informed me he had a complete tally of the stock on the place we were going to purchase, and he had informed Corporal of that fact. I thanked him, as I was concerned about the price the widow wanted. Dulce and Olga went off to inspect the Hacienda, and I got a report from Juan and Salvador.

I asked them to give me the tally. Juan stated, "Our count was 821 mother cows, 33 bulls, 219 yearling steers, 172 yearling heifers, and 429 mixed calves."

I informed José and Salvador they needed to take no fewer than 800 head to Pueblo, and they must be there no later than April 30th. "You will need to mark the 600 head, so we know where they came from, as we will owe the ranchers that pastured them over the winter 15 percent of their price. If there are cull cows or bulls from any of the herds, which include the stock on the new property, they should be sent to market at this time. But, in no case can we sell, under this contract, more than 2,000 head, of which 1,400 are on the trail at this time."

I then indicated that Juan needed to go with us to the closing, so he could get the papers proving we were the owners of all cattle with the brand of the new ranch.

I then asked the two of them how the roundup was going and if they had enough hands for the roundup on the Hacienda and to participate in the roundup of our feeders on the other ranches as well as a roundup on the new ranch.

Juan stated, "We have completed the roundup and branding on the Hacienda, and we have about 200 steers that are of the weight we can ship from here. The other ranches, with the 600 head, are well along, and we have representatives there who are separating the feeder steers we contracted for. They will make sure there is a notch on either the right or left ear representing which ranch they came from. As soon as I return from the closing, we will move the roundup crew over to the new ranch, where we will begin branding all unbranded stock. What brand do you want us to use?"

I told him to use the Hacienda brand, which we had registered with the State and the Association. "I will see that Señor Leven registers the brand of the new ranch in our name in both places. In the future, we will decide if we want to keep that brand for some uses."

I then went on to bring up the next problem. I looked at Salvador and asked him, "Do you feel you will have any difficulty starting the drive to Pueblo before Juan returns from Hacienda Oriental? I will want him to leave here no later than March 20th."

Salvador stated, "We have mapped out the drive, and it should not take us more than 26 days to reach Pueblo. We have our wagons ready as well as the horses and mules to make the drive. I do not feel I would have any problem getting started before Juan returns."

I then dropped the hammer on him. "I want you to start by March 25th. This will give you a safety margin in case you run into weather problems at La Veta Pass. I have discussed this with Señor Deus, and he has agreed to accompany you on the drive as a guide and confidant. You will be in charge of the drive. Juan and Dulce can return to Pueblo from Hacienda Oriental on the 15th of April. I am relying on you to get this done. Juan will be there to see that the paperwork is completed."

I then turned to Juan and said, "When the southern herd reaches Albuquerque, Corporal will meet them and take care of the paperwork. He will then meet you either in Pueblo or Denver. Where you meet will be determined by you and Corporal, as you will need to keep each other informed of where you are. In addition, Running Bear will accompany Corporal on his trip to Colorado, and I will want you to show him the ranches we purchased, the name of which will be changed to just Hacienda Colorado.' Do you anticipate any problems with this?"

Salvador replied, "I appreciate your faith in me, and it will be done as you ordered."

On the 11th of March, I sent Señor Leven the following telegram: "I want the compensation for the ranch we are buying from the widow to be changed from $6,000 dollars to $9,000 dollars. I will explain when we arrive."

Corporal, José, He Who Hunts, and Olga attended the closing with me, at which time I explained I felt the widow had asked too little for the ranch. "I have raised my offer to $9,000 dollars, as I have no intention of being known to take advantage of a widow. I instructed Señor Leven to assist her in seeing that her funds are secure and transferred to wherever she wishes, and his fees are to be at my expense."

At 2:00 pm on the 12th of March, we boarded our train for the trip home. I had a wire in my hand stating that Juh had requested He Who Hunts to meet him at a place known to both of them called El Tigre when he returned.

CHAPTER 18

We arrived back at Hacienda Oriental on the evening of March 17. The next morning, He Who Hunts left in the company of El Tigre, who was making a trip to the Tarahumara camp at El Tigre to take a survey of the watchers on the southern border. He reported that during my time away, there had been four conflicts involving watchers. The first two ended with the cuatreros losing their animals. It appeared that the warning shots were being heeded, as the next two cuatreros left when a shot landed close to them.

I told him we might need to modify our actions, as it was evident the cuatreros were still willing to take a chance they may not be spotted and, if at all possible, the warning shot may need to be placed in their trailing pack animal at the watcher's discretion.

El Tigre said there had been no confrontations in the north, but the watchers reported there had been riders coming from the north, moving across the range and then going back to the north. It was only a matter of time.

On March 25th, both grooms arrived, and the Hacienda was abuzz with preparations for a double wedding. It became evident we men were in the way, and we were all too happy to remove ourselves.

We had received word from El Paso that Victorio had raided around Alma, in the New Mexico Territory, which was on the trail we used to move our cattle north. At the time of the raid, our trail herd was well north of the area. They had killed six miners northwest of Alma and many settlers in the vicinity of Alma, which were mostly sheepherders and their families. The news was that at least 41 people were killed before soldiers arrived from Fort Bayard. It was being referred to as the "Alma Massacre."

Included with the wires we received was a request from Presidente Díaz summoning me to meet with him in Ciudad Mexico at my earliest convenience. I wired him that I would leave the Hacienda on April 2nd. When I informed Olga and Mother that I had been summoned by the Presidente and would be leaving the 2nd, Olga told me she would be traveling with me. Mother's response was that she needed until tomorrow to make plans for my trip and asked me if anybody else was going with me.

I did not think I needed someone to make plans for my trip, and I had not stopped to think if I needed someone else along, but I knew it would be best not to voice these opinions, as Mother was a product of the social fabric of Ciudad Mexico and had many connections there including two brothers and three sisters.

Tío (Uncle) Peter Baker was the oldest of her siblings and, at an early age, had started working under his father in the British Embassy. He was presently the informal representative of British interests in Mexico, as there had been no formal envoys to Mexico since the French intervention.

Tío Joséph Baker Castro was highly placed in the Mexican government under Presidente Díaz and oversaw much of the interior agricultural business of the government.

All my tías (aunts) had married well. One of them was married to the owner of a hacienda, and the other was married to a successful businessman, both of whom leaned more toward the conservative society of Mexico. The third was married to a Liberal-leaning general.

After I had a drink and had been sitting on the veranda for a few minutes, José came over and sat down. I stared at him for a moment and then said, "José, I have been summoned to see the Presidente. I do not know why he has called on me, but I think we have an opportunity to meet people who can help us with marketing while I am there. I need your advice. Do you think you could persuade Angélica to join Olga, me, and yourself on a trip to the capital?"

José sat his drink down, gazed at me, and said, "You know, of course, that nearly all of our management, including Running Bear, Roman, Juan, and Corporal, are either not at their jobs or are traveling on business?"

I replied, "Yes, I do, but I also know we have good people, and Roman will be here for a significant amount of that time. Are you concerned that Hacienda Oriental might suffer due to your absence?"

José replied, "Not in the least. I have good people working here, and Angélica would be delighted to go to Mexico and see her aunts and uncles."

I ended the conversation saying, "We leave the morning of the 2nd."

José went up to inform Angélica that she was going to Mexico and further complicating Mother's plans.

When I went down to Pedro's kitchen for breakfast, I was informed that Mother had ordered my breakfast up to her rooms, and it would be on its way shortly. I headed up to Mother's suite and knocked on the door. Her maid opened the door, and Mother was sitting at her table waiting for me. We had our coffee, and she brought up her agenda. She was concerned about where Roman and Juanita would stay once they were married. Her solution was, since Olga and I were leaving, that it might be best if we spent our last night in one of the guest rooms, so our rooms could be made up for the newlyweds.

I indicated I was sure Olga would be happy to give up her space for one night. Mother went on to say that Juan and Dulce could stay in Dulce's rooms. In addition, since the Honeywells were losing two more of their children, they had indicated they had two extra rooms, and it was her intention to make a suite of those two rooms for future use.

I wholly concurred, and she moved on to what I wanted to discuss—her plans. Mother said, "I have sent wires to all my siblings letting them know that you and Angélica are going to México (the common way of referring to la ciudad de México or Mexico City) with your spouses. I have asked Joséph to extend the hospitality of his home to you. I am sending Running Bear's granddaughter, Autumn Moon, to help Angélica and Olga on the trip. I have ordered the grand coach to be made ready, so you will arrive there in an impressive style." She paused, and then continued, "I will not have you taking my daughter-in-law on a non-stop trip. You must stop every evening, so she can rest. Plan your trip around her comfort. If she appears fatigued, or if Autumn Moon or Angélica say she is fatigued, delay your trip. She is carrying a Pérez, and that must be uppermost in your mind."

I agreed and told her both José and I would be ever vigilant.

On the afternoon of the 31st of March, He Who Hunts arrived with Juh, who was here to represent the fathers at the wedding. He Who Hunts informed me that Naiche, who was at San Carlos, had sent word to Juh that his thoughts were that He Who Hunts should continue to live at the rancho and learn the ways of the Mexicans and Americans, so he could help to guide the people in the future when they would no longer be free to roam the land.

Juh, He Who Hunts, and José joined me in the library for a private conversation. Shortly after we got settled, there was a knock on the door. Pedro had sent up some beer and tamales. I then told Juh and He Who Hunts that I had been summoned to Mexico by Presidente Díaz, and I would be leaving the day after tomorrow. I went on to explain that Presidente Díaz, although he had always been a Liberal, was traveling in a forest where the tall trees of the Liberals were on his side of the trail and behind them were the smaller trees that were ever pushing to gain the trail and enforce their ideals. "On his left side are the industrialists, businessmen, and many representatives of the haciendas who are interested in gaining wealth and developing Mexico for the betterment of all. But just behind them are the ever-encroaching Conservative thorn bushes that want to re-establish the rights of caste and church and take Mexico back to an era of privilege for 'the rightful' few. They are supported by many who would like to gain that privilege. He will need all the help he can get from the moderates on both sides to keep his path clear. We, at this hacienda, have followed the path of my father, which was a path of non-involvement in the pettiness of national politics. The journey of the Estancia del Pérez is to follow a path that is best for all who live on the Haciendas.

"Presidente Díaz did not tell me why he wants me to come, but my assumption is it has to do with the many encroachments of campesinos and miners on the Hacienda's borders. As you know, we have followed a path of accommodation rather than confrontation, because, in the end, confrontation will be the death of the Hacienda. I am sure this is what we are to discuss. It would mean ceding parts of the Estancias to the government, and I do believe it will be extensive.

"My father told me that Presidente Díaz is a shrewd man. He will present the problem to me to solve, and he will be ready to negotiate. My solution to his problem will be to make these concessions to ensure a stable political peace if the government will grant the Hacienda the ownership of the ridge line and the east face of El Tigre as well as an extension of our southern border to encompass much or the municipality of Bavispe, with the southern border along the same parallel as the village of Bavispe."

I then turned to Juh and asked, "Father, what do you think the fathers and people will think about the Hacienda expanding its borders in the mountains south of our present borders? That land would become part of the Hacienda and, therefore, the peace and the protection of the Hacienda would expand to them. There could be no raiding from those mountains, and the government of Mexico would honor the peace and sanctuary of the Estancia del Pérez. I would insist on that in our agreement."

Juh replied, "My son, I cannot speak for Naiche or the other fathers. I can only say what is in my heart. My band lives in Mexico the year round. It would be good that, in a greater part of where we live, we could live in peace, and the women could sing again."

I then announced I would like for He Who Hunts to accompany us to Mexico. I pointed out that he would need to check his wardrobe and get his hair shorn once again, as he was going to see the Presidente de Mexico. Juh and José laughed, while He Who Hunts gave a good-hearted grunt. We all went out to the party that was beginning on the ball field and the veranda.

On April 1, 1880, I walked Dulce down the aisle and put her on the arm of my friend and confidant. I then walked over and stood by my brother as his bride came down the aisle on Edward's arm. Mother had asked Juh to escort her and Niñera Juanita down the aisle, and he was sitting beside her.

We had a grand feast, and the new couples retired after dark. Olga and I were not far behind, as we were leaving early in the morning.

CHAPTER 19

We arrived in Ciudad Mexico on Sunday, April 25th. We traveled a route that took us through Janos, Ciudad Chihuahua, Ciudad Durango, Ciudad San Luis Potosí, and Ciudad Queretaro—a distance of approximately 1,150 miles. We stayed at haciendas and mesónes (inns) along the way, and the women arrived fresh and well. Mother's instructions, which had been wired to us in Durango, were that we were to go immediately to the home of Tío Joséph.

We arrived to great fanfare. The women of the house took our women away, and we men sat down to drinks on the veranda. Tío Joséph informed me that I and my guests were to have a public audience with Presidente Díaz and his staff at 11:00 am on April 27th, which would be followed immediately by a private working lunch. The lunch would be attended by Presidente Díaz and himself. He went on to say it was anticipated there may be several more meetings before our business was over.

Olga and Angélica were occupied with visits to the homes of tías, tíos, and primos. Olga was concerned she may not remember everyone's name, and I allayed her fears by saying, "I have always relied on Angélica to keep me straight on such things. Just tell her of your fears, and she will deftly give you the name in conversation."

I informed José and He Who Hunts they were to go with me on the 27th to the formal audience with Presidente Díaz. He Who Hunts said, "Juh gave me a present to give to the Presidente. Will I be able to give it to him then?"

I told him, "I will ask Tío Joséph, and he will instruct you on the proper way to make the presentation."

The following morning, José, He Who Hunts, and I paid a visit to Tío Peter at his offices. We were graciously received, and José scheduled a working lunch with Peter for the following day. Tío Peter informed us that the women had planned a grand dinner at his home for tonight, and it was good we were doing our business in the office. I was surprised about the dinner, as I had not heard of it.

He laughed and said, "You are still newly married. Olga was informed, and she assumed you knew. Get used to many surprises like that. A wife expects you to know by the fact that she knows."

Our formal audience went well. Juh had given his war bow and a quiver of arrows to be presented to the Presidente. He Who Hunts made the presentation by saying, "El Presidente, mi jefe, Juh, the jefe de lo Janeros de los Ndendai and el grupo de los Chiricahua, me ordenó que presentara este arco de guerra con la esperanza de que el Presidente lo fuera a usar para enviar sus flechas a sus objetivos para el bien de todos los pueblos de México." ("Presidente, my chief, Juh, of the Janeros of the Ndendai group of the Chiricahua, ordered me to present his war bow to you in the hope the Presidente will use it and the arrows with the objective of good for all the people of México.")

The Presidente was greatly moved and gave He Who Hunts his sword to present to Juh with his warmest regards.

My working lunch with the Presidente was all I expected it would be. He stated, "Mexico has made an accommodation with the United States to affect orderly trade. This accommodation was the opening of formal ports of trade along the Chihuahuan and Sonoran borders. We are going to run into conflict with your Estancia as a result of the crossings that are to be established. We will be establishing one just northwest of your Hacienda Este by the small village of Palomas, and it will be called Puerto Palomas (Port Palomas). We will need 520 hectares of flat land to legitimize the village of Palomas and take care of expansion of the port if need be in the future. The second one will be at the village of Aqua Prieta in Sonora. We will need 1,040 hectares of the valley land adjoining the frontera to legitimize Agua Prieta and the Puerto Agua Prieta. A third port is to be established on the frontera just north of the Sierra San José. There are large copper deposits north of the frontera, where there is a small village in the Montañas Mulas by the name of Bisbee. We will need 1,040 hectares of the valley land for the Puerto de Naco.

"General Ygnacio Pesqueira García made an accommodation with your father in 1868. He reopened the old Spanish workings in the area of Cananea and laid claim to them. Of course, his claim was somewhat tenuous in that Cananea is on your rancho. Your father compromised with the most powerful man in Sonora. He granted a 20-hectare piece of land and gave General Pesqueira a permit to mine in the Cananea area. For that concession, General Pesqueira signed a document giving the Estancia del Pérez five percent of the gross proceeds of the mine.

"Since that time, the mine has grown in size, and many ore reserves have been discovered. A town has sprung up in Cananea, and we will need to call upon you to make further concessions. It will be necessary to grant 520 hectares of land adjoining the land granted to General Pesqueira to the municipality of Fronteras so a village may be built to house the workers and merchants the mine attracts. In addition, General Pesqueira needs to build facilities to support the mine such as mills, smelters, and a headquarters. He would like a lease for any of the facilities that may be built on the land, which is in the hands of the Estancia or its assigns.

"So far, I have been asking you for accommodations that are political in nature. But, the accommodations to General Pesqueira are not political in that he stands to gain greatly from these accommodations. I have persuaded him that, for seven percent of the gross proceeds of any mine within the historic boundaries of the state of Sonora after the settlement of the frontera, you may grant him those leases and rights to the minerals in any mine he has developed or will develop. He has reluctantly agreed that such an agreement would be just. In addressing the Cananea concessions, what is your gut feeling?"

I replied, "In principle, I agree to the concessions on Cananea and minerals on the Sonoran side of the Estancia. Of course, the devil is in the details, as I would not want minerals extracted from any of the properties I cede to the municipalities to be reserved for the Estancia. The Estancia will retain the mineral rights to all the lands within its historic borders." I paused for a moment, and then I added, "I feel we are not through, however, as there is the nagging problem of the Fronteras."

"Exactamente, Don Francisco" exclaimed the Presidente. "We have further business and, now that you mention it, we should look at the Fronteras problem. There is not much conflict except for a few ranchos that were established prior to the granting of the land. I feel that if you were to cede to the municipality of Fronteras the Rio Fronteras Valley north from your border five kilometers, there would be no problem.

"I have one other accommodation. As you may know, there is a large, landlocked mine at Nacozari. A railroad has been planned to be built between Nacozari to the frontera with the United States at the new Puerto Aqua Prieta. We will need a legal right-of-way established. Don Francisco, do you have any concerns to discuss?"

"Con su permiso, mi Presidente, I am sure you are expecting requests from the Estancia for certain things to balance out the ledgers?"

"Por supuesto (of course)," replied Presidente Díaz.

I went on to say, "I have anticipated most of what this discussion would be and have some requests of my own. I know we can come to a harmonious accommodation.

"I am sure you are aware the Estancia has purchased ranches in the United States and we are moving cattle back and forth as well. In addition, we have a large agricultural component and are exporting cotton and other goods. In the past, there has been no hindrance to commerce by the governments, but, as you say, ports are being planned. We market not only for ourselves but have many neighbors that sell cattle and goods in cooperation with us. We need to have our own import and export license as well as an official on hand to issue visas, so free trade will not be hindered by petty bureaucrats. This would go a long way to cover the losses of the use of our land to the railroad right-of-ways.

"I have been studying the maps, and I have a request for a grant of land to cover the loss of the lands the government requires. The land the government requires is flat, arable land and, in some cases, within river valleys. I would like the government to cede to the Estancia del Pérez the following mountain lands: At a point just north of La Pitahaya on the west slope of San Luis, our border would be extended in a straight line on the western slope of the pointed mountain that is cut off by the Rio Bavispe. After crossing the Rio Bavispe, the boundary would run southwest; just above the western side of Sierra El Tigre to a point parallel with Sierra San Diego and the village of Bavispe on the east slope of Sierra El Tigre. It would cross the Rio Bavispe just north of the village of Bavispe and continue east across the Sierras de San Pedro to a point two kilometers west of the headwaters of the Rio Janos. The line would turn north, following a line that remains two kilometers east of the Rio Janos, until it becomes parallel with the northern tip of the Sierras de San Pedro. It will turn west and run on a straight line to a line that is parallel to the eastern flank of the Sierra Los Azules until it reaches the present southern border of the Estancia. If, in the valley of the Rio Bavispe and any other areas that come under the care of the Estancia, there are people who are farming arable land or have farmed it in the past 10 years, that land will be deeded over to them, and they will have legitimate title.

"As you are aware, mi Presidente, the lands of the Estancia have been neutral in the wars of the Apache and Comanche with the Americanos and the Mexicans. All who respect this neutrality can come onto the Estancia without fear from any of the combatants. We would need to extend that neutrality to the new lands."

Presidente Díaz replied, "I can see you planned for this meeting. I congratulate you on your foresight. You are truly a son of General Gregorio Pérez Adame, and he would be proud. As you said, the devil is in the details. It will be up to you and your Tío Joséph to work out those details. I will get frequent updates, and I expect drawn papers by the first of next week."

Tío Joséph and I spent the next few days working on the details. The rights ceded to General Ygnacio Pesqueira García would be limited to the Cananea area and would include an area of a circle with a 12-kilometer diameter in the center of the present concession of 1868 with the addition that the Estancia del Pérez would be paid seven percent of the proceeds of production on the lands.

The Estancia del Pérez and anybody who marketed their animals or farm goods would pay an export duty of two percent of the market value to the government of Mexico and one percent to the state of origin. José Gallego had agreed to accept the appointment as the gerente (manager) de los Puertos of Palomas, Agua Prieta, and Naco. He would see to the construction of the puertos and the manning of them. He would establish offices in both Palomas and Agua Prieta, which would provide consular services. He was to man the ports with the personnel necessary to run them efficiently, and he would have the duty of overseeing the issuance of visas and the collection of duties as prescribed by the government of Mexico. This appointment would be in effect as long as Presidente Díaz remained in office or until José resigned.

The lands requested by me would be granted to the Estancia and all provisions, including neutrality for all combatants that honor the stipulations of the neutrality, would be honored. The government of Mexico would become a partner to these stipulations. These would become effective when the jeffes of the tribes signed an agreement to honor them. It would be up to the Estancia del Pérez to see they did not raid from the rancho and use it as a safe haven.

We met with Presidente Díaz. He signed the papers and stated, "I know the frontera is in good hands."

He then handed me a telegram he had just received from Comandante Francisco Neri stating that Hacienda Oeste had been raided by banditos with a loss of many cattle and horses as well as the death of some vaqueros. It also stated that Roman had been gravely wounded.

I begged permission of the Presidente to immediately leave for the Estancia. He granted the permission and stated, "I have arranged for a carriage to leave here at your discretion and take you to a port to the west where a clipper will be waiting to take you to Guaymas. In addition, I will be sending a strong letter of protest to the government of the United States, which will let them know of my concerns regarding the continued lawlessness north of our frontier that jeopardizes not only the citizens of Mexico but also the citizens of the United States who are being granted concession for development in Mexico."

I stated, "We are grateful for the help, and we will be ready to leave this evening as soon as I can make arrangements for the passage of the other people in my party."

Presidente Díaz replied, "The carriage will be at your Tío Joséph's home within an hour and waiting for you and my new friend, He Who Hunts."

I thanked him and left to find José and Olga to tell them of the change in plans.

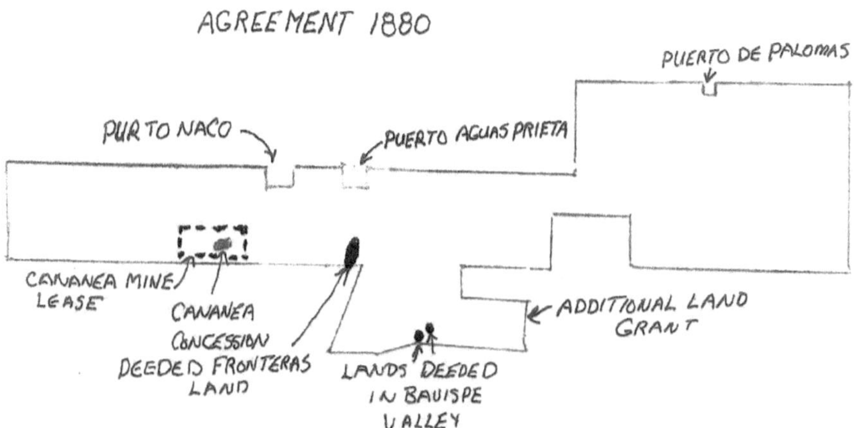

AGREEMENT 1880
PUERTO DE PALOMAS
PUR TO NACO
PUERTO AGUAS PRIETA
CANANEA MINE LEASE
CANANEA CONCESSION
DEEDED FRONTERAS LAND
LANDS DEEDED IN BAUISPE VALLEY
ADDITIONAL LAND GRANT

CHAPTER 20

Three hours later, on the evening of May 3rd, He Who Hunts and I were in a presidential carriage headed for the west coast and a fast clipper. On the evening of May 11th, we landed in Guaymas and were met by two Rurales, who had been dispatched by Comandante Neri. They gave me the news that Roman was healing well from his wounds. The attack was on Hacienda Occidental itself, and eight of our people died. Antonio Sapia had kept the Hacienda running even though he lost his oldest son in the raid. By now, Corporal would have arrived. El Tigre had sent scouts into the States to find the stolen animals. Captain Alfredo Carrillo was at Hacienda Occidental and had patrols out all a long the frontera.

The Rurales went on to report that the raiders were Cowboys, and they attempted to burn the Hacienda. There was extensive damage, but the Hacienda still stood. In addition to Roman being wounded, his wife, Panchita, received an injury to her leg, but she continued to see after Roman and other wounded for two days before she collapsed due to an infection that arose from her wound. She was in serious condition, but the ladies said she would recover. There were an additional 16 persons wounded, and all were expected to recover.

One of the Rurales said, "Capitán Carrillo instructed me to tell you he sent a courier to Captain Whiteside. Captain Whiteside sent back a note to Capitán Carrillo stating he has been detailed to the hunt for

Victorio, and there will be no troops to patrol the frontier in the near future."

When I arrived at the Hacienda on May 14th, two of the large coaches from Hacienda Oriental were there, and I knew Mother had ceased her mourning. Edward Honeywell met me on the veranda, and beside him was Pedro Gonzáles with a drink for me in hand. Edward informed me my mother would be down to talk to me shortly and that Juliana had taken over the care of the wounded.

He Who Hunts grabbed some food from a platter and said he was going to find El Tigre. I told him to bring El Tigre and any of the older hands that were around, as we were going to recover the stock and avenge our dead.

At that moment, Mother came out onto the veranda and said, "My son, our home and people have been attacked and murdered. I will be here taking care of the Hacienda. You have a good man in Antonio Sapia, and I have instructed him to take care of Hacienda Occidental and report to me with any problems. You must avenge this sacrilege. The governor of Sonora offered troops, and I thanked him and told him the Estancia will clean up its own mess." She then gave me a hug and said, "Go get our animals, and see that our people rest in peace." She then turned and went back into the house.

I noticed Captain Carrillo and Corporal were waiting off to the side of the veranda. They came up when Mother retreated, and Captain Carrillo commented, "I will never do anything to make your mother go after me!"

I said, "Mother ran the Estancia when my father was away, which was often during all the intrigue of the revolutions and the French intrusion. She considers everyone on this Estancia to be her family, and her family has been attacked."

I then turned to Corporal and said, "I have missed you, my brother. I know you have news about the ranchos in Colorado, but I am too consumed with all I have heard and learned over the past days to hear it now. Has Running Bear returned with you?"

"He has," replied Corporal, "and he begged me to tell you he will have 40 extra vaqueros stationed at Campos Berrendo, San Luis, Angélica, and El Lobo. They all have been communicating with a mirror telegraph and will be awaiting your orders."

I replied, "This is not his first campaign. I wait for He Who Hunts and El Tigre. Both know what must be done and will have made a plan. Corporal, would you please ask Antonio Sapia to join us?"

Corporal left to get Antonio, and Pedro Gonzáles came out with a large platter of tamales and tacos. I had noticed that Captain Carrillo's lieutenants were standing around below the veranda and asked him to tell them to join us for supper.

Once all our plates were full, I addressed Captain Carrillo and his lieutenants. "The outlaw groups known as the Cowboys, who are led loosely by the Clantons, are undoubtedly responsible for this outrage. I would like nothing more than to hit them with the strength of an army and wipe them out. But that will trigger an international crisis. Instead, I propose we raid the two ranchos of the Clantons. The San Pedro ranch should receive our attention first and then the ranch at the head of the Animas Valley. They will be simultaneous attacks. My goal is to take every animal off their range. They have found it advantageous to not brand their cattle and falsify bills of sale; therefore, they are never in danger of being caught with running irons.

"It is my suspicion that Victorio's war has made it impossible for the Clantons to move the stolen cattle they are not selling to the hungry market in Tombstone to the Mogollon Rim. The cattle and horses will be on the ranches. We will take every head, separate the brands, and notify the ranchers both in Mexico and the United States that we have some of their cattle. They will be able to come and claim them at anytime. Also, I intend to let the people in Tombstone know the

Estancia can supply them with all the beef they need at the prices they are now paying.

"When we raid the ranches with overwhelming force, the Cowboys will assume our revenge is something that will soon pass. It will not. It may be some time before they try again on the Estancia, but the time will come, and they will find themselves in a trap."

Captain Carrillo said, "As you know, I, as well as my comandante, still burn with the fire of revenge for the time you lost your father and we lost our men to their savagery. I would like to send half my force, who will be your volunteers when you make your raid. They, of course, will go as vaqueros of the rancho." I replied, "Of course."

Corporal returned with Antonio. I thanked him for taking charge and gave him my condolences and those of the entire rancho for the loss of his son. I then went on to ask him if he had made any decisions for Hacienda Occidental regarding the recovery of the stock stolen.

He replied, "I was at a loss as to how the Estancia would react. When El Tigre came in with a contingent of scouts, he left Running Bear here. Running Bear came to me while I was alone and told me the family will not let this stand, and I should start moving extra men toward the campos close to the San Pedro crossing. I have ordered 30, well-armed vaqueros to slowly drift in to Campos San Pedro and Huachuca and to the Hacienda. They are all in place and appear to be working, so they will be ready at a moment's notice."

I said, "Thank you, Antonio. When we ride, I will want you by my side. Please see that the 20 volunteers from the Rurales have proper vaquero clothes for that ride."

Antonio replied, "See, mi jefe. It will be my honor." "Oh, Antonio," I said, "is Running Bear still around?" He replied, "No, mi jefe. He rode out with He Who Hunts."

I had accomplished all I could until I heard from the scouts, so I excused myself, as I needed to see Roman and Juanita. I entered

Roman's room to find Mother and Juliana there ministering to his needs. I sat next to his bed and put a hand on his arm.

He smiled weakly and then asked me what was being done, and I gave him a rundown of all that has passed. He stated, "I will be ready to ride when the scouts get back."

Mother looked at him and said, "The only riding you will do is sitting in the coach heading to Hacienda Oriental when Panchita is ready to go. Until then, you will ride the bed."

I got up and said, "I will be back in the morning. I will keep you updated, but you have your orders, and they are final."

It was the evening of May 16th when I was notified that El Tigre, He Who Hunts, Running Bear, Cachorro, and several other scouts rode in. I gave them all a glad greeting and spent time talking to Cachorro, who had been visiting his abuelo for the summer when he got caught up in the excitement. I told them all to get something to eat, and we would have refreshments on the veranda in an hour, when they could give me their reports. I let Pedro Gonzáles know we would need refreshments, and I sent a young boy to apprise Capitán Carrillo, Corporal, and Antonio that the scouts were back and would be making their reports on the veranda in an hour.

To my surprise, Mother, Edward, and Juliana joined us on the veranda to hear the reports. El Tigre began his with an apology. "Mi patrón, Señora Pérez, and all that were affected by this tragedy; I offer my apologies that the warning system did not work." I asked, "Why did it not work?" El Tigre answered, "The watchers on each side of the passage of the bandits were killed."

I replied, "Then I am at fault for not using the precaution we started with of having a second person with each watcher. We grew too confident in the skills of a few. Please go on with your report, as you can see there is plenty of blame to go around."

El Tigre stated that our cattle and horses were indeed on the Clantons' San Pedro ranch. They were scattered south of the ranch headquarters along the river. "There are five careless riders stationed with them at all times. It appears the thieves do not believe they could be robbed. Three or four men with bows could slip in and take care of the herders in the early morning hours after a shift change, and no one would be wise to us until siesta time. We plotted out routes back to the Estancia and places to ambush any pursuers."

I thanked El Tigre for his report and asked him, Corporal, He Who Hunts, and Running Bear into the foyer for a private word. When we were in the foyer, I said, "I do not believe our watchers were lax. I believe they were betrayed. I want you to leave in separate directions and see if we have a spy listening in on our plans right now."

I went back to the veranda and offered everyone a drink before we began with our plans. In about 15 minutes, the scouts returned. They had flushed out a young vaquero from under the veranda, and he was, at that moment, being led with a rope around his neck by He Who Hunts while protesting he was only looking for a cool place to rest. I told everyone we would adjourn our meeting for about 30 minutes while He Who Hunts thoroughly questioned our young guest, who no one seemed to know well. El Tigre grabbed the rope and headed off while He Who Hunts started stropping his knife and walking beside the weeping young man. I noticed Cachorro was following. I stopped him and told him I was worried about the safety of mi madre in case there were any other spies. I told him I needed him to stand by her to keep her safe. He reluctantly returned to take on the responsibility of guarding my mother while the intrigue was going on.

Corporal returned in about 10 minutes and said the young man did not even make it to the barn before he was confessing to spying and letting the Cowboys know where the watchers were. He was now tied up in the barn.

I noticed that Mother and Juliana had slipped out with Cachorro in tow. I found them in the kitchen with pan dulce and glasses of milk.

I sat down, helped myself to both, and thanked Cachorro for watching after the ladies. I told them the meeting would now resume.

We were fortunate to find the spy so easily, but he had done his damage. He was a nephew of Florentino Cruz, and he had been blackmailed into spying on us. It was unfortunate he did not see that his new family would stand beside him against Cruz and the Cowboys. We would take him back to the Cowboys.

Back on the veranda, I continued with my plan. "El Tigre, will you, He Who Hunts, and Running Bear be able to dispatch the night herders without an alarm being sounded?"

El Tigre replied, "I am certain we can. I have a couple of young scouts that I know will be able to ensure that certainty."

I said, "That is under your control, but I do not want Cachorro to be one of them. I have a far more important job for him."

"He is not," replied El Tigre, "and I am honored you have trust in my grandson."

"He has earned it. I would like for you to leave early in the morning. I want you to tell five extra scouts where you want the men placed. They will be the guideposts for the main body. There will be 50 men in the main group, but they will be traveling in bunches of 10 during the day and leave an hour apart. They will also be taking different routes to our destination. All five groups will use the foothills of the Montañas Huachucas for cover.

"Antonio, I will need you to find a reliable man to create a diversion. He will need to take 30 riders—anyone who is willing to make a long ride. They are to leave at dawn, ride up the river to the frontera, turn toward the Montañas Mulas, and cross the frontera. I am sure the Cowboys will still have someone watching their back trail. When they reach the Montañas Mulas, they are to make camp and take a long siesta. Then they are to ride to Campo San José and spend the night.

"Cachorro will guide me and Antonio to a place of observation. He Who Hunts will come to us and let us know the guards have been taken care of. Cachorro and He Who Hunts will come up with that location this evening. I will send Cachorro back to bring the main body in to start moving all the cattle and horses they can find south in the river valley. I know this is complicated, but I feel it will work and avoid detection. Does anyone see any problems?"

El Tigre said, "It is complicated, but it is cautious and takes in the safety of our men."

Capitán Carrillo said, "I feel this is not your entire plan."

I replied, "Sin duda (Without a doubt), mi Capitán, I will need to employ you and your volunteers as a rear guard to ambush any pursuers and continue to fall back. When the cattle are moving, I will want Tall Runner to lead the way down the valley. He Who Hunts and El Tigre are to follow behind you and keep you advised as to pursuit. As we cross the frontera, we will send back vaqueros to help you if necessary, which it may be.

"The Cowboys are not finding Tombstone as hospitable as it was in the past now that Virgil Earp is the town Marshall and his brothers, Wyatt and Morgan, are deputies. However, the Earps may become sympathetic to the Clantons if they ride in and give the alarm they were raided by Mexicans, and several of their herders were killed. The citizens of Tombstone will begin to wonder where their meat will come from as will the soldiers still garrisoned at Camp Huachuca. It is possible there may be quite a force headed our way. Because I don't know how the Earps will react, I must request, Capitán Carillo, that the rest if your force be in place to protect the frontera, if need be.

"This leads me to the next phase of our endeavors." I turned to Corporal and said, "Mi hermano (My brother), you have been quietly listening and waiting for the next shoe to drop. I hope you are rested, as I need you to ride tonight. As you know, Running Bear has already situated vaqueros around the head of the Animas Valley. Most of you know that Old Man Clanton has established a ranch in the Animas Valley near the border, so he does not have far to drive the cattle he steals out of Mexico. I want you to have the vaqueros in place. I anticipate Old Man Clanton will get news of the raid on his ranch on the San Pedro by Saturday evening or early Sunday, and he and some men will leave immediately for the San Pedro ranch. Make sure they have gone over the pass before you ride down on their ranch. I want every head of stock on the ranch moved to Hacienda Oriental, and I hereby order you to destroy every building on the ranch.

"On your way east, I want you to alert the jefes at Campos San Juan and Aguas Frescas. Tell the jefe at Aguas Frescas to bring his vaqueros and as many fresh horses as he can gather to Campo San Pedro by tomorrow evening. Tell the jefe at Campo San Pedro to gather in his vaqueros and fresh horses and have them in camp by tomorrow evening. Also, inform him that the diversionary forces will be coming into his camp tomorrow evening as well as the forces from Campo Aguas Frescas. Tell him he and his vaqueros are to leave Campo San Pedro the next morning and meet Capitán Carrillo's forces at the border. They are to place themselves under the command of the lieutenant in charge of protecting the frontera and ourselves as we bring the cattle across, and also provide us with fresh mounts.

"Today is Monday, May 17th. The raid will take place on Wednesday, May 19th. It will be a very good day for the rancho and the beginning of a cascade of problems for the Cowboys and the Clantons. I would suggest to everyone that it is time to retire, as there will not be much time for rest. Pedro Gonzáles has prepared a package of food for you, Corporal, and a companion. Have Antonio pick a good rider to accompany you. Vaya con Dios, mi hermano."

The raid on the Clanton San Pedro camp came off with complete surprise. The Cowboys watching the herds were quietly dispatched, and the nephew of Florentino Cruz was left tied to a tree by his neck with his entrails airing. We netted over 1,500 head of cattle and 200 head of horses. Nearly all the cattle had brands. Most of the cattle were ours, but there were some from estancias to the south and west of our estancia, and there were some American brands among the herd.

Capitán Carrillo began fighting a rear-guard action about an hour away from the border. We could hear occasional gunfire in the distance. As we crossed the border, I gathered some vaqueros and headed back to help the Capitán.

He hailed us as we were riding up and said, "We have everything in order, but there is a large group of riders arriving from the rear. We will need to make a stand at the border."

When the riders approached the border, they found a barricaded army waiting for them. Three men separated themselves from the mob and came forward under a white flag. As the three men approached us in their dusters, we could see badges on their chests.

Capitán Carrillo and one of his lieutenants accompanied me as I went out to meet them. They introduced themselves as Virgil, Wyatt, and Morgan Earp and said they were the law in Tombstone. They went on to state that normally they would not intervene in a rustling event, as that was the purview of the sheriff. However, there was a real threat to the palates of the people of Tombstone if the rustled cattle were not returned.

I introduced myself to the Earps and presented Capitán Alfredo Carrillo, explaining that he was the top Mexican law officer on the Mexican frontier and had the confidence of his comandante and of Presidente Díaz of Mexico, who charged him with the recovery of our stolen cattle and the apprehension of the raiders called the Cowboys.

Wyatt Earp replied, "Is it your contention that you made a raid to recover stolen cattle?"

I replied, "I am in charge of this rancho and the son of Gregorio Pérez. I am not a thief, and I do not tolerate thieves."

Virgil Earp said, "Can you provide proof that you recovered stolen cattle from the Clanton Ranch?"

I returned with, "I would normally become offended by such a brash question, but, in the interest of peace, I will say I have proof that would stand up in a court in either Mexico or the United States, and I would be happy to present that proof to you now. Would you care to ride with me to the Hacienda? You will be my guests and, in the light of day tomorrow morning, I will present you with the proof."

Virgil said, "Fair enough. I need no proof, as you are my proof, but I would like to send a couple of the town's outstanding citizens with Wyatt, so they can see for themselves and report back to the people of Tombstone."

I replied, "That will be fine. And while you are talking to the citizens of Tombstone, please tell them that I, Francisco Pérez Castro, hereby declare I will provide them beef for a lower price than what they paying for in stolen beef. I will wait here for your people."

In just a few minutes after Virgil reached the crowd, several men separated from it and came toward us. Capitán Carrillo ordered a lieutenant and 30 men to pull back from the border and camp for the night. I told the jefes from Campos San Pedro and Aguas Frescas to camp beside the lieutenant's men for the night, and they could head back to their homes when the Rurales broke camp in the morning.

I rode back to join Wyatt Earp and the important citizens who had joined him. Earp smiled and said, "You might be a very good poker player, as a good poker player will always hedge his bet."

I retorted, "I think you would not hesitate to take a shotgun to a gun fight."

He laughed and said, "I expect this to be a very pleasant evening."

He Who Hunts took two horses and raced off to the Hacienda to warn Pedro Gonzáles and Mother that we were to have guests that evening. We passed the herds on the way to the Hacienda and, when we arrived, drinks had been set out on the veranda and the house was alive with activity, as a grand feast of traditional Mexican food was being prepared.

The two important citizens were introduced to me as Dr. George Goodfellow and C. S. Fly. I shook hands with Dr. Goodfellow and gave "Buck" Fly a warm abrazo. I turned to an amazed Earp and said, "Uncle 'Buck' is well known on the Estancia. There are many photographs of families in the homes on the Estancia, and Señor Fly has always been an honored guest not only of the people of the Estancia but the Apache that reside there as well. The rider that left here in a hurry is an Apache brave, and he told me that Tío Buck was among you. My mother and family wait to greet an old friend."

Tío Buck said, "I am so glad your mother is here. I have wanted to give her my condolences of the loss of Gregorio."

I replied, "Yes, she broke her deep mourning when she heard Roman and Panchita were wounded. She is now wearing gray and will be very happy to see you."

I turned to Dr. Goodfellow and said, "Doctor, your excellent reputation precedes you. My brother and sister-in-law were gravely wounded during the raid on the Hacienda. They are both slowly recovering. I would greatly appreciate your looking in on them while you are here and on the other wounded as well."

Dr. Goodfellow said, "Of course. I will see them immediately."

Mother approached at that moment, gave Tío Buck an abrazo, and then turned to Dr. Goodfellow and said, "Doctor, I stand ready to take you to see my son and daughter-in-law, but I insist you take some refreshment before we go. Señor Fly, when I return, we will have time to catch up on our lives."

Señor Earp looked somewhat puzzled at what had just passed. When we had drinks in hand, Tío Buck and I stepped with him to the end of the veranda, where I told him what had transpired during the raid on the Hacienda. Tío Buck told him about the circumstances of the loss of my father. When he understood the history that my family had with the Cowboys, he stated, "I marvel at your and Capitán Carrillo's restraint during your raid. If my family and men had been so attacked, I do not believe I could show such restraint."

I replied, "It has been very hard, but I must remember my responsibility to the Estancia and the people on it. I have had some revenge, but it is not yet complete. So, when you hear about other portions of it, please remember the Cowboys have earned all the grief they will reap. I think it is time to join the others."

Wyatt said as we were walking back, "You will receive no grief from the Earps. We, as with your family, hold our families first, but we remember our responsibilities."

When we had rejoined the others, Mother confronted us and said, "Doctor Goodfellow says the bullets in Roman and Juanita must be removed. I have persuaded him to join us at the table this evening and perform the operations in the morning, as he appears tired. He is making them comfortable with Juliana, and he will be down shortly to join us."

I met Señor Earp, Tío Buck, and Dr. Goodfellow at the head of the stairs the next morning, and we went down to breakfast. Pedro was serving in the dining room, as the kitchen table was not as large as the one at Hacienda Oriental. We appeared to be somewhat late, as even Capitán Carrillo was deep into his plate.

After we had eaten, I addressed our guests and said, "Señores, we will leave to examine the herd when everyone is ready to go. Almost all the cattle are branded except some nursing calves, and not all the brands are from the Estancia. There are Mexican brands from neighboring estancias and American brands from north of the border. As good neighbors, we are familiar with all the brands, and riders will be sent to the owners of the brands to inform them we have recovered some of their stock and will hold them here to be picked up—no different than any stray stock caught in a roundup."

Dr. Goodfellow declared he would have to abrogate his responsibility to Señores Earp and Fly, as he was needed here. "I must stay here for two more nights to tend to these patients. If you need to return right away, I will make my way back on my own."

Señor Earp looked at Señor Fly and then turned to me and said, "Would it be an imposition for you if we wait to leave until the good doctor is ready?"

I replied, "You would honor us if you would extend your stay beyond the business at hand. If you would care to draft a note to your brothers, I will see it is delivered to them today."

On the evening of May 21st, after supper, I informed our guests that, when they arrived back in Tombstone, they may be greeted with the news that a Clanton ranch situated in the Animas Valley of the Territory of New Mexico had been attacked and razed by Mexican bandits. "I would like you to remember that the grief the Clantons and the Cowboys have reaped is not total."

Señor Earp said, "It is a piece of justice."

Walter Vail rode in with ten vaqueros and some of his neighbors in time to sit with us for breakfast. I introduced him to our other guests, who were somewhat astounded at the level of cooperation going on between ranches despite the rhetoric of the politicians in Arizona, Washington DC, and Mexico. Walter told Señor Wyatt he had admired his history and would stand with him and his brothers any time they needed his help against the Cowboys.

I wanted to pay much more than a standard doctor's fee, but Dr. Goodfellow would not hear of it. I consulted with Tío Fly and Señor Wyatt as to any need I could fulfill for Doctor Goodfellow. They both agreed he had often expressed the wish of having a small hospital where he could operate and his patients could recover. I charged them with locating a piece of land, which I would pay for, that would be central to Tombstone. I told them I would send a construction crew with the materials to build his hospital.

CHAPTER 21

We reluctantly watched our guests leave. Mother was promised a visit from Tío Buck in the near future, and I exacted a commitment from Dr. Goodfellow to assist us in setting up clinics at both the Haciendas. Dr. Goodfellow ordered a week of bed rest for Roman and Panchita before they could be moved to Hacienda Oriental.

The following morning, I informed everyone that El Tigre, Cachorro, and I would be leaving for Hacienda Oriental the next day. Corporal would stay and see that all was running smoothly and that Antonio Sapia had picked an adequate segundo to help him with the running of Hacienda Occidental. They must start the Fall roundup immediately and move the market cattle to Hacienda Oriental. It would be several months before Roman would be returning, because, when he recovered, he would be going on an extended honeymoon.

When Corporal had everything in order, he would meet me at Hacienda Oriental. He Who Hunts had the responsibility of making sure the coaches made it back to Hacienda Oriental safely. I was entrusting him with my family. Tall Runner was in charge of the watchers and the safety of Hacienda Occidental.

I went up to say goodbye to Mother.

She said, "We have been very busy with the immediate problems at hand, and I have not been able to speak with you about some needed changes at Hacienda Oriental. I will be following you there within a week. I am sorry I will not be there to help you when you get there, but you will have Señor Blanco and José."

I walked out of that meeting with many questions in my head.

Regarding Hacienda Oriental, it was evident that Running Bear had things in hand. The roundup was in full swing, and Emilio Vásquez had the harvest going. When I reached the Hacienda, I settled into the work of running the rancho.

Four days after my arrival at the Hacienda, the grand coach arrived with Olga, José, and Angélica, and there was a second coach following. In her correspondence with my uncles and aunts, Mother had neglected to tell me it had been decided that six of my cousins were to come to live at Hacienda Oriental.

I had no idea how much I had missed Olga until I saw her. I was no longer able to be just me. I was a part of "we."

Señor Blanco came to the house that morning and said, "We have some urgent business to talk about concerning some of the changes in the education requirements on the rancho. Would it be possible for you to set aside tomorrow to discuss these things?"

I replied, "Of course. Is there anything in particular I should be prepared for?"

He answered, "You may want to have a construction foreman at the meeting."

Of course, that made me curious, but I said nothing. I asked one of the house boys if he could see if José was available to meet with me.

It was several hours before José arrived.

He greeted me with, "I finished my pressing business this morning, as I believe you and I are going to be together the rest of the day. I am anxious to hear about the agreement with the Presidente and how you plan to stop the predation of the Cowboys."

I answered, "You have some news as well, which I need before I tell you about what is going on. Señor Blanco has asked for my day tomorrow for some important matters and said I should probably have my construction foreman at the meeting. Can you enlighten me about what may be coming up?"

"Unbeknownst to any of us, Doña María has been busy planning the next phase of the education of the rancho," replied José. "She has been in contact with her siblings all along, and she has agreed to take the cousins of yours whose parents want to further educate them at the university level. She has ordered a language school to be established, so they can become proficient in English before they go off to college, if Señor Blanco feels they are university material. In addition, Señor Blanco has taken you up on your offer to further educate children of the rancho that he feels would benefit from higher education."

"So that explains the six cousins we are being graced with," I said.

"No, not entirely," countered José. "Originally, there were to be only four. The evening before we were to leave for the Hacienda, we were at a family gathering at your Tío Peter's house when your Tío Joséph arrived with appointment and authorization papers for the new post you acquired for me. He asked if he could speak to Olga, Angélica, and myself privately. He explained that his wife, whom he loves dearly, is not a disciplinarian, and the Presidente keeps him going all the time. This has led to his two younger sons developing into willful remolones (slackers) and dandies. It is his belief that a hard life on the rancho will make useful men out of them."

I did not respond to that bit of news in the manner dictated by my blood other than to say, "Evidently, we are not too far away to feel the results of the privilege that has spawned one revolution after another. When our meeting with Señor Blanco is over, I want Running Bear, Bull Tamer, Hungry Fox, El Tigre, and the two young men to come in for a meeting with us."

José replied, "Twice I have heard the meeting is no longer a meeting with you. It is a meeting with us."

"Eso es exactamente correcto (That is exactly correct), Don José de la Hacienda Oriental," I retorted.

"I can give you several reasons for the need of the construction foreman," José continued. "We will need a new wing on the Hacienda. With a growing family, the addition of cousins, and this being the headquarters of the rancho with guests coming and going, we are out of space. Señor Blanco's school here at the Hacienda is overflowing, and now we are adding an English language school that I am sure your mother will be adding students to. This necessitates a doubling of the size of the school building.

"Also, I have here the papers signed by El Presidente with an order to build a building at the location of Hacienda Oriental to serve as the office of the Consular of Puertos Palomas, Agua Prieta, and Naco. This building will consist of a private office for the Consular and an additional office for an Assistant Consular, who is to assume all the clerical duties of the consular offices and oversee the clerical duties of the puertos. In addition to the offices, there should be adequate living quarters for the Assistant Consular and his family. The cost of the consular building will be covered by the rancho and reimbursed by the Mexican government through fees collected at the puertos."

I replied, "That is not all. I have insisted on building a small hospital in Tombstone for Doctor Goodfellow. We owe him that for the care he has given the rancho."

I paused a moment and then said, "I know we should discuss what you and Tío Peter came up with as far as markets in England, but, frankly, José, right now I am consumed with thoughts of Olga, so you are just going to have to hold those thoughts for tomorrow or when it becomes necessary. I am going up for a siesta, and I will see you at dinner."

Señor Blanco had a large agenda for our meeting, as we had Emilio Márquez, the head of construction, there as well as Running Bear and Angélica. He began the meeting by talking about the construction needs. "As you are well aware, we started our small school here at the Hacienda when Angélica came of age and there were 12 students. By the time you started school, Don Francisco, we had two classrooms and 20 students. Presently, we have three classrooms and 60 students. At the same time we built the schools here, your father followed up on his promise to your mother about the education of all the children of the rancho, and an additional school was set up at Hacienda Occidental.

"Two things have happened at both Haciendas. The first is that our schools are overflowing, and we need to expand them. I would like to double them both in size, so each child can receive a quality education. The second thing is, as you know, many of the children travel from a long distance to go to school, and they are away from their families for long periods of time. This has put an extra burden on families that live near the Haciendas, as they have taken the children in. It has been incumbent on each family to take in more than one child. I want to build two dorms at each Hacienda that could be expandable but at the present would house at least 30 students. In addition, we need housing for teachers. At the moment, I need two houses on both Haciendas, and I would like to have the authority to be able to work directly with Emilio in the future to address these problems before they become as critical as they are now."

I replied, "Señor Blanco, as you know, the creation and operation of the schools are reserved for my mother. She has ended her deep mourning and is in gray. In addition, she has delegated many of those responsibilities to Angélica. However, I do appreciate you bringing this to me, not because either my mother or Angélica would need my permission to address problems of education on the rancho but for the coordination of manpower and the assets and expenses of the Hacienda. Of course, these problems will be addressed immediately. I would very much appreciate it if you and Emilio would work out the specific needs of the present and future that require construction and bring them to me, so I can oversee the allocation of funding. As far as the allocation of personnel on each of the Haciendas, that will need to be addressed by José or Roman at Hacienda Occidental. José is here and knows the needs. Roman will be here in the next few days, and they will be working with you to get the work completed.

"José, it might be best if you arrange a meeting with Señor Blanco and Emilio so you two can address specific needs as immediately as possible. Emilio, it has been understood for a long time that you are the head of construction on the rancho, but, in addition to this, when you send people to work at other haciendas, you will have to be able to delegate responsibilities. There are many pressing jobs that José and I will need to discuss with you later today.

"Señor Blanco, in my preparation for this meeting, I was made aware we were to discuss the continuation of education of the family and the children of the rancho. Angélica and I are ready to discuss that with you while these gentlemen continue to address the logistics of the construction demands, harvest, and roundup."

I then said to Tall Runner, "Don José and I will need to discuss some additional problems with you after my meeting with Señor Blanco. I would appreciate it if you would bring your sons to that meeting."

The meeting broke up with a chorus of "Sí, Don Francisco. Entiendo (I understand)."

Olga came in and joined the meeting just as Señor Blanco said, "On the subject of the continuing education of the family, while you were traveling, your mother received communication from Javier stating he is not really happy with the education he is receiving in New Jersey. As you are well aware, Javier is much more scientifically oriented, and he thinks more as a mathematician or engineer than a philosopher or language professor. He feels he is wasting his time at Princeton. Your mother and I have discussed this. You had mentioned the new Colorado School of Mines, and we have arranged for him to start this semester."

I replied, "I will leave those decisions to you. Did Javier and Roberto get their citizenship, and how is Roberto progressing toward his degree?"

Señor Blanco responded, "They both have become naturalized United States citizens. Roberto is finishing up his summer internship at Drexel, Morgan, and Company, and all reports suggest they were very impressed with him. He is starting his junior year in September, and he is on track to finish his Bachelor's Degree in January 1882."

Senor Blanco went on to say, "I have a distant cousin, Andrew Dickson White, who is the President of Cornell University. We have communicated over the years, and he is fascinated with the history of the rancho and its ordeals through the revolutions. I wrote him recently to tell him about a young man who has a gift for learning and a great instinct regarding the care of animals. His reply was, 'That is all well and good, but is he university material?' I replied, 'He has always gotten top marks with me.' He passed on my information to Dr. James Law, who established the School of Veterinary Medicine at Cornell University. Dr. Law was intrigued with the idea of having an indigenous native of Mexico in his classroom, but his reply letter stated, 'Very few of the applicants to the Veterinary School pass the entrance exam, and passing the exam is the prerequisite for entry.' My answer to him was that, if he sent me information about what was asked in the entrance exam, I could make a determination about whether this young man has a chance. I received those materials, and I can say without reservation that Hungry Fox can pass the entrance exam."

I asked, "Have you discussed this with Running Bear and Hungry Fox?"

"Yes," he replied, "and Running Bear is eager for Hungry Fox to be a credit to the rancho, his tribe, his band, and his family. To say the least, he is honored that we would consider his son. Of course, the main concern for all is that he would be alone.

"As you know, Cornell University is a land-grant college that was set up on the principle that children of families that work the land need education, and agriculture, as the largest segment of the economy at the time, needed college graduates. The United States Government set up a method whereby each state could have a land-grant college of agriculture. Essentially, the government granted lands to each state that were to be used to establish a college and sustain it for a period of time. One of the requisites for a land-grant college was that every male that attended must undertake military studies.

"Cornell University was an innovator in the field of education. Because of its location in Ithaca, New York, there was not much in the way of housing for students, so it built dorms for this purpose. In continuing with its innovative programs, it began admitting women to all its colleges as equal students in 1870. In 1872, it built a dorm exclusively for women."

He paused for a moment, and then continued, "As you know, your mother insists that all the children of the rancho receive an equal education regardless of who their parents are or their gender. She has been equally adamant that the girls be judged just as the boys as to whether they are college material.

"Although Cornell was founded on the concept of a land grant college, it is a university, and it has a College of Medicine. Rosa Honeywell has taken the entrance exam to the College of Medicine and is hoping to become a nurse. In addition, my daughter, María, has qualified to enter the Cornell College of Agriculture to study home economics and will use her education to teach on the rancho.

"I have two more students that have qualified to attend the School of Agriculture at Cornell. Emilio Cortez, whose father is a vaquero at Hacienda Occidental, will attend with a boy from this Hacienda whom you know well—Cachorro."

I was obviously overwhelmed with all I had heard and with the thoughts of what needed to be done and how that would affect the efficiency of the harvests and land acquisitions due to the strain on personnel.

At that point, Angélica spoke up and said, "Señor Blanco, we thank you for bringing us up to date on the education of the children on the rancho. We trust your judgment and will do all in our power to expand the school."

Olga then entered the conversation with, "Señor Blanco, you know best what needs to be done to get these young people into the University and get them settled. Would it be possible for you to make the arrangements and oversee their entry into Cornell University? My husband has many duties at this time, I am heavy with child, and I would prefer that he stay near until the child has arrived. We all appreciate your hard work, and I hate to ask, but my husband will not be able to properly oversee their entry into college and take care of his responsibilities."

Angélica said, "Señor Blanco, we will leave the education of the children of the rancho in your capable hands. Whenever you need help, please call on me or Olga, as we will be able to assist you."

I then injected, "Thank you for your report and all of your work. This rancho would not have a future without you. I will always be here to talk to you about goals and needs, but I trust you, Angélica, and my wife will be better off discussing the mechanisms of getting done what must be done. I am relieved to leave these problems in your capable hands." I then said, "El Tigre has been with me, so does he know about the plans for Cachorro?"

Señor Blanco answered, "Cachorro's parents are discussing it with El Tigre now, as he is the head of the family."

I then turned to my sister and my wife and asked, "Have you considered that it may be difficult in the United States for Hungry Fox and Cachorro to negotiate officialdom with their given names?" Señor Blanco answered for the women with, "I have mentioned that to the families, and they feel the problem can only be addressed between the heads of the families and you. They are ready to discuss it with you."

I replied, "Running Bear and his sons are waiting to talk with me, but I am no longer prepared to talk to them. Would you please tell them that something has come up, and I need to talk to them and El Tigre after breakfast tomorrow morning? By then, I will have my thoughts gathered, and we can make some decisions."

As Señor Blanco left, I asked Angélica if she could come to our rooms in about three hours, as Olga and I needed a siesta and quiet conversation. She agreed, and we all departed to our rooms.

As Olga and I lay on our bed in each others' arms, I asked her if she had problems living in a house where her husband was the head of the household but my mother and sister had more to say about the household than she did.

She replied, "Your mother is my godmother, so she is my mother. Your sister is my sister. We discuss the household. We discuss the rancho. My opinion is considered. I am very happy with living in the bosom of our family. Someday, I may want my own home to rule over, but that day is not near."

All our plans for the rest of the day were cancelled when a knock on the door told us that two coaches were approaching, and mother was arriving with her patients and the rest of the household.

The next morning, Mother joined José, Roman, and me in my meeting with Running Bear, El Tigre, Bull Tamer, Hungry Fox, and Cachorro. I started the meeting by congratulating Running Bear and El Tigre on having a son and grandson who had reached so far as to attend a university in the United States. I then went on to state I knew they were aware of the problems of a single given name and had been thinking about a solution to the problem. I asked if they had solved this issue.

El Tigre stood up and said, "Con su permiso, mi patrón. He sido elegido para hablar por ninguna otra razón de que yo soy el mayor (I have been chosen to speak for no other reason than I am the eldest)."

I replied, "Esperamos su sabiduría por favor. Hable (We await your wisdom. Speak)."

El Tigre continued, "We are children of the Tarahumara and the clans of the people. Running Bear and I have spent our lives following your father and you in war and peace. Your father invited us to join him on this rancho and told us to treat it as it is ours as much as his. We have done so and have always felt we were working for our future as well as that of our children. Doña María has seen to it that our children have had the same opportunity to advance in life as have her own. Con su permiso, nos gustaría que el segundo nombre fuera de Pérez (With your permission, we would like the second name to be Pérez)."

I looked over at Mother.

She stood up and replied, "En este día, usted nos hace a todos un gran honor. No tengo ninguna duda de que estos jóvenes reflejarán el honor hacia todos nosotros (This day, you do us a great honor. I have no doubt that these young people will reflect honor on us all)."

After Hungry Fox and Cachorro left, Angélica, He Who Hunts, and Olga joined us, as it was time to tell of the results of our trip to Mexico. I told all about the concessions we were to make for the puertos, Cananea, and the railroads, and the land we were to gain on El Tigre. I told them I wanted to immediately use the new barbed-wire fencing to fence the boundaries of our new acquisitions as well as to set up grazing pastures based on the sources of water, so we could rotate our cattle and not overgraze any one area. I concluded by saying I had intended to turn the responsibilities of the fencing over to Bull Tamer and Hungry Fox, but, due to the changes made today, these will be the responsibilities of Bull Tamer alone. "Bull Tamer is to survey the border and see to the fencing crews. He alone will make the decision as to who he needs to employ, with the exception of two individuals—we will assign my two cousins to his crew. He has absolute authority regarding what work they must do, but it is my intention that they learn the work of a man, and I expect Bull Tamer to see they learn how to be men."

I turned to Bull Tamer and said, "I do not envy the trials you are sure to have with them, so pick your other men wisely, as they can be good examples of what it means to be a working vaquero.

"El Tigre, you and Running Bear lived in these mountains as children, and you know the water and terrain. I want you to spend as much time as you can with Bull Tamer in helping him to best utilize the water. Set aside the traditional sites of the summer villages of the Tarahumara, so their farming and grazing lands will remain for their use.

"He Who Hunts will accompany Bull Tamer on his first survey and point out the trails the Apache use and the sites of the camps, so gates can be placed on the trails and their graze can be preserved. Presidente Díaz has accepted that these lands will come under the protection of the rancho and that the conditions of peace on Estancia del Pérez will extend to them and the tribes on them."

I ended with, "He Who Hunts needs to contact Juh. I will consult with him and through him with all of the fathers, so they may know of the changes to the rancho."

CHAPTER 22

We were taking a siesta on the afternoon of Tuesday, September 21st, 1880 when Olga felt a pain. I caught one of the house staff and told them to alert Mother. It seemed to take a long time for anyone to arrive, as Olga was starting to experience stronger pains, and the mattress in the bed was all wet. Angélica finally came rushing in, checked Olga, and told me I must leave. I gave Olga all the love I possessed and Mother came through the door, pointed to me, and said, "Out!"

I retreated to the veranda, sat down in a chair, and stared out into the valley below me. *I am Don Francisco of the Estancia del Pérez, and I am relegated to a helpless spectator at my own child's birth.* I was wondering what I could do when Eduardo showed up with a stiff drink and a cigar.

He said, "I know you're feeling helpless. For the upcoming hours, your job is very hard: You are to do nothing but wait. I have always found this is a good time for the company of friends, drinks, and cigars. All is in God's hands."

Well-wishers came and went, and it was as if time stood still, but I knew it did not. The world became dark, and Mother eventually told the staff not to disturb her with my frequent requests for updates. The hours passed, and my despair became darker than the night.

As light began to peek over the hills, my constant companions Corporal, Roman, He Who Hunts, and José joined me in rum-spiked coffee and pan dulce.

A few moments later, Angélica came onto the veranda and announced I had a son, and he and Olga were waiting for me.

I had no idea how I got upstairs, as I do not remember moving my legs, but I found myself standing at the door to our rooms wondering if I should knock. But before I could raise my hand, Mother opened the door and said, "Go meet your son."

Lying against Olga's shoulder was a small bundle of blankets and, peeking out of a hole in the blankets, was a small, red face haloed by hair—my son! As I stood there, every bell at the Hacienda began tolling.

Ariel Pérez Celaya made his introduction in the Grand Room the following Sunday, September 26th, with his parents and family in attendance. The people of the rancho came in to meet him and partake of food, drinks, and cigars on the veranda. It was a grand party befitting a young Don, and many toasts were made to his health.

October 20th was a busy day at the Hacienda. Emilio had crews from Ascención and Chihuahua working on the new southeast wing of the Hacienda and doubling the size of the school. He had been to Tombstone and drawn up plans for the hospital, which were awaiting Doctor Goodfellow's approval. A site for the consulate had been laid out, and the foundation had been installed for two dorms—one for girls and the other for boys. Long pine logs arrived on wagons. A new sawmill that had been built next to a cotton gin to utilize the power of the steam engine was producing lumber. The cattle drives had reached their destinations in Albuquerque and Pueblo, and the drovers were on their way home. Cotton and all the farm products were being shipped to markets in the United States, Mexico, and Great Britain.

Late that night, He Who Hunts rode in with Juh. We had breakfast together the next morning, and I had just finished bringing Juh up to date on the changing of the borders of the rancho and the agreement that the peace of the Estancia del Pérez would extend to the new borders. Juh was happy that El Tigre was now included in the rancho and safe from raids by the Mexicans.

As we were finishing, Maria, Mother's maid, came in and said, "Señores, a mi señora le gustaría que vinieran a sus habitaciones, ya que tiene un asunto (My missus would like for you to come to her rooms, as she has some business)." We left immediately for my mother's suite, as María had said the business was urgent.

When we were let in, standing in the middle of Mother's parlor was Lozen. Both He Who Hunts and Juh let out the Apache expression of surprise: "Wah!" Lozen, a sister of Victorio, was a female warrior of great acclaim as well as a prophetess who could predict the actions of the enemy. She was Victorio's most valued confidant and was credited with being the originator of Victorio's strategy that allowed him to prevail over seemingly unwinnable odds.

After we had all settled down, Lozen addressed us. "I have some very bad news. It has gotten harder and harder for us to escape the traps set by the large American forces that have been sent against us. The Mexicans have given the Americans the right to pursue us into Mexico, so we no longer have the opportunity to escape here to avoid them. Eight days ago, I went through the American lines to deliver a pregnant woman to the Mescalero reservation, and Nana went east with warriors to raid for supplies. One day later, the American army, with the help of the Rurales, surrounded Victorio and his band at Tres Castillos. They were negotiating with Victorio when the Mexican army, under Joaquin Terrazas, arrived. He thanked the American commander for his help and told him permission for the American army to enter into Mexico was revoked. He then dismissed the Rurales, and the Mexican army attacked and killed all the braves, elder ones, and any women that resisted. A few young women escaped and caught up to Nana. The rest of the women and children were gathered up and marched off to be sold as slaves in the mines and Haciendas of Mexico."

Juh knew he had no chance of recovering any of the people that had been taken as slaves and was in great despair. He Who Hunts was boiling and ready for a fight, and Juh had his hands full keeping him in line.

I asked Lozen if the bodies had been prepared and buried. She stated they were as they died. I sent a houseboy to find Corporal and have him come to me immediately wherever I was in the Hacienda. I then stated I would take a burial crew to properly bury the bodies.

Lozen said to me, "If at all possible, please bury Victorio in the Warm Springs area high on a mountain."

I told her I would do my best for my father and would send riders to determine where the captives had been taken. He Who Hunts declared he was going along, and I told him no. "They will be waiting for any braves that come to properly bury the bodies. They will not arrest a Don of a hacienda and a friend of the Presidente."

Juh said to He Who Hunts, "My son speaks wisely. You are to remain here at the Hacienda. Some that got away will come here. You are to remain to direct them to my camp or the camp at El Tigre."

I left to inform my wife and our new child that I must leave them. Corporal arrived at our quarters, and I told him of the events and that we needed to take a burial detail and some able scouts who could discreetly find where the captives had been taken. He said, "When do you want to leave?" I replied, "Now."

Mother came to our rooms and said, "Do not worry about your son and Olga. I sent for Juanita Celaya to come and care for them. If I know Juanita, she is already on her way to see her grandson and care for her daughter."

In two hours, we were on our way to Tres Castillos. Corporal had a burial crew of 10 and five extra men that would begin the hunt for the captives. José had drawn up a letter of credit for Corporal wherein he was authorized to buy any of the captives he found and authorize payment on the accounts of the rancho.

I supervised the burial of the braves. They had been lying in the sun for 10 days, subject to the carrion-eaters, and it was very difficult. I was able to identify Victorio by some Tarahumara footwear I had given him when we last saw each other. After two days, all were buried, and their graves obscured by riding horses over them and then sweeping the desert clean. We wrapped Victorio in blankets and left for the Warm Springs country.

We never made it to Warm Springs. We were intercepted shortly after we crossed the border by an American patrol looking for refugees to take to San Carlos. We were escorted to Mesilla, where a federal judge told me it had been ordered by the American government that Victorio was not allowed to return to Warm Springs—dead or alive. He then went on to say that a man from Colorado by the name of Charles Deus had bought a gravesite at a local cemetery and had requested that it be held for the body of Bidu-ya if he should need it. So, Charles Deus finally paid his debt to Victorio for his help in recovering his niece.

We arrived at the Hacienda on November 1st to await the success of the trackers and Corporal. The next evening, one of the trackers that had gone with Corporal came in with Corporal's report. I immediately sent for Lozen, He who Hunts, and Juh, so they could hear the report. When they arrived, I told the scout we were ready for the report.

He began, "We followed the army, and it became evident that they were headed to ciudad Chihuahua. Corporal took two men and started a forced march to the ciudad. I and two others were to follow the tracks of the army. Along the way, we found six Apache babies with their heads bashed in, and we buried them. We also buried the corpses of four young boys that had somehow raised the ire of the army. The day we arrived in Chihuahua, Corporal and an abogado were meeting Joaquin Terrazas at the Banco Chihuahua, where he was to obtain the return of 78 captives. Corporal met with Comandante Francisco Neri, who had wired Presidente Díaz for permission to escort Corporal and the captives to the Hacienda. The Comandante had made it known that

16 of the young women had already been sold to brothels in Chihuahua. The Presidente ordered the Comandante to use all the men he needed to recover the young women and escort the captives to the Hacienda. The captives were to leave Chihuahua that day. Most would have to walk, as there was no transportation. Corporal requested that you send wagons and coaches to meet them on their line of march."

I turned to He Who Hunts and said, "Make it happen. Go tell our sisters and children. Mother Lozen and I will arrange for food and medicine as well as people to care for the injured."

Juh rose to go with He Who Hunts and I stopped him with, "Father, I will need your help and guidance in preparing for the arrival of our people."

I needed things expedited, and I was not the supreme authority in the Hacienda. Mother Lozen, Juh, and I went up to apprise Mother of the events and our needs. Mother called Angélica, Eduardo, and Pedro and told them we needed blankets, food, water, medicines, and medicos (doctors) ready to leave in two hours.

I then addressed Lozen, "Mother, I know you are feeling the need to go to meet your people and see to their welfare. I also know you are not in fear for your safety, but I am. As long as you are on the rancho, you enjoy the peace of the rancho. The route your people are taking to get here is not on the rancho, and they are being escorted by Rurales. The Rurales know He Who Hunts and do not think of him as an enemy. He is a friend of Presidente Díaz and therefore enjoys safe passage. I do believe you can best serve the people by helping Father Juh and me prepare a place for your people when they arrive."

Juh turned to Lozen and said, "Our son speaks with wisdom. We must think of the needs of our people rather than follow the heat of our blood."

We left Mother's rooms knowing that all would be ready in two hours.

Lozen, Juh, and I retired to the great room where Juliana met us as we came in. She asked if we could use some coffee and pan dulce. I said we could but voiced reservations about interfering with the preparations for the rescue mission. Juliana assured me she had been detailed to see after us while the preparations were being made, and she was never a bother to Pedro. I thanked her and asked her if she could send people to fetch Roman, José, Running Bear, and Emilio Márquez, as they would need to be at this meeting.

Juliana said, "It will be done, Pancho."

With Juliana, I would always be that little boy.

I stepped out onto the veranda and called in the scout that had brought the news. I told him a rescue column would be leaving here in about two hours. I then asked him if he would be able to go back to meet Corporal and tell him that transportation, clothing, and food were on their way and that he would need to find a wet camp and wait for their arrival.

He replied, "Mi jefe, puedo salir de inmediato (I can leave immediately)."

I told him he need not leave immediately, as he should take a siesta after we had gotten some food down him.

Juliana came in with our coffee, and I asked her if she could find something to eat for this man and a place where he could take a siesta for a couple of hours. I then apprised her that he would be riding back to meet Corporal and the captives.

Juliana looked at the scout and said, "Come with me to the kitchen. We will get you something to eat, and I will show you a place to sleep. In two hours, I will see that you are awakened. There will be a horse out front with food for your trip."

I was beginning to see that the management of the Hacienda should not be exclusively accredited to the efforts of Edward Honeycutt.

Everyone arrived in short order, and I brought them up to date. "He Who Hunts will be in charge of the rescue mission, and the people of the Hacienda are gathering all that will be needed. We will need temporary housing for as many as 100 people, and we will need it within two days. It will be up to Juh and Lozen to design how the camp should be laid out and what amenities will be needed. Emilio, you are herein charged to use all our resources to make this camp appear. I know you will have to be resourceful, and you have little time to get it done. At all times, you are to listen to the direction of Mother Lozen and Father Juh as to what the needs are and fulfill those needs. These young people have had their world turned upside down and have seen and experienced unmentioned brutality. I want them to know they are safe in the bosom of the Hacienda.

"José, it will be up to you and Running Bear to see that He Who Hunts has all the resources and help he needs to be on the road within two hours and then to aid Emilio with his great task as well as keep the business of the Hacienda going.

"Roman, my brother, you are still recovering, so you have a unique task. You are to remain on the veranda and, while He Who Hunts, José, Running Bear, and Emilio are making this happen along with the household staff, it will be your job to anticipate roadblocks and problems that may come up and give orders to head them off as well as be the sounding board for problems and see they are solved. When all is completed, we will need to gather and begin to plan for a long-term solution to the settlement of these young people. It is my hope that Juh will be able to consult with the other fathers and give us some direction."

By November 10th, directives started coming in from San Carlos via Naiche and Loco. They were unanimous in believing the Americans may want to ship the women and their children to Florida. There was still a large fervor against the Chihenne because of the long success of Victorio's war. Nana was still at war, and Geronimo was raiding. The Mescaleros were willing to take any that wanted to come to their reservation, although food was very short.

It finally came down to Juh, Lozen, and He Who Hunts to create a reasonable solution. They asked to speak to Roman, José, Mother, Señor White, and myself. They began by stating the obvious. "Winter is coming, and the refugees are weak. They will not survive if we send them out on their own, and the clans in Mexico have no supply of food to feed themselves and the refugees through the winter. It is the wish of all the fathers that the refugees live free from predation from the Americans or the Mexicans, and they feel this can only happen on the Estancia del Pérez. So, it is their humble plea that their sons and sisters take them into their family."

Mother spoke up and said, "When we were weak and vulnerable, we approached the fathers and the fathers of the fathers and made a bargain we all would live on this land together. The Chihenne as well as all the other clans are our brothers, sisters, and children, and this is their home as well as ours. They need not ask to live here."

He Who Hunts spoke up and asked, "Mother and Señor White, will the children be able to go to school, so they can prepare to face the world that is coming?"

Señor White replied, "The law was established long ago that the children of the rancho will go to school. It will not be broken. However, I can see one problem in that most or all the children speak only their native tongue. My solution for that is to find Chihenne women who also speak Spanish to assist the teachers. We will need at least 10, and they will be employed by the rancho, so they will be earning their own way while they help to educate the children. I know there may not be 10 women among the refugees that speak Spanish, so I leave it to Juh and Lozen to recruit some elder women among the clans who do."

I spoke up and said, "It will be necessary for all that are able to contribute to the welfare of the rancho by doing chores. In addition, we have yet to address the education of the children in the ways of the people. He Who Hunts is assigned the task of reserving village sites on San Luis and El Tigre, so they will not be compromised by the fencing.

I propose that the three of you oversee the building of a village on San Luis where the children can go when they are released from school by Señor White and be taught by the elders in the ways and traditions of the people in safety. I know you might prefer El Tigre, but security is my responsibility, and I can secure San Luis."

Mother ended the meeting with, "José, you have been very quiet, but all of us realize the logistics fall on you. It is you who will need to see that all the parts come together at the Hacienda. Do not hesitate to call on any of us for assistance. You are invaluable."

By Saturday, November 20th, Mother had deemed Roman and Panchita fit to leave on their honeymoon. They had decided they would prefer to meet up with Juan and Dulce in Colorado. Both couples would then travel to Princeton, where they were to pick up Roberto. They then planned to travel to Boston and then on to Wellesley to pick up Elizabeth and then head down to New York where all were to spend Christmas and New Year's Eve.

Roberto would head back to Princeton on Tuesday, January 4th, 1881, and the honeymooners would deliver Elizabeth to Wellesley and retire to Boston for a week before taking a ship from Boston to Veracruz. From there, they would take a coach to Mexico, where they would visit with the family for several weeks before making their way to the west coast. On or near the 15th of February, Roman and Panchita would take a ship to Guaymas, where they would secure transportation to Hacienda Occidental.

Juan and Dulce would secure passage on a ship to San Francisco, where, after a few days' rest, they would begin the journey by train back to Estancia Colorado.

Olga, Ariel, and I were to remain at Hacienda Oriental until after the new year and then move to Hacienda Occidental until the honeymooners returned. Corporal would be leaving within the week to represent the family at Hacienda Occidental.

CHAPTER 23

I t was Sunday, January 16th. Olga, Ariel, Juanita, and I had arrived at Hacienda Occidental the day before and, that morning, we woke to a blanket of snow.

I had left orders with José to arrange for the sale of 2,400 hundred to 3,200 head of cattle averaging 900 pounds per head to be delivered the first of April for shipment on the Santa Fe Railroad. The Santa Fe Railroad would meet the Southern Pacific, which had arrived from Tucson on December 18th the previous year at the old customs place on the Mimbres River called Deming. The projected arrival of the Santa Fe was March of 1881, which would complete the second continental railroad.

I wanted our delivery point to be at Deming. José was to contact our neighbors that market with us and let them know we would reserve an allotment of 800 head for them to fill if they cared to. That allotment was to be reserved by them no later than January 31st, and it would be on a first-come basis. I had given Corporal orders to alert the neighbors of Hacienda Occidental.

At the same time, I asked Corporal and José to relay to the neighbors that we will be delivering cattle to the railhead on October 1st, and we would like to know by January 31st how many head they would like to ship at that time. It was my hope that José could lock in a price by the end of February for the delivery of the cattle to Deming.

In addition, some of the cattle would be exported through Puerto Palomas, and the rest of the cattle would cross the border at Pozos de Antílope (Antelope Wells). It would be up to José to acquire the health certificates newly required by the United States government for importation of beef. The regulation was implemented due to the prevalence of Texas Tick Fever, which had never been found in Mexican cattle.

As expected, Emilio Márquez came up with a grand solution for the inclusion of orphaned Chihenne children when adding on to the boys' and girls' dorms: an addition would be constructed between the buildings to create a gathering area. There would be private rooms facing the gathering area for the adults who had the responsibility of watching and caring for the kids in the dorms.

In the meantime, a makeshift village had been built under the direction of Juh, Lozen, and He Who Hunts. All the children were attending school and had responsibilities assigned to them.

We were still being raided by cattle thieves but not on the grand scale of the past. It was becoming apparent to me that we needed fencing along the frontier to keep our cattle from straying and to give our vaqueros that had to ride fence a point of location for the movement of cattle across the frontier. I sent a request to José to increase his purchase of wire two-fold.

I then talked to Corporal and Antonio Sapia and told them of my plans to fence the frontier of Hacienda Occidental and eventually to fence individual pastures in the interior. It would be up to Antonio to choose a fencing crew and a foreman of that crew to fence the frontier. I suggested it might be in Antonio's best interest to make a trip down to El Tigre and observe how the fencing was progressing. He might find an experienced hand that he would like to make the foreman as well as a couple of hands that would be the nucleus of the fencing crew. I then told him that Corporal would be going along, so he could report back to me on the progress of the fencing and let me know when we could begin to stock the range. As an aside, I said, "Corporal will curb Bull Tamer's urge to shoot you for raiding his crew."

I asked Corporal to leave word with the watchers along the way that I would like to have El Tigre and Tall Runner come to Hacienda Occidental to report to me on the watchers.

It was a new experience for me to be tied down to a location with my wife and baby. We dined together every evening, and Ariel ruled the table. Anything he wanted, he got.

February 2nd was a great day, as Olga and I were lying in bed watching the sun go down behind the mountain, Olga informed me I was going to be a father again. I forgot all thought of sleep and, after holding her in my arms all night, I got up, feeling ready to conquer the world. I went down to Manuel's kitchen to grab some breakfast. When I came through the door, I was greeted by the sight of Corporal, He Who Hunts, El Tigre, Tall Runner, and Antonio Sapia with plates of tortillas, beans, chorizo (a spicy Mexican sausage), and eggs. Over at a side table were two young Apache women that Juanita was instructing on how to prepare a breakfast tray.

I gathered myself up, tried to not look startled, and announced, "Señores, I am glad you are here, as I have the privilege to announce that Olga is with child."

Everyone got up, shook my hand, and congratulated me. I then went on to announce we would have a small fiesta in celebration of a new addition to the family.

During breakfast, He Who Hunts explained that Mother knew Juanita needed to get back to her family, and there was too much help at the Hacienda Oriental. "She sent these two young women, who have no family with them, to be of assistance to Olga and Hacienda Occidental." Bringing the women was a detour on his trip to San Luis.

I responded with, "En cualquier momento que veo a mi hermano, mi corazón está lleno de alegría (Any time that I see my brother, my heart is overjoyed)."

We adjourned to the veranda with coffee and pan dulce, so Manuel could begin the preparations for a proper fiesta. Corporal began the conversation by relaying the commitments for market from the neighbors of Hacienda Occidental. He had a commitment of 1,200 head for Fall shipment and 500 head for Spring shipment. He had written down the dates of the commitments, and José would compare them with the neighbors from Hacienda Oriental and fill out the 800 head on a first-come basis.

The report from El Tigre was not encouraging. "We are beginning to receive increased attention from pandillas susurrantes both in the United States and in Mexico. The forts and mining ventures are providing a market for beef in the United States, and the enterprising Cowboys are trying to stock that market with our beef. Most of the incursions are coming from the Animas Valley, where Old Man Clanton has re-established his ranch after it burned down. It is next to impossible to patrol the border or to keep strays from crossing, whether they are just looking for food or are being pushed. Two or three head a day for a month make for a marketable herd at the mining camps or the forts. The Cowboys and the banditos to the south have learned that raids are big and visible and easy to defend against. In addition, we are beginning to lose cattle to the stomachs of the miners at Cananea. It appears, right now, the only places we can really protect are the mountains and the adjacent grasslands," said El Tigre.

I thanked El Tigre for his report and told him and Tall Runner I was gradually fencing the border and the pastures. "It will still be necessary for the watchers to continue their work, and we will start looking at recovery of stolen cattle. The watchers will need to stealthily follow the cuatreros and report back, so a plan can be developed to recover our stock." I went on to say, "It will be necessary to set up forces of well-trained men to pursue and recover our stock. I would prefer that you two begin recruiting and setting up such forces at each of the camps. I would like each of the forces to be no more than five men with a backup force of five men. I am going to need to talk to Comandante Neri about the proper way to go about this without encroaching upon his orders and responsibilities."

I then asked El Tigre to return the next day to Hacienda Oriental with the information about the amount of stock our neighbors would like to ship as well as to consult with José and Running Bear about the strike forces. Tall Runner would stay at Hacienda Occidental and began the task of setting up the strike forces here and managing the watchers.

CHAPTER 24

On February 28, Panchita and Roman gave us the news there was a new family member on the way. In addition, they told us that Dulce was expecting. It looked like the rancho was going to be very busy around August, September, and October.

The next morning, we started making preparations to return to Hacienda Oriental. Roman got down to the business of running the western branch of the rancho, and we discussed fencing, rustling, roundup, and shipping dates. The neighbors of Hacienda Occidental were to send 470 head for the drive north, and those cattle should arrive road branded no later than March 5th at Campo Guadalupe. I said, "Antonio Sapia has already started the movement of the 1,450 head toward Campo Guadalupe, and they should be there on or near March 5th. The cattle should be rested and on the move no later than March 7th for Campo Berrendo and be ready to cross the frontera on or near March, 15th." I then went on to state, "Roman, I would like you to leave Antonio in charge of Hacienda Occidental and accompany the herd from this Hacienda to Campo Berrendo. You will be met by someone from Hacienda Oriental who will have all the papers necessary to cross the frontera at Pozos de Antílope.

"An escort of three vaqueros is to accompany Juanita back to the Celaya home in the coach you arrived in. I would appreciate it if you could persuade Panchita to accompany Olga and the two young Apache women back to Hacienda Oriental in the grand coach. Corporal and He Who Hunts will escort the women along with two vaqueros. Ever since He Who Hunts brought the two Apache women to the Hacienda, he and Corporal have done nothing but hang as close as they could to the Hacienda, so they could 'accidently' meet up with the women while they were doing their chores. Olga informs me the attention is not lost, and the two young women are infatuated, too.

"I and a vaquero are to leave here tomorrow at the same time as the women, but we are going to ride straight through to Hacienda Occidental, where I can assess the business of the rancho and accompany the herd that is to pass through Puerto Palomas to the Santa Fe railhead in Deming. I will meet you there, and we will be able to ride back to Hacienda Occidental together. I have some ideas I want to mull over with the family as to the direction of the rancho and our businesses. In addition, we will need to meet with the fathers on the state of our relationship."

It was mid-morning before the women were ready, and we all left together. I rode on top of and in the coach until we reached Campo San Bernardino, where the women were to rest for the night. I said my goodbyes to the women, Olga, and Ariel. The vaquero and I took our saddles off the coach and picked out two horses each to ride on our trip to Campo El Lobo, where we would rest for a while before we rode on to Hacienda Occidental.

We left Campo El Lobo before daylight and were each on our second horse when we arrived at Hacienda Occidental around midnight. When we arrived, a houseboy was waiting to take the horses and had given the vaquero instructions as to where to sleep. I was not curious about how Eduardo had anticipated my arrival, as I had caught the flash of mirrors on our ride. When I went up to our rooms, I found a warm bath drawn and my bed turned down.

I woke up at dawn and hurried down to Pedro's kitchen to be greeted by the smiling faces of José, Running Bear, Emilio Vásquez, and

Emilio Márquez. After breakfast, Pedro shooed us out to the veranda where he had coffee and pan dulce awaiting us. stating, "My kitchen is not a meeting room!"

José opened the meeting by saying, "Don Francisco, it would be good if Emilio Márquez gave you his report, as the workers are already on the job, and he is anxious to oversee how they are starting the day."

Emilio began with, "Don Francisco y caballeros (gentlemen), the expansion of the school is complete. The dorms for the students are nearing completion and should be complete in five more days. The headquarters office and living quarters have been laid out, and the foundation rocks have been set. We will be starting on the framing this morning. The addition to the Hacienda has been laid out, but I am hesitant to begin laying the foundation without Doña María's and your approval."

I replied to him, "I appreciate your hesitation, but you will have to wait a few more days, as I would not want to make a decision on the Hacienda without including Olga's and Angélica's input also."

Emilio smiled and said, "That is very wise, Don Francisco."

I then asked, "Emilio, can you tell me about the progress on the hospital for Dr. Goodfellow?"

Emilio said, "I left my son, Hector, in charge of the construction of the hospital. Dr. Goodfellow, Hector, and I laid out how it was to be built. The last news I had was that the walls were up, the roof was on, and they were working on the inside per Dr. Goodfellow's instructions. Dr. Goodfellow also sent me home with drawings as to how a clinic should be constructed here and at Hacienda Occidental."

I thanked him for his complete report and then asked José how the roundup was going and whether the neighbors here had come up with the 300 head for the Spring shipment.

José replied, "I will reserve the report on the roundup for Running Bear. We received a request to ship 400 head from the neighbors of the Hacienda. I have confirmed the first 300 and have told the holders of the extra 100 that the allotment is filled. I also told them I would keep them in mind if someone falls short."

I said, "I am going to need to hear Running Bear's report on the roundup before I comment further on that subject."

Running Bear started with, "Mi jefe, the roundup is all but complete. All the early Spring calves are branded, and we are ready to road brand the market animals. We can easily provide any amount you need by including older and barren animals up to about 2,400 head that will meet the 900-pound requirement at the shipping point."

I asked Running Bear if any of those animals would benefit by waiting to be shipped with the Fall market stock.

"I am concerned about graze and not harming the land. I feel we should ship as many as we can from the lowlands and, with winter rains, both El Medio and the eastern slope of San Luis will have extra graze, which will ease the pressure on the eastern lowlands."

I turned to José and said, "What is the maximum number of head we can ship on this contract?"

"We must provide 3,200 head at 900 pounds each, which is 2,880,000 pounds of beef cattle. Our contract allows for a maximum of 3,150,000 pounds, which is approximately 3,500 head."

I asked Running Bear "If we only ship 1,650 from Hacienda Occidental, will that cause too large a burden on our graze?"

He replied, "No, we can manage very well, as we will keep the smaller stock for the fall shipment."

I replied, "I will not want more than 200 head to be culls."

Running Bear replied, "Llevará a cabo (It will be done),"

I then told José and the men that I needed to report to the Doña and that I would like to take this conversation up again after breakfast the next day.

After Running Bear and Emilio Vásquez had left, I asked José if Angélica would be with Mother.

"I do not know, but I can send a boy to request that she be there if you would like."

I replied, "I would like that."

We waited about 30 minutes for the women to prepare for our arrival, as I knew Mother would send down for refreshments. José and I followed the maid with the tray.

Once we had settled and Mother had put down her cup, I said, "Mother, you will be interested to know you are about to be a grandmother again."

Mother looked up, startled, and inquired, "Olga is pregnant?"

"Yes, she is, and she has company. Both Juanita and Dulce had eventful honeymoons and are expecting." I then went on to tell her that Olga and Juanita should be arriving here at the Hacienda some time the next day, as I had called a family meeting. "Roman will be accompanying me on my trip back from delivering our cattle to Deming."

On March 14th, Corporal and I left the Hacienda for Deming in the New Mexico Territory. I had all my documents in hand for the herds to be presented to the customs house there. On our trip up, Corporal confided to me that he and Saguaro Blossom, one of the Apache women, had decided to marry. In addition, He Who Hunts and Singing Brook had also decided to marry. He went on to say they would get married at the new summer camp being set up on San Luis with Juh and Lozen conducting the ceremony. I told him this news was not unexpected and very welcome. I asked him if April 15th would be a good time for the ceremony, as my family would like to be there, and this would give time for everyone to make the journey.

He stated, "That is a long time to wait, but I and He Who Hunts would want all our family who want to attend to be able to do so."

We arrived in Deming and were met by officials of the Santa Fe Railroad and the packing house in Chicago. We had supper with the officials and agreed to meet with them the following morning—after I had presented my papers to the custom house—to go over the need for a holding area and tour the loading pen area.

The customs officials accepted and approved all our papers, and I paid the import fees. They were somewhat mystified as what to do about the certifications about ticks, as it had never been a problem in cattle from Mexico, but the law had been directed at Mexican cattle instead of the cattle from Texas, where there was Texas Tick Fever.

The cattle from Hacienda Oriental arrived on March 26th, and the holding area was ready for them. It was situated north of the town site of Deming, and wells had been dug and windmills set up for water, so the cattle could graze and be rotated near water. There was a train of 25 cattle cars already set up to be loaded, and the vaqueros assisted in moving the cattle to the scales where a whole carload of 30 head could be weighed at once and then moved into a car. Within five hours, 750 head were weighed, their brands checked, they were loaded into cars, and the train was on its way to Albuquerque. There, the cattle would be offloaded, fed, watered, and then moved on toward their final destination, which was Chicago.

Empty trains arrived within hours of departure of a loaded train, and the cattle were loaded day and night. Three thousand one hundred and twenty head were loaded on the trains for a gross weight of 3,800,000 pounds. The cattle shipped by our neighbors weighed out at an average of 952 pounds for a total of 889 head delivered to the railhead for a total of 846,328 pounds for a price of $27,929 at a contract price of $3.15 per hundred weight plus a bonus of $0.15 per hundred weight for an average above 50 pounds over the contract price per animal.

The rancho netted $73,711 for the Spring shipment. On March 30th, I received a wire at the station in Deming that a sum of $101,640 had been deposited into my account at Drexel Morgan. All the vaqueros headed back to their respective homes, and Corporal, Roman, and I boarded a Southern Pacific Train headed to El Paso.

Once we arrived, our first stop was to see Samuel Schutz and order dress material as a present for Olga, Mother, Juanita, and Angélica. We ordered sacks of rock candy for the children at the Hacienda and some that Roman could deliver to Hacienda Occidental. We asked that the goods be delivered to the westbound train in the morning and for Herr Schutz to join us for supper that night.

We then invaded José and Salomé Adame's house, where Roman and Corporal found a place for a siesta and I drafted instructions to Drexel Morgan to wire specific sums to the individual banks of our neighbors.

We boarded our train west early the next morning and, by 10:00 am, we were on our horses towing six pack animals headed to the Hacienda. Before we had cleared sight of Deming, we saw 10 horses approaching, and I recognized Running Bear in the lead. As they pulled up to meet us, Running Bear said, "Banditos south of the Floridas stopped some of the vaqueros on the way back, looking for the proceeds of the drive. It was decided that he lead some men to escort us back. As we were riding south, we saw the dust of some riders that rode toward the north end of the Tres Hermanas, where they abruptly stopped. He Who Hunts was with us, and he went to investigate."

I thanked him for his concern and intuition, as we would have been easy prey for men hiding in wait.

As we were approaching the east side of the Tres Hermanas, we saw a dust cloud made by riders heading north along with the dust of a lone rider headed toward us. When He Who Hunts caught up to us, he reported there were six riders. He got close enough to them that he could hear them arguing. It seems this was no longer an ambush of three Mexicans, as more riders had joined them. One man was arguing that "a few more Mexicans ain't going to make a big difference," but the rest weren't convinced. The man decided he would make the odds against them greater by climbing up, making himself visible on the skyline, and shouting to the other Indians where they were. That did the trick, as they quickly mounted and fled to the north.

As we rode into the Hacienda with our goods, we were met by the beginnings of a fine fiesta celebrating the selling of the herd, the gathering of the family, Corporal's and He Who Hunts' upcoming weddings, and the news of three more additions on the way to join the next generation.

It was well after midnight when I joined Olga in bed. I hope I whispered some sweet words, but I just don't remember.

It was mid-morning on April 6th when the family gathered with me in the great room so I could relay to them my thoughts about where we were going with the rancho.

I started out by telling them how we had developed a cooperative marketing strategy that included our neighbors and whoever else wanted to join us in the marketing of farm goods and cattle. I explained how José had further developed markets in Mexico, the United States, and Great Britain. We were now contracting cotton and other farm goods for shipment to Great Britain. The Mexican Central Railroad was to be completed by 1884, and we would be able to ship goods through Ciudad Mexico to Veracruz.

I went on to say, "We are in the process of joining with British entrepreneurs to ship frozen meat from Veracruz to Britain. We will be able to ship our cattle to Veracruz by train, where they will be slaughtered and then shipped to European ports. It is now possible to ship from Deming and other locations to Galveston, and we are investing in the facilities to ship frozen meat to Europe through Galveston. The main problem will be whether we can join with others to force the Southern Pacific into becoming a partner in development. In addition, our consortium is entering talks with the large packing companies in Chicago and New York to initiate the slaughter of animals in locations such as Kansas City or Denver for shipment as frozen meat to the eastern market as well as Europe.

"Our Colorado ranches are doing well, and we are looking at further expansion in Colorado and California. The California market is growing, and it can help us expand into other markets.

"I firmly believe that our future is in marketing not only our goods but the goods of others that would join with us. I want the Pérez family to secure itself by not being vulnerable to the political whims of any group or country.

"Our Haciendas are tenuous because of politics and distance. We are spread across a long, thin line extending from near Juárez to within a short distance of Nogales. We must be vigilant at all times against thieves from both our northern and southern borders. What were villages 20 years ago are now small, growing towns that are putting pressure on our borders. We have made some large concessions in the past year, have deeded some of our land to municipalities, and have received a further grant of land on El Tigre.

"It is my intention to fence the frontier of the rancho, and we are proceeding with that as we speak. It is also my intention to further continue to fence the domains of all the campos. Once that is done, we will fence in pastures, so cattle can be rotated through those pastures, and we can better husband our grass.

"It is also my proposal that we begin to sell portions of our rancho that are too cumbersome to manage from either Hacienda due to distance and neighbors. I propose to offer those ranches to the families of the rancho. They will be in charge of their own land and will join us cooperatively in marketing their goods and cattle. I propose we help them by providing financing and advice when requested. I would like to see our rancho shrink to a manageable size by centralizing it at El Medio, San Luis, and El Tigre for our cattle. If we can control those mountains and the valleys extending from them, we will be able to manage our graze, cattle, and borders much more efficiently. If, occasionally, our neighbors would like to sell their holdings that are contiguous with our rancho, I would be agreeable to exploring that possibility. However, I would be much more amenable to offers to purchase in Colorado and California as well as states farther north, as I want this family to be safe from the politics of both nations. I am not afraid of confiscation of lands in the United States. In Mexico, that is and has been a real possibility, as we are not through with revolution. By gaining ownership of lands in the United States, we gain legitimacy and will not be run out as foreigners trying to take jobs away from Americans.

"I have been speaking mostly about cattle, as that is our heritage, but our future is also dependent on the raising of crops. I propose that certain of our lands that are arable and have good water sources be developed both by the rancho and by those who would join us cooperatively. It is our cooperative ownership of gins and other means of marketing farm products and ownership of the knowledge of how to run the machinery that will insulate us somewhat from revolution. We just need to take care we do not get too big in any location as to excite envy.

"Therefore, I propose that you, my family and partners in the ownership of the Estancia del Pérez and all its related businesses, consider what I have said and come up with some plan wherein the people of the rancho become holders in the future welfare of the rancho and their own lands and families." Mother asked, "When do you plan on implementing these changes?" "We should have a plan worked out soon after the fencing of the frontier of our present boundaries is in place. Once we begin to fence within the boundaries of each campo, we should have an idea of how we might want to divide up some of the land into ranches. I expect that will be next spring." Mother said, "It is up to all to consult their minds on this project, and I want to hear what you come up with."

CHAPTER 25

On April 15th, José, Angélica, Mother, Roman, Juanita, Running Bear, El Tigre, Olga, and many more joined me in traveling to the summer camp that had been set up for the Chihenne survivors on San Luis to celebrate the marriage of Corporal to Saguaro Blossom and He Who Hunts to Singing Brook. Lozen officiated at the ceremony to give away the Chihenne brides. Naiche was there to represent the Chokonen band of He Who Hunts as well as the Chiricahua. Juh was there, as this place was built on the ancestral lands of the Ndendai band of the Chiricahua. Many of the Chihenne survivors at Hacienda Oriental had made the trip as well as a large contingency of the Ndendai.

Running Bear made sure that five fat steers had been tied up at the site, and they were quickly butchered to provide a feast for all the participants.

I stood with Mother, who represented Sargento and María Guzmán, the parents of Corporal, and his siblings, whom she had adopted. Both Corporal and He Who Hunts elected to stay on at San Luis for a few days, and we headed back to the Hacienda the next morning.

On April 17th, I received a letter from Edward and Walter Vail stating they had found several ranches in southern California that were for sale. They were only looking for one, and they remembered I was interested in that territory. Their letter went on to state they would be going to Los Angeles on April 23rd. I wrote back to them that I and my party would be in Los Angeles on the 26th of April and would be staying at the Pico House.

I sent a rider to get Corporal and He Who Hunts. The message I sent them was that we had some land to look at in Los Angeles, and I wanted them and their wives to join Olga and me on a trip to Los Angeles, San Francisco, and to our ranches in Colorado. I told them we would need to leave the Hacienda no later than the 22nd. I sent a rider to Deming with an order for a private railroad car to be situated in Deming on the 22nd of April and to send a telegram to Gerald Pitney in Sacramento, California asking him to meet me in Los Angeles on the 26th at the Pico House or send a competent surrogate, as I would be looking at purchasing a ranch or ranches in the Los Angeles area.

We arrived at the Southern Pacific Station in Deming at noon on the 23rd in the grand coach with six outriders. Our car was on the siding, and it was to be connected to the next train coming through at 3:30 pm. By late evening, we had cleared Tucson, and we arrived in Los Angeles on the morning of the 25th. A coach picked us up and delivered us to the Pico House, and our car was placed on a siding to await the continuation of our journey.

Ariel was enjoying the ministrations of his mother and three more women who were in total awe throughout the trip. For the two brides, the Hacienda was the largest building they had ever been in. Their previous experience with abodes was wickiups and the slave quarters they temporarily shared in Chihuahua.

We met with the Vails on the morning of the 26th and, happily, were greeted by Gerald Pitney when we went in for breakfast. The Vails explained about the three ranches for sale and that they were interested in one, but they felt it would be advantageous for both themselves and us if we became neighbors in this venture.

Later that morning, Gerald Pitney, the Vails, and I met with the three owners of the ranches and their attorneys. We had lunch and discussed ranching and their ranches. It was decided we would leave early the next morning to inspect the ranches. After we parted ways, the Vails asked me if I would have any objections to them consulting with Gerald Pitney, because the sellers had lawyers, and they did not want to be at a disadvantage. I wholeheartedly assented and left them in the care of our lawyer with the orders that they and Gerald were to be our guests in the hotel dining room that evening.

Mother insisted that Corporal Juan Cortez accompany us on our trip as a caretaker of the women and Ariel, and she would not allow her grandson to travel without a nurse. At this moment, I could see the total value in that advice. I would have had no idea how to see to the safety of the women, since it was necessary for me to travel to ranches for inspections. Olga would be held captive to Ariel's needs and not be able to enjoy the cities we were to visit.

The Vails, Corporal, He Who Hunts, the three owners of the ranches, and I left early the next morning for the inspections. After three days of looking at the headquarters and making short rides out onto the ranches, Edward Vail and I returned to Los Angeles. Walter Vail, Corporal, and He Who Hunts stayed to do a more thorough inspection of the ranches, as our preliminary inspection was favorable.

Saguaro Blossom and Singing Brook had obtained suitable clothing from Mother, Angélica, and Olga for the trip, but Olga was determined to take them shopping for clothes in Los Angeles. By the time we arrived back at the hotel, she had them all set up as young señoras, ready to take the town by storm. It became my pleasure as well as the pleasure of Edward Vail and Gerald Pitney to escort three beautiful women to two productions at the Merced Theater next door as well as dining at some of the finest restaurants during the eight days it took Walter, Corporal, and He Who Hunts to thoroughly explore the three ranches.

On the morning of May 8th, the Vails, Gerald Pitney, Corporal, He Who Hunts, and I met for a breakfast meeting in a reserved room at the café in the hotel. It had been an accepted fact that the Vails, by virtue of discovery, would have first choice of which ranch they wanted. The ranches were laid out on true north/south and east/west lines, with the northwest corner on the Pico Madulce and the southeast corner on the Pico Santa Paula, all of which were northeast of Santa Barbara, California. The ranches had been evenly divided into 210 sections each. The Vails chose the ranch on the east side, and I was to take the ranches on the west side.

We had discovered one major problem with the ranches, which was that not all the land was patented. On the Vail ranch, the patented land was a total of 12, 160-acre homesteads on water. The land we were looking at had 21, 160-acre homesteads we could hold deed to that surrounded the available water. The rest of the land was government land we would not hold title to.

The owners of the ranches were seeking $20,000 per ranch, and I was less than enthusiastic to buy land I would not own. Gerald Pitney asked me to not turn down the purchase until he could do a title investigation of the land. I assented and told him I would not pay $40,000 for five and a quarter sections of land even if those sections hold the water. I went on to say I was looking at a future not a gamble. "If I am to gamble, I will not pay anymore than $15,000 for both ranches, as our investigations and conversations with long-time families in the area say have revealed that, although there is plenty of grass today, it is subject to drought and is not as strong a feed as our desert grass. Therefore, although the sizes of the ranches are large, their carrying capacity is less than the Colorado properties we currently own, of which the 50 percent that is not in the mountains is patented.

I announced to the Vails and Gerald Pitney that I would be moving on to San Francisco on May 10th, arriving on the 11th, and we would be residing at the Palace Hotel. From San Francisco, we would be moving on to Colorado on the 20th of May, where I had just received word there was an additional ranch contiguous to the property we currently owned that had come on the market and was being held for our inspection.

Gerald Pitney asked if he had the authority to continue to negotiate for me, and I replied he certainly did, and I would sign a document to that effect, but it would be incumbent upon him to keep me informed about the negotiations. I would have the final say of acceptance or denial.

We arrived in San Francisco, where we settled into a suite with three bedrooms and two rooms for the newlyweds at the Palace Hotel. On the 12th of May, I received a wire from Gerald Pitney stating the title investigation did not turn up any better news on the titles to the ranches. He stated the Vails had come around to my argument and were offering $8,000 for the eastern ranch, and he asked if he had my authorization to counter with $15,000 for the two ranches. I sent him a wire giving him the authorization to proceed with a counteroffer.

Olga and I attended plays and dined with our entire entourage, but half the time we enjoyed exploring San Francisco on our own or just staying in our suite with Ariel.

I received a wire from Gerald Pitney on the 15th of May stating the sellers had reduced their price to $25,000 for the two ranches combined and had countered with the Vails. I sent a wire back to Gerald stating I would raise my offer to $18,000 and gave them until the 18th of May to accept with a closing date of June 20th. This would give me time to have managers on the ground at the time of closing.

I received a wire from Gerald late on the 18th stating we had a deal based upon my counteroffer. I sent back a letter giving him my congratulations on closing the deal and stating I would hold off on leaving San Francisco for two days if need be and book him a room at the Palace so we could consult about the closing if he could be there no later than the 20th. He wired back saying he would be leaving on the evening train and should arrive by the evening of the 19th.

Gerald arrived late that evening, and we met for breakfast the next morning. I told Gerald I would send Corporal to attend to the closing and bring whoever I was going to have manage the new ranches. I would be paying by wire from Drexel Morgan and asked him to get the information regarding to whom the sellers wanted the wires addressed. I went on to say, "You will have the funds in hand to disperse at the closing. In addition, I would like you to let me know what your expenses are as well as your fees, and you will receive that wire at the same time made out however you dictate."

Gerald asked me if I would be interested in any more acquisitions in California, and I replied, "Definitely not for the next couple of years, as we have a lot to swallow from the acquisitions I am presently making. In addition, the Vails and I have come to an agreement wherein they will market through the marketing cooperative I have set up from their Empire Ranch, and I will let them lead in setting up a local market in California for most of the beef produced there."

It was possible we would be in the market for agricultural land in a few years, and it was possible we would need Gerald's help in negotiating the purchase of mines in California in approximately three years.

I ordered our car, and we departed for Colorado the next morning. We used our car until we got to Pueblo, Colorado, where we were to proceed on the Denver Rio Grande Railroad, a narrow-gauge railroad, through the mountains. We stopped in Walsenburg on the 25th of May, so I could consult with Silas Leven on the particulars of the property that was for sale. Silas informed me he had received a wire from Henry Pitney stating his firm had been successful in getting the incorporation of The Crossed Arrows Corporation through the New Jersey legislature and signed by the governor. The statutory agent listed was the Pitney Law Firm, and the President/CEO was Francisco Pérez with Roberto Pérez listed as the Secretary/Treasurer. In addition, they filed a dba, La Corporación Flechas Cruzadas (Crossed Arrows Corporation), and a trademark with the federal government featuring the brand of the Estancia del Pérez.

This indeed was good news, and I asked Silas to do what was necessary to change the title of the Colorado properties to the name of the corporation and to wire Gerald Pitney in Sacramento with the particulars, so the ranch we were purchasing in California would be put in the corporate name.

Silas told me the ranch I was to look at was contiguous with the properties we had already purchased, was the same size as the properties we presently owned, and was billed as 1,800-head spread. The asking price was $18,000.

We arrived at Fort Garland in the mid-afternoon. Corporal, He Who Hunts, and their ladies were anxious to ride out to the ranch. I told them the five of us would remain in Fort Garland for the night and see that adequate transportation was available to move Olga, Ariel, and our entourage to the Hacienda in the morning as well as secure a horse for me.

After a good Alemán meal, we all turned in, as we had a big day ahead of us. By the time we were ready to move to the Hacienda, two carriages arrived escorted by Juan Gonzáles and Salvador Honeywell. Juan explained that we would pass by the Hacienda on our way south to see the property, and Corporal and He Who Hunts took advantage of sleeping in until we arrived. It was so good to see Dulce. Mother had sent presents, all of which were clothes for a pregnant lady.

The ranch house was adequate for a campo, but the land had been overused. It was apparent it had been grazed to excess, and it would take several years to return it to good shape. Corporal, He Who Hunts, and Salvador spent the next four days combing the entire ranch. They reported finding adequate water, but the graze was poor throughout. It could take up to five years for it to fully recover and, in the meantime, it could handle no more than 400 to 500 head the first year, which could be increased slightly every year until it reached a maximum 1,400 head.

I spoke with Juan about our purchase of two ranches in California. I told him I was in need of someone experienced in setting up a Pérez ranch business. I only had two men presently that had gone through this process.

Pedro looked at me and said, "Pancho, I know you are not talking about me moving to California, and you know that Dulce has just finished building her nest. So, I am assuming you would like to take Salvador away from me. It would be a great loss, but you could not get anyone better equipped for the job. I also have two American men that are top hands. I respect and trust both of them. Either one of them could be very valuable to Salvador and me as foreman. We do have one problem. Salvador is very serious about a niece of Señor Deus by the name of María Gallegos. I am not so sure he will leave her here."

I replied, "Let us put it to him and see what he says."

When Salvador came in, I said, "Salvador, I have a problem, and you are the only man I can think of who can solve it. We are buying a large ranch in California. It is mostly in brush country but has a lot of rolling, grassy hills. It is a large and beautiful place. My problem is I need a man to get it into shape and run it. Juan highly recommends you and states there are two American men here, either of which would make a good foreman. It would be your choice—if you can persuade him to move to California. Juan also informs me there is another problem by the name of María Gallegos. Are you interested in the job and, if I may be so bold, what are your intentions toward Señorita Gallegos?"

Salvador answered, "Mi jefe, I am indeed eager to move to the ranch in California. I only hope I live up to the faith you and mi jefe Juan have in my abilities." He paused. "I understand your question regarding my intentions toward María Gallegos. Señorita Gallegos is the daughter of a very prosperous man, who is the cuñado (brother-in-law) de Senor Deus. He has told his daughter many times he will not give her in marriage to a vaquero. María and I are eager to marry, but we are afraid to approach him, because he may send María away and forbid my seeing her."

I asked Juan, "How far is it to the home of Señor Deus, and how far it is to the home of the father of Señorita Gallegos?"

"It depends on your mode of transportation. It is about equal distance from here to the home of Señor Deus as it is from Walsenburg, which is a day's trip. The trail from here is by horse only, as you must go over the mountains. There is a wagon road from Walsenburg, and there are coaches to rent. Señor Gallegos is a neighbor of Señor Deus."

I said, "Very well, then. We must look at this as one would a military objective. Salvador, He Who Hunts, Singing Brook, Corporal, Saguaro Blossom, and I will ride to the home of Señor Deus. We will take along a couple of pack animals with camping and cooking gear and a fat steer. I am aware that Señor Deus has a home with many rooms, but we will be invading him, and I am sure that both He Who Hunts and Corporal would prefer sleeping out.

"Once we arrive, I will explain to Señor Deus the objective we seek and apologize about the invasion. It will be up to Salvador to speak with María and let her know the reason we are there, as we do not want to address this if she has had a change of mind or does not want to go to California. The next morning, Corporal will ride to Walsenburg to meet you, Dulce, Olga, Ariel, and the maid. If María is ready to commit, he will escort your coach to the home of Señor Deus.

"It is my plan for Señor Deus to hold a parilla (barbeque). At the parilla, Señor Deus and his wife will formally introduce me to María's father. I will then introduce everyone in our entourage and Salvador as the general manager of our new and very large ranch in California. I will explain that he has been Juan's assistant in setting up our ranches in southern Colorado. It will be up to Salvador to ask for the hand of María. I will then explain that we would like to hold a grand wedding at Hacienda Oriental for Salvador and María and host her parents at the Estancia del Pérez. I will state it is up to María's parents where the wedding is performed, and we, as well as Juan's parents, will be in attendance wherever it happens."

The plan went off perfectly. We left the home of Señor Deus on Sunday June 5th and headed home. It had been decided by the Gallegos family that they would prefer to have the wedding at their home, so their extended family would be able to attend the festivities. I persuaded Señor Jesus Gallegos to let us donate two fat beefs and the personnel to prepare them for the wedding feast. He also agreed to us donating two barrels of our wine and a barrel of blue agave tequila. The wedding would be on July 18th, and Señor Deus said he would throw his house open to the wedding party from the rancho.

Salvador, his new foreman, Corporal, and Saguaro Blossom would be leaving in two days to become acquainted with the ranch and make plans to fix up whichever house they chose to be the headquarters. After the wedding, Corporal would take five volunteer vaqueros from the Estancia del Pérez to help start the new ranch and remain to work it. It would be up to Salvador to hire vaqueros from California when the need arose.

We arrived in Walsenburg on July 16th and hired two coaches to transport Mother, Edward and Juliana Honeywell, José, Angélica, Roman, Panchita, Olga, Ariel, Juan, Dulce, two maids, and myself. Corporal, He Who Hunts, Saguaro Blossom, Singing Brook, and six vaqueros from Hacienda Colorado left with the steers and the pack goods early in the morning and would arrive close to the same time we would.

When we arrived at the home of Señor and Señora Deus, the first persons to greet us were Salvador, Elizabeth, Roberto, and Javier. Mother was overwhelmed with tears of joy. All her children had gathered in one place for the first time in six years, thanks to the miracle of transportation that was knitting the world and our family together.

Roberto had gone to Wellesley to pick up Elizabeth, and Javier joined them in Denver. They had hurried to a livery to hire horses and gear, so they could ride to the Deus home. They had sworn the livery people to secrecy, so they would not spoil the surprise.

Roberto, Elizabeth, Javier, and I found some time to talk about their education and goals. Roberto said he would be graduating before Christmas and wanted to pursue his law degree. Henry Pitney, Reverend McCosh (the President of the College of New Jersey), J. P. Morgan, and Presidente Díaz had all written letters of introduction to Harvard University on his behalf, and he had been accepted for the Spring semester at Harvard Law School.

"Instead of reading law, I will be getting a Doctorate in Jurisprudence from Harvard University," he explained.

I expressed how happy I was about the honor he not only brought to himself but to his family and the Estancia del Pérez.

Elizabeth carried herself with a degree of confidence I had never before seen in her. To be sure, she was a daughter of the Estancia del Pérez, but her attendance at Wellesley for just one year had made an undeniable difference in her carriage and assurance. We all knew she would be a great ambassador for her family.

Javier was gushing with happiness in his choice of school. He was learning not only geology but engineering, and he had spent his first summer working in a school-owned mine to gather hands-on experience.

With Mother in attendance, we all made plans for the entire family to have a Christmas at Hacienda Oriental. Salvador and María had agreed to be there as well as Jesus and María Gallegos, who would be accompanying Charles and Juanita Deus.

The wedding went off well and, by the 20th of July, we were on our way home—except for Mother, who was staying with Dulce.

CHAPTER 26

On the 23rd of July, I had a breakfast meeting with Roman, José, Corporal, and Running Bear. I explained to them what I felt were the logistics of getting the ranch started in California. I felt we needed to move at least 400 heifers and 20 bulls to California. The heifers would have to come from Hacienda Occidental and the bulls from Hacienda Oriental. We needed to get this moving rapidly.

I turned to José and said, "Cuñado, I am again going to complicate your life. I need you to go to El Paso and negotiate with the Southern Pacific Railroad for the transportation of 400 heifers from Tucson to a siding at a railroad stop called Santa Clarita, which is northwest of Los Angeles. In addition, I want you to negotiate the transportation of 20 bulls in two cars from Deming to the same destination. I am to meet the Vails at the Porter's Hotel in Tucson on the 26th. I will need your information wired to me in care of the hotel. Also, I need the following information regarding the marketing of our cattle this Fall. Juan says he will have 600, market-ready steers to deliver to the Santa Fe rail yards in Pueblo, Colorado."

I turned to Roman and said, "Can you give me a low estimate of the market-ready steers and culls you will be able to deliver?"

"I can safely say I can deliver 1,600 market-ready steers to Deming. I do not know the number of culls that would be market-ready."

I then turned to Running Bear and asked him the same question I had asked Roman.

Running Bear stated, "We can be sure of sending 1,200 market-ready steers. Like Roman, I have no way to estimate the number of market culls we may have."

I turned back to José and said, "The Vails indicated they will have 600 head of market-ready steers to deliver to Deming. They will negotiate rail transportation to Deming and decide whether they will freight them or drive them. We, too, are still undecided as is how to get our heifers to California. You may sign an agreement for the transportation of the bulls, but the transportation of the heifers will need to wait for my meeting with the Vails. You already have a figure from our neighbors as to what they will be sending you. I know you already have a price set on the delivery of a quantity of cattle to Deming, and we will honor that, but we have no agreement on the cattle from Colorado. In addition, you will need to negotiate the amount of extra cattle above the amount we are committed to have in Deming. I would add another 200 head that will be market culls.

"Mis Hermanos, I have contracted to purchase 10 purebred Hereford bulls, 20 half-breed Hereford bulls, and an additional 200 head of half-breed Hereford heifers from John Chisum. We are to take delivery as of September 15. During the roundup, I will need to move 200 head of heifers from Hacienda Oriental to Hacienda Occidental. It is imperative that none of the heifers moved are crossbreeds. In the Spring, we will have to move all crossbred, two-year-old heifers that have been produced on the Oriental to the Occidental. I will be purchasing additional purebred bulls this winter in Maine to be delivered to the Colorado ranches. I will be delivering some additional crossbred bulls from Oriental to Colorado and moving the original purebred bulls and all our crossbred bulls on the Colorado ranches to both Oriental and Occidental. Within two years, my plan is that we have no more bulls that do not have Hereford in their background and, within four years, that we have no heifers without Hereford in their lineage. Next year, I plan to ship all viable, non-lineage Hereford bulls to California. On this roundup, I do not want any non-lineage Hereford bulls reserved. I want you to use caution and preserve enough Hereford-lineage bulls, so we do not run into a shortage.

"Corporal, it will be your task to see the 20 bulls that Running Bear has picked out to be shipped to California are at the railhead. You will need to work out the timing with Running Bear and José, but I will want them shipped out immediately. Send the five vaqueros that will be moving to California to escort the bulls. Once you have done that, I will want you to meet me wherever I am. After I finish my negotiations with the Vails, I will be headed to Hacienda Occidental.

"I have news from El Tigre that the theft of cattle is becoming an everyday thing on our frontier with the Animas Valley, and I will need you at my side to help us retrieve our cattle and deliver another blow to the thieves. It will not be a place for wives, as I plan on moving swiftly, and it will be dangerous. I have already sent word to Comandante Neri that I am planning these actions to occur on or near the 10th of August. It will be least expected by the cuatreros at that time, as we will be conducting a roundup. I know this will put a hardship on you, Running Bear, and Roman, but I will need a strike force in place at Campo Central of at least 30 men that know how to fight and use a gun. I do not want married men, as they have other responsibilities. At the same time, you must not leave the herds unprotected. The appearance of insurmountable odds will deter the cuatreros.

"Roman, mi hermano, I would never direct you about the management of your family, but the conditions I have just described will not give you any time at the Hacienda and, as Panchita is with child, we would all worry if she is at the Hacienda alone and vulnerable."

Roman replied, "Mi hermano, no offence is taken. I will be leaving in the morning in the company of He Who Hunts, who is headed to Campo San Luis to escort the Chihenne back to Hacienda Oriental for the winter. He will leave me at Campo Central, where a capable vaquero will join me as a segundo for the duration of the roundup and this crisis."

I closed with, "Mis Hermanos, estén seguros. Yo sé que el trabajo que les he dado es mucho, pero es mi esperanza de que todos nuestros aflicciones hayan sido cumplidas por el 15 de agosto (My brothers, be safe. I know the work I have given is much, but it is my hope that all our trials are behind us by August 15th)."

I spent the entirety of the next day playing with Ariel. He had a great grip, and he followed me about the room on his knees asking me to pick him up and pay attention. He had a slight cough, but it was not slowing him down a bit.

In the morning I said goodbye to Olga and Ariel and left on my journey to Tucson, where I arrived on the evening of the evening on the 25th and checked into Porter's Hotel. I met the Vails down in the restaurant for breakfast. Mrs. Porter served a marvelous spread, and no one walked away hungry.

When I showed the Vails the wire I had received from José laying out the costs to ship 400 head to California, they immediately said they would drive their herd to California. I agreed and offered to throw my 400 heifers into their trail drive with vaqueros to help them.

There was another apparent problem in that they also needed to drive 600 head to Deming. I alleviated their concerns by saying, "Why not drive your 600 head south to Hacienda Occidental, and Roman will move them to Deming with the other stock from the Hacienda?"

Their immediate concern had to do with the Rurales and their mandate to collect import duties. I told them I was again having trouble with thievery, and I had received a wire from Comandante Neri that a troop of Rurales would be meeting me at Hacienda Occidental on July 29th. "I can wire José, who is still awaiting my reply on the transport of the heifers to California in El Paso. He is the jefe in charge of the ports east of El Paso, which is not inclusive of Nogales. He can wire us official passage for your cattle, as they are moving in and out of Mexico for easy transport to market."

Walter looked at Edward and said, "Let us get it done. Is there any way we can join you in shipping 20 bulls on the same train?"

I wired José and received a reply that Southern Pacific had agreed to have two cars at the stock corrals in Tucson on July 30th to be loaded and joined with our cars on the 31st for double the price I had contracted for. The expected time of delivery was August 4th at Santa Clarita. The Southern Pacific had agreed to leave the stock at sidings with corrals, water, and feed for a period of at least eight hours after approximately 10 hours of transportation. I told the Vails I had five men accompanying my two cars and, if they could contribute two men, which would assure a man was watching each carload 24 hours a day.

We sent our request for a document authorizing the passage of the Vail cattle through the rancho to Deming and José along with the agreement to the contract he had set up with Southern Pacific for the transport of the bulls from Deming and Tucson to California. José sent a wire back to me saying he was sending the authorization of the passage as well as the papers of transport for the 400 heifers from Hacienda Occidental to the United States as well as a certificate of health that would be needed by the authorities at the border. These papers would arrive at the hotel the next morning.

I asked the Vails if they would mind having company for the ride south, as I was headed for Hacienda Occidental. They immediately agreed to my joining them and said they had several extra horses at the stable, so I would not need to buy one.

The next morning, we started out for the Empire Ranch and arrived there in the early afternoon. I was a guest at the ranch for the night and, the next morning, I left for the Hacienda with the escort of a rather fierce-looking vaquero the Vails had dispatched to keep me company. We arrived at the Hacienda on the evening of the 28th to find Captain Carrillo was already in camp there.

After a good meal, we lit cigars and each had a drink in hand. I explained to Captain Carrillo the Vails would be sending 600-plus head of steers to the Hacienda, where they were to be joined with our herd to be exported to Deming for shipment east.

He said, "Don Francisco, there is no need for papers, as your word is always good with me."

I replied, "I bask in your friendship and trust but, nevertheless, mi amigo, the existence of authorized papers protects both you and me."

He assented, and we moved on to the next topic.

I explained to him that the man who was the head of a gang of cuatreros had a small ranch in the Animas Valley and, from that ranch; there was continual illegal acquisition of cattle from the rancho. "I do not know if they move the cattle across the border or they wander across the border and are appropriated by them. It is my and Roman's objective to cross the border into the Animas Valley and reclaim our cattle. We propose to do this with only personnel from the rancho, but it is our sincere hope that the Rurales will be at the border to welcome us home and discourage any pursuit."

Captain Carrillo replied, "Comandante Neri has authorized us to pursue the cuatreros across the frontier and dispatch them if we can find them, but I will accede to your wishes and assume a backup role."

I replied I thought that would be the best path, if it can be accomplished, as we would not arouse the disdain of Capitán Whiteside at Camp Huachuca.

Capitán Carrillo left the next morning on a sweep along the frontier and agreed to arrive at Campo Central by a trail from Campo Angélica on August 8th. I rode into Campo Central on August 5th, and the first people I saw waiting for me were Corporal, He Who Hunts, Running Bear, El Tigre, and Tall Runner. We were ready to engage. The first order of business was to find where our cattle were. El Tigre, Running Bear, and Tall Runner had already anticipated the need for scouts.

Among the men pulled out of the roundup to make up the 30 men I required were the sons and grandsons of scouts in my father's army.

By that evening, He Who Hunts had left for Campo Guadalupe, where he was to pick up two scouts to perform a reconnaissance that would include Guadalupe Canyon and as far north as the southern face of Guadalupe Montaña. Particular attention would be paid to the Canyon and scouting the Clanton Ranch.

At the same time, Tall Runner was to visit Campos Angélica and El Tigre and then head for Campo Berrendo. Tall Runner was to pick up two scouts and proceed up the chain of mountains on the east side of the Animas Valley with a special focus on the Gray Ranch. El Tigre was to take two scouts and approach the Animas Montaña from its east side, surveilling the small ranches in the area as well as the small ranches north of the Gray Ranch.

Corporal was to take two good vaqueros from the Campo Central and start out on August 7th at the frontier. They were to spread out and appear to any observers as if they were looking for strays.

On the August 8th Roman, who had joined us, and I left with eight vaqueros and picked up Corporal and his two vaqueros. We preceded up the west side of Valle de Animas and remained in the cover of the foothills. By evening, we had met with He Who Hunts and his scouts, and they described where they had found many grupos pequeños (small groups) of our cattle.

On the east side of the valley, Tall Runner and his scouts as well as El Tigre and his scouts had met up with Running Bear, who was leading eight vaqueros. They planned their attack as instructed and, on the 10th of August, we swept down and reclaimed our cattle.

By midday on August 11th, we were moving south down the Animas Valley with our reclaimed cattle. When we were south of the Clanton Ranch, we saw dust behind us. When the riders came into sight, we saw 25 Americans riding hell bent to keep the Mexicans from stealing their cattle.

I had put a contingency plan in place. I had no desire to deal with the political fallout of a pitched battle for my cattle, as that was not what would appear in the papers. I also had no intention of losing any of my loyal vaqueros. Even though we outnumbered the Americans, we had the added burden of the cattle.

As was planned, we scattered for the frontier with He Who Hunts and his scouts to the west and Running Bear and his scouts to the east, where they were to observe where the cattle were taken. On the evening of the 11th, Running Bear and his scouts returned to Campo El Lobo, where we had gathered with Capitán Carrillo and his men. Running Bear reported that it appeared the cattle had been taken west toward the Clanton Ranch. Shortly after dark, He Who Hunts reported the cattle had been moved past the Clanton ranch into Guadalupe Canyon. He had left his two scouts to observe. The Americans were moving slowly with the cattle, and there were seven riders tending them.

Capitán Carrillo spoke up and said. "We will not sit on the sidelines this time".

I replied, "Very well, but I have been waiting for this opportunity for a long time, so please listen to my plan. The cuatreros from the Clanton ranch in the Animas Valley have been using Guadalupe Canyon to move their cattle west to their ranch on the San Pedro River and on to market. This is the first time we have had the opportunity to catch them in the canyon. So, this is my proposal. Tall Runner and He Who Hunts are to leave immediately to locate the herd. Early tomorrow morning, El Tigre and six vaqueros will accompany Capitán Carrillo on a trajectory toward Pico de Guadalupe. Running Bear, Corporal, Roman, and the rest of the vaqueros will accompany me. Our objective is surprise; therefore, I want to catch them tomorrow night in their beds. Capitán Carrillo will be in charge of the east attack group, and Corporal will be in charge of the west group. When we attack it be up to Tall Runner and He Who Hunts. It will up to Tall Runner to advise Capitán Carrillo as to the best way to approach the cuatreros from the east and He Who

Hunts to advise Corporal on the west group. They should arrange some sort of signal about when to start the attack. I only ask that I be among the first to put bullets into Señor Newman Haynes Clanton."

Capitán Carrillo replied, "I feel the plan is very good, but I have one request. Don Francisco, Roman, Corporal, and I have suffered much at the hands of Señor Clanton. It is my proposal that, when the signal is given, Don Francisco, Corporal, Roman, and I will fire the first shots at Señor Clanton, and the sound of our gunshots will be the signal for all in our party to begin firing."

Corporal assented with, "I like that plan."

I then stated, "Mi amigos, we have our plan. Let us get some sleep. Tall Runner and He Who Hunts, sean seguros y guíenos bien (be safe, and guide us well)."

It was dark on the night of the 12th, and we were moving slowly up the canyon. He Who Hunts had joined us about an hour before. Our group was split into three. One group was to remain in the canyon bottom to catch anyone trying to escape to the west. Corporal and I went with the southern group to form an arc on the southwest corner of the cuatreros' campo. He Who Hunts placed men on the northwest corner and then climbed up to a bluff that was visible to only the men on the southwest and southeast corners.

As dawn peeked into the canyon, the signal came as a sudden flash of light—He Who Hunts and Tall Runner had lit some powder.

At that moment, Señor Clanton was bent over the breakfast fire reaching for the coffee pot. Four shots rang out, and he fell into the fire. The shooting quit after what seemed a long time, but it was no longer than 60 seconds. Seven men were lying around the campfire, and I gave the order to leave them be and start moving the cattle west.

The cattle were delivered to Campo San Bernardino to be dispersed. Those of us who would be heading to Hacienda Oriental rode back to Campo Central and collapsed with exhaustion. The rest headed for their homes, and Capitán Carrillo headed toward Hacienda Occidental, where his men were to remain for a day before he rode on to meet and report to Comandante Neri.

Running Bear, Corporal, He Who Hunts, and I took off for home to be hailed as the returning conquerors. We made a mad dash, changing horses twice along the way. It was still light when we arrived. My companions headed to their families, and I handed off my horse to the young groom waiting to take him.

As I looked up at the veranda, I was greeted by the sight of Edward standing at the door, and Angélica was with him. I bounded up the stairs onto the veranda and only then became aware that Edward was not smiling a greeting, and my sister was in black. I froze in place. The conqueror had fled and been replaced by a man about to lose his footing.

Angélica escorted me into the parlor, where she told me the story of the previous day—the last day of Ariel's life.

She said, "His coughing worsened, and someone was with him at all times. Toward evening, after a long bout of coughing, he fell asleep. Not long after that, Niñera Juanita let out a scream and, when we rushed into the room, Ariel had just quit breathing and his heart was no longer beating. We lost our angel!" she sobbed, throwing herself against my chest.

I tried my best to console her and then asked her about Olga.

Angélica, her face wet with tears, said, "She has been inconsolable, and we are worried about her and the baby she is carrying. My brother, I know you have suffered a terrible blow, but you need to be extra strong for Olga. Father Salvador will be here in the morning, and we are to have a funeral mass. We will bury Ariel near your father, who will look over him until we can come to help. Go, brother, tend to your wife."

The funeral passed as a nightmare. After Father Salvador's benediction, Lozen placed an eagle feather in Ariel's coffin, accompanied by a low chant from the Chihenne, so he would have an easy flight to the heavens.

CHAPTER 27

Mother returned on August 20th with the news that Dulce had delivered a little girl, which Juan had named after her mother. We informed Mother of the loss of Ariel.

On August 31st, Olga went into labor. By our calculations, it was early, and the baby would be premature. Nevertheless, the baby was coming, and the household was in turmoil. That evening, my son, Rene Pérez Celaya, entered the world.

I walked out onto the veranda, proclaimed the birth of a son, and announced there would be a grand fiesta the next day to celebrate his arrival.

It was September 3rd. I had been exclusively attending to the needs of Olga and my family, although the rancho was never out of my mind. That morning, I met with José, Corporal, Running Bear, Emilio Vásquez, and Emilio Márquez.

I started out the meeting by praising Emilio Márquez for the excellent construction of the buildings and the rate at which the addition to the Hacienda was being accomplished. I reminded him we were going to have a full house by Christmas, and it should be completed by then. I ended by saying, "I do not need to remind you to call upon us if you need our help. I know I have put a heavy task on you."

I turned to Emilio Vásquez and said, "Old friend, I am not going to bother you with demanding a report on the harvest. It is enough for me that you and José are communicating on this. It is my wish, however, that your status on the rancho be raised, so you are now in charge of all agricultural pursuits of the rancho and our holdings in the United States. You will report to José and, if we have farming interests in Hacienda Occidental, to Roman. You will be looking at agricultural interests in Colorado and California. It is imperative that you find people you can trust to manage and run the everyday business. From now on, it is up to you to manage the managers. I do not see us expanding our ranching pursuits for a while, but our agricultural pursuits—especially those we can irrigate—are only in their infancy. In three to four years, you will receive help from the children of the rancho that are going to college."

I turned to Corporal and said, "Mi amigo, can you ask Señor Blanco to join us?"

Corporal replied, "I will do that immediately, mi jefe."

While we were waiting, I dismissed Emilio Vásquez and Emilio Márquez with my appreciation of their work. I then asked Running Bear how the roundup was going.

He replied, "We have our quota of steers and market cattle, and we are near finished with the road branding. The health inspectors have cleared them for shipment, and we will be driving them to Deming on the 13th of September. We have had a very good calf crop despite the dryness in the valleys this year. I am concerned we may have a drop-off on calves next year if we do not start getting more rain in the valleys. The mountains are doing very well, and we will need to ship those Hereford steers that were not fit to be bulls."

I asked, "Are you going to have a problem releasing 10 vaqueros to ride with Corporal on the 10th to pick up our purchases from John Chisum?"

"I will be able to do that," he said.

I went on to explain to him that Lozen would be returning to the Mescalero reservation with them, and I wanted to send 10 head with her as a gift from the Estancia del Pérez.

Corporal returned with Señor Blanco, and I wanted to wrap up my conversation with Running Bear, as I knew I had interrupted his day. I thanked him for all his help in the successful completion of the incorporation of our American interests.

I then addressed Señor Blanco. "Several years ago, El Tigre gave a young vaquero by the name of Mario Cortez a difficult task. One of the reasons he gave for appointing him to the task was that he spoke English. I would like for you to give me an evaluation of him and tell me why he was never recommended as a candidate for further education."

Señor Blanco explained, "When Mario graduated from our school, there was no student more accomplished. You ask me why he was not recommended. The easy answer is that Mario was just two years behind you and, at the time, we were not offering a continuing education to all the children of the rancho. Another answer would be that, six months after graduation, Mario was a parent. The third reason is that I am not sure Mario is a good candidate for further education in that he has boundless energy and is always ready to explore the unknown."

I replied, "What you have said gives me hope that my evaluation may be correct. I have been asking Corporal to be constantly on the move, and that is only going to get worse. He needs one or two young men to do some of his footwork and learn the rancho as well as be comfortable going to our other properties to do some tasks as he directs."

Señor Blanco assented. "Mario is the best candidate I could recommend."

I thanked Señor Blanco for his help and asked him if he could return around 10:00 am on the 4th to enlighten us about candidates he may have for the upcoming term and what he knew about the progress of the students already in school.

I then turned to Corporal and said, "Will you take on an assistant?" Corporal replied, "Absolutely, mi jeffe."

I then turned to Running Bear and asked, "Can you do without Mario, and can you have him here to ride with Corporal to the ranch of John Chisum?"

Running Bear stated, "I am reluctant to give him up, as I was going to make him a head vaquero at one of the campos. But, I think this new job will better fit his skills, and he will be more of a credit to the rancho."

"Well said, mi Compadre," I responded. "Please have him here at the Hacienda to accompany Corporal to the rancho de John Chisum. We have further need to talk to you, but that conversation can wait until the drive has left. I will need to have Bull Tamer at that meeting. Can you summon him to the Hacienda at that time?"

Running Bear replied, "Se hará (It will be done), mi jefe."

José and I spent the rest of the day on the business of the rancho and our plans for the future.

Señor Blanco arrived promptly at 10 am on the 4th, and Edward escorted him into the parlor where Mother, Angélica, Olga, and I were waiting.

He started out by saying, "Three students are starting the Spring semester at Cornell University. One is Dishosa, a daughter of Emilio Vásquez, and she has qualified to enter the School of Agriculture. She is to be joined at that school by Benito Hernández, a son of Armando Hernández. In addition, Gregorio Sapia has been accepted into the School of Agriculture's degree track in Animal Husbandry. Also, my son, Franklin, has been accepted at the College of New Jersey.

"I have a special request," he continued. "I would like to accompany these students to their enrollment at Cornell and see to the welfare of our other students that are there. After having done that, I would like to take a month to visit with relatives and friends."

I told Señor Blanco I would appreciate him escorting all our students to college and that no one had earned a vacation more than he. In addition, I suggested he should take Frank to see the house we had there and which I would maintain until we had no more students there. I then turned the meeting and planning of logistics over to Mother, Angélica, and Olga and left them to it.

Later that morning, our courier to Juárez/El Paso brought us some newspapers. I was anxious to see if our raid made the news. It did. The headlines read, "Massacre at Guadalupe Canyon." The story said that Rurales, under Comandante Neri, had ambushed and killed ranchers and cowboys as they lay in their beds. "The persons massacred by the Mexicans were Newman Haynes Clanton, a rancher in the New Mexico and Arizona Territories; Dick Gray, a rancher in the New Mexico Territory); Jim Crane [who was wanted for stagecoach robbery and murder], Charley Snow [a ranch hand who was on our list for the murder of Gregorio], and Billy Lang, another rancher in New Mexico. Harry Ernshaw, a dairy farmer, was wounded in the nose, and a drover by the name of Billy Byers [Myers] played possum and escaped death."

An earlier edition of the paper featured the headline, "Mexican Bandits Foiled." In this report, the story went that a large band of Mexican bandits invaded the Animas Valley and attempted to steal the cattle from hardworking ranchers. The ranchers gathered together and pursued the Mexicans. They were successful in recovering their cattle. It then went on to praise these hardy people who were not being protected by our government. There was no mention of the Estancia del Pérez in either article, and all was just as it should have been.

On September 17th, Running Bear showed up with Bull Tamer. I asked Bull Tamer how the fencing was going on El Tigre. He stated the frontier of the El Tigre addition to the rancho had been fenced except for the north face, which he had been ordered not to fence. Some pastures had been fenced in around available, all-year water.

I asked him how my cousins were working out.

He replied, "Mi jefe, it was difficult at first. On the second day, they took some horses and attempted to ride to Mexico. I treated them as ordered, and they walked for a month. It soon became apparent to them their condition was set, and they began to participate. Both of them are now foreman of their own fencing crews and are valuable members of my crew."

I then asked Bull Tamer, "How are our neighbors taking the fencing of the rancho?"

Bull Tamer replied, "That has not gone well, and I have one of my fencing crews continually mending our fences on the east side. On the west side, there are occasional breaks."

I inquired about why he thought these breaks were happening, and he said, "The people in the valleys have always used the mountains for various purposes, and they do not like being shut out. The biggest crossers are goat herders and sheep herders, who have traditionally used the mountain."

I then turned to Running Bear and asked him if he had been able to utilize any of the pasture yet on El Tigre.

He replied, "We have yet to move any cattle into the mountains but, as the valley areas are fenced, we are moving our Hereford bulls and heifers to those pastures. When winter is past, we hope to begin to utilize the mountains."

I replied, "During Christmas, when all of us are gathered, we will need to meet and decide how we are going to utilize the mountains in a much better way than we have in the past. For now, I would like to talk about the most immediate problem I have. I am not only fencing the El Tigre acquisition but the total frontier of the rancho. And I not only want the frontier of the rancho fenced but the Fronteras and Cananea concessions as well."

I then said to Bull Tamer, "The reason I left the north frontier of El Tigre unfenced is I want to run a fence three miles east of the Rio Batepito and follow the contours of the rio to a point parallel to Campo Guadalupe. At that point, I will want you to run the fence two miles west of Campo Guadalupe and then north to the frontier. We will discuss further the west side of San Luis in the future.

"We have bought two more ranches, and we need to start fencing in the frontiers. In Colorado, we have four contiguous ranches for which we need to fence in the frontier. As you can see, there is a lot of fencing being done and that will need to be done. I need someone to manage all the fencing projects and coordinate with José on the ordering of materials to keep all those jobs going. It will be up to that manager to see the fences are installed in the right places and the jobs progress in a timely manner.

"You have the experience and knowledge to gauge that work and oversee all the projects. It would be your job to hire managers for all the jobs and oversee them. It will be their job to hire the foremen of crews and oversee those foremen. It will be the job of the foremen to see that the work gets done. What I am offering is not an enviable job. Its very nature requires you to move around a lot and be responsible for the actions of others. This is the job that your father, Don José, and I do, so we sympathize, but, of course, you will also bask in the success of the enterprises. My question to you is, are you ready to take on the responsibilities of the job?"

Bull Tamer responded with, "Mi jeffes, I am honored by your faith in me, and I will not make you regret your choice."

I responded, "Very well, you will need to go back to El Tigre and begin to delegate. Once you have done that, you need to evaluate the fencing of the frontier and make changes where necessary. You will need to go and consult with Juan in Colorado and Salvador in California. José will be awaiting your report, and it is my hope to be here to receive it, also."

Bull Tamer walked out of that meeting standing tall alongside his proud father.

Corporal arrived with the purchase from John Chisum on the 22nd, and Running Bear took the cattle over and proceeded with the movement of the Herefords as I had prescribed.

On September 24th, Panchita went into labor. He Who Hunts rode with me to intercept Roman on the drive to Deming and sent him to the Hacienda. It was nearly impossible for Roman to get there before delivery, but, with women, I find that thought and effort count for a lot.

When we got into Deming with the herd, José was there taking care of business. We left him in charge and headed home to find out if the new addition was a boy or girl. We were greeted on the veranda with cigars and drinks. Roman declared his oldest son would be named Gregorio.

On the 27th, I convinced Roman that his duty at the moment was to his son and wife. He Who Hunts, Singing Brook, Corporal, Saguaro Blossom, and Mario Cortez left for Hacienda Occidental to fill a void in management and check on the thievery. Olga was tending to Rene and still emotionally frail, so I, too, stayed where I belonged.

It was October 31st when Corporal, He Who Hunts, and company returned to Hacienda Oriental after having been relieved by the return of Roman, Panchita, and their son. They brought great news.

On October 25th, Ike Clanton and Tom McLaury had a confrontation with the Earps and ended up getting pistol-whipped. The following day, Billy Clanton, Frank McLaury, and Billy Claiborne rode in to join Ike and Tom. At the first bar they hit, they were told about the fate of their brothers and friends, and the three left to find them. The Clantons, McLaurys, and Claiborne got together behind the OK Corral. The Earps, along with Doc Holliday, found them there, and a gun fight started. When the smoke cleared, two of the Earps and Doc Holiday were wounded. Billy Clanton and the McLaury brothers were dead, and Ike Clanton and Billy Claiborne had fled the fight.

In just a few seconds, the Earps and Holliday had wiped out three of the people on our list, and now Johnny Ringo, Florentino Cruz, Curly Bill Brocius, and Ike Clanton were at the top.

We were also told the fencing was proceeding east and west and had crossed the old lakebed at the head of the Animas Valley. The vaqueros were adapting to not only checking on the cattle but taking seriously the patrolling of the fence line. Presently, that was being done in twos—one man patrolled and the other stayed in the brush watching for danger. It appeared the cattle were not drifting across the frontier, and the Cowboys must have been busy elsewhere.

On December 15th, Emilio Márquez and his crew finished construction on the Hacienda. It was nearly double the size it had been previously. We awaited our holiday guests.

Roman, Panchita, and Gregorio arrived on the 18th. On the 20th, Roman and I, with an escort of 20 vaqueros, greeted our guests from back east at the Deming Depot. Juan, Dulce, and little Dulce arrived with Elizabeth, Javier, Roberto, Salvador, María, the five Gallegos, and the five members of the Deus family. We had brought the grand coach and another coach plus 15 extra horses for those who cared to ride.

It was evening when we arrived—just in time for the grand Christmas parade. The Hacienda and many of the buildings were lit up with luminaries (a lighted candle embedded in sand inside a paper bag). The veranda was covered with verderón Navidad (Christmas bunting), and Mother, along with all the family and staff, were standing on the steps or in front of them. Maríachis led the way into the square, followed by the rest of the people, who watched us go by and then joined the parade circling the ball court, which had been prepared for a grand fiesta.

The coaches stopped at the steps, and the new mothers and babies as well as all who needed to freshen up were hustled up to their rooms. The babies met the nannies that were to help care for them during their stay. The men, who did not need to freshen up, remained on the veranda for drinks and cigars as we prepared to have a party. The Maríachis continued to play on the ball court and were interrupted only by the Chihenne—who did a series of celebration dances—and the call to eat.

It was a very Feliz Navidad (Merry Christmas) that all would remember. On Christmas Eve, the children of the rancho created and performed the Natividad de Jesús (Nativity of Jesus). It was moving for all of us. Even the old vaqueros were wiping tears. Father Salvador held Mass on Christmas morning, and we all gathered in the ball field for a gran cena de Navidad (great Christmas dinner).

CHAPTER 28

By January 4th, 1882, all the guests were gone as were my siblings. Mother was both glowing with having basked in the love of her family and, at the same time, rather ready to settle into a gentler pace. Olga and I were spending time together ministering to Rene's needs. We still had a great hole in our hearts from the loss of Ariel, but Rene's presence kept us in the here and now.

I settled down to the everyday life of a husband and rancher. José had negotiated a price of $4.96 per hundred weight for steers and heifers, with no cull cattle, in Deming, with delivery no later than April 15th of a minimum of 1,500 head at 850 pounds per head on average. The maximum was to be no more than 5,500 head. We would need to give a firm amount that would be within a 200 head, más o menos (more or less), of that number by February 28th.

We called in Running Bear and stated we had a very good price for Spring delivery and would like for him to tell us how many head weighing 900 pounds we could ship from this Hacienda. We sent the same message to Roman, the Vails, the Bakers, and our neighbors in Mexico and asked them the number of head they could commit at that price and we needed to know no later than February 10th.

José negotiated prices for delivery at traditional delivery times at set future prices in the same manner and contacted those who cooperatively marketed with us. By February 10th, we had a total commitment of 5,500 head for delivery.

It was March 5th, and it was time to plot the eradication of the Cowboys. The Earps were having more difficulties with them, including the ambush of Virgil Earp by members of the gang on December 28th of the previous year. He had been maimed and was still recovering. It was well known that this assault was an attempted revenge killing for the killings at the OK Corral.

I ordered signals to be sent to summon El Tigre and Tall Runner to the Hacienda. When they arrived, we got down to the business of moving watchers into the States so they would be in a position to keep an eye on Tombstone, the Clanton ranch on the San Pedro, and Galeyville. Young, English-speaking men or boys were sent with the watchers to infiltrate each town under the pretense of looking for work. Watchers were stationed on the mountains, so a chain of communication reached to the rancho.

All this was in place and, by the 19th of March, we received news that Morgan Earp had been assassinated on the night of the 18th. Based on my previous conversations with Wyatt on the frontier and at Hacienda Occidental, I knew war had broken out between the Earps and the Cowboys.

On March 19th, Wyatt helped escort Morgan's body to the train station in Contention. James Earp and five family friends escorted their departed brother to the family home in Colton, California.

On March 20th, Wyatt, along with his brother Warren and Doc Holliday, escorted Virgil and his family to Benson, where they were to catch a train to Tucson and then on to Colton. When they arrived in Benson, a young man from a hacienda south of the border informed Wyatt that Ike Clanton and Frank Stillwell had taken an earlier train to Tucson. Wyatt changed his plans, and the escort continued on with Virgil to Tucson.

In Tucson, Wyatt was met by Deputy United States Marshall J. W. Evans, who handed Wyatt a letter appointing him a United States Marshall. He was given a badge. Virgil and family, along with Warren, Wyatt, and Doc Holliday, went to the Porter's Hotel for a meal and returned to the station to load Virgil and family for their trip.

While Virgil was getting aboard, a passenger warned Wyatt there were two men lying on a flatcar on the train south of Virgil's train. Wyatt spotted them and realized that, as Virgil's train was moving out, they would have a clear view of the passengers. The train began to move, and so did Wyatt and Doc Holliday. They could see the two men were Stilwell and Clanton. Clanton rolled off the other side of the flatcar, and Stilwell got up to move. People heard gunshots, but no one went to investigate. In the morning, Frank Stilwell's body was found lying by the flatcar.

At the coroner's inquest into the death of Morgan Earp, the wife of Pete Spence stated she was present when her husband, Frank Stilwell, Fredrick Bode, and Florentino Cruz planned the killing of Morgan Earp. All four were immediately arrested by Sheriff Behan.

During their trial, their lawyer argued that the only evidence of their involvement in the murder of Morgan Earp was the testimony of Pete Spence's wife, and the lawyer pointed out a wife cannot testify against her husband. The judge agreed and dismissed the case, but he kept Pete Spence locked up on other warrants.

A Pima county Justice of the Peace issued a warrant for Wyatt Earp and Doc Holliday related to the death of Frank Stilwell. Sherriff Behan received a wire from the Pima County sheriff with a warrant to pick up Earp and Holliday. When Behan approached Wyatt and Doc on the 21st to arrest them, Wyatt showed him his badge and told him Holliday and the other four men with him were deputy U. S. marshals and that Behan was interfering with them in their duty. Wyatt wired a federal judge and got federal warrants for Pete Spence, Fredrick Bode, and Florentino Cruz.

Wyatt and his posse left on the 22nd and headed for Pete Spence's ranch, only to discover that Spence had been arrested on a Pima County warrant and was in jail there. He was informed that Cruz was up a canyon cutting wood. As the posse was riding up the canyon, they heard gunshots at the ranch.

It was Wednesday, April 5th, in the late afternoon when the alarm sounded as six mounted men approached Hacienda Oriental. He Who Hunts met me on the veranda and stated that among the group was the lawman from Tombstone. As they got closer, we could see they were mounted on horses that wore the brand of the Sierra Bonita Ranch, which was at the head of the Sulphur Springs Valley in Arizona.

I mounted a horse tied in front of the house and was joined by He Who Hunts, Corporal, Running Bear, and José. As I rode up to Wyatt, I waved. I then dismounted and approached him with my hand out, giving him a hardy welcome to Hacienda Oriental.

Wyatt said, "We are weary, and I wonder if we can take you up on your invitation to visit."

I said, "But of course. I have news of your exploits over the past month. May I ask, do you think Behan is still pursuing you?"

Wyatt replied, "We have not seen any sign of him, but he has been rather persistent."

He Who Hunts and Corporal put spurs to their mounts and rode off.

José left immediately to tell the Hacienda that today was a day of celebration, as friends had come to visit. Wyatt stated on the ride back that our mutual enemies, Frank Stilwell, Curly Bill Brocius, Florentino Cruz, and Johnny Barnes had gone to the devil. I thanked him for the news, as we had longed for the chance to meet them ourselves. Then I said, "You are to be the guests of Hacienda Oriental of the Estancia del Pérez, and nuestra casa es su casa (our house is your house)."

On the 7th, Wyatt and his men left with an escort of vaqueros for El Paso, where they had the intention of catching the train to Albuquerque. As they rode out of sight, I called José, He Who Hunts, Corporal,

Running Bear, and El Tigre together and stated it was now time for us to go hunting. "I am very happy that Señor Earp has dispatched some mutual enemies, but he has cooled and is leaving the field. It is time for the Hacienda to exact its vengeance on the Cowboys—especially the Clantons and Johnny Ringo."

On April 10th, I kissed Olga and Rene goodbye and stated we would be back once we had eliminated the threat to the rancho and had the revenge we so richly deserved. I sent riders ahead to notify all the old soldiers that the rancho was going hunting for its enemies and, if they could ride, to please join us. If not, they could send a son or have that son accompany them, as we were about the business of avenging Don Gregorio. They were told to gather at Campo Angélica by April 20th.

As we rode away from the Hacienda, I turned to El Tigre and Running Bear and said, "I would like for you two gentlemen to take us to the place where my father fell. I want that to be where we make our plans. I would prefer that Roman was there with us to help to plan our war for the peace of the rancho. Is it possible for you to work your mirrors so Roman is informed to meet us, along with two able compañeros, at Campo Central as soon as he can?"

El Tigre replied, "It will be done, mi jefe, but I will need to leave you to do so. I will meet you at Campo Central."

I told him to do what he needed to do. "However, since you are going to leave us, please bring 10 reliable men, of which one must be Tall Runner, when you return. It would be best that they read the mirrors and are prepared to spend the next two to three months away from their families."

On April 27th, we were all gathered at Campo Central and began our journey north to Cañon Bonito. I expressed my desire to El Tigre, Tall Runner, Corporal, and He Who Hunts that we not be discovered making the trip. "My plans rely on stealth and surprise, so we cannot do as Wyatt Earp did and ride to face our prey without arousing the ire of the other Americans."

We rode across the border in the high country to the west of the Animas Valley. After we had crossed Guadalupe Canyon, all trace of our passage was wiped out, and we followed the Apache trails on the ridges of the Sierras Peloncillo until we reached Cañon Bonito. Our camp was made just north of the Cueva de Refugio (Refuge Cave) in a hollow the Apache had been camping in for hundreds of years as they waited for prey to avail themselves of the passage.

Corporal took Roman and me to the place where our fathers fell, and we swore upon the mountain that we would seek the death of all who participated. We went back to the camp and joined our companions. I began to lay out my plans. I started with, "Mis amigos, tenemos dos objetivos—la seguridad de la estancia y la justa retribución por la muerte de nuestros padres. En este caso, tenemos la oportunidad de realizar ambos (My friends, we have two missions—the security of the estancia and the just retribution for the death of our fathers. In this instance, we have the opportunity to achieve both goals)."

I then went on to state we were to begin a silent war against the assassins who were called the Cowboys. "This war is to be relentless, because the safety of the peoples of the rancho dictates it must be. That will always be our first objective. It has come to pass that some of the assassins have already met their just ends—either as a result of the dangers of their pursuits or the revenge of the Earps. We are still tracking three of the leaders, and it is my hope that two of them will meet their ends at the hands of the peoples of the rancho. For the next four days, we will do nothing, as it is up to Roman and Running Bear to send four men back to organize a trap at the border. Those men will need to have the Mexican end of the Valle de Animas sealed off, and anyone that crosses it is to be killed. I want no living witness to give the alarm.

"For those that remain, I want them to accompany El Tigre, Tall Runner, He Who Hunts, Running Bear, and Corporal to keep watch on the Valle de Animas and the restored ranch of the Clantons. He

Who Hunts will be in charge of the east side of the valley, and no one is to pass from the ranch that way. El Tigre will seal off the north and Running Bear the west. It is your job to make sure anyone who flees can only see one way out, and that will be into the hands of our compañeros at the end of the valley.

"Roman, Corporal, Tall Runner, and five volunteers will join me in attacking the ranch and wiping it out for all time. Corporal will be in charge of the attack, and it will be up to him to pick the volunteers. Each man on this expedition has a job that is very important, which is: When we are finished, there will be no answers if anyone asks what happened here. It must not be traced to the rancho.

"The 10 men picked by El Tigre will return to the camp above Canyon Bonito as will El Tigre, Running Bear, and He Who Hunts. The rest of you are to return to your jobs on the rancho, but be aware we are still at war, and we will most likely be calling on some of you very soon. Keep your guns oiled."

It was dawn when we began our assault on the Clanton ranch. There was no one stirring, but there were 16 horses in the corral next to the house. It appeared there were way more people there now than what we had seen in our reconnoitering. Many of the horses had a dusting of dried salt on their coats, and it was obvious they had been ridden hard.

Corporal adjusted his plan from an assault to a siege. We would not fire a shot until several of the Cowboys were outside or at the corral getting ready to start their day.

There were eight Cowboys doing morning chores outside when a dog alerted them to our presence. All eight men had guns, but they did not have the opportunity to use them. The men fell where they stood. Instantly, men came boiling out of the doors and windows of the house. Some were immediately wounded or killed, but many made it to the corrals and the horses. As is the habit of all men of the horse when startled, they grabbed their hat, gun, and bridle in that order. At the corrals, they were not interested in saddles, and most just put the bridle on, leapt aboard, and forked the horse into a gallop. Even though we were there to kill them, I took a moment to admire their craft.

Six men escaped the trap and headed south away from us, but that was not their goal. El Tigre and his men sped past us headed south in pursuit. The rest of us stayed to eliminate all possibility of a Clanton stronghold in the Animas Valley. We heard some gunshots to the east, and then some guns went off to the west. Our prey was now committed to running for the safety of the Mexican border.

We were just mopping up at what had been the Clanton ranch when a rider came in from El Tigre. He stated there was a large herd of mixed cattle on the west side of the valley, and there were many with the brand of the rancho. I decided it would be a good idea to start the cattle toward Canyon Guadalupe. I told the rider that, when he met up with Running Bear at the border, to tell him to send a crew to relieve us and have them move the cattle to the Haciendas.

I gave the report to Corporal, who was running this contingent, and he sent half his riders under Tall Runner to begin to move the herd. He said he would hang back with the other half to make sure there was no pursuit.

It was near noon when we were met by a large group of riders who took over the herd and the security. Running Bear reported the herd would be in Mexico by late evening, and the cattle would be taken to Campo San Bernardino. The owners of the cattle that were not ours would be notified about where they could pick up their strays. It was time to leave the mop-up in capable hands and return to our camp. El Tigre, Tall Runner, He Who Hunts, Running Bear, and Corporal begged off, as they wanted to backtrack and make sure there was no pursuit from the upper Valle de Animas.

It was April 30th when the scouts returned, and a report came in that the cattle were at Campo San Bernardino. It was time for step number two. I wanted to place watchers all over the Chiricahua Mountains. I wanted watchers above Galeyville, Portal, and Dos Cabezas as well as in the Mule Mountains. I wanted additional English-speaking people to infiltrate the aforementioned towns as well as Tombstone and Charleston to join those that were already there as laborers. These men were to be on the lookout for three individuals—Johnny Ringo, Ike Canton, and Poney Diehl. These extra men would signal the watchers to pass the information on to Hacienda Occidental.

El Tigre said that, since the watchers were his responsibility, he would see to them. Running Bear asked to go with El Tigre and Tall Runner, as he wanted to remain on the hunt. He Who Hunts, Corporal, Roman, and I returned to Campo Central.

On May 4th, we arrived at Campo Central and were informed that Doña María and Doña Olga as well as Singing Brook and Saguaro Blossom were on the road to Hacienda Occidental. They were under escort and should be approaching Campo Central by that evening. It was welcome news, although I felt somewhat annoyed the women did not respect that we were about men's business.

I received another report that two of the escaping Cowboys had been killed by the east and west crews, and six of the Cowboys met their end as they crossed into Mexico. Three vaqueros were wounded but none seriously. Our campaign had been a great success and, so far, there had been no news from the United States that poor American ranchers were being murdered by Mexican bandits. They just disappeared from the face of the earth.

We met our women not as conquering heroes but more as lonely husbands who were hungering for their wives. We all knew that anything but complete boyish glee upon seeing them would not be good and, besides, we were indeed happy to see them. We all continued on to Hacienda Occidental and, that evening, Mother called for attention and stated that three more babies of the rancho were on their way. I immediately turned to Olga to find a big smile on her face. He Who Hunts and Corporal found the same on the faces of their wives. Our immediate concerns were laid to rest. The births were about five months away for each of them. It would be an exciting October.

On May 20th, I left our nest with Corporal and headed to Tombstone. The mirrors had reported Johnny Ringo was there and spending most of his time drunk.

I went immediately to see Uncle Buck, who had just returned from Gunnison, Colorado where he had been visiting with Wyatt. I asked him how Dr. Goodfellow was doing with the clinic and if it was adequate.

He replied, "The clinic seems to be adequate for his needs, but the practice of medicine is not enough for him, as he has a wandering mind. He would be very happy to see you, and he might be persuaded to travel to the Hacienda if you were of a mind to ask him."

I replied, "We had a very grand Christmas this past year and are prepared to outdo it this year. You would honor the whole rancho if you would consent to be the guest of honor, and I would very much want to have Dr. Goodfellow attend also."

Uncle Buck replied, "Consider it done if Doña María is out of mourning and will be presiding."

I smiled and said, "She is out of mourning and presides over the Hacienda. She is summering at Hacienda Occidental, and you would be a welcome guest."

Uncle Buck smiled and said, "Look for me in a week."

With that, Uncle Buck hung a "Closed" sign on his studio, and we went to gather Dr. Goodfellow for some drinks and food.

That night, I had my first glimpse of Johnny Ringo, who was drunk and unruly at the Crystal Palace. I let the conversation go where it may when I found out that Poney Diehl had been arrested in New Mexico. He was presently a prisoner of the Territorial Prison at Santa Fe and would be there until 1887.

As the evening went on, the conversation got around to the Cowboys and the fact that a rider had come back to the Clanton ranch after having been sent to deliver orders to the Animas ranch. When he arrived, the cattle and Cowboys had disappeared. The prevailing theory was it must have been vigilantes. I was also told that Ike Clanton had left the country when the Earps went on their vendetta ride, but he'd shown up at the ranch several weeks ago. When he got the news about the vigilantes, he took a large herd to the Mogollon Rim and had not been seen since.

I thanked Uncle Buck and Dr. Goodfellow for the company. I told them I had planned to check out some country east of the Huachucas, but I would be back at Hacienda Occidental in less than a week.

Dr. Goodfellow readily accepted the invitation to accompany Uncle Buck not only to the Christmas fiesta but to Hacienda Occidental so he could check in on his patients and visit the mothers-to-be.

We camped northwest of Tombstone and took turns standing watch. It was noon when we approached Camp Huachuca and paid our respects to Capitán Whiteside. We were invited to stay for supper, and we accepted. We discussed the problems the cavalry was having with the raids by both Geronimo and Nana, and I was informed there were negotiations going on with the Mexican government to allow the cavalry to pursue the raiders into Mexico. The captain went on to state the American government was aware of the peace the Estancia del Pérez had with the Apaches, but proof had been given to Presidente Díaz that Geronimo, Naiche, Nana, and others were taking advantage of the peace to raid in the north and pass through the Estancia to the Sierra Madres.

He continued, "It would be wise if all non-combatant Apaches in the Sierra Madres moved to the Haciendas, which will be respected as a haven, and both nations will accept the word of the Haciendas that these Apaches are non-combatants."

I thanked him for the warning and told him I would inform all the Apaches that those who request it were welcome to join the family of the Estancia del Pérez.

We made our way back to Hacienda Occidental through the Santa Cruz Valley and over the Cerro de la Cruz (Hill of the Cross) to the Hacienda.

On July 8th, a signal came in that we had been waiting for. Johnny Ringo had been overheard saying in a drunken stupor, "You gentlemen can go to hell. I am headed to Galeyville where there are still men who can appreciate the wild side." By the 9th, Roman, Corporal, He Who Hunts, and I along with several of the old hands were riding for the Chiricahuas. By the 11th, we had joined El Tigre, Tall Runner, Running Bear, and many of the watchers on the mountain above Galeyville. The reports were that Ringo was not finding Galeyville to his pleasure and was threatening to ride for Texas or back to Tombstone.

We still had watchers on the peaks above the east side of Paradise Creek observing Galeyville. Just before dark, the signal came that Johnny Ringo had left Galeyville and was heading up Whitetail Canyon for Whitetail Pass. He never made it. We were aligned all along the pass and on both sides, but no rider came through. Before dawn, He Who Hunts, El Tigre, Corporal, Tall Runner, and Running Bear slowly started down the canyon. Within 45 minutes, the signal came that Ringo had been found and secured.

I ordered my men to surround the site of his capture at a distance. The last thing I wanted was to be surprised by a traveler, hunter, or resident from nearby. No one who wandered in was to be captured, but they were to be run off in such a way that they would be hesitant to come back. I then told the old ones who served my father that I wanted them to come see this murderer of my father and their colonel.

Roman and I went down to join the captors. Lying on the ground was a man. He was not remarkable in build, but he was nattily dressed, and his hands were small and smooth from never having worked them. He had a prominent nose and black eyes. He was awake and alert, which was indicated by his wide eyes as he looked up at me and the men gathered around him.

I began with, "It is now my pleasure to address myself to you, Señor Johnny Ringo. You are the person who has been referred to on the Estancia del Pérez as 'el hombre muerto caminando,' which, in English means 'the walking dead man.' I am Francisco Pérez Castro, and this man standing next to me is Roman Pérez Castro. We are the sons of Gregorio Pérez Adame, the man you bragged about killing when you gave the graphic details at Big Kate's saloon.

"It is also my pleasure to introduce to you my friend and mi mano derecha (my right-hand man), who is the son of that old Mexican, Sargento Primero Guzmán, who came to the aid of our father and whom you also bragged about killing.

"Now, I want you to meet your captors." I gestured toward El Tigre, Tall Runner, and Running Bear. "These men served as scouts in my father's regiments. They have distinguished themselves honorably in battle many times, they joined my father in creating the Estancia del Pérez, and, most importantly, they are members of the Tarahumara nation and have ruled the mountains of northern Mexico for many centuries.

"Let me now introduce to you my brother, He Who Hunts, who counted my father as among his own fathers and, being a Chiricahua warrior, has learned the best way to exact revenge upon the enemies of the Apache nation and the Estancia del Pérez.

"So, my brother and I are going to step out of the way while others of my father's regiment join these four men in assuaging their grief by making the last hours of your life hell. It is time for breakfast, so they will be taking turns on you while we all eat and rest."

As I walked away, He Who Hunts and Running Bear called in men to take pieces of canvas and drag in cholla cactus, agave spears, and mesquite limbs. Roman and I sat on a hill so we could observe the hombre muerto as he was stripped and strung by his arms and legs to green saplings, which had been bent to facilitate tying him to them and then released to stretch him out with a cracking of joints. The Indios were very methodical as they kept him conscious while allowing all who wished to brush his entire body with pieces of cholla cactus. As time went by, he enjoyed the sinking of mesquite thorns into the soles and heels of his feet and the breaking off of the agave spears in his thighs.

The old ones had scouted around and found a tree with a large fork in it on a trail a rancher used often and was not more than a mile from his home. We all accompanied Ringo to this spot. The hombre muerto was dressed in his pants, which were intentionally put on him backwards. The placement of his clothes over the cholla thorns brought sweet terror to his eyes, and it was necessary to keep reviving him.

He was put on his horse, and his boots were tied to the stirrups. He was led down the valley with a rawhide cord tied around his testicles, and, once again, we were all part of his escort. When we arrived, he was taken from his horse, and Corporal led him to the tree 30 yards away. He had to be revived several times and made to continue the walk. When he reached the tree, Roman, Corporal, and I stood near him.

I said, "Hombre muerto, I am going to tie your pistol to your wrist and place it in your hand. It contains one bullet. We have decided to show you the mercy of death. Your wrist will be tied to your neck, and you will be given a chance to end this yourself. If you decide not to do that, we are going to pull on this rawhide tether until it comes free."

We had stepped away only a few feet when the gun roared. Roman removed the tether from Ringo's testicles, untied his wrist from his neck, and pulled up his pants. We shooed Ringo's horse into the valley.

As the story goes, the rancher came up the valley and found the hombre muerto in the fork of a tree with a pistol in his hand. He later located the horse with boots tied to the saddle. To the rancher, it appeared Johnny Ringo had lost his horse and settled in the tree fork, where he ended his life. The county coroner acquired the body about three days later and, after listening to the rancher's testimony, declared the death a suicide. On July 13th, the body was buried without any further investigation.

It was July 20th when Juh, Naiche, Geronimo, and Nana rode into Hacienda Occidental. We had a great feast and toasted each other many times. The next morning, I told them of my conversation with Capitán Whiteside at Camp Huachuca. I told them I had confirmed with the Mexican government that the peace of the Estancia del Pérez would not be recognized by either the American or Mexican government in the future, as they had proof that raiders were using the rancho as a safe haven from which to raid. I went on to explain that all Apaches discovered on the rancho would be treated as enemies except those that resided at the Haciendas.

"I am going to build a third Hacienda at the location of Campo Ocelote, but that will take time. So, any of the people residing presently in the mountains of the rancho will need to move to the Haciendas immediately. It will be the choice of the people what they wish to do, but I am absolutely certain the next raid into the United States will invite a hot-pursuit incursion into Mexico and the rancho, just as any raid in Mexico will bring the Mexican army and the Rurales to the rancho to seek revenge upon the people. Please go and discuss this with the people. If some want to go to the reservations, I will try to arrange safe passage, but they are always welcome at the Haciendas, as it is their home also. My fathers, it is not my place to judge raiding, but it is my place to protect all the people of the rancho. It is my hope that you honor the rancho as a place where your children can live without fear, as those lands are quickly disappearing."

October 12, 1882 was the day that Olga Pérez Celaya enriched the lives of Olga, Rene, and myself. October 13th was a great day of celebration, as I got to show off my daughter to the people of the rancho at a fiesta to celebrate her birth. Olgita would have playmates her age in that Saguaro Blossom and Corporal had a new daughter and Singing Brook and He Who Hunts soon became the parents of a son.

CHAPTER 29

It was December 22nd, and our home was filling up. Uncle Buck as well as Dr. Goodfellow would be arriving in the afternoon. Roberto graduated from The College of New Jersey after the Fall semester that year and had been attending law school at Harvard University. He picked up Elizabeth at Wellesley, and they were joined by two of our cousins who were now attending school at Cornell. They picked up Javier, joined the gang from the Hacienda Colorado, and had all arrived on the 18th.

Most of the older refugees from Victorio's Warm Springs band had chosen to move to the San Carlos Reservation to join with Loco's band of Copper Mines Chihenne, who had relatives there. Some of the young men and women joined Geronimo. The orphans and others who had no relatives had found a home at Hacienda Oriental.

Pedro Gonzáles had been persuaded by Mother to teach some of the elderly and middle-aged women how to use a kitchen for preparing food so they could help with food preparation for all of the students at the school. It took him one week to give Morning Sun, a middle-aged woman, the title of assistant cook in his kitchen.

Roberto had just finished his first semester of law school and was ecstatic about Harvard. At that moment, though, he was on his way in the grand coach to the Deming depot to pick up a young lady from Boston by the name of Mary Beth Machen, who was being accompanied by her parents and her younger brother. Roberto had declared he intended to marry her in June. I truly hoped they loved the Hacienda and could think of no other place to hold the wedding.

Elizabeth was starting her senior year at Wellesley. I was looking for Mother to give me direction as to where she should go from there. Javier would be starting his senior year at the Colorado School of Mines. We had been conversing about all the opportunities open to him and how he could be a benefit to the rancho. Emilio Cortez and Cachorro had modified their original plans at Cornell. Emilio was concentrating on Plant Science and Cachorro was going for a Bachelor of Veterinary Sciences and had passed all the exams. Hungry Fox had announced that his goal was to obtain a Doctorate of Veterinary Medicine, which was a six-year program. All the young people of the rancho that had gone on to further their education were on a good track.

I had received news that my friend, Mahlon Pitney, had passed the bar in New Jersey and was setting up his own practice in Dover, New Jersey. I sent him warm congratulations and let him know I faced the dilemma of whether to continue to do business with his father, Henry, or move it to Mahlon. I received an equally warm letter from Mahlon in which he said I would be served far better by his father's law firm than I would be by a one-man law shop with no national or international connections.

The Sonoran Railway had been completed between Guaymas and Nogales and had joined the Santa Fe Railroad's track that extended from Nogales to Benson. The port of Guaymas was now open to the United States.

Overall, the world was right. I was a 24-year-old man going on 50. My pleasure was my family, and that was where I longed to be, but the fateful words of my father kept ringing true. The revolutions were not over yet. The unrest between the haves and have-nots was growing. I had continued and would continue to make the people of the rancho aware that the Pérez family considered them essential to the rancho and wanted them to have all the advantages available to the family.

The fencing of the frontier of the rancho was near completion, and I directed that the lands to the west and southwest of Hacienda Occidental and on the eastern frontier of Hacienda Oriental as well as the eastern side of the Ajuste de Septiembre 16, 1865 were to be surveyed into viable economic ranches that had adequate water and graze.

It was my plan to offer these lands first to soldiers that had served with my father or their families. It would not be a grant of land but a contract wherein the family would be deeded the land if they improved upon it over the following 10 years. We would enter into a contract with those who chose to obtain seed cattle for their herds from the rancho. This contract would state they were to market their cattle through the associations we had set up with our neighbors, and 25 percent of the proceeds from the sale of the cattle would go toward the retirement of the debt for the cattle. There would be no price for the land, as it had always been theirs as much as that of the Pérez family. I emphasized that those who availed themselves of the opportunity of land would still be considered part of the people of the rancho, and their children would have the opportunity to obtain an education as if nothing had changed.

I discussed this with Mother, and she was in total agreement. We were to have a grand feast on Christmas Eve, and I was to announce this plan at the feast. I would also be announcing the creation of another Hacienda, which would be called Hacienda Montañas. It would be my headquarters and the home for my children. As with all the Haciendas, it would be open to the people of the Estancia del Pérez.

During the Christmas Eve feast, which was held on the ball court surrounded with luminaries, I rose to speak while the dulces (sweets/desserts) were being passed out and the cordiales (cordials) were being poured. I thanked everyone for attending this gathering of friends and family. "I would like to first introduce you to our guest of honor, Cornelius Sydney Fly, who is known to most of you as Tío Buck, and his lovely wife, Mollie. I would also like to introduce Dr. George Emory Goodfellow. Some of you may remember that Dr. Goodfellow treated our brother, Roman, and his wife when they were wounded by the cowardly Cowboys who raided the Hacienda Occidental."

Everyone stood and applauded.

I continued with, "Sitting beside the good doctor is a lovely woman by the name of Katherine Colt Goodfellow. We all know her as Kate. I want you to know that Kate is a member of the Colt family, and her cousin is the maker of the famous Colt pistol. You señoritas should remember that when you go batting your eyes at the good doctor."

A few people chuckled at my joke.

"It is now my pleasure and honor to announce the betrothal of our brother, Roberto, to Mary Beth Machen of Boston, Massachusetts. Mary Beth and her parents, Cornelius and Susan Machen, are here with their son, Raymond. The wedding is set for June, and it is our hope they have it here at the Estancia del Pérez."

There was a standing ovation and many pleas for them to allow us to throw them a grand wedding.

I then got down to the announcements I had prepared. Much of what I said was unknown to this gathering, and they were stunned about the possibility they could become landowners. I told them these lands would become available once they were fenced, and they would go to the families that had seniority of service to the rancho and to my father, in that order. I then went on to say, "Now, it is my pleasure to bring before you mi madre, la Doña María Elizabeth Baker Pérez Castro."

My mother stood and announced, "Es un gran placer para mí estar en compañía de mi familia y de amigos sin los cuales nada de esto habría llevado a cabo sin su amistad y devoción al rancho y a mi esposo, Gregorio. Independientemente de que usted tome la oportunidad de poseer su propia tierra y negocio, quiero que usted sepa que usted será siempre parte de mi familia. Es hora de que comience la diversión! Deje que los niños vayan mientras las piñatas están subiendo, y es hora de ganarse su riqueza." ("It is a great pleasure for me to be able to be in the company of my family and friends for whom none of this would have come to pass without your friendship and devotion to the rancho and my husband, Gregorio. Whether or not you take the opportunity to own your own land and business, I want you to know you will always be part of my family. It is time for the fun to begin! Let the children go, because the piñatas are rising, and it is time to gather in their wealth.")

I left José and Running Bear in charge of deciding which areas on the eastern frontier and along the border of the Ajuste de Septiembre 16, 1865 should be fenced off as land to be settled. Their instructions were that I wanted to consolidate closer to the Haciendas, and I wanted a friendly buffer between us and the rest of Mexico. The same instructions were given to Roman and Antonio regarding the lands designated on Hacienda Occidental.

The first Thursday of 1883 found Olga, Rene, Olgita, and me headed for Hacienda Colorado in the company of Saguaro Blossom, Corporal, and their daughter, María Elizabeth Guzmán; Bull Tamer; and Mario Cortez. We had a car waiting for us at Deming and, once the women were comfortable with the babies, we men sat down to talk over drinks and cigars.

I started with, "Caballeros, we are going to be making a tour of properties in Colorado and California. I will be visiting and riding the range with the managers, and you gentlemen will be riding with other guides. I need to know what each one of you thinks about the ranches. I want to know about the progression of the fencing on the frontiers, about graze and water on all the sections, how we should proceed with the fencing of pastures, and how we should utilize those pastures so we can achieve the best benefit over generations—not just this year or next. I expect two separate reports—one from Bull Tamer and one from Corporal, with your input, Mario. When you feel you know these ranches and are ready to make these reports, we will have a meeting with the managers, the foremen, and the top hands. I will need the input from all to make sound decisions. So, this is no vacation. Take all the time you need, but I want you to know we will be going from report to implementation. I feel time is short."

I then turned to Mario and said, "I understand you have a family. Tell me about your family and where they are."

Mario replied, "Yes, mi jefe, my wife and I have two sons, and they are all at Campo Nogales."

"Since you have been at your new post, how much time have you spent with them?"

"Only a few days, when I get close to them in my travels," replied Mario.

I said to Mario, "On this rancho, family must come first. If I feel you are neglecting that prime duty, I would begin to think you might neglect other duties in the future. Where are you spending your time when you're not traveling?"

"At Hacienda Oriental," he replied.

"That is where your family needs to be. If they had been there, you would have had the opportunity to bring them along on this trip. This goes for you, too, Bull Tamer. There will be times when you cannot have family along, but, when you are going to the other Haciendas, I expect to see your family or parts of your family with you."

I continued, "My first responsibility is to my family. My second is to the Estancia del Pérez. In my case, they are near one and the same. I will not tolerate you letting the work of the rancho cause hardship for your families."

Both men replied, "Sí, mi jefe."

I poured us all another drink, and we bragged on our children until we all needed to go to sleep. I crawled into my bed, grabbed my family into my arms, and slipped into a contented sleep.

We arrived at Fort Garland the following day and were met by a coach and wagon plus horses to ride. We were at the Hacienda by late afternoon, and I asked Juan if he could summon Abe and Jake. When they arrived, I introduced them to Bull Tamer and Mario, as they had met with and rode in with Corporal. I asked Jake if he could guide Corporal and Mario over the entirety of both ranches so they could make an assessment of the graze and water. I then told him I wanted him to also make the same assessment based upon his experience here. They were all to make their reports to me and Juan in a private meeting. I told Jake I would appreciate it if he would not try to influence their reports. I then turned to Abe and asked him to show Bull Tamer around under the same conditions. They both said they were ready to go.

I said, "Good. Take as long as you need, and you gentlemen work out when you are leaving."

Juan and I had discussed this visit over Christmas, and he was ready to proceed with our own inspection of the entire ranch with me and his new foreman, Martin Smith.

The next morning at breakfast, I met Señor Smith and was impressed by the way he spoke and carried himself. We rode for five days, and it was good to get back to the Hacienda and my family. By the next morning, all had arrived back at the Hacienda, and the reports were made.

The fencing of the ranches was about 50 percent complete, but that percentage was mostly in the valleys, although it had started in the mountains. It would take at least nine more months to complete, as the top lines in the mountains would not be done until the snow melted.

It was unanimously agreed that the additional ranch that had just been purchased would need at least three years to fully recover, but there were many areas in the mountains that would need to be grazed. The other portions of the ranches were in good shape. I asked whether the ranch would be able to sustain two-year-old steers and heifers in the Spring for the next three years if we left the mother cow numbers where they were and how many steers and heifers we could send. The answer was that the high country would sustain between 1,000 and 1,200 head, conservatively, and continue to recuperate as long as we didn't add to our cow-calf operation.

My next question was how many breeding-age Hereford crossbred heifers there were in surplus if the culls were replaced. The answer was approximately 200. I told everyone I would need to huddle with José, and we could meet after breakfast the next morning early enough for us to catch the train back to Trinidad that afternoon.

In the afternoon of the next day, I met with Juan, and we discussed our plans. The 200 head of breeding-age crossbred heifers would be shipped to California at the earliest convenience along with one, purebred Hereford bull, as the ratio of bulls to cows was high here and low there. One thousand two-year-old steers would be shipped to Hacienda Colorado from the rancho in the early Spring to take advantage of the summer graze, but most would be shipped in the Fall as part of our market quota if they reached the weight limit. This would be the goal for the Estancia Colorado for the next three years. All the crossbred heifers of breeding age would be sent to California.

At the meeting in the morning, Juan took the floor and spelled out what was going to happen for the next three years at Hacienda Colorado. Recommendations had been made as to how to divide the ranches into pastures. Juan and Martin Smith would meet with Bull Tamer to finalize those decisions and notify José as to what would be needed in the way of materials.

We arrived at our car in Pueblo, which was joined to a train that would be leaving for Cheyenne in the morning. There, it would be attached to a train that would eventually deliver us to a siding close to the ranches in California.

Three days later, our car was shunted off to a siding, and a coach was waiting for us as well as riding horses along with the smiling face of Salvador Honeywell. When we arrived at the houses, we were greeted by María and some hands to help us get settled.

I explained to everyone what was going to happen. Salvador and his foreman, Donald Parker, had a couple of old hands that were familiar with the ranches and were descendants of the original ranchers and vaqueros of California. Salvador, Don, and I left the next morning on a tour of the ranch. We arrived back in four days.

When the survey crews arrived the next day, we got down to our meeting. The reports we heard told us the obvious. The fencing crews were not progressing well, even though the terrain was the easiest terrain of any of our ranches. Bull Tamer would need to stay behind to assess the problem and find a solution. Presently, the number of cattle for the grazing areas was woefully low. I apprised Salvador that 200 head of breeding-ready heifers and one purebred bull would be shipped from Colorado in a short time. He would be notified about the approximate date of delivery. In addition, some bulls would be sent from the rancho once we got back and made assessments.

In a private meeting with Salvador, I expressed my disappointment in the progress of the fencing.

He said, "Donald Parker brought it to my attention, but I felt he had no authority, since Bull Tamer is in charge of fencing."

I told him, in no uncertain terms, that he was the manager of the California ranches and anything that happened on these ranches was his business and responsibility. Beyond that, it was my responsibility, and I didn't need additional problems.

Salvador replied, "And you will have none from California in the future."

I patted him on the shoulder and said, "That is good to hear."

We arrived in Deming on the morning of January 25th after staying in Los Angeles for three nights and two days so the women could avail themselves of the shopping. Olga had invited María to join us in Los Angeles to catch up on her shopping also.

Salvador wanted to beg off, as he needed to take care of some problems.

I looked at him and said, "Salvador, if you do not accompany your wife so she can do some shopping, your problems will multiply."

He decided to come along.

A coach with escort and three extra horses were waiting for us at Deming, and we headed for the Hacienda. Once all were settled, I went out on the veranda to meet with José, Emilio Márquez, Corporal, Running Bear, He Who Hunts, and Emilio Vásquez. I began the meeting by asking Emilio what he had found in the way of arable land with water on the rancho that had not been utilized.

He began with, "Mi jefe, there is much arable land on the rancho, but we are already using the lands that have available water. The only land that has available water that is not being utilized is in the Rio Batepito Valley."

I interrupted with, "But are there not some small farms already there?"

"Yes, mi jefe," replied Emilio, "but they are concentrated in small groups up and down the valley, and I doubt they are farming more than 200 hectares in total. There is a narrow band of land of several thousand hectares that is good agricultural land with available water."

I said, "Thank you for the report. I would like for you to make yourself available to me so we can tour these lands hasta el lunes (until Monday)."

Emilio replied, "Si mi jeffe, but there is more to the report. May I go on?"

I smiled and replied, "Sí, Emilio, continúe con tu informe (continue with your report)."

Emilio went on to say there was ample arable land on the rancho that had no available surface water. However, he had been informed by salesmen that in parts of Texas and Oklahoma, farmers and ranchers had drilled for water that was under the ground. He also said he had discussed this with our mechanic and machinist as well as the blacksmiths, and they felt certain if we could find one of those machines that drill into the ground, we could manufacture more and with our available pump knowledge. "I am sure we can bring water to the surface," he said.

I turned to José and asked, "Have you been informed of this?"

José replied, "Yes, I have, and I think Emilio's report is worth considering. Along those lines, I have found a company that is manufacturing drilling rigs in Houston, Texas. We can purchase one for $800. In addition, there are men who know how to drill with these rigs and set pumps. Presently, these men are out of work in Houston. We would have no problem hiring about four of them to run the rigs."

I said, "How do we get training for men on the rancho?"

José replied, "It takes a three- to four-man crew to run a drilling rig."

I asked if we could order two rigs, and José replied, "I have them reserved."

I smiled and told them to let me know when and where they would start drilling.

I thanked Emilio Vásquez and turned to Emilio Márquez to inquire if he had the plans for Hacienda Montañas drawn.

He replied, "I have a conceptual plan, but I cannot draw a building plan until I see the ground we are to build on."

I agreed. "You will need to accompany us on our trip on Monday."

I then turned again to José and informed him about the decisions that had been made about the cattle at Hacienda Colorado and that 200 head of crossbred heifers and one purebred bull would be sent to the ranches in California. I added, "I would like for you to see that Juan ships them on the Santa Fe and includes enough young, crossbred bulls to service the rest of the heifers. It will be necessary for Running Bear to send someone with the cattle that will be able to teach the hands our manner of keeping track of which bulls and cows produce which calves. I will be happy to send Corporal or Mario Cortez along to see the cattle are delivered."

Switching topics, I stated, "I want you both to understand that the progress of the fencing on the California ranches is not anywhere up to the standards here or on the rancho in Colorado. Fencing is Bull Tamer's responsibility, but his responsibility covers the ranchos in Colorado, California, and here. There has not been a shortage of materials, but there is a shortage of output. I addressed this problem with Salvador, and his response was he did not know if he had any authority over the fencing crews. I have informed him that his authority is that he is the manager of those ranches, and all their problems are his. I left Bull Tamer there to sort it out. My assumption is my cousins slipped back into their slothful ways once they were out from under Bull Tamer's immediate supervision. It will be interesting to see how Salvador and Bull Tamer solve this problem.

"Another development at Hacienda Colorado is that we will be unable to turn those ranches into cow-calf operations for at least three years, as the lower pastures on the newly acquired land are overgrazed and need rest. Therefore, I will want to send 1,000 to 1,200 head of two-year-old steers to arrive there in mid-March so they can be fattened and shipped from there in the Fall. We will need to follow this plan for the three years, and then we will re-evaluate how we are to proceed. Given the large number of cattle, I believe it would benefit us to drive the cattle rather than freight them.

"I also have agreed to participate in a Spring drive with the Vails to California. I will want to send 500 head of heifers to our California ranches from the Hacienda in that drive. I want those heifers to be Hereford or Hereford crosses as much as possible. It will be necessary to freight enough young bulls to service the heifers. I would prefer that the bulk of those heifers come from Hacienda Oriental. The decision as to how many can be shipped will be made after we know how many heifers we need to replace culls."

Running Bear was shifting in his seat uncomfortably, and a light came on in my head. I turned and addressed him. "I appreciate your subtle way of expressing the obvious, and I am still your student. Instead of freighting the heifers from Colorado all the way to California, we will off load them at Deming and add them to the herd with the Vails, which will easily allow us to reach our 500-heifer target. We can send any extras—up to 700 head—on to California. Juan can send the bull we have here, and we can put him in our rotation along with an adequate number of bulls that will be needed to service the heifers.

"So, there you have it, hombres (men). We must conduct Spring and Fall roundups. We will need to send a cattle drive to Colorado in the early Spring and also participate in another cattle drive to California with men and materials at the same time. We will be shipping bulls to California within the month. José will have come up with a fairly solid number of animals that can be shipped to market in the Spring and Fall to get us a market price as well as commitments from our other shipping partners.

"Corporal, you have an assistant, and someone is needed to accompany the drive to California and to Colorado. There will be a Hereford bull sale in Maine on March 15th. I will need someone along who can take charge of any cattle purchased and accompany them back to the Hacienda. Consult with the managers of the Haciendas, and let me know how you decide to address the problems I have outlined."

I then announced to all that a plant was being built in New Orleans by a British company called The British Beef Producers and Shipping Corporation. The purpose of this company was to slaughter and freeze American and Mexican beef to ship to Britain and other parts of Europe. "The Crossed Arrows Corporation holds 15 percent of the shares in this corporation. When the railroad from Mexico reaches El Paso, an additional plant is planned and has been funded for construction at Veracruz."

I turned to He Who Hunts and said, "I would like for you to accompany me when I leave Monday on my trip to the site of the new Hacienda, so you can see the possible farmlands in the valley of the Rio Batepito as well as other adventures I have in mind. Mi compañeros, it is time for me to seek my wife and children and take a rest from the worries of the rancho. As you can see, I have put those worries on your shoulders."

CHAPTER 30

It was February 18 when He Who Hunts and I returned to Hacienda Oriental. The site had been chosen for Hacienda Montañas in a high valley on the eastern side of the Teras Montañas with an easy access to the short grass prairie to the east and a good, gentle slope from the top of the pass into the Rio Batepito Valley.

Our visit to the farming areas in Valle de Rio Batepito was informative, and I had given Emilio Vásquez orders to begin development of the unused lands and water along the Rio. The first order of business was for him to establish ownership rights of those who had improved on the land and were farming it then. Once that was done, he was to see to the fencing of all the lands by working with Bull Tamer. The fencing would include not only our farmlands but also a fence protecting our neighbors from the intrusion of our animals. Lanes would be left open so cattle could go to water at the river, and our neighbors had to be informed that the maintenance of fences adjoining their land was on their shoulders. We were not going to patrol the protection of their properties. I also directed him that, in developing the water of the river for irrigation, he was to always protect the water rights of the existing farmers.

He Who Hunts and I headed south down the Valle de Rio Batepito until we crossed the Rio Bavispe and began our climb toward El Tigre, where we would begin our inspection of our southernmost lands. The cross fencing of pastures was complete and, at our newly established

Campo El Tigre, I learned that Juh had a rancheria in a small valley on the east slope. He Who Hunts and I found a fat steer and drove him to the location of the rancheria.

He Who Hunts and I were alarmed by how much Juh had declined. After we had enjoyed the beef and Tiswin, Juh informed us his time was short, and he was concerned for the wellbeing of the Janeros. He requested we take all the children and the elderly to the Hacienda, so they would not have to live in fear of the Mexicans and the Americans. He went on to say that many of the young men had joined with Geronimo, Naiche, and Nana, and there were none left to guard the people.

I told him anyone who wanted to come to the Hacienda was welcome and, within a year, there would be a Hacienda in the mountains. I also requested he come as well, so he could receive medical care. His response was that this rancheria was built by his wives on the same ground that his mother had built the rancheria where he was born, and he would remain there.

He Who Hunts told Juh he would return as soon as he could outfit the wagons to transport the people.

I reluctantly left the father, as I knew this would most likely be my last time to sit and hear his wisdom.

I had expected Corporal to accompany me on my trip to Maine, but he informed me he was sending Mario Cortez in his stead, as Saguaro Blossom was heavy with her second child and would be delivering before we could return. In addition, he would be needed there to coordinate the drives with José. I replied that I would sorely miss him, but I understood that his family was his first responsibility. I went on to inform him it was my intention to buy as many as 24 bulls, and Mario was going to need additional help, as those bulls would be divided between California, Colorado, and Hacienda Oriental and would be delivered directly from Maine.

I had asked José to arrange for a car to be ready for Olga, the kids, and our entourage on February 26th, as the sale would be on March 20th.

I had also asked him to arrange for accommodations at the Gilsey in New York from the time we would arrive through March 30th.

While He Who Hunts and I were on our trip, Mother had informed José that she and Angélica were going to be accompanying us, and José had made arrangements for an extra car to carry them as well as María Gomez; Salomé, Mario's wife; and Corporal Juan Cortez. In going over our itinerary, I found we were adding an extra person at the La Junta Station in Colorado—Dulce would be joining us

This was strictly a trip for adults. Olga had not been away from Rene and Olgita since their birth, and I was concerned she may not want to leave them. However, it appeared she might even be relishing the respite.

Mario had made arrangements for nine young vaqueros to meet us at the hotel no later than March 18th, and José had arranged for lodging for them.

This was Mother's coming-out party after her long mourning. She had notified friends in New York that we were traveling there and should be arriving at the Gilsey on March 2nd. Mother received a wire back that Richard Wagner had died on February 13th, and The New York Philharmonic was performing a memoriam in his honor on March 10th. Mother's friends had reserved a large box at New York's Academy of Music so they could all attend.

On March 4th, Mother summoned me to let me know Juan Cortez had been sent to fetch Elizabeth at Wellesley, and the ladies would want to do some shopping as well as participate in the New York pastime of seeing and being seen. It would be the duty of the remaining two men—Mario Cortez and me—to escort them.

Mario was beginning to show signs of stress early in the shopping spree, as there is nothing in this world that makes a man feel so non-essential and in so much danger as to go shopping with a significant female. I tried to explain to him that anything he says either for or against the clothes she is modeling for him will get him into trouble.

I then proceeded to give him an example. "Let us say Salomé comes walking out of the dressing room in a very nice dress and asks you, 'How do I look in this dress?' You have no idea what answer she wants. Maybe she thinks it is too sexy and you say, 'You look ravishing in that dress.' You just hit on her preconceived notion it might be too sexy. Then she fires back, 'You only like me in sexy clothes?' You want to run, because you know the train is about to leave the station. Here comes the bomb: 'Do you want me to dress like one of your whores?' You have not had a chance to utter a word other than uh, uh, uh. Then you will be dismissed with, 'Why not go live with one of them and see if you ever get another breakfast?' Mario, my friend, my suggestion to you is to never offer an opinion, look extremely bored, and, if relentlessly pushed for a response, you should have a prepared answer such as, 'It's okay.' At which time, she will return to the dressing room with the confirmation that you have no clue and probably would not know what to do with a whore if you ran into one. After a time, you might even develop a question that always seems to keep me in cool water, which is, 'I don't know, dear. What do you think?'"

Juan Cortez returned with Elizabeth and Roberto, and they attended the memoriam for Wagner with us. Roberto informed us that Mary Beth and her family had decided that a grand wedding at the Hacienda would be perfect and wanted to set the date for June 16th. Of course, this necessitated more shopping for the wedding.

We bought 26 purebred Hereford Bulls at the auction, and I helped Mario set up the freighting. Eight bulls were put into a car bound for the ranches in California. The remaining 18 bulls were placed in two cars—one with eight bulls to be sent directly to Deming and the other with 10 bulls to be sent to Trinidad, Colorado. Juan would meet the latter shipment and arrange for the shipment of four bulls to Hacienda Colorado. The remaining six bulls would be then shipped on to Deming. Mario split his vaqueros into three per car, so one vaquero would be on or in the car with the bulls at all times to prevent any of them from going down and getting trampled.

Mario made one vaquero of each car the jefe vaquero, and it was his responsibility to wire José as to the various locations of the cars and condition of the bulls' everyday when they were offloaded in a rest area until the next train came through after six hours of rest.

Mother had made plans to travel by ship from New York to Veracruz and then on to Mexico to see her siblings, but the impending wedding of Roberto and Mary Beth changed those plans. When we checked out of the Gilsey on March 30th, we boarded our cars for the trip home and arrived before the bulls did.

José and Running Bear had arranged for four bulls to be kept near the Hacienda and the rest to be transported to the new summer grounds that had been fenced into pastures on El Tigre. In addition, they had shipped six bulls, whose heifer calves were now long two-year-olds, to Hacienda Oriental. This provided for the movement of other heifers to unrelated bulls as well as the introduction of some home-raised, crossbred bulls to certain pastures and the retirement of native bulls and cows.

In my absence, two drilling rigs had arrived, and Emilio and José had picked locations to drill. This was good farmland near our established fields west of the Hacienda that was too high to receive ditch water.

Emilio Vásquez reported that the fencing in the Rio Batepito Valley was coming along well, and he had hired crews to clear land as well as to construct irrigation ditches from a diversion dam being built on the Rio further north.

I received reports that although rustling from the Tombstone area and the Animas Valley had tapered off considerably, a group of small ranchers recently arrived from Texas had aligned east of the Cienega in the San Simon Valley and were exercising what they assumed was their right as Texans to rustle small herds in Mexico, some of which happened to be on the rancho. Many of the original watchers were becoming too old to pull down that duty, and they had been replaced by younger men they had trained. Fortunately, for the rancho, most of these small ranchers were slovenly, lazy, and took the easiest path. In this case, they went straight down the valley and were not as professional as the Cowboys were. However, they were ruthless and had no qualms about killing any vaqueros they came across.

I gave orders for armed vaqueros to be dispatched to ride the high country and be alert to the mirrors of the watchers. They were not to present themselves to the rustlers if their force was not double that of the rustlers. Their job was to intimidate and scare the bullies so they would slink away until a better time. I told them, "If they fire, protect yourselves, but do not fire first. I have other plans."

I had been informed that Capitán Carrillo had arrived at Ascención with a large troop of Rurales. I sent an invitation for him and his aide to spend the weekend with us on April 14th and 15th, as we would like to have his company as well as discuss some business. He sent back that he would be eager to spend time as a guest of Hacienda Oriental. I informed Mother, Angélica, and Olga of the plans and the reason for the sudden invitation.

When Capitán Carrillo arrived, Mother, Angélica, and Olga greeted him and had him seated on the veranda where refreshments had been set up. Mother praised and thanked the Capitán for his attention to the recovery of the body of Gregorio and the foresight to meet his family in Ciudad Chihuahua.

Edward Honeywell had seen to the Capitán and his aide's gear, and grooms had taken their horses away by the time Corporal, José, and I arrived on the veranda. Shortly after our arrival, Mother, Angélica, and Olga begged off to attend to other duties and admonished us that dinner would be at 8:00 and that it would be formal.

After cigars had been lit and glasses filled, Corporal asked the Capitán about the situation to the south of us. Capitán Carrillo informed us the mining activity of the big United States companies was growing rapidly, and spurs of the newly built railroads were reaching into many of the rural areas of southern Sonora. "Overall, the wealth generated by the employment of miners and construction workers has enriched the society, but growing discontent is prevalent in rural villages that are not in mining districts or large agricultural areas. Instead of moving to the jobs, many of these rural citizens are joining leaders who tell them they need to unite to get what is coming to them. The era of bandito gangs has begun, and the Rurales are sorely equipped to chase those gangs and patrol the northern borders."

I entered the conversation with, "One of the reasons I asked you here was to discuss the northern border and the ramping up of rustling out of the San Simon Valley. We are experiencing small-time rustling by desperate and low men. If we catch them, we can deal with them, but the loss of these men will be noticed by their neighbors and friends who know what they are doing. It is not the same as the Cowboys, who preyed on their fellow Americans. These are Texans who have a belief it is their sacred right to steal cattle in Mexico.

"I am hoping we can approach this problem another way. I propose that the Rurales not spend their time patrolling the border in large forces. We, at the rancho, are prepared to build accommodations for four Rurales—or however many you think is necessary—at two different campos. I think Campo Aguas Frescas and Campo El Lobo would be best. I now have armed men patrolling the border and watchers signaling them as to the constant movement of one small group or another. I would put them under the command of your stationed Rurales, so it will be a fact that the Rurales are patrolling the border, and the rustlers will understand they are facing the Mexican government and not a few Mexican ranchers. I would go on to ask that the rustlers that do not offer resistance when confronted be escorted back to the border to report to their neighbors that the free market on beef no longer exists in Mexico. You and Comandante Neri are much more knowledgeable than I in how to deal with these intruders, but I do need help, and I think this might be beneficial to both our interests. The Rurales get the credit for protecting the border, and we on the rancho can live in peace and safety."

After drinks had been freshened, Capitán Carrillo replied, "I think your proposal has great merit, and it addresses the fact we are undermanned. I will be seeing the Comandante in Chihuahua at the end of the week. I am almost certain he will also see great merit in your proposal, and you may have your stations by the end of next week."

I replied, "Then I will issue orders that the accommodations be constructed."

Capitán Carrillo replied, "Very good, then. I need time to freshen up so I arrive for dinner promptly at eight. I have no intention of disappointing your mother."

Javier graduated from the Colorado School of Mines on May 5th and was charged with the control of mineral exploration on the rancho and our lands in the States. It was also his duty to look for investments in minerals throughout both the United States and Mexico and to access the ownership rights that we owned in royalties, and make sure that we were receiving our shares.

On June 9th, Roberto, Mary Beth Machen, and her family arrived at Hacienda Oriental. There were a series of dinners and parties as preparations were made for the wedding. Guests arrived from all over the United States who were friends or family of both the groom and the bride.

On the morning of June 16th, 1883, Roberto Pérez Castro married Mary Beth Machen. Three pits had been dug, and El Tigre was in charge of barbacoa en un agujero de dos novillos y dos cerdos (barbequing in a hole two steers and two pigs).

On June 17th, the new Pérez couple left on their honeymoon to New York and then on to London, where Mary Beth could meet our extended family. The newlyweds would arrive at Harvard in mid-August.

On Sunday, July 15th, after dinner was complete, Olga and I stood to announce that Olga was again with child. Rene and Olgita were to have an additional sibling. This, of course, led to many toasts on the veranda and, when I joined Olga in bed, the sun was sending its promise of light.

In November, the worst of news arrived at the Hacienda, which sent He Who Hunts, Corporal, and myself to the site of our father's birthplace in the Sierra Madre. By the time we arrived, the people had concealed the grave of our great father who, with Mangas Coloradas and Cochise, had stood tall over his country and his people. Juh, as the chief of the Janeros group of the Ndendai band of the Chiricahua Apache, had controlled the wilderness areas of the Sierra Madre in northern Sonora and Chihuahua. In the Apache language, these were called the Blue Mountains, and the Ndendai were known as the Blue Mountain People. Juh's band controlled an area that stretched from the Animas Mountains and the Florida Mountains in the north, Lake Guzmán on the east, Sierra de Carcay at the southeast corner, and west to the Bavispe. In the south, the territory included Sierra San Luis and Sierra El Tigre. It was Juh who first negotiated the agreement my father made with the fathers. It was the consent of the Ndendai that was brought before the principal chiefs—Cochise of the Chiricahua and Mangas Coloradas of the Mimbreño—and was agreed upon by all parties. Juh was truly the father of us all.

Elizabeth graduated from Wellesley and returned home for Christmas. It had been decided that the Crossed Arrows Corporation was to purchase an estate on the southwest end of Manhattan in New York City that would serve as our business headquarters. Mother, Roman, and I, as the sole directors of the Crossed Arrows Corporation, voted to add José, Javier, Roberto, and Elizabeth to the Board. It was decided we would ask the Pitney law firm to establish a subsidiary corporation, which would have the responsibility of minerals and would be named the Western & Mexican Minerals Corporation. The sole stockholder of this corporation would be Crossed Arrows. Javier was to be the President of the Minerals Corporation, and the members of the Board of Directors of the Crossed Arrows Corporation would serve as the Board of Directors. I would remain the chief executive officer of both corporations.

CHAPTER 31

On February 21, 1884, Olga delivered a beautiful baby girl, which we named Angélica Pérez Celaya. I was walking on clouds.

In March of that year, the railroad from Ciudad Mexico to El Paso was completed, and The British Beef Producers and Shipping Corporation had begun building a slaughter and freezing plant at the port of Veracruz, which would be receiving and processing beef by the Fall.

Our experiment of having the Rurales stationed on the paths of the rustlers was working. There had been contact with rustlers from the San Simon Valley every day in the first months of the change, but, by the middle of 1884, there was little to no contact with rustlers on our northern border. However, the banditos—whose ranks had grown due to an influx of the disenfranchised or those who were unwilling to move to areas where there was work—began to overwhelm our southern borders, and the Rurales were becoming overtaxed in manpower.

In May, a small, deadly looking man came to the rancho and introduced himself as John Slaughter. He informed us he had bought the rights obtained by Ignacio Pérez to the San Bernardino Valley.

Capitán Juan Bautista de Anza had arrived in this valley in 1773, and a garrison was established in 1775. In 1822, an Ignacio Pérez bought from the governor of Sonora a land grant of 73,000 acres for the ridiculous sum of 90 pesos. Pérez and his family moved into the valley, but the garrison was long gone, and the Apache ran him off. He never established a ranch, and his title was suspect, as the governor of Sonora had no right to sell the land in the first place. The grant our family received from the federal government specifically stated that our right was supreme as an original land grant.

In addition to this problem, all land grants included within the Gadsden Purchase were cancelled by treaty in the sale of the Gadsden land. Mr. Slaughter had bought land the seller had no right to sell. Also, two thirds of his purchase was in the nation of Mexico, and Mexico would not recognize a purchase of Mexican land without permission from Mexico. Mr. Slaughter was highly agitated, and his reputation as a gunfighter had reached our ears before he showed up.

Mr. Slaughter and I sat on the veranda with drinks in the presence of Mother, Olga, and Angélica, who were ministering to his needs. I asked him what he planned to do with the land. He replied he had sunk all his funds into the land and the cattle he had coming to stock it.

I sipped on my drink and asked him what he intended to do about the rustling that was prevalent, because the Rurales would not waste manpower on protecting the interests of a gringo that were suspect at best.

He replied, "No man alive can boast he stole from John Slaughter."

I retorted, "And if they state their intentions to pass through to raid your neighbor?"

Slaughter's reply was, "My neighbors are like family. If there is no harmony in a family, life becomes a trial, and I cannot accept that. I am always prepared to protect my family and neighbors."

"I am glad to hear that," I said. "Are you traveling alone?"

"No, I left my family camped just north of the border, as I had been told you and I would have a conflict, and I needed to find out if that were so."

Mother spoke up, "You and your family are to be our guests, as we also treat our neighbors as family. A coach will leave here immediately to bring them to the Hacienda."

Corporal left the veranda to summon the coach, and I turned to Señor Slaughter and said, "It is done. We have been made to submit to a higher power." I smiled slightly. "Do you want to accompany the coach, or would you like to send a reassuring note to your family?"

Señor Slaughter smiled and said, "I think a note will do."

John Slaughter, along with his young wife, Cora, and his two children, Addie and Willie, remained at the Hacienda for three days while an agreement was reached between the Slaughter Ranch and the Estancia del Pérez. This provided for the division of the San Bernardino Valley on the Mexican side of the border and defined the obligations of each party to protect the interests of their neighbor. John Slaughter and his wife received a lifetime lease of 19,700 hectares for the sum of one dollar. This lease was not transferable to a third party and would remain in effect for the lifetime of the surviving spouse.

The area covered by the lease started at the Mexican-American border and followed the Rio Batepito south approximately seven miles to extend east-west from the center line of the rio approximately 11 miles. Campo Bernardino would remain in the hands of the rancho and would take up one square mile along the rio, with the center of the Campo at the center of the square mile. It was understood there was an established road between the Haciendas that extended east and west through the land, and the use of the right-of-way was not only for personal or business transportation but for the movement of stock. It was further agreed that the lease land would be fenced off from the rest of the rancho, and both parties would pay half the cost of the fencing.

When Señor Slaughter and his family left the Hacienda, they were escorted by Running Bear, Bull Tamer, and five vaqueros. Running Bear was introduced to Señor Slaughter as the capataz (foreman) of Hacienda Oriental, and he would see that once Señor Slaughter had settled his family, he would be introduced to Don Roman, as the San Bernardino Valley was part of the land of Hacienda Occidental.

It was Bull Tamer's job to locate the corners of the lease land with the approval of Señor Slaughter and proceed, along with the employees of Señor Slaughter, to fence in the lease lands.

On Friday, June 6th, Olga, Rene, Olgita, Angélica, and our entourage joined me at our new home at Hacienda Montañas. The following day, Mother and her entourage arrived to claim her rooms, as she had declared Hacienda Montañas was to be her summer home.

Mother's entourage, which included her maids, the Honeywells, and the house staff, had decamped from Hacienda Oriental as well. The kitchen at Hacienda Montañas had been designed and built to the specifications Pedro Gonzáles required, and he moved in as the chef of the new headquarters.

Mother had ordered the building of a schoolhouse to be ready for classes in the Fall along with dorms to house not only the children of the near campos but the children of the Blue Mountain People who had joined the orphan children of Victorio's band at the summer camp. This camp was overseen by He Who Hunts and Singing Brook, who had been assigned by Naiche the duty of seeing to the old ones and the children on the Estancia del Pérez. Lozen had traveled from the Mescalero reservation when school was out and was overseeing the education of the children in the ways of the people.

Olga was the mistress of Hacienda Montañas, just as Angélica had assumed the duties of mistress of Hacienda Oriental. Mother was mistress of the Estancia del Pérez and all its sister estancias and ranches as well as the business headquarters. All would have rooms as she required.

As this was my home, Hacienda Montañas was now the headquarters of the Estancia del Pérez.

As per the agreement with The British Beef Producers and Shipping Corporation and the Crossed Arrows Corporation, we began shipping steers to New Orleans and to a new slaughterhouse and packing plant in Veracruz. In cooperation with our neighbors in Mexico and the United States, we shipped 4,500 head of market-ready cattle FOB from Deming to Chicago.

En el 15 de septiembre de 1810, un sacerdote llamado Miguel Hidalgo y Costilla salió por los escalones de su humilde iglesia en la aldea de Dolores Hidalgo y dio un discurso que se llama, "El Grito de Dolores." Ese discurso resonó a través del país y al día siguiente un ejército de revolución fue formado por los peones de México contra la regia española. El 16 de septiembre, se convirtió en el Día de la Independencia de México. (On September the 15th of 1810, a priest by the name of Miguel Hidalgo y Costilla walked out on to the steps of his humble church in the village of Dolores Hidalgo and gave a speech referred to as "The Cry of Dolores." That speech resonated through the country and, the next day, a revolutionary army was formed by the peons of Mexico against Spanish rule. September 16th became Mexico's Independence Day.)

On September the 15th of 1884, Father Salvador blessed Hacienda Montañas and, after a formal speech, recited El Grito de Dolores on the steps of the small capilla (chapel) that had been built on the opposite end of the ball park in front of the Hacienda. A formal dinner was served at the Hacienda for our distinguished guests, and the day was spent in quiet celebration and reflection as the preparations for a grand fiesta to celebrate September 16th were being completed.

Early in the next morning, the sounds of trumpets were heard as the Maríachis began to play. The Hacienda was alerted that the Fiesta de Independencia was starting at Hacienda Montañas. The cooking fires were at work preparing bacon and eggs, and stacks of tortillas were warming on irons placed on dying coals from the cook fires. All were waiting with eager hands to grab tortillas and stuff them with chili, bacon, and eggs.

Sides were being chosen on the ball field, and soon there was mayhem, as all who were able crowd onto the field joined in. At noon, the field was cleared, and all the players participated in its transformation into a glittering garden that any king would have been happy to dine in.

Children chewed on impaled corn that had been cooked in a pit as they eagerly awaited the adults feasting on barbacoa and pit-cooked carne asada. The children were anticipating that, any moment, they would be given permission to attack the many piñatas hanging from the branches of tall trees.

Rene sat in front of me and held on to the pommel of my saddle as I walked our horse down to the corrales (corrals) where we watched young men try their hand at taming three-year-old bronquios (bronks)— which ended by raining young vaqueros into the dust.

I tired of the duties of Don Francisco and yearned to enjoy the fiesta with Olga and the children. Don Roman and Don José began to deftly take on the formal reins, and I retreated into the bosom of my family. That evening after the children were safely in the hands of their nanny; Olga and I started the gran danza (grand dance) on the veranda. A dance floor had been erected on the ball court and was the scene of swirling dresses as the fiesta continued into the morning.

Early on the morning of September 17th, we received the news that slave raiders, many of whom wore federal military uniforms and were commanded by an officer, had attacked the Apache village and the school dorms at Hacienda Oriental. They had captured 63 young women and children and headed toward Chihuahua.

I immediately informed Capitán Carrillo, who was a guest of the fiesta, and he sent his aides to inform Comandante Neri of the raid. He informed him that five vaqueros were lost who had sought to defend the Hacienda, and vaqueros of the Hacienda were in full pursuit of the raiders.

I also informed Capitán Carrillo that not only Apache children were taken but Yaqui and Tarahumara children as well. "All the vaqueros from the territories of Hacienda Oriental and our neighbors are in pursuit. There will be no quarter given, even for those in federal uniforms."

Capitán Carrillo said he understood and would ride with us.

We left Hacienda Montañas with a group of 42 avengers. Roman and José rode to intercept the vaqueros in pursuit and inform them we would be cutting off the fleeing slavers before they reached Chihuahua.

As we arrived at the area of Casas Grandes, a dispatch rider met us and handed Capitán Carrillo a telegram. Capitán Carrillo was to ride post-haste to Chihuahua on orders from Presidente Díaz and secure any officers at the garrison. He was not to proceed with the distressed and aggrieved parents of kidnapped children, and he was not to interfere with the retrieval of the children in any way. There would be no official federal or state military or police presence.

Each rider led a spare horse, and we made a forced march, exchanging horses with our friends along the way. Running Bear and He Who Hunts stated the raiders were aware of the pursuit but had not spotted our approach. They had stopped at the southwest corner of the Laguna del Sueco (Swedish Lake) and were watering their exhausted horses. It was decided we would approach the northwest side of the laguna and fan out toward the southwest. The pursuers were to apply gentle pressure on the slavers so they would begin to move up the west side of the laguna and we could encircle them there.

When it became apparent to the slavers they were surrounded, their lieutenant rode out with three soldiers to inform us he was on official army business, and we were interfering with the duties given to him by his commander. I showed him a telegram from Presidente Díaz stating that any federal officer or soldier acting as a slaver was decreed to be a renegade and subject to execution on sight.

At that moment, Roman rode up and shot the lieutenant out of his saddle. The members of his escort were similarly dispatched by He Who Hunts, Corporal, and Running Bear.

The rest of the slavers abandoned their captives and made to escape—initially by fleeing south. They ran into withering fire, switched direction, and headed west and then north. Each time they turned, they were repelled. In a last-ditch effort, they rode their mounts into the laguna, where the horses bogged down in the mud.

Not one slaver escaped the revenge of the Estancia del Pérez and, by evening, the children were being taken home.

The battle of Laguna del Sueco is officially recorded as a raid by banditos on soldiers and civilians that had sought refuge at the laguna. By the time this atrocity had been discovered, the banditos had melted back into the Sierra Madres and were untraceable.

Comandante Neri and Presidente Díaz announced the government would not rest until the perpetrators were brought to justice.

The commanding officer of the raid died while cleaning his gun.

CHAPTER 32

Our agricultural lands were beginning to pay dividends. Wells began to produce water and opened new land for development. Over the previous five years, cattle had been the primary economic producer for the rancho, but our crops were beginning to look like a much more sustainable business, because the price of cattle had declined slightly as the production of beef accelerated during the 1880s in the Midwest. Wyoming and Montana were brimming with cattle due to mild winters and abundant rain as well as good rail transportation to market.

Many of the older hands were taking advantage of our offer to set themselves up in business. The first lands that were put into the cooperative effort were the lands east of the eastern line of Ajuste Ascención-Janos and north of the southern border of the rancho. Running Bear, who had the most seniority, entered into a contract for eight sections two miles east of the Ajuste line and four miles north of the southern border. He also took the eight sections immediately south of Laguna de Santa María. The rest of the land was claimed by the end of the first day in which people could sign up for it.

Plans were under consideration to offer land along the northern border within the next two years as well as 48.5-hectare portions of agricultural land on the borders of our croplands. Our well rigs were operating year-round, and two more were to be delivered no later than February of 1885.

Like Running Bear, most of the old hands would be developing lands they had acquired for their children, and they had no intention of leaving the employ of the Hacienda until they felt it was time for them to retire. Each family would enter into a purchase agreement for seed cattle, wherein they would repay the value of the cattle when they marketed their steers and heifers.

The bulk of our cattle was being marketed through The British Beef Producers and Shipping Corporation's slaughter and freezing facilities in New Orleans and Veracruz. It seemed prudent to sell any of our steers and heifers as well as our culls, because the market was declining. With our coop partners, we shipped 6,500 head to market from Mexico and our ranches in the United States.

The birth of Javier Pérez Celaya occurred on August 21, 1885, at Hacienda Montañas. It was a great day of celebration, and our family had grown to six. The Hacienda was alive with children, and Rene was a very proud big brother.

Elizabeth had the New York headquarters up and running and had become a naturalized American citizen. She hired two of her classmates to help her run the headquarters, as it was the terminus for not just the Crossed Arrows Corporation but for the business of the Estancia del Pérez and The Western & Mexican Minerals Corporation as well. José, Mother, and I received weekly and sometimes daily reports on business opportunities as well as income and expenses for all our enterprises within the States.

Roberto and Mary Beth moved into the expanding headquarters and established the Robert Pérez and Partners law firm, of which the Crossed Arrows Corporation was a 50 percent partner and, at that time, the law firm's sole client.

Several of the stockholders of The British Beef Producers and Shipping Corporation visited our New Your Headquarters, as we were among the top five percent of the stockholders, with 16 percent of the stock. They were inspecting production holdings the corporation had along the Wyoming-Montana border plus checking out the facilities of stockholder producers throughout the Midwest. They were then scheduled to be at Hacienda Oriental on August 30th and would proceed with José and Mother to Hacienda Montañas on Wednesday September 2nd to inspect the rancho and hold some business discussions.

When the four gentlemen arrived with Mother, I was introduced to two of my mother's cousins that were on the Board of Directors by the names of Lord William Baker and Sir Percy Baker—sons of her father's oldest brother. Accompanying the cousins were two young men who appeared less than happy. The benefits of the rancho's finishing school for young, privileged sons had crossed the pond from Mexico City, and the elder Bakers had been in touch with Mother as to the possibility of enrolling their sons in the school of hard knocks. When I was informed that I had two more indulged children to make men out of, I could say nothing other than, "Of course, it will be an honor to be of service to the family."

In our discussions, I received some alarming news that certain portions of western Wyoming and Montana had received less than two inches of rain over the summer, and herds were presently being drastically culled in those areas. The ranchers, who were to be producing for delivery in 1886 and 1887, would not be able to meet the quota of prime beef animals for slaughter at New Orleans. They felt certain they could lock in this year's prices in a delivery contract with FOB if we could ship 1,000 head of beef every month of 1886 and 1887. I told them I would be able to do that by working deals cooperatively with both my neighbors in Mexico and the United States. They went on to say they would make the same deal with us for the shipment of 400 head to Veracruz every month.

I replied, "I need to discuss this with my neighbors who have contracts with The British Beef Producers and Shipping Corporation."

Lord Baker said, "We would appreciate your locking in your supply. Would October 15th work for a reply, so we can enter into agreement?"

I agreed to the deadline.

Sir Percy informed us they had more warning signs about the market and said it may be good if we imparted this information to individuals we might want to coop with. He went on to say, "In our trip across the Midwest and into Wyoming and Montana, we were struck by the immense change in the quantity and quality of the grasses compared to five years ago. It is very evident the country is overgrazed. Five years ago, everyone was touting the great graze, and there was no need to supplement during the mild winters. I and others talked to people who had moved into that country 20 and 30 years earlier. Their pastures seemed to be in great shape, and they had fenced them to protect them from the speculator ranchers that have been moving in over the past 10 years. Their assessment was the last five years have been mild and abnormal. There are usually two to three heavy snows every winter, and it was necessary for animals to be fed to get them through. The old timers always cut and stored grass hay for those occasions." He paused. "There could be a disaster coming wherein people will sell off their herds for whatever they can get before they die of starvation. We are offering a sure profit for the next two years for quality beef. We have no intention of buying culls and bones. If we cannot work a deal, we will have to start looking at the South American market to meet our obligations."

I replied, "I hope your dire predictions do not hold true, but, even here, we put up supplemental feed for emergencies."

Mother stood and said, "Gentlemen, as you can see, the sun is in the trees. It is time to have a drink, smoke a cigar, and then retire to your rooms to get dressed for supper. I will have no more business spoken this day. You are our guests."

It was midmorning the next day before our guests joined us for cigars and coffee on the veranda. Lord William began by saying, "We have several more subjects to discuss with you."

I replied, "By all means. This is the perfect setting for a discussion among friends."

Lord William said, "Our lines of communication take way too long. The plants are being managed and run efficiently, but they are not equipped to take care of the business end of the corporation. The business of the two plants is to butcher beef animals and freeze them for transport to market. This is being done efficiently at the plants. What is not being done efficiently at the plants is arranging for beef to be delivered at opportune times. We have determined we need a headquarters in New York to coordinate the contracting of product and its shipment to our processing plants. In addition, many of our ships are sailing empty to the States, so we are in the process of talking with shipping companies to bring British exports to the United States and Mexico.

"The reason we are discussing this with you is we visited your New York headquarters. We saw how efficiently Elizabeth and the other two young ladies are running it, and we feel it would be the ideal place to establish our headquarters for the American continent. We discussed this with Elizabeth and Roberto—who we would like to handle our legal business on this side of the pond. Both feel they have the capacity now to handle both businesses but would need your approval to proceed. We are prepared to build a headquarters on your present site and lease back space from the Crossed Arrows Corporation at a nominal fee that could cover taxes for the entire complex as well as insurance costs for a 30-year lease. We are prepared to pay for permanent employees to run our business under the watchful eyes of Crossed Arrows Corporation personnel."

I replied, "In general, gentlemen, I am inclined to accept your proposal, but the devil is in the details, and the man that handles details is my brother-in-law, José Gallego, whom you already know. I would prefer you hash it out with José and bring me the final product to consider. But, I sense there is more to come."

Sir Percy replied, "Yes, there is, but it is all in the conception stages. Some of these are business ideas we have had for some time, and some arose after observing your business. We have many investors that are champing at the bit to place their money in the United States. Most are interested in the cattle market, but some are interested in what could be lucrative investments. Many of the products we will be shipping to the United States and Mexico are textiles. We are in preliminary talks with companies to deliver reliable stocks of cotton at prices that will fluctuate only on an annual basis. We know our cousins are brokering your cotton and that of members of your coops in the English market. We are considering incorporating their business into ours and beginning to export farm products from both the United States and Mexico, which would lead to the need for expanding the office building on your property in New York. In addition, we have investors eager to get into the minerals business, both in the United States and Mexico, and we would be amenable to going into a partnership business in any viable minerals adventure that Javier and the rancho or the Crossed Arrows Corporation are ready to invest in."

José and Mother took over hashing out the details with the Lords Baker, and Rene and I went down to the corrals to get our horses saddled. We picked up Olgita at the house and rode up to some waterfalls and a cool swimming pond.

Javier was a one-man show as President of Western & Mexican Minerals Corporation. His offices were situated at the New York headquarters, but his focus was the western portion of the United States and northwestern Mexico. His first order of business was to assemble a staff. Upon graduation from the School of Mines, he had convinced two of his classmates to go into business with him. His major concern was that there were presently several projects on the rancho that required immediate attention.

The Palacio de Minería (Palace of Mining) had been established as a school of mines and mining engineering in Mexico City in 1797. It was an off-and-on school during the military upheavals and revolutions. In 1867, it regained its scientific purpose and began to graduate geologists and mining engineers. The new graduates of the Colorado School of Mines were to spend six months at the Palicio de Minería to learn the mining laws of Mexico and to find two, compatible Mexicans who were educated in geology and engineering that would like to hitch their wagon to a start-up mining company.

By January of 1885, all four geologists were working out of an office set up at Hacienda Occidental, and Javier was back in New York, where he and María Hundhausen, who was one of Elizabeth's classmates, began to set up a business plan for the mining corporation.

My offer to the vaqueros in 1879 to participate in the profit of any minerals located had brought many discoveries. As discoveries were made, we properly entered them on the books for posterity. The geologists at Hacienda Occidental had been concentrating on what appeared to be major discoveries of copper ore bodies, which were west of the Cananea lease. It was decided that Elizabeth would accompany María and Javier to the rancho to observe the sites and hear the reports and projections of costs and benefits.

On September 22nd, the grand coach arrived, and Elizabeth sprinted out the door on her mission to see her new nephew and his siblings. Two of the geologists had already arrived and were busy setting up an exhibit. Javier joined them, leaving Mother and me to get acquainted with María Hundhausen. She was the product of a Prussian family that had made its fortune in mining speculation in the iron fields of Minnesota and then moved to the Boston area. Mother and I observed an uneasiness in both Javier and María when he left with a geologist. We felt it would be just a matter of time before the management of the mining division would become a family affair.

The presentation by Santiago O'Toole, who was a graduate of mining engineering from Mexico, as well as a description of the discovered mineral body by Reginald Baker, one of Javier's classmates, was convincing. The geologists were dismissed while we had a meeting with Javier to digest what we had been told. They joined Corporal and others on the veranda for libations and cigars. María sought to excuse herself, but Mother asked her to stay, as she was part of the management of the mining division and should know how decisions were made and what the direction of the company was.

Javier started out by saying it appeared we had a major discovery, and the realization of this discovery into a mine was going to be beyond the means of the rancho. He felt we should either look for investors to help us develop it or start courting some major mining companies to purchase a stake in a new development.

I agreed and told him about Mother's cousins and our discussion about having British investors on line for mineral exploitation. I turned to Javier and said, "Do you think you can gather the expertise necessary to develop this property into a major mine?"

His answer was, "Yes, we can. I feel our connections with the Palicio de Minería will get us all the expertise we will need."

I turned to Mother and said, "If we do this, we will ruffle feathers in Hermosillo, as they are being courted by the Phelps Dodge Mining Company, which has assumed the lease at Cananea. I feel you and I should contact Tío Joseph and get an audience with Presidente Díaz before we completely jump in and commit ourselves and our reputation to this adventure. This would stave off any noise from Hermosillo and demands for patrónage. It would also be very prudent to give Tío Peter the opportunity to obtain investors if we proceed ahead."

Mother said, "I will go to Hacienda Oriental and start the communications. Of course, you know it would not be good to take Olga on that trip."

I replied, "Yes, it will be a hard sell, and I doubt I can pull it off. In the meantime, I want to go with Javier and the geologist to the site of this discovery. Would it be all right if I request that Elizabeth and María remain here with Olga? I know you would like to catch up with Elizabeth."

Mother replied, "Send them to me when you return. I will make plans for our trip to Mexico."

By sunrise, the geologists, Javier, Corporal, He Who Hunts, and I had topped the peak of San Luis and were in the shadows as the sun struggled to reach us on our journey into the Valle of the Rio Batepito. The conversion of the lands along the Rio that Emilio Vásquez had accomplished was amazing. There was a diversion dam, and corn was drying in some fields. Alfalfa was being put up, and the valley was alive with industry.

We stopped at Campo Bonito for a late lunch and exchange of horses and then proceeded on to Campo Aguas Frescas, where we spent the night. On fresh horses, we rode on to Hacienda Occidental to be greeted by a hardy abrazo from Roman and some much-needed cold beer and cigars.

The following morning, we decamped for the mine site, and I was highly impressed by the professionalism of our young geologists. They had crews digging exploratory tunnels into all corners of the expected mine. They had ordered what amounted to a small drill to bore down and locate the ore body. They had drawn maps as to the location of the known body, and there was provable ore near the surface.

They also knew their limitations. They readily stated they did not have the expertise to determine the proper way to extract the ore. They needed consultants to not only determine how to mine the ore but also to calculate the most efficient way to mill and extract the metals. I was struck by the enormity of the enterprise we were considering embarking upon and the enormous costs entailed prior to seeing any money flowing into our coffers. I was reminded of Gregorio's caution that everything can disappear in a revolution.

After we had made a thorough investigation of the site, I was told of another site to the northwest that was not quite as large as this one but significant. I was overwhelmed by the immensity of the impending enterprise, and I knew we did not have enough information yet to sell it to investors or mining partners.

After supper, I had a private meeting with Javier, Roman, and Corporal in which I discussed my trepidation in getting too financially involved in a large mining adventure. It was decided that many more discoveries must be made for us to be able to market these ore bodies, and it was necessary to map the northwest ore body, also. I would proceed to Mexico City to talk with Tío Joséph and, if necessary Presidente Díaz, to gain concessions against future nationalization.

I received a communiqué from Mother stating that she, Elizabeth, and Angélica would be leaving with Olga and my children (so much for, "They should not go") for Mexico on October 15th. It was now October 5th, and I needed to start back toward Hacienda Oriental.

Roman was left with the task of loosely monitoring the progress of the geologists and sitting in on their planning meetings at the Hacienda. It appeared they relied on majority decisions on whatever tack they were using in their explorations, and it seemed to be working, as Javier could not be there to monitor their activities.

Roman had brought me up to speed on the fencing of the Slaughter lease land and what he knew of John Slaughter's activities. There was no intrusion from either the San Simon Valley or the areas to the west of it by cattle thieves. I stated my intention to ride straight to the Slaughter ranch to check on my neighbor on my trip back to Hacienda Oriental.

When I arrived at the Slaughter ranch, Cora produced a wonderful supper. Afterwards, John and I were settling down with some mescal and cigars I had brought as a gift when He Who Hunts and Corporal appeared with an exhausted young vaquero who delivered a message that began, "Mi patrón, please pardon my intrusion upon your evening. I have been charged with the task of delivering a message from El Tigre. The message is that cattle rustlers struck a camp of vaqueros south of El Tigre. One vaquero is dead, and two are gravely wounded. The bandits escaped into the Valle de Rio Bavispe with 40 head of mixed cattle. El Tigre sent three Tarahumara vaqueros to observe the rustlers. One of the vaqueros left the pursuit and returned to a watcher site to send a message. The mirrors say the bandits are headed to Nacozari de García, where they will be paid well for beef for the mines."

I prepared to leave immediately in pursuit. He Who Hunts rode out to Campo San Bernardino to get us fresh horses, as this was going to be a long march south. Señor Slaughter asked for permission to accompany us south, as he was planning to run for sheriff of Cochise county, and he thought it would be advantageous to get the lay of the land and see how Mexican justice was achieved.

At Campo San Bernardino, we parted ways with Javier. He wanted to ride with us, but I told him he had our women to look after. They were to proceed to Mexico, as I would leave for Mexico through Guaymas once our cattle were retrieved and the perpetrators had paid for the life of our vaquero. I also charged him with alerting Comandante Neri about our pursuit of the bandits and letting him know they were headed with the cattle to Nacozari de García.

He Who Hunts had ridden on ahead and alerted the camps along the way that we would need remounts and food when we arrived. Daybreak came, and Corporal began signaling to the areas where the watchers were. He quickly received an alert. He signaled that we would need 20 well-armed vaqueros to meet us at the confluence of the Rio Batepito and the Rio Bavispe. We would need food and a siesta when we arrived, and then we would ride to recover our stock and avenge our brother.

As we rode, we kept receiving signals from watchers on the movement of the banditos. They were still in the Valle of the Rio Bavispe and were moving slowly. At the rate of our pursuit, we should reach them just as they turned to climb the mountain on their way to Nacozari.

After a short siesta, we continued our journey south, and the mirrors of watchers kept us informed of the progress of the banditos. Instead of turning up the mountain, they made camp in the valle, where they had water. When we were within a mile of them, we were met by He Who Hunts and one of the Tarahumara pursuers. He outlined how we could surround the banditos.

I held a conference with the others and told them we would surround the camp. "There are 11 banditos, so I want 15 men to surround the camp. The rest of you men will secure the cattle once the shooting begins. I will hail the camp and, when I do, at least one of the banditos will jump up firing. I want every one of the banditos killed. I then want a branding fire built. The corpses will sport the brand of the rancho, so all will know these are the bandits that stole from the rancho and met justice.

We approached the camp, and, as predicted, when I hailed, one of the banditos jumped up and started shooting. Corporal and He Who Hunts pursued two banditos that escaped up a small ravine and, by the time they joined us, they signaled they were no more.

We moved a mile north of the site of the battle and butchered a steer to feed our lot of hungry men. There were soon steaks frying and supplies of tortillas were broken out of saddlebags.

About midnight, a lieutenant of the Rurales rode into our camp with his sergeant and said, "I received orders from Comandante Neri that I was to pursue and make an example of the banditos. As you have already delivered justice all that is left to me is to advertise your work. When the people of Nacozari wake up in the morning, the branded bodies will be neatly laid out in the town square."

The watchers were able to receive and pass on the signal that Don Francisco would be able to leave with his family on the 15th of October. Corporal, He Who Hunts, Javier, and I started on our way to Hacienda

Oriental via Hacienda Montañas to pick up Saguaro Blossom and Singing Brook. This trip was going to be a family affair, and the family was getting large. The mirrors had informed Mother of the additions and the request that Javier accompany us also. I am sure José was scrambling to get all the cars necessary to handle this entourage.

On October 15th, four coaches left Hacienda Oriental for El Paso. Two wagons left with clothing and presents we were taking to Mexico. We arrived late on the 16th and went immediately to the three cars that were sitting on a siding at the Santa Fe depot that would connect us to the Mexican Railroad. We were hooked up and rolling south of Juárez by 10:00 am on the 17th and arrived at the depot in Mexico City at 2:00 am on the 19th. Coaches were standing by from the homes of aunts and uncles. Olga and the children as well as Saguaro Blossom, Singing Brook, and their children joined He Who Hunts, Corporal, Javier, and myself at Tío Joséph's home.

It was Wednesday, the 21st of October, when Tío Peter arrived with Mother, José, and Angélica at the home of Tío Joséph. After pleasantries, the men retired to the smoking parlor and got down to the business of how we could protect our investments in large mines in the country of Mexico. Tío Joséph had consulted with Justices of the Supreme Court at the behest of Presidente Porfirio Díaz, and it was explained to us the only way we could avoid nationalization of the minerals of any mine in Mexico was to be a foreign entity that had obtained control of minerals in Mexico through purchase of land containing minerals, and that purchase had to be approved by the government of Mexico. Said entity also needed to be registered with the government of Mexico. Those actions would allow the entity to own the property, but it would not keep the country from nationalization in the future.

The way to keep future governments from nationalizing the mine was to deed the mine over to the government, which would result in the government issuing to the entity an irrevocable lease on the mine for a 75-year period. The lease would be nine percent of the net annual proceeds of the mine.

Tía María Aguilar Baker and Mother came into the meeting and said there were several social events that were going to require our attention. "Therefore, it is a requirement that the ladies be dressed well in the latest fashion and, to do that, they will need to spend the day shopping and will need escorts," explained my mother.

Sometimes, I do think well on my feet. I replied, "It is with great regret that I must excuse myself from such an opportunity to be with you lovely ladies, but I am to meet with Presidente Díaz shortly. Tío Joséph and Tío Peter are here to coach me on what should and should not be said. It is my duty to the rancho. I must leave the sweet duty of escorting you to He Who Hunts, Corporal, and Javier."

Mother smiled, looked at me, and said, "Your father taught you well."

On October the 29th, Tío Joséph escorted Singing Brook, He Who Hunts, Tío Peter, and myself into the office of Presidente Porfirio Díaz. He Who Hunts and Singing Brook were dressed in formal Apache garb. Tío Joséph reminded the Presidente he had met He Who Hunts on my last visit, when he had presented the bow from Juh. He went on to introduce Singing Brook by saying, "Mi Presidente, you may remember the occasion when Victorio and many of his Warm Springs band were surrounded and killed. Some of the young women and children were spared and taken to Chihuahua to be sold into slavery and the brothels. You ordered the Rurales to assist the rescue party from the Estancia del Pérez, and this is one of the women that was rescued. She would like to thank you for your assistance."

Singing Brook stepped forward and stated, "Mi Presidente, if it were not for your assistance, the last survivors of the Warm Springs band of the Chihenne would have been lost, and our band would be no more. The women you saved have all contributed to the making of this blanket, which commemorates our being saved."

She handed to him a beautiful woven blanket, which he graciously accepted.

The Presidente then ordered drinks and went on to request that Singing Brook tell him the story depicted on the colorful blanket. This she did, most eloquently.

After He Who Hunts and Singing Brook were escorted from the room, the Presidente turned to me and said, "Don Francisco, explain to me this business you have in Veracruz with los británicos (the British)."

I explained that I had joined a marketing company in England, and this arrangement would allow our cattle to be slaughtered in New Orleans and Veracruz and frozen prior to shipment to England and other markets. "Presently, the beef we send to Veracruz are few, but we also ship cattle from our neighbors, who market part of their herds cooperatively with us. The plant is now up and running and we will be sending cattle on a year-round basis instead of just in the Spring and Fall. We now own ranches in the United States and are also shipping cattle to New Orleans from those ranches as well as from the Estancia."

Presidente Díaz then asked, "How is a cooperative set up, and do you market other goods for your neighbors cooperatively?"

I replied, Sí, mi Presidente. We market all manner of farm goods in Mexico, the United States, and England. We have no formal legal structure, and our neighbors trust us due to our honor. It would be good, however, to be able to set up formal structures such as corporations as we have in the United States and in England. Presently, the laws in Mexico are such that if one does so, he must sign over the management to law firms, and no one in their right mind would have lawyers running their business."

Presidente Díaz retorted, "You would have us change our laws so you and others will do business in Mexico?"

I replied, "Those laws are precisely what are keeping Mexicans from incorporating and, therefore, unable to attract capital to compete in the international business world."

The Presidente changed the subject and said, "Am I to understand that you want to start up mining ventures with an American corporation in Mexico?"

I replied, "Sí, mi Presidente. We have a corporation that holds our land holdings in the United States and a subsidiary corporation that is currently seeking investments in mining in the United States. That corporation is managed by my brother, Javier, who is a naturalized American citizen born in Mexico. Mexican law stripped him of his Mexican citizenship when he naturalized and pledged loyalty to the United States. My brother, Roberto, graduated from Harvard with a doctorate in law and is representing the corporations and other clients in New York. He has the same dilemma regarding citizenship."

El Presidente stood up and said, "It is time to change this discussion from my education about your business to our familiar give and take. It is my understanding that you need permission to mine in Mexico through an American corporation, and you want to protect your mines by selling them to the government with an irrevocable lease-back at a rate of nine percent of the net profits for 75 years. In addition, you would like to change Mexican law so a business can incorporate, both to shed liability and garner capital by selling shares. Third, I sense you would like me to make exceptions for both your brothers and grant them Mexican citizenship so they would be dual citizens."

Before I could respond to any of this, Díaz continued, "I am prepared to do what you ask, but I have some conditions. Your brother, Roberto, is to move to Mexico and, with the submission of his credentials to the Supreme Court; he will be given a license to practice law in Mexico. He will work with the members of the Supreme Court to craft laws that permit corporations to sell stock to capitalize in which the stockholders are protected from liability resulting from the actions or liability of the corporation. These laws will also need to provide for non-profit corporations or cooperatives in which small producers of goods can band together to compete in this world and receive the benefits of their contribution to the common market.

"Finally, you have been educating the youth of the Estancia. I am going to rely on the Estancia to use the expertise it has acquired to start the cooperative movement across Mexico and make it viable by establishing business locations in New York and England right away. I understand your corporate headquarters in New York has provided space for the Ingles beef corporation and you will set up a headquarters for the Mexican corporations as well. Is that correct? I also understand your Tío Peter has some locations identified to set up a marketing headquarters in London, and he states you are ready to do this. Are we agreed?"

I replied, "I, Don Francisco, agree, but I will need to discuss this with both my mother and Don Roberto before I commit the Estancia del Pérez and Roberto to this endeavor. Can I give you a final answer by November 30th?"

Presidente Díaz took my hand, shook it, and said, "I await your favorable reply. Mexico will live up to our bargain."

When we returned to Tío Joséph's home and had settled down to cigars and drinks, Tío Peter started a conversation about the state of the cattle industry, observing that the drought that had started in Texas had spread to Oklahoma and was now threatening Kansas. "It is apparent the lack of feed is forcing a large sale of not only market cattle but even year-old steers and heifers. The dumping of all these Texas cattle is causing beef prices to collapse. The prediction is that the market for seed cattle will collapse completely by the end of 1886.

"In that light," he continued, "The British Beef Producers and Shipping Corporation, which the Estancia del Pérez has invested in and markets cattle with, has sent representatives from the Board of Directors to meet with me on Monday, November 2nd. I know enough to state they are concerned that some of their substantial stakeholders got caught up in the Wyoming cattle boom and leveraged their stakes with considerable debt. Presently, they owe more than their cattle are worth, and graze is becoming scarce. They will want to pitch a solution that could get you heavily involved in the rescue at what could be a real profit for you, but it is fraught with danger to the economic wellbeing of the Estancia del Pérez."

I replied, "In something of that magnitude, I will need to have all my immediate family in the room to hear the proposal, as it not only affects the welfare of the Estancia del Pérez but the family. I will need their counsel."

CHAPTER 33

In the meetings with The British Beef Producers and Shipping Corporation that took place over several days, their original proposal was essentially to see if the Estancia del Pérez would be interested in bailing out the investors in a large ranch in Wyoming. It was proposed we assume the debt of the investors and gain the ranch as it was presently stocked. In addition, we would gain an additional five percent stake in the corporation.

Our counterproposal was that we would be happy to help in the rescue of our British brethren, but we had no intention of assuming their debt, which far exceeded the present value of their holdings. "We have been told there are nearly 20,000 head of cattle on the ranch, and the ranch boundaries encompass approximately 300 sections of both private and government lands, of which 100 sections are patented and control the water. We also have reports the ranch has been heavily grazed and cannot support the cattle presently on it, of which many are farm animals brought out from the eastern states.

"Therefore, we propose that, on March 1, 1886, we start a roundup of all existing cattle on the ranch. This would give us the opportunity to see the ranch and its condition as well as conduct a count of the cattle. Depending on our assessment of the quality of the seed stock, we would purchase such stock that met our standards, if there was graze to support them. We would purchase market steers and heifers that met our requirements, as we would have to move them to either our California or Colorado ranch to finish them out. The prices at which we would purchase the stock would be 25 percent below the market price at the time of purchase.

"In addition, all cattle we cull would be marketed in the manner that best suited the present owners, and we would provide the labor to move them to a railhead. The present owners need to have representatives at the roundup to verify the counts. Also, the Crossed Arrows Corporation would pay three dollars a head carrying capacity for the verifiable patented land. The carrying capacity would be agreed upon by the sellers and buyers at roundup and before the purchase of any cattle. The government lease-land held would be at one dollar per head carrying capacity to be agreed upon at roundup. The addition of an extra five percent stake in The British Beef Producers Corporation—which would raise our holdings to 21 percent—is acceptable.

"Lastly, the Board of Directors of The British Beef Producers and Shipping Corporation would agree to the addition of a third processing plant in the Los Angeles area to take advantage of the natural market that The British Beef Producers and Shipping Corporation has in India, Hong Kong, and Singapore."

Lord William heard our counter-offer and stated, "We were chosen to represent both The British Beef Producers and Shipping Corporation and the members of the corporation who find themselves in this predicament in Wyoming and are in need of help. We are well aware our relationship to your mother and her brothers here in Mexico is highly weighted on our being chosen as representatives. Therefore, we demanded strict negotiating guidelines and, instead, were given somewhat wide latitude in the negotiations. Your offer is well within those latitudes.

"The story of you paying a widow more than the negotiated price for her ranch reached the Board of The British Beef Producers and Shipping Corporation, and they felt you would not take advantage of a situation.

You have not. Your offer is herein agreed to, and we are prepared to sign on behalf of the owners with their written authorization. We will present your request to open a plant in Los Angeles to the Board of The British Beef Producers and Shipping Corporation, and I am sure it will be favorable to that endeavor. The idea is not new to the Board and, among us; we now control 33 percent of the stock.

"Cousin Peter, do you think you could find a lawyer to draw up the papers and authorize them as legal?"

Tío Peter replied, "I think a member of the Supreme Court would be sufficient to authorize that the papers are legal."

Everybody agreed, and we turned to brandy and cigars.

On November 16th, we started our trip back to the rancho. During the trip home, we had many discussions about my meeting with Presidente Díaz. I had received an agreement from Roberto regarding the conditions put forth by Presidente Díaz. Roberto had taken on a partner, with whom he had attended law school and who would keep the office manned during the next year. He and Mary Beth were in contact with Tío Peter and Tío Joseph, who were setting up housing arrangements for them, and he would be departing to Mexico just after the new year.

Our conversations then turned to our returning students and how best we could utilize them in the business of the Estancia del Pérez as well as in setting up formal cooperatives. Mother was interested in them helping with the training and education of the children of the rancho, and I wholeheartedly agreed. Rosa Honeywell would be returning at Christmas with a degree in nursing from Cornell, and María White would graduate in Home Economics and Emilio Cortez in Agriculture. Cachorro would be returning at the end of the Spring semester, as he had changed his major from agriculture to veterinary medicine and would graduate with a degree of Doctor of Veterinary Medicine. Hungry Fox would not return until December 1886, when he would also have a doctoral degree in veterinary medicine. It was imperative we offer them the chance to work with and for the Estancia del Pérez or its outlying businesses as well as to benefit their family and Mexico. These students were but the vanguard, as there were many more attending schools of higher education, and most would be returning to the rancho for opportunity.

Mother had volunteered to represent the rancho at the graduation ceremonies, and she was accompanied by José, Angélica, and the parents of all the graduates that were able to make the trip. They were met by Roberto, Mary Beth, Javier, and Elizabeth at Cornell. A grand fiesta was held, and this was quite an experience for the people of Cornell. Mother did know how to throw a party, and I suspect she brought along a few vaqueros to properly produce the barbacoa.

María Hundhausen and Javier departed Mexico via Veracruz, where they took an ocean liner to New York. We arrived at Hacienda Este on November 24th. Two days later, He Who Hunts, Saguaro Blossom, Olga, the kids, and I were on our way to Hacienda Montañas. Corporal and Singing Brook were on their way to pick up Juan and Dulce in Colorado. From there, they would go on to Wyoming to do an initial assessment and determine what assets we would need to fulfill our obligations under the agreement with the owners. It would be tight, as we would be in the midst of roundup on all the ranchos.

When Juan and Dulce finished their examination, they continued on to California, where Corporal was to determine how many cattle could be shipped to California and then bring back his report. I needed a report from Juan and Dulce on how many cattle they could take at the Colorado ranches and their assessment of the Wyoming property.

When we arrived at Hacienda Este, José explained to Running Bear there was a possibility we may be bringing steers and heifers to the rancho also. We had initiated a strict breeding program, so it would be his task to manage where these animals went and what stock they were mixed with.

The official Christmas celebration in 1885 was held at Hacienda Este, just as it had been since the Hacienda was originally built and became the headquarters of the rancho. Javier arrived with Mary Hundhausen, who was accompanied by a brother and sister. Javier and Mary announced their betrothal and their plans to marry on February 20th, 1886. Javier explained they wanted to have the ceremony in March, but he knew we would be in the midst of Spring roundup at the Wyoming ranch. They did the next best thing and set it for February, so many of us that would be headed to Wyoming could go directly there. Javier asked Roman to be his best man, because he felt that was the only way he could get him to leave the rancho. He asked me, as the head of the family, to escort Mother and Olga.

The wedding was beautiful. Mary's maids of honor included Elizabeth and other classmates that were now working at the New York headquarters, which was already feeling the brunt of all the paperwork of not only the Crossed Arrows Corporation but the shipping manifests as well as the coordination of cattle shipments to the slaughterhouses in both Mexico and New Orleans on contract with The British Beef Producers and Shipping Corporation. They were also involved in setting up a business structure for the Mexican marketing cooperatives as they came on line. The cooperative arrangements were created by the Crossed Arrows Corporation, but they were locally controlled by the individual cooperatives, which could elect to market through the Mexican Cooperative Market Association created and managed by Crossed Arrows Corporation at the behest of the managers elected from each participating cooperative in Mexico.

Presidente Díaz was apprised of the structure and wholeheartedly agreed—with the provision that the Mexican Ambassador to the United States be the observer of the business of the marketing cooperative for the Mexican government.

Mother had obtained permission from Mary's parents to throw a lavish fiesta after the wedding ceremony. As we were in Boston, the barbacoa was accompanied by all manner of lobsters, crabs, shellfish, and fish fillets. The guests quickly developed a taste for guacamole and calabacitas. Along with the Boston baked beans were pots of steaming pinto beans as well as many trays of mild chili rellenos (battered and fried, cheese-stuffed green chilies) and sopapillas. The fiesta was thoroughly enjoyed by Boston society.

To our complete surprise, we had extra guests on our side at the wedding. Boston society as well as the Hundhausen family were thrilled that the wedding had attracted the attention of some British royalty—relatives of the Mexican side of the family. Lord William Baker and Sir Percy Baker arrived in time to attend the wedding, as they were to be the representatives for the sellers at the roundup and participate in final negotiations regarding funds owed.

For the men, there were cigars, rum, and—for the adventuresome—tequila. The women indulged in sherry and tea as well as pan dulce. Señora Hundhausen and Mother became fast friends and were not above sending a maid over to the men's bar for a sample of rum. Señor Hundhausen was old enough to be my father, but he treated me as an equal and readily accepted an invitation to come to the Estancia del Pérez for the fiesta on the 16th of September.

As planned, we left Boston on the 22nd of February for the Wyoming ranch and the roundup. Corporal, Running Bear, and Mario Cortez had stayed at the rancho to prepare for the shipment of horses, men, and materials to the Wyoming ranch to expedite our ability to proceed to the ranch when we arrived by train.

Corporal's examination of the ranch was extensive, and it included an evaluation of the ranch hands. He was not impressed with the foreman, but the top hand impressed him very much. Corporal had secured the commitment of six of the present hands that were satisfactory to both him and Billy Machelson—the top hand—to remain under our employment. Corporal also gave Billy Machelson the right to hire six more good men out of a huge pool of cowboys in Montana and

Wyoming that had recently become unemployed. They would be under our employ as of March 1st. Billy Machelson was under our employ the moment Corporal picked him as were the six hands. They were to prepare for the roundup, scour the high country, and move all stock to the flats as long as they could find shelter from the wind and snow.

The Wyoming ranch was located approximately five miles north of the Little Snake River, with its southeast corner in the middle of Slavery Creek. The eastern boundary was Slavery Creek, and it extended into the Sierra Madre range to a point parallel with a line drawn east and west 20 miles south of Rawlings, Wyoming. The western boundary extended north and south between Wild Horse Butte and Muddy Mountain.

In early December, Mario Cortez accompanied Emilio Márquez, Hector Márquez, Emilio Vásquez, and Armando Hernández to the Wyoming property. The trips to the Wyoming property were always by train to Rawlings, Wyoming, where the travelers would obtain horses to head south to the ranch headquarters. Emilio and Hector Márquez were to assess the adequacy of the buildings on the ranch for a Hacienda as well as the buildings for the employees at the headquarters and the campos, and to stake out a school for any children.

Emilio Vásquez and Armando Hernández were to assess the lands in river valleys that would be good for farming. They needed to check for good soil and accessibility of surface water and possible drilling sites. We needed to begin immediately raising supplemental feed for cattle.

The car I had ordered for the 22nd of February was waiting for us as well as the car that Lord William and Sir Percy had ordered. Because I was to be away for some time, Olga had informed me she and the kids would be accompanying me to Wyoming. In addition, she had persuaded Pedro Gonzáles, with Mother's help that he could part with Morning Dew, one of his two assistant cooks, so she could become the cook at the new Hacienda. His complaints were loud and full of lament, but, in the end, the promise of two more assistants to replace Morning

Dew was accepted. So, Morning Dew was part of our entourage as well as two house maids and a nanny. It was beginning to look like we needed an entire train just to move the Pérez family. Corporal assured me the owner's quarters at the ranch would be adequate for my family, and I realized I always needed Olga by my side.

Mother and the rest of the family all headed back to the rancho. Roundup was pending as well as the expansion of farming and the assimilation of our incoming students for the good of the Estancia del Pérez and Mexico.

We arrived at the ranch headquarters on February 28. The headquarters were expansive, as the owners liked to entertain family and friends when they were in attendance so all could experience the American West. One striking feature of the headquarters were the large fireplaces in every room. Corporal, who had arrived with his contingent on the 23rd, had made sure plenty of firewood was available, as we were still in the throes of winter. Olga began immediately to set up a home with the two housemaids, who, like Morning Dew, were widows from Victorio's band.

Morning Dew went immediately to her kitchen and began to assess her domain as she contemplated supper for the household and guests. Her daughter, Bright Moon, had accompanied her and was to be her assistant. It became apparent that Morning Dew had been one of Pedro Gonzáles's students, as she made all aware the kitchen was her dominion.

Billy Machelson had lived up to Corporal's expectations, and the men he picked were top quality and had all arrived early. Corporal had put Billy in charge of the men from both the rancho and the ones he had hired, and the roundup had begun. It was apparent we were woefully short on personnel to roundup every head on the ranch, but, as we began to work with the crews, we easily could pick out top hands that could manage simultaneous roundups across the ranch.

Mario Cortez was to coordinate the roundup in conjunction with Billy Machelson, who spoke no Spanish, and relay Billy's orders to the vaqueros from the rancho. Corporal escorted Sir Percy on the range, and I escorted Lord William. It was Running Bear's responsibility to observe the roundup and follow up by looking over the areas where the cattle had been moved out. He had three vaqueros to assist him, and his orders were to report directly to me. He was my extra eyes and ears.

As was the custom, Billy had notified all the neighboring ranches about our roundup, and they had sent representatives to claim animals that had strayed from their range onto ours. The owners or managers of the adjoining ranches would, at some point, drop in on the roundup. It was both Billy's and Mario's responsibility to invite them to the headquarters for a meal and to meet the new owners, if Corporal or I were not there. The invitations were readily accepted, and counter invitations were extended. At those meetings, which Bull Tamer and the Bakers attended, we came to an agreement as to property boundaries and the fencing of the exterior of the ranch property.

All the bordering ranches began their roundups, and we picked up stray cattle on those ranches through our representatives. Billy had put out the word that if anyone was looking for a job, we were hiring good hands, and only good hands need apply. Chuck wagons were being built at a rapid pace to keep up with the expansion of the personnel, and unemployed ranch cooks were coming in daily looking for a position.

As the ranch had been woefully overgrazed, Billy had located a few areas that could sustain cattle until we had feed to supplement the graze. It was agreed with Lord William and Sir Percy that the culls would be removed from the range when an adequate herd had been assembled to ease the pressure on the meager graze. It became Sir Percy's duty to see to the marketing of the culls, and he spent considerable time in Rawlings arranging for the marketing of the cattle in Chicago, as the quality was not up to the standards established by The British Beef Producers and Shipping Corporation.

When the Wyoming boom began, investors began to push the building of large ranches in an area where they found endless grass and ample water. This pushed up the price of cattle and sharply limited the number of breeding cattle. These investors were paying higher prices for breeding cattle than the beef market was paying for beef. Farmers in the eastern and southern states could sell their heifers and young cows for higher prices than they were getting in their local beef market, and there was a great migration of breeding cattle to the West that had no experience in hunting forage, because they were usually fed.

We weren't surprised that the tally of all the cattle on the ranch would be significantly less than the tally on the company books. The snow was so deep in the mountains that the vaquero needed to trail two horses behind him when he was checking the sheltered valleys for cattle. The vaquero would ride one horse to break trail until the horse needed a rest. He would put that horse at the end of the string and put his saddle on the first horse trailing. In this manner, he could cover ground and have a trail broken to move cattle back toward the roundup. When he found a bunch, he would start pushing them down the trail, and the cattle, once they gave up resisting, would soon string out on the trail, so the rider had little trouble moving them through the snow. Most of the cattle were in the low foothills or in the valley in places they could find shelter from the cold wind as well as fodder. There were many carcasses of mixed breeds of dairy and beef cattle that did not learn from their elders to go to shelter and where to find the hardy dry grasses of winter as well as what browse may be available.

The total count of cattle on the range was 13,296 head, of which 6,109 were breeding cattle, older market cattle, and culls we could not use and were being marketed by Sir Peter at prices not seen in decades. The flood of beef, even of poor quality, began to severely depress the market. As the market's customers began to adjust to very cheap beef, demand slowly rose. It was apparent we did not need to be in a hurry to begin producing beef on the Wyoming ranch, and we let it rest while we built it up to become a long-term economic enterprise. In the meantime, we had to deal with the cattle that were not going to the slaughterhouses. It was easy to see it had been a hard winter, as not many of the cows had carried their calves to term or had milk for them when they were born. So, the final tally of cattle we would be purchasing at market price was 7,187. In addition, there were 1,186 young calves for which we paid $0.50 per head.

May 3rd found Olga, Saguaro Blossom, Corporal, Lord William, Sir Percy, and me in Rawlings, Wyoming. The children had stayed with the maids at the ranch, and Mario Cortez was left in charge as the representative of the owners. It became apparent I was going to be the interim manager of the ranch in Wyoming until I could make other arrangements. Therefore, when I was absent, which could be often, either Mario or Corporal would be my interim representative.

Running Bear had taken the vaqueros back to Hacienda Oriental. The extra hands had been paid, and Billy Machelson had been promoted to foreman with the duty of hiring the hands necessary to take care of the cattle that were left on the ranch—which was no small task, as they had to keep moving them to good forage and try to keep them in one bunch until we moved the steers and most of the heifers to the Estancia del Pérez or the other ranches.

My first order of business while we were in Rawlings was to arrange for payment as agreed upon. Drexel, Morgan and Company of New York had a subsidiary bank—Drexel, Morgan and Company of London—which was affiliated with the Bank of London. The Bank of London was the bank used by The British Beef Producers and Shipping Corporation. As the Bank of London would be holding the funds for Drexel, Morgan and Company of London, it became apparent to all sides they would escrow the sale. The agreement was that copies of ownership papers would be sent to Crossed Arrows Corporation in New York, where they could check the papers and consult with lawyers in Wyoming to make sure all was proper. Once that was done, Drexel, Morgan and Company of London would authorize the transfer of the funds and take charge of the ownership papers for Crossed Arrows

Corporation. Upon receipt of notification from Drexel, Morgan and Company of London that the papers were in hand, we would start moving on setting up farming, branding all the cattle, and doing any necessary construction.

It was May 6th, and our destination was San Francisco and the Palace Hotel for three nights so the ladies could do some much-needed shopping. We arrived on the morning of May 9th, and I informed Corporal he and Saguaro Blossom were on their own, and we would meet them for breakfast in the morning. Corporal and I had the unenviable duty of escorting the ladies on their shopping trip and the pleasure of taking them out on the town in the evening.

On the morning of Wednesday, May 12th, we left San Francisco for the Pico House Hotel in Los Angeles, where we were to meet Salvador Honeywell and María as well as a maid for the women and a chaperon, as Salvador, Corporal, and I would be leaving the next day to inspect the California Ranch.

We spent three days on the ranch and met with Bull Tamer, who had preceded us. Bull Tamer's report was that the fencing crews were a month away from completing the pasture fencing and would be moving on to Wyoming. Corporal reported the California ranch was well recovered, and he and Salvador felt it could support an additional 4,000 head. I requested they refigure what it could support, as the cattle we would be sending them would be cows carrying calves along with yearling calves, which should be ready for market by the time the slaughterhouse in Los Angeles was up and running.

I rode the range for two days, and I was impressed by the fencing and the condition of the range. Salvador and Corporal came back and stated they felt it would be a safer bet to take no more than 3,200 head. I commended Salvador and his foreman, Martin Smith, on the condition of the ranch. I asked them if they would need a larger crew with the addition of an extra 3,200 head, and they said they would. I then talked directly with Martin and told him it was my policy that the foreman hire hands or that I send hands from the Estancia del Pérez I regarded as competent. "In this case, there are many good hands in Wyoming and Montana, and I trust the foreman of the Wyoming ranch to know who would fit well."

Martin, who had moved from Colorado with Salvador, asked; "Could you tell me the foreman's name?"

I replied, "Billy Machelson."

Martin said, "I rode the grub line with Billy, and I trust his judgment."

I asked Salvador and Martin how many men they needed. They felt 15 men would be good for the present, and they could hire short-time labor in the Los Angeles area.

When we returned to the Pico House, I had a wire from Lord William and Sir Percy Baker, who had preceded us to the Los Angeles area, asking if they could meet with us at the Pico House. I responded that I could delay our trip to Hacienda Oriental until they could meet us, and they replied they would be there the next day.

I met with the Bakers on May 20th, and they expressed that they had located a suitable spot for the headquarters in an area called Long Beach by the locals. There was a fine harbor for seagoing vessels that was thriving. Their major problems had been solved by Elizabeth, who had stated that the office in New York could handle the purchase and the construction as long as employees of either the Crossed Arrows Corporation or the Estancia del Pérez were used to do the construction, so people from the office in New York would not need to be on the ground while the construction was proceeding. I told them I could have the construction manager and his foreman meet with them and go over the plans from the previous construction of plants and tell them whether they could do the job. I also informed them they also had jobs to do at the Wyoming ranch, but those would not start for several months. I told them I felt sure, from past experience, they could do both jobs simultaneously. "I will wire them to come and consult with you, and I will leave Corporal here at the Pico House to help you converse and make plans with them."

The Bakers agreed, and Corporal and Saguaro Blossom stayed at the Pico House Hotel waiting for Emilio and Hector Márquez to arrive for their meeting with the Bakers. I instructed Corporal to return to Hacienda Oriental with the Márquezes when they were completed here. I told him it would be best if he wired me when they were to arrive in Deming, and Olga and I would meet them there to proceed on to the Colorado Ranch and then back to Wyoming for a reunion with our children.

It was Monday, May 24th when we were notified by the Southern Pacific railroad that a car was ready for us. Olga and I departed the Pico House and, by evening, we were headed out of Los Angeles. We arrived at the train depot in Deming on the 26th and found the grand coach with six vaqueros waiting for us. By nightfall, I was sitting on the veranda of Hacienda Oriental with a tequila-and-lime and a cigar. It was good to be home if even for a couple of days.

I met with José and Mother and brought them up to speed on the Wyoming ranch. After our meeting, we all came away knowing we had taken on a heavy responsibility. I informed them I would stay at the ranch headquarters until the Fall, when I would be coming back to Hacienda Montañas. "I know this is a great opportunity for the family, and I need to become familiar with every valley and mountain on the ranch. In addition, I need to set up banking, join the Cattlemen's Association, and learn the character of our neighbors."

We met with Emilio Vásquez and Armando Hernández and went over their recommendations for farming. They felt there was great opportunity to farm in the river valleys, and they had located some fertile areas in some of the valleys. They informed me they thought it would pay to bring in a well rig to test for the availability of water for the crops in those areas. I informed them that, for the present, my major concern was the production of winter fodder for our cattle.

Emilio replied, "Mi jefe, I have discussed this project with Armando, and we feel we need to let you know what we are thinking and get your advice. We decided it would be best that I return to the Wyoming ranch with Armando and Emilio Cortez, because both have degrees in agriculture from Cornell University. Armando will stay with Emilio Cortez until they get a crop in and will oversee him as they develop the farming on the Wyoming ranch. Of course, I will be checking on the progress all along. Benito can handle the responsibility, and he knew farming prior to going to college."

I answered, "Mi amigo y confidant, I totally respect your judgment as to all endeavors of farming that we have on our lands as well as the personnel to do the work. Will Armando be coming back to the rancho when he feels Emilio Cortez has the farming in hand?"

"Oh, yes," Emilio replied. "Armando has no intention of having his family anywhere but on the rancho, and I will need him to help get farming starting in Colorado and California."

We adjourned the meeting, and I asked José to be sure and set a priority of building a home for the farm manager on the Wyoming ranch at the headquarters.

I turned to Mother with my next query. "Have you had an opportunity to speak with Dishosa Vásquez since she returned to the Hacienda?"

Mother's reply was, "Yes, I have, and I am very impressed with her intellect and the manner in which she presents herself."

"Do you think she can handle the major responsibility of eventually overseeing the finances and marketing of our agricultural goods from all our farming endeavors and do so under the supervision of Elizabeth and the direction of José? This will entail getting a thorough education in the development of the marketing for both the Mexican cooperatives as well as the crops raised by the rancho and all the American haciendas."

Mother replied, "I have no reservations about her capacity to do the job, as she completed her education at Cornell in three years. However, we must first discuss with her whether this will fit into her plans for herself and, if so, I will need to convince Emilio and her mother that she will be performing a valuable task for the Estancia del Pérez and will be safe under Elizabeth's tutelage. I feel certain I can do this, and I will take her to New York and see she is well established, along with her mother, if she is willing to go."

My next request of Mother was to ask her thoughts on what name we should apply to our Wyoming endeavor. Her reply was quick. "My son, from the moment Olga returned to the rancho, she has been gushing about the beauty of the Wyoming ranch. The naming of the ranch should be her privilege."

On May the 30th, Corporal and Saguaro Blossom returned with Emilio and Hector Márquez. They met with José and me the next morning and gave us a report on the impending construction of The British Beef Producers and Shipping Corporation's new facility at Long Beach, California. It was apparent this endeavor was going to be the largest construction project the Estancia had ever taken on, and I tasked José with assisting Emilio and Hector with the hiring of competent construction personnel to make it happen. I made a suggestion that he contact Tío Peter to see if he could find the construction foreman and management personnel that had built the plant at Veracruz. The job was to be directed and managed by Emilio with Hector's help, but it might be advantageous for them to hire the management personnel that had successfully built an identical plant and, with them, oversee hiring construction workers in the Los Angeles area.

It would also be a great help for the future if José would consult with The British Beef Producers and Shipping Corporation and request them to send whoever was to be the manager of the plant when it was constructed to help oversee the construction as well as to look into obtaining construction workers that were totally knowledgeable about the nuts and bolts of the plant to help with getting it up and running.

CHAPTER 34

Both Olga and Saguaro Blossom were eager to get back to their children, and we started our trip north to the Colorado ranches on June 12th. We arrived at Fort Garland at noon on the June 14[th]and were greeted by the smiling faces of Dulce and Juan. We proceeded to Hacienda Pérez de Colorado.

After riding the range for five days and getting reports from Juan, it was decided we could ship 1,500 yearlings from the Wyoming ranch to the Colorado ranches, and it was time to bring the new additions to the ranch on line. I had surveyed the farming areas that had been recommended by Emilio Vásquez and Armando Hernández and discussed the management of the farming. It was decided that Benito Hernández, the son of Armando, would manage the farming operation under Juan. Juan would contact Emilio Vásquez to get things started by moving two drilling rigs to the area. Sites were to be established to erect barns for fodder, and shelters would be ready to receive crops by Fall of the next year.

On June 25th, we boarded a train in Fort Garland and headed for Wyoming. Our arrival at the Wyoming headquarters was a time of joy and tears, as Rene and Olgita led a procession of all the children into the arms of their parents.

For the next two weeks, I remained with my children at the ranch headquarters and went on discovery missions with Rene and Olgita, who had learned to ride their ponies as well as participate in swimming picnics with the family. I had informed Mario that, for the present, I would be the manager of the Wyoming ranch, but I would be leaving in early winter for Hacienda Montañas, and he would manage the ranch when I was away during the winter. Therefore, I told him, he must go and fetch Salomé and his family, so they could make a home here for the near future.

Fields were being laid out, and diversion dams were being built to irrigate them starting in the Spring. Corporal headed for Nebraska in the hope of finding at least six carloads of winter feed to supplement the meager grass.

Bull Tamer had fencing crews on site, and they were busy fencing off the farming areas. New crews were coming from California and the rancho to begin fencing off the mountains from the plains and fencing the borders of the ranch starting on the western side. All fencing in Wyoming would cease when winter came, and the crews would head to the rancho to apportion the remainder of the southeast and southwest areas for small ranches to be granted to our long-time employees.

It was July 20th. Billy Machelson had done a marvelous job of dividing the cattle headed for California, Colorado, and Wyoming into separate herds and moving them to separate grazing areas. He had left his top hand in charge, and he and Bull Tamer joined me on a trip to Cheyenne.

On the morning of the 22nd, we walked into the Wyoming Cattlemen's Association headquarters, registered all the brands, and the Crossed Arrows Corporation formally joined the Association. For the next three days, I established bank accounts in Cheyenne and set up a subsidiary arrangement with a bank in Rawlings. Billy and I set up arrangements to begin on August 9th for shipping cattle to a point close to the California ranch and, on August 23rd, to ship cattle to Fort Garland.

Each evening was spent dining in the Cattlemen's Association dining room and lounge, and we discovered it was certainly worthwhile to meet Wyoming cattlemen and hear their struggles and solutions to problems. I was especially heartened that rustling was not one of those problems.

We arrived in Rawlings on the 28th, and Billy immediately sent a note to his top hand to start moving the cattle destined for California to the holding pens at the rail yard in Rawlings with the goal of having all of them there no later than August 8th. We then began a trip down the western border of the ranch with the purpose of stopping in at our neighboring ranches to discuss the fencing project that was about to start. Two of the ranches had previously fenced portions of their range and welcomed our completing the job. The other two neighbors offered to send hands to help with the fencing and agreed to participate in the purchase of materials. Billy worked out a month-on-month-off agreement with the foremen of the ranches regarding who had the responsibility of maintenance. We were met with cordial and happy neighbors who were pleased to have new neighbors that were interested in the husbandry of the land. After eight days of traveling, wining and dining, Bull Tamer and I started for the headquarters, and Billy went to meet the herd in Rawlings.

The month of August was again family time. The reports were that Elizabeth and her crew in New York had a firm control of the logistics of the Crossed Arrows Corporation and were keeping a steady supply of beef moving to the slaughterhouses in New Orleans and Veracruz with the cooperative participation of our neighbors in both Mexico and the United States. I had discussed this marketing with our neighbors to the west, and they were enthusiastic about a steady market for beef animals. I forwarded their information to Elizabeth. The news from The British Beef Producers and Shipping Corporation contained nothing but praise for Elizabeth and her crew. The construction of their New York headquarters, which adjoined the headquarters of the Crossed Arrows Corporation, was nearing completion.

Dishosa had settled into the headquarters and, under the watchful eye of José and Elizabeth, was quickly learning the business of marketing farm goods. The British Beef Producers and Shipping Corporation was establishing markets throughout the British Empire for farm goods and already had ships en route to the ports of New Orleans and Veracruz. Mexican coops were being created, and their members were beginning to produce crops for an international market. The ambassador had relayed Presidente Díaz's happiness about the gradual increase in Mexican exports.

Both Roberto and Javier had gained dual citizenship and were licensed to practice law and mining engineering in both the United States and Mexico. The mine west of Cananea was being developed by a Mexican and United States consortium created through the efforts of both Roberto and Javier. The mining division was the lead entity in the development of the mine as well as the running of it.

Daniel Barringer was a classmate of mine who graduated in my class of 1879 at the age of 19. He went on to Harvard and obtained a law degree. He then went on to the University of Virginia, where he obtained a degree in geology. Daniel was consulting at Cananea when he ran into Javier, who was working on our mine just west of there. They struck up a friendship and established a working relationship on some projects, as Daniel was exploring the mineralization of northern Sonora and Arizona. He became a working partner of Javier's, and they were actively looking at many projects for the future. Daniel would serve as consultant on the development of the Cananea mine and others.

Things were running smoothly. I could easily address the correspondence coming in, and it was all good. All the parts to our business were in good hands and, for the first time in seven years, I could relax and spend time with my family. We had found a stream an hour's ride from the ranch house where the surface of the water was constantly disturbed by cutthroat trout rising to seek flies and grubs floating on the water. The children were eagerly trying to catch the trout, and I was brought back to the times I had enjoyed with my parents at Hacienda Oeste. It was a wonderful way to spend the month of August.

Mario and Salomé had arrived and become acclimated, so there was no reason to linger other than the whole family loved it there. On September 18th, Olga and Saguaro Blossom ushered the children into our car followed by Corporal and myself, and we started our journey back to the rancho. We arrived at the Deming depot to be greeted by José and Running Bear, who had brought the grand coach and another coach to transport us and our baggage to Hacienda Oriental. It was nice to be home, but we were going to miss the easy living in Wyoming.

On the morning of the 23rd, I walked into Pedro's kitchen and grabbed a cup of coffee. Before I could sit down at the table, Pedro informed me my food was being sent up to Mother's rooms, where I was to have my breakfast.

I walked into Mother's rooms to find José and Dulce with Mother. Olga came in behind me. We all sat down to breakfast and, after we had settled into her lounge chairs with coffee and pan dulce, Mother brought us all to attention. "I have an announcement to make. We are going to have a new addition to our family. Olga is with child."

I choked on my pan dulce and spilled my coffee as I jumped up to hug Olga. After the spilled coffee was cleaned up and I regained my composure, Mother went on to say, "Panchito, you asked me for a recommendation on a name for the Wyoming ranch, and I told you the name should be Olga's choice. Olga tells me you never brought it up." She gave me a look and then immediately continued, "So, I asked her for a name. Her immediate answer was 'Tierra Hermosa (Beautiful Land).' For us in Mexico, the name of the ranch will be Estancia de la Tierra Hermosa, but, in the United States, it will be the Tierra Hermosa Ranch. If you do not have my quarters ready there, you have the winter to get them ready. Take your wife and leave me now. I know you are eager to be with her and celebrate the life she holds."

I could tell Mother was upset with me for not bringing up the question of the name of the ranch with Olga, and I had just been chided for it. From then on, I vowed to consult with Olga first on decisions of this nature.

It was the morning of the 25th when two riders came with bad news. We had been raided by banditos from the south and rustlers from the north. In the south, banditos had attacked the ranch that Running Bear had established and killed his wife and his youngest son while raiding their home for horses and cattle. To the north, they killed a vaquero and made off with 12 head.

Running Bear and Hungry Fox, who had returned from Cornell, were rabid to pursue and avenge their loss but, at the same time, they needed to go home and take care of their loved ones. Mother called Running Bear to her and told him that she, Angélica, and Rosa Honeywell would go to their home, retrieve the bodies and the rest of the family, and bring them to the rancho where they would be safe until justice had been served and they returned.

I ordered José to notify the Rurales and told He Who Hunts that he was to ride with José to find the perpetrators of the northern intrusion in the United States. Once they found them, José was to return to the Hacienda while He Who Hunts was to observe and await my coming, which I would do once I had helped Running Bear obtain justice and the rancho had exacted its revenge. In an hour, Running Bear and I, along with 13 vaqueros, left well stocked for a campaign with food and extra horses. Hungry Fox and Corporal had taken two horses each and headed out in hot pursuit. They would leave us a trail to follow.

As we rode, neighbors of Running Bear joined us and gave us the news they had seen Hungry Fox and Corporal ride by. It was becoming apparent the banditos were headed for safe havens in the Sierra Madres north and west of Casas Grandes.

When they reached the foothills, they were met by Apache and Tarahumara scouts that had seen the mirror talk from Corporal. Fellow braves had sighted the banditos and were following them from the sides, as the banditos were looking for pursuit from behind. Two of the Tarahumara scouts came to meet us on foot, as they could outlast a horse at a high gait, to guide us on parallel paths to the banditos.

In Casas Grandes, the banditos sold the cattle they had taken and continued on with the horses. I told three vaqueros to break off from the pursuit and find out who bought the stolen cattle and await our return to point them out.

On the evening of the fourth day, we surrounded the banditos hideout and were waiting for morning to exact our revenge. The following morning, the vaqueros and Tarahumara tightened the noose and killed all 26 individuals in the bandito stronghold while the Apache picked up six hapless souls who believed they had escaped the killing. All the corpses were branded with the brand of the rancho as well as the brand of Running Bear's family. They were placed on horses and packed to Casas Grandes.

We were met by Capitán Carrillo on the way to Casas Grandes, and he followed us into the town in the middle of the night as we placed the bodies in front of the homes of the buyers of the stolen cattle. When they awoke in the morning and saw the bodies, the men in the family were arrested by the Rurales and taken to Chihuahua. Unfortunately for them, they never saw a court.

Six days later, the people of Deming woke up to find the naked bodies of a rancher and two cowboys from a ranch on the east side of the Floridas with the words "killers" and "thieves" branded on their chests. When some of the town folk went to the ranch, they found the carcasses of 12 Mexican cattle and a burned-out home. In that part of Mexico, it was not a right to steal from or kill Mexicans.

It was October 3rd when we arrived at Hacienda Montañas, and it was good to be home. At the school Señor White had established at the Hacienda, Rene began his education along with the children from the surrounding campos and Hacienda as well as the Apache children. He was in a class of 11 that covered the first two grades. When classes were over, he and all the boys began their apprenticeship under the watchful eye of two of the old vaqueros who had moved to the Hacienda to steward the young men in the skills of a vaquero. Their first lessons were in the care of their animals, which started with keeping the horses' living quarters clean. They were no longer boys. They were referred to as vaqueros jóvenes (young cowboys).

Dulce was busy helping throughout the house and eager to join Rene in school. My children were becoming little adults before my eyes, and it was my duty when I was there to help them escape all the watchful eyes and have fun. I knew too well that responsibility would come soon enough, and childhood would melt away.

Pressure from the have-nots and derelicts of society who were banding together along our southern borders and stealing what they were unable to earn was being felt throughout the rancho. Three more times, we pursued and dealt with bandit gangs that would kill for just a few head of cattle. The resentment felt by los desamparados (the needy) toward our efforts was beginning to grow. We could not allow them to steal with impunity or kill in the act of doing so and, at the same time, we couldn't punish every starving human being that sought to obtain food. I came to the conclusion we needed to act to alleviate the effects of poverty in those citizens who were less fortunate than us.

I called a meeting on December 1st of the family at Hacienda Montañas that included those individuals who opted to purchase land and work cooperatively with us. It was decided by the family that we would open 600-hectare plots for settlement by anyone who would like to purchase them from the rancho in the same manner that our hands could purchase their own land. They would market their stock through the coop and pay us back for the land at 25 percent of their production. In addition, we would open tierra cultivable (arable land) on the outskirts of our cultivated lands to farming in 20-hectare plots with a 20 percent interest in a well-share agreement with four neighbors. They would pay back the cost of the lands and wells with 25 percent of their crops. The Estancia would retain 100 percent of all mineral rights. The children of those who took this offer must attend the rancho's schools, and the students that qualified would be offered a college education. This offer was made for only the lands the rancho designated and was on a first-come basis. The lands would become available once they had been fenced. The rancho would continue to offer the land and the association to all the people populating the land adjacent to the rancho.

The announcement was made that anyone residing within 45 leguas (leagues; a league is three miles) of the Estancia's borders was eligible to buy land in a cooperative purchase if they could establish they were of good character and could demonstrate they had skills in either ranching or farming. Immediately, a flood of applicants began to beat a path to Estancia Oriental, where they made application and were guided to the lands being offered. The decision of which lands were to be included in this offer was made by the rancho. This offer was not a right. It was a business arrangement to those who wanted to take advantage of it.

CHAPTER 35

As was the tradition, Christmas was observed at Hacienda Oriental. Roman, Dulce, Elizabeth, Javier, and Roberto and their families joined in the celebration with Mother, Angélica, José, Olga, and me. The house was alive with children, and it was a memorable time for all.

A family meeting was called on the 27th of December, and I reported on Estancia de la Tierra Hermosa and Estancia Santa Barbara (which Olga had named the California Ranches near Santa Barbara). I gave an overall view that our family was now secure from the ravages of the revolution that was sure to come, because the haves were far fewer than the have-nots. It was my goal that Hacienda Oriental would remain an agricultural headquarters of the northern Mexican cooperatives, if they remained viable after the revolution. I foresaw we or our progeny would be able to hold on to Hacienda Montañas, and the Pérez family would remain in a profitable cattle business in the mountain ranges as well as their adjoining foothills. Most of the western and southern portions of the lands of Hacienda Occidental would be or would have been portioned out.

Juan and Dulce reported on Hacienda Pérez de Colorado and said the first purchase of the property had recovered well with ample snow and rain. The second addition was overall in the best shape, and it could easily handle the cattle that were on it. The third purchase was in the worst shape, as the lower lands were badly overgrazed and would need some husbandry, but the mountain portions were doing well and could provide good summer graze for cattle already marked for shipping to market.

The well drilling was a success, and the valley portion of the third property had the best soils for the plow with ample water available. Benito Hernández could have 300 acres of winter fodder in cultivation by Spring. It was expected that, by the Spring of 1888, there would be an additional 600 acres that could be dedicated to wheat and summer vegetables for both the Hacienda and the Denver market. It could be shipped there within eight hours after harvesting.

Elizabeth then reported that the Crossed Arrows Corporation was now not only supplying a large portion of the beef to The British Beef Producers and Shipping Corporation but was also shipping to them its entire cotton crop as well as a large amount of grain.

She turned over the floor to Javier, who reported the copper mine northwest of Cananea would be on line by July of next year, and that two other mining projects had been started north of that project as well as a project in the state of Durango. He estimated we would need to inject approximately $150,000 in the mines in the next six months to make that happen. The proven reserves of the first property alone were $1.7 million. He also indicated we were in the process of looking at deposits both in New Mexico and Arizona.

At that point, Elizabeth called upon Roberto, who stated a new corporation had been established in Mexico to purchase and develop mining properties in that country. This corporation would be known as La Corporación Minera de México (The Mining Corporation of Mexico). La Corporación Tenedora de Pérez (Pérez Holding Corporation) would be the major stockholder with 88 percent of the stock, and the Mexican government would hold 12 percent of the stock. All our crop-producing lands as well as machinery and production plants in Mexico would be put under the La Corporación de Producción Agrícola de

México (Corporation of Agricultural Production of Mexico), which would be owned by La Corporación Tenedora de Pérez at 92 percent and the Mexican government by eight percent. The Crossed Arrows Corporation would hold 100 percent of La Corporación Tenedora de Pérez's stock.

Elizabeth then took the floor again and stated the Mexican coops were coming on line, and The British Beef Producers and Shipping Corporation was ramping up its capitalization in shipping, dock space, and warehousing. She stated, "The Crossed Arrows Corporation now has a 21 percent stake in the corporation. Our assessment on the 193,000 pounds of beef needed should be approximately $210,000, and our share of the profits for the past year were $286,000. The reserves in the United States are $1.26 million, and that should be sufficient to continue expansion and capitalization. Our net income from the ranches and farms for 1886 will be approximately $490,000."

I then adjourned the meeting until 10: 00 am on the 28th.

That evening in our private rooms, Olga and I had a discussion about our life and where we wanted to go with it. We came to the conclusion we would like to take our children to the States and, for the time being, live at Estancia de la Tierra Hermosa. It was important for us to afford our children every opportunity and, therefore, we would seek to naturalize ourselves and our children. We could start by having our sixth child born in the United States. I was head of all the business of the family. We had no illusions that we could live happily ever after in Wyoming, but we decided that should be our home for most of the year, and most winters would be spent at Hacienda Montañas. It was agreed we would move during the first weeks of February. It was also agreed that, whenever possible, Olga and the children would travel with me wherever my duties took me.

I convened the meeting on the 28th, which was focused on my thoughts about what direction the business of the Estancia del Pérez should take. I started the meeting by saying, "I do not feel we should limit our expansion in the United States and, therefore, I would like to direct Roberto to look into the purchase of both ranch land and crop land in Colorado, New Mexico, California, Montana, Wyoming, and Arizona. I feel crop lands in the Sacramento Valley of California will be extremely profitable, and there are areas of Arizona and New Mexico that will be lucrative for the cattle business and agriculture. Montana has many opportunities similar to the one we just obtained in Wyoming. I will always let people know I am looking at expansion for the future. In addition, I would like to expand more into the San Luis Valley of Colorado, where there is good opportunity for both the cattle industry and crop raising.

"I want to continue with our program of sending the children from our schools to college, both here and in the United States, and I want to be able to employ them once they graduate. I need all your help in providing employment opportunities, as I cannot know the capabilities of each graduate, and our need for expertise is great. Dishosa is an example of someone who is a great credit to Estancia del Pérez, as is Benito Hernández and others. We need their blood, as our business cannot run without them. They need to know this business is theirs as well as ours. It is up to each of you to know the capabilities of these students. Our need is already great, and we must couple these young people with the old hands. They will then not only have the knowledge they learned in school but will experience for themselves the history and the workings of the ranchos, so their ideas will be heard and their skills utilized. Already, Presidente Díaz knows of our graduates, and he is looking to utilize them for Mexico. We should be proud of their accomplishments, but we should also keep expanding so we have a place for them and their families.

"I envision a future for our children where they can use the advantages they are born with to not only maintain the ranchos but to steadfastly protect the welfare of the people of the ranchos. We all know an upheaval is coming; we just do not know when. Each of us has a duty to the land and the people to see that both survive. The United States will have no more revolutions, although there will be despots and those who want to go backward to what they imagine was a better time in the past. However, the people of the United States will always appreciate and honor the labor and success of its citizens, and it has always upheld the premise that no one is above the law. The dandies that dance in Mexico and do not dirty their hands have doomed Mexico to another revolution that will rip Mexico to the core. It will be up to us and others to slowly bring it back to the position where it is right now and, at the same time, bring all its citizens with us.

"We must make it known to all the children of the Estancia del Pérez they are valuable to the ranchos, but their life achievements are theirs alone, and we want them to be, first of all, valuable citizens of the world."

It was Tuesday March 1, 1887, when Olga, our children, and I were joined by He Who Hunts and Singing Brook, and their children; Corporal; Roman; nannies; and household staff on our return to Estancia de la Tierra Hermosa. The cars were on the siding waiting for us in Deming and, on March 2nd, we headed north. We had scheduled a stop in Santa Fe to see the sights and partake of the social entertainment for which it was highly noted.

While we were there, He Who Hunts, Roman, Corporal, and I took many rides to survey the mountains and valleys in all directions out of Santa Fe. We let it be known we were interested in cattle and farmland in northern New Mexico, and I engaged a law firm to contact the Crossed Arrows Corporation if a suitable property came on the market.

It so happened that, by coincidence, Pony Diehl, who had been residing in the Santa Fe Territorial Prison for the past five years, was released while we were there. He purchased a horse and, on March 7th, rode out of Santa Fe toward Taos with the eventual objective of visiting relatives in Denver.

On March 10th, we resumed our journey north. Corporal and Roman returned to the rancho. For some unknown reason, Pony Diehl must have run into calamity. His horse returned to Santa Fe with his clothes tied to the saddle. Not even the law was interested in finding out what might have happened to him.

It was the 18th of March when we arrived at Estancia de la Tierra Hermosa. The coaches rolled through deep snow up to the front of the house. The children hit the ground running, as maids and mothers worked to get them into the house and in front of a grand fireplace whose fire radiated warmth throughout the room.

On April 22nd, Roman Pérez Celaya was born. It was April 26th when I received a wire that Mother had decamped from Hacienda Oriental and was headed to Wyoming. Her expected arrival was on the 29th. We had three days to have her quarters ready.

On Sunday, May 8th, a dispatch rider rode in as we were sitting down to an elk feast that Morning Dew had prepared carrying a message from José. It stated that, shortly after 11:00pm on May 3rd, a strong earthquake had struck the area around Hacienda Oriental. Most of the adobe homes were destroyed including the adobe portion of the Hacienda. "No information had arrived from the other Haciendas," the message read. "Angélica and the children survived, although there were some broken bones. We will be departing to stay with Dulce. There were many deaths."

Within an hour, He Who Hunts and I were in the saddle headed north to catch a train. There would be no special car. Billy Machelson and Mario Cortez were not only in charge of the ranch but also charged with watching over our families and any others who may be evacuated here.

I had noticed that Billy had often been around since Mother arrived. What was even more curious was that mother, at 50 years old, was radiant.

On the 12th of May, we arrived at Hacienda Oriental in the company of José and Running Bear. Signs of the earthquake were evident in Deming, where several adobe and brick homes had collapsed or were seriously damaged. Nothing in my mind could have prepared me for the scene at the Hacienda. More than half the buildings had been demolished or damaged. Many of the homes of vaqueros and farm workers were partially or totally destroyed, and there were 22 new graves in the graveyard including those of Edward and Juliana Honeywell.

José had ordered a carload of canvas for temporary housing to be delivered to Deming from Georgia and an additional carload from Mexico to be delivered to Juárez. Two sawmills were being set up, one on the east flank of San Luis and the other on the west flank of El Medio. Our cooperative partners on the rancho had been notified they should put in their orders for lumber as soon as they could and, if they could spare any labor, to send those men to the mills. Most of the wells on the agricultural lands had been destroyed, as the land had shifted, and the bottoms of the wells were no longer in line with the pumps.

Five new well rigs had been ordered, and the well rigs on hand were busy drilling new wells for not only the rancho but for our cooperative members, who were contributing labor to run the rigs. The rigs were running 24 hours a day until the damaged wells were replaced. The gins and agricultural facilities were fairly intact, as they were made of lumber and steel. Much was still to be done, and labor was arriving from all over Mexico to get the facilities up and running as well as restoring irrigation ditches for both the rancho and the cooperative owners.

Running Bear reported many stock tanks had been destroyed, and many creeks had been either diverted from their original course or were no longer running. The vaqueros were all working on the restoration of water for the stock and moving them to where there was ample water.

Corporal had taken Saguaro Blossom and their children to Hacienda Montañas, which had been damaged but was still functional. This was surprising, as it was located on the east flank of San Luis. Only 18 miles away, on the west flank, the earthquake had torn a large scar that extended for miles north and south. We could only surmise that, because there was solid bedrock below the Hacienda and it was built solely of lumber, these were the reasons it had withstood the tremors.

José had Hacienda Oriental in hand, and I had the rest of the rancho to inspect. I left José with one order: "Delegate as much as you can, but do not delegate visiting every one of the cooperative-member homes to find out their needs and let them know the rancho is there to help."

It was May the 14th when He Who Hunts and Running Bear departed with me for the west to Hacienda Montañas with a goal of stopping at each of the campos on our way west. All along the way we found devastation. Since most of the homes at the campos were adobe, they collapsed in on themselves or outward, with the roof coming down on top of whatever was inside. This was also true for the homes of the cooperative members. As many of the homes were low-roofed, the mortality rate was much less than at the two-story Hacienda. However, the injury rate was high, with many broken bones, and some were left paralyzed.

It was apparent we needed to intervene, and I ordered Running Bear to return to the Hacienda and see that all the coaches at the Hacienda visited all the campos and transported the injured to the closest place for care—whether it be Douglas, Bisbee, or El Paso—at the expense of the Hacienda. Those that could be cared for at the clinic at Hacienda Montañas would be transported there, as it was built out of timber and had survived intact. I wanted no one to suffer needlessly on this rancho due to lack of care. In addition, I wanted to see that the women and children were transported to the closest Hacienda for shelter until their homes could be rebuilt.

When we reached Hacienda Montañas, I was amazed at the lack of damage to the Hacienda or the outlying homes. I vowed that no longer would the rancho allow construction of homes that could kill. I ordered the staff at the Hacienda to prepare to receive refugees, and finding them housing was paramount. All the available space must be utilized.

Roman, Panchita, and their children were in residence at the Hacienda. Panchita said, "We were traveling home to Hacienda Occidental when Roman decided we must stop for the night. We had a family camp-out, with the children asleep in the coach, and Roman and I were in blankets under the coach when the earthquake struck. Roman waited until light before he would allow the coach to move on to the Hacienda, as he was sure there would be damage to the road. As we were preparing to go, we were met by vaqueros from the Hacienda, who said it had been totally destroyed, with much death. Roman ordered that horses be obtained to transport the family back to Hacienda Montañas and that the coach be left at the first campo it could be taken to. He then went on to Hacienda Occidental."

Panchita went on to tell me she had gotten the news about the loss of her parents through the signals. I told Panchita I would like for her to go to Dulce in Colorado with Saguaro Blossom and others in the family to make room for refugees that had no home.

I told her, "I will confirm this with Roman, and he will signal his agreement to you."

He Who Hunts asked the Apaches to build wikiups to shelter themselves so refugee families who had been unable to build them could take the buildings at the Hacienda until we could build new homes for them. Many had already done so and were living in both places, as it was hard to give up the old ways.

I told Corporal he was in charge of the Hacienda, and his first order of business would be to send a crew to open the coach road between Hacienda Oriental and Hacienda Occidental. I informed him I would send him a signal to transport Panchita and Saguaro Blossom and the children to Colorado. I asked him to see that José sent a message to Olga and Mother in Wyoming to tell them the family was being evacuated to Colorado. "I am sure she will intervene, and you may have to take

Panchita and Saguaro Blossom on to Wyoming, if Mother wishes it. Once you have seen to your family and my family, you will be sorely needed here."

He Who Hunts and I proceeded on toward the Hacienda.

Our worst expectations of the damage to the Hacienda were far exceeded. The Hacienda and its outlying buildings were mostly rubble, and there were 36 new graves in the cemetery. I discussed the transport of Panchita to Colorado and possibly Wyoming, and Roman concurred and said he would see a message was sent to Corporal. Given the total destruction of the Hacienda and the partition of much of the western lands, we decided it would be best if he moved his headquarters to Hacienda Montañas. I told him about the evacuation of women and children to Hacienda Montañas. Unfortunately, the road was blocked in many places between the Haciendas, and he would need to send road crews toward the east to meet the road crews that Corporal had sent west. I told him he needed to see to the care of not only the people of the rancho but the cooperative owners, too. There was almost no transportation available to take the injured for medical help.

Roman informed me there was a small hospital in Cananea, but he had information that some tunnels in the mines had collapsed, and there were many wounded. I told him to stop by the hospital and see if they could take some wounded at the expense of the rancho. I said to him. "Make every effort to get the road open to the east, as I will go to Tombstone to see if Dr. Goodfellow can set up a care center at Hacienda Montañas and make sure there are caregivers on a temporary basis."

I also asked him to stop by the mine that was about to open to get a report on damage and relay it on to me. I suggested he keep his foreman busy with the cattle and he should take responsibility for visiting all the campos and cooperative ranches and farms in his jurisdiction to offer help, send only the most gravely injured to Cananea, and relay his information about the mine by a courier who could also inform

Hacienda Montañas as to the progress on the road. He Who Hunts and I would leave for Tombstone early in the morning.

He Who Hunts and I arrived in Tombstone on May 24th. My first stop was at Dr. Goodfellow's clinic, where I made my case to him. He immediately began to gather all the medicines he had on hand and alerted his nurse they were going on a journey. He Who Hunts and I left in the company of Dr. Goodfellow and his nurse for Hacienda Montañas within hours of our arrival in Tombstone.

We passed one of the road crews that was approaching the western flanks of the climb over the north end of San Luis. They reported making contact with the eastern crew, which had peaked from the east and was headed down toward them. Their job was to make the road passable, which meant removing boulders and stabilizing the surface so the coaches could get through. It had to be passable for coaches, but it would be some time before it would be a proper coach road.

We turned southeast at Campo Guadalupe and took the trail to Campo Central, where we turned east and dropped down to Hacienda Montañas.

When we arrived, Corporal had a clinic set up in the grand room of the Hacienda. My rooms would be used to house Dr. Goodfellow and his nurse. José had sent Rosa Honeywell to this Hacienda, as the clinic at Hacienda Oriental had been set up as a regional hospital, and two doctors had arrived from Chihuahua with nurses. I was also informed the government was sending doctors from Hermosillo to Hacienda Montañas along with nurses, because there were many casualties south of the rancho, and they would be transported to the Haciendas and the clinic at Cananea.

Corporal handed me a telegram that Presidente Díaz had sent to Hacienda Oriental via Ascención. In it, he offered the facilities of the government in rebuilding roads so wounded could be moved and commerce restored. José replied to the Presidente that I was out surveying damage and putting plans together to take care of the people and restore their homes. He also told Presidente Díaz the offer was very much appreciated and needed, and he gave him a rundown of the roads that needed to be restored in northern Chihuahua. He stated I would be sending him a list of roads that needed restoration in northern Sonora once I was in communication.

Felix Francisco Maceyra, the governor of Chihuahua, sent a road crew of six men to open the road between Hacienda Oriental and Palomas on Presidente Díaz's orders to give all assistance necessary.

I immediately sent a wire to Presidente Díaz and outlined the roads that needed immediate repair, including the roads up the Rio Batepito Valley and the Bavispe Valley as well as the road from Nacozari de García to Aqua Prieta and the road from Cananea to Aqua Prieta and Naco, all of which, if left in disrepair, would completely shut down the repair of the railroad between Nacozari and the smelter in Douglas, Arizona.

Carlos Ortiz, the governor of Sonora, sent engineers from Hermosillo with authorization to rebuild all roads of commerce damaged by the earthquake as soon as possible.

On June 7th, we received news that Ike Clanton had been killed by a range detective named Jonas V. Brighton in the hire of the Arizona Cattlemen's Association. Clanton was killed at Jim Wilson's ranch near Springerville, Arizona. The hunger for revenge for the death of Gregorio Pérez Adame had been sated.

It was June 11th when Carlos Pacheco Villalobos left the office of governor of Chihuahua and Lauro Carrillo, the governor of Chihuahua, sent engineers with the authority to hire all necessary help to repair the roads of commerce due to the damage of the earthquake.

On June 18th, He Who Hunts and four grateful vaqueros escorted Dr. Goodfellow and his nurse back to Tombstone, and the clinic in the grand room of the Hacienda was closed. The mills were turning out lumber, and new houses were being built for those who lost their homes. On July 2nd, I moved back into my quarters—which I shared with Roman—after living in a wickiup I had also used as a headquarters for Estancia del Pérez.

There were 37 new graves in the cemetery at Hacienda Montañas. In all, the death toll at the Rancho was 151 souls, many of whom had died because of lack of timely medical care. However, some 764 people had been treated at the clinics at Hacienda Montañas and Hacienda Oriental.

There was very little agricultural production in the Rio Bavispe Valley due to the destruction of the diversion dams and canals. The diversion dams around the Hacienda Oriental were repaired in time to get out about 60 percent of the normal production. Expansion of our agricultural lands would be in full force by wintertime. Water catchments and dams had been built and would be continuing to be improved upon. Our shipment of market cattle had continued at the same rate as before, but the calf crop was about 80 percent of our annual average.

It was apparent that any expansion in the next year should be in properties adjoining our existing lands, as the price of beef was recovering, but the market was still low. Our prices, and those of our cooperative members, were better than the market due to our participation in The British Beef Producers and Shipping Corporation, and demand would improve considerably with the opening of markets in China and India from our Los Angeles slaughterhouse. I felt confident the downturn in cattle production on the rancho was a one-year event, and we would have no problem obtaining cooperative members to fill in the gap.

As of July 22nd, Roman had things well in hand at the new headquarters for the Occidental portion of Estancia del Pérez, and it was time for He Who Hunts, Corporal, and me to head to Hacienda Oriental.

On August 11th, He Who Hunts, José, Corporal, and I boarded a train for Colorado and then on to Wyoming. In Colorado, we stopped off at Hacienda Pérez de Colorado and spent five days with Dulce and

Juan. We inspected the stock and grazing land as well as the newly opened crop lands. The expansion of the crop lands was looking good, but I decided the crew members should begin work after they had gone to the rancho and seen to the welfare of their families and help get the agricultural lands back into production around Hacienda Oriental as well as the Rio Batepito and Rio Bavispe Valleys.

I asked if any of them would like to work here on a permanent basis, and 11 of the 26 said they would rather stay in Mexico. I instructed José to ask the agricultural workers at Hacienda Oriental if any wanted to move to Colorado and Wyoming to work the farms there, and we would transport them with the men that wanted to stay at Hacienda Pérez de Colorado when the farms were back in shape in Mexico. I told them I would send them back with Mario Cortez when he returned with the men we would send back from Wyoming, which should be in about 15 days. José gathered his family along with all the refugees that had been evacuated to Hacienda Pérez de Colorado, and he and Corporal headed back to Hacienda Oriental, where they were sorely needed.

On August 21st, I arrived at Estancia de la Tierra Hermosa, hungrily rushed into Olga's open arms, and buried my head in her bosom. The next month was spent solely with my Olga and the children. It took some coaxing to get little Roman to warm up to me. Rene took many rides with me to inspect the rancho and, when we would not be riding a long distance and stopping at a pool to enjoy lunch and a swim, Olgita joined us on her pony.

I received notice on September 15th that Silas Leven had been contacted by a rancher who had a 1,800-head ranch north of our holdings and was interested in selling. Also, there were two sections of agricultural land southwest of Fort Garland that had come on the market. I wired Silas we were interested, and I would be sending people to inspect the properties immediately. They should be on site within two weeks. I then wired Corporal to contact Antonio and Gregorio Sapia and ask them to accompany him to inspect a ranch in Colorado. In addition, I would need either Emilio Vásquez or Armando Hernández to accompany him to inspect some agricultural lands. He was also to contact Mario to let him know he needed to be at Estancia de la Tierra Hermosa for winter duties and should leave immediately.

I also contacted José and let him know I would be decamping to Wyoming for the winter as Rene would be starting school, and there was no school at Estancia de la Tierra Hermosa. "I need to know if my rooms at Hacienda Oriental are available and in condition for occupancy. If that is not possible, please talk to Señor Blanco and ask him if he has someone able to tutor Rene, which might be the best solution, as the tutor could accompany us as we travel."

On October the 2nd, I received word from Corporal the ranch land was as advertised and was in good shape. The agricultural land was highly regarded by Armando Hernández, who praised not only the fertile soils but the availability of water. He also went on to state there was a fine, large ranch home that went with the property. I spoke with Olga, and she agreed we should consider staying at the house for the winter.

José had sent a message that the reconstruction at the Hacienda was still in progress, and Señor White was sending a tutor. I responded to both Corporal and José that Olga, the kids, and I would be moving to the new house in Colorado and asked that the tutor be sent there. I also contacted Silas and told him we would purchase both properties. I asked him to contact Roberto in New York and make arrangements to close on the properties, as I would not be able to make a closing in the near future. I told him I would like it to be closed right away, as I was moving my family to Colorado.

As things were being finalized, I approached Mother to tell her what was happening and that we would be moving the family to Colorado. Mother asked her maid to fetch Billy Machelson. Olga came in, and we had coffee and pan dulce until Billy arrived. When Billy arrived, Mother announced that Billy had asked her to marry him, and she had accepted. I was not totally in shock, as it seemed they were together often.

I asked her what plans she had made, and she said, "It is my wish to get married at Hacienda Oriental, where my family and people can gather to enjoy my happiness. For now, I would like to accompany you and Olga to Hacienda Pérez de Colorado to consult with Dulce on the wedding plans. Would it be possible for us to have our wedding over the Christmas holiday?"

I replied, "I do not know if Hacienda Oriental will be sufficiently repaired for such a large gathering. I know the arrangements could be made at Hacienda Montañas, but that would require a lot more traveling for family in New York. Of course, it may be easier for Roman and his family to join Angélica and her family on a trip to Hacienda Pérez de Colorado, and it would be a train trip for Elizabeth, Roberto, and Javier from New York. Would you consider that as an alternative?"

Mother looked at Billy, who said, "Whatever arrangements need to be made so I can marry your mother is just what I want."

Mother agreed to having Christmas and the wedding at Hacienda Pérez de Colorado. My next question was, "Where do you want to live?"

Billy replied, "Estancia de la Tierra Hermosa."

I said, "Billy, it is going to take me until mid-October to settle the family into the ranch house on the newly acquired land in Colorado. I would like for you to travel to Hacienda Pérez de Colorado to arrive around October 20th. You and me, as well as Corporal and He Who Hunts, will tour Estancia del Pérez in Mexico, Estancia Santa Barbara, and Hacienda Pérez de Colorado for 45 to 60 days, and we will end up at the Colorado ranches prior to your wedding date. Will you be able to leave the Estancia de la Tierra Hermosa in time to be in Colorado on the 20th?"

Billy replied, "I will."

I went on to say, "I will make sure He Who Hunts and Corporal are at the ranch on or before October the 15th."

I ordered champagne to toast the engagement and announced there would be a party with a pit-roasted steer the next day to celebrate.

We had just settled into our home on the new ranch when Billy Machelson arrived with Corporal and He Who Hunts. We began by touring the newly acquired ranch, which took several days. From there, I opted out of touring the other ranch lands and asked them to notify me when they were ready to tour the new farmland. I asked Billy to give me his opinion of all the ranch lands after he had seen them.

I then took my time to ride with Rene and Olgita touring the sites as well as traveling down to Hacienda Pérez de Colorado to visit Mother and hear what plans Juan and Dulce had for the husbandry of the lands of the Hacienda. I also took the opportunity to take Mother, Billy, Dulce, Juan, and Olga to the restaurant Alemán (German restaurant) in Fort Garland, where we were served beef stroganoff followed by Black Forest cake. During the meal, I announced that when Mother and Billy returned from their honeymoon, Billy would become the manager of the Estancia de la Tierra Hermosa and that he should name who would be the foreman before they left.

After touring the lands in Colorado, Billy, Corporal, He Who Hunts, and I headed south to Hacienda Oriental. I so did not like leaving Olga, but she was somewhat cheerful to see me go, as she needed to feather her nest without me being in the way.

At Hacienda Oriental, Hacienda Montañas, and the campos we visited, it was my duty to inform all my brothers and sisters and the hands that Doña María was getting married to Billy Machelson on December 20th at Hacienda Pérez de Colorado, and all that wished to be at the ceremony need only inform us, and we would see that transportation was provided. I do believe Billy began to suffer from too many hugs and handshakes.

We left the rancho and rode north to Tucson, where we boarded a train to Los Angeles. My first visit there was necessarily the new processing plant and facilities of The British Beef Producers and

Shipping Corporation in Long Beach. The capacity was already being expanded, as the demand coming from both China and India had greatly increased.

We toured the California ranches and looked at some farmland in the Sacramento Valley that had been recently put on the market and that Gerald Pitney had sent a wire about. I informed Gerald we were interested, but I needed to have my farm experts examine the properties before we purchased them. I had wired José to send someone to check them out and report to me his approval. I had Gerald contact Roberto about the funds authorization. Funds to purchase the land would be in the name of the Crossed Arrows Corporation.

We arrived at Hacienda Pérez de Colorado on December 12th after stopping in San Francisco to get Billy outfitted properly to marry my mother. Carlos Deus arrived on the 14th, and the priest oversaw rehearsals to ensure all would go off perfectly.

The wedding was spectacular, and Billy joined the Pérez family. It was December 28th when Mother and Billy left in the company of Elizabeth, Roberto, and Mary Beth on their honeymoon's first leg, which was to be in New York. They would eventually embark on a cruise ship to London, where Billy was to be immersed in British aristocracy. From there, they would go to Mexico to meet the Mexican aristocracy before they headed back to Wyoming.

CHAPTER 36

Patricio Pérez Celaya was born on March 17, 1889 and was followed by Ricardo Pérez Celaya on June 5, 1891. It is now December of 1901; I cannot believe how quickly the years passed since I sat in that cantina in Chihuahua in 1879 and was addressed as Don Francisco.

Our expansion into the cattle business has ebbed. We are now owners of large tracts of farmlands in the Sacramento Valley of California as well as the San Luis Valley of Colorado. Much of the ranch land of Haciendas Oriental and Occidental has been broken up into ranchos, of which most are under the husbandry of old hands of the Haciendas or their children. The cattle lands under Hacienda Montañas remain intact, and Roman is in charge of the cattle production at the Hacienda. José remains in charge of the farming productions we have developed both in the United States and Mexico.

Many of the children of the hands of the Haciendas graduated and have gone on to work in the businesses of the Crossed Arrows Corporation in the United States and the La Corporación Minera de México or La Corporación de Producción Agrícola de México. We have graduates working in the government in Mexico City as well as in Chihuahua and Sonora.

Rene is a second-year student at the College of New Jersey, which was renamed Princeton University in 1896. Olgita is a first-year student at Wellesley. Gregorio, Roman's son, decided he wanted to strike out on his own, and he started a ranch in the Santa Cruz Valley where the river begins its bend to flow northward into the United States. José's and Angélica's oldest son graduated from Princeton and is studying law at Harvard University with the goal of joining Roberto in the family law firm. Roberto and Mary Beth have three children at Cornell.

Mother is now 64 years old and is residing with José and Angélica at Hacienda Oriental. Billy passed away in 1899.

I am 44 years old and have been head of the family for the past 22 years.

We built our own market through our participation in The British Beef Producers and Shipping Corporation. The decline of cattle prices during the 1880s and the 1890s affected our bottom line, but, having a steady market helped us to weather the declines. People continue to want to eat beef, and our market is the world.

Our investments in mining ventures throughout Mexico, the United States, and Peru are not totally invested in any one mineral. Copper was king, but we invested in coal, steel, and other minerals. The economic downturn in the 1890s had a significant effect on our bottom line, but the mining ventures remained on the positive side of the ledger.

The collapse of many of the banks, especially in the United States, were marginally significant to us. We had few funds in Mexican banks, and the J. P. Morgan Bank (where our American funds were deposited) remained sound as did the Rothschild Family Banks in England, where the proceeds from our business with The British Beef Producers and Shipping Corporation are deposited as are the dividends.

Having secure funds enabled us to invest in more farmland in the Sacramento Valley of California as well as the Río Bravo (Rio Grande) Valley of New Mexico and Texas.

Due to the collapse of the Union Pacific, Northern Pacific, and Atchison Topeka and Santa Fe railroads and their subsequent placement in receivership, The British Beef Producers and Shipping Corporation and the Crossed Arrows Corporation gained modest ownership and representation on the Boards of both of the Union Pacific and the Atchison Topeka and Santa Fe Railway, which helped assure we were not subject to the gouging of our agriculture and mining interests by the railroads.

My goal has been and always will be the security of my family and the people who work alongside us in all our endeavors. It has been our policy that those who work with us reap the benefits of their work, secure the future of their children through education, and have the opportunity to achieve according to their abilities and wishes.

I would be remiss if I did not pass on to you the warnings my father made part of my being. In Mexico, there is a large disparity between those who own the means of production and those who work to exist. Those who work to exist far outnumber those who own the means of production. This disparity will continue to lead to revolution.

Many of the great landowners live in Mexico City and are not of the land. They have done nothing to give back to the land or to better the living situation of the people who work on their land. In the end, the workers will take the land. Unfortunately, Mexico, as a whole, will be the loser, because those that will acquire the lands will neither have the means nor the knowledge to make them produce more than a subsistence living, and Mexico will decline as a nation.

Even now, corridos (folksongs) are being sung about the banditos Ignacio Parra and his brothers. Federico Arreola and Refugio Alvarado are cited along with the Parras as defenders of the disenfranchised who rob from the rich and give to the poor. They are the heroes of the poor.

The corridos of the young José Doroteo Arango Arámbula are sung everywhere. At the age of 16, Arámbula killed a hacienda owner by the name of Agustín López Negrete, who had raped Arámbula's sister. The songs tell of how Arámbula fled into the mountains of Durango, became a protegido (protégé) of Ignacio Parra, and assumed the name of Francisco Villa. He is now in the Sierra Madres of Chihuahua and has his own gang of banditos. The newer corridos are now singing the praises of Pancho Villa.

I mention all of this because my siblings, my children, and I feel this wave of banditos will be a major threat to the wellbeing of the Estancia del Pérez and all its environs. Sometime in the future, an ambitious man will come along and organize those bandits into an army for revolution.

La Vida Seguirá (Life Continues)…

CHARACTERS IN THE BOOK

Character	Description	Appeared in
Abe and Jake	----Old hands on the Colorado ranches	Ch. 14
Ada Howard	----President of Wellesley College	Ch. 15
Andrew Johnson	----President of the United States	Prologue
Angélica Pérez Celaya	----Second daughter of Francisco and Olga Pérez	Throughout
Antonio López de Santa Anna	----Gregorio's cousin dictator of Mexico	Prologue
Antonio Sapia	----Foreman of Hacienda Occidental	Throughout
Ariel Pérez Celaya	----First-born son of Francisco and Olga Pérez	Chs. 22,23,26
Armando Hernández	----Trusted foreman of Emilio Vásquez	Chs. 27,34
Autumn Moon	----Running Bear's granddaughter	Ch. 18 on
Benito Hernández	----Son of Armando Hernández	Chs. 27,34
Benjamin Franklin White	----Tutor (Señor Blanco)	Throughout
Benito Juárez	----President of the Supreme Court, President of Mexico	Prologue
Billy Machelson	----Foreman on the Wyoming ranch Mother's second husband	Chs. 33,34,35
Bull Tamer	----Oldest son of Running Bear	Throughout
Cachorro (Cub)	----Grandson of El Tigre	Throughout
Cochise	----Principle chief of the Chiricahua Apache	Prologue
Comandante Francisco Neri	----Commandant of the Rurales	Throughout
Capitán Alfredo Carrillo	----Captain of the Rurales	Throughout

Cora Slaughter	----Wife of John Slaughter	Chs. 31,32
Carlos "Charles" Deus	----Prussian explorer and soldier	Throughout
Captain Whiteside	----First commander, Camp Huachuca	Throughout
Clanton Cowboys	----Johnny Ringo, Curly Bill Brocius, Florentino Cruz, Frank and Tom Mc Laury, Jim Hughes, Rattlesnake Bill, Joe Hill, Charlie Snow, Jake Gauge, Charlie Thomas, Poney Diehl	Throughout
Consuela Angélica Pérez Castro	----Daughter of Gregorio and María	Throughout
Corporal José Ochoa Guzmán	----Son of Sargento Primero, Francisco's playmate, friend, and right-hand man	Throughout
Corporal Juan Cortez	----Women's bodyguard	Ch. 1
C.S. 'Buck' Fly	----Historic photographer in the Southwest	Throughout
Daniel Barringer	----College classmate, partner in mineral exploration	Throughout
Dishosa Vázquez	----Youngest daughter of Emilio Vásquez	Ch. 27
Doctor Emory Goodfellow	----Renowned surgeon in Tombstone	Ch. 20
	who became an expert in the treatment of gunshot wounds	Throughout
Donald Parker	----Foreman of the ranches in California	Ch. 29
Dulce Pérez Castro	----Second daughter of Gregorio and María, wife of Juan Gonzáles	Throughout
Edward Honeywell	----Mayor domo (Butler) of the Estancia	Throughout
Edward Vail	----Owner of the Empire Ranch	Chs. 8,9,10,25
Eduardo Honeywell	----Playmate, son of Edward and Juliana	Prologue

Elizabeth Pérez Castro	----Third daughter of Gregorio and María	Throughout
El Tigre	----Tarahumara Indian and soldier in Gregorio's commander in charge of the watchers	Throughout
Emilio Márquez	----Head of construction	Throughout
Emilio Vázquez	----Head of the farming on the Estancia	Throughout
Father Salvador	----Missionary Franciscan who ministered to the Haciendas and the chapels	Chs. 13,31
Felipe González	----Watcher along the Animas frontier	Ch. 7
Francisco Pérez Castro	----Main character and storyteller	Prologue
General José Urrea	----Gregorio's commander and mentor	Prologue
General Zaragoza	----General of the Liberal army	Prologue
General Zuloaga	----Conservative President of Mexico	Prologue
Gerald Pitney	----Cousin of Mahlon Pitney and lawyer in Sacramento, California	Chs. 14,25
Geronimo (Goyathlay)	----Chief of the Bedonkohe band of the Chiricahua Apache	Throughout
Gregorio Pérez Adame	----Father and founder of the Estancia	Prologue
Gregorio Pérez Honeywell	----First son of Panchita and Román	Ch. 27
Gregorio Sapia	----Son of Antonio Sapia	Chs. 27,35
Hector Márquez	----Son of Emilio and his foreman on jobs	Chs. 24,33
He Who Hunts	----Apache brave, boyhood companion	Throughout
Henry Pitney	----Father of Mahlon and senior partner of the Pitney law firm and on the Board of the College of New Jersey	Ch. 15

Hungry Fox	----Son of Running Bear, student	Chs. 18,21,33
Ike Clanton	----Son of Old Man Clanton and brother of Billy Clanton	Throughout
Javier Pérez Celaya	----Third son of Francisco and Olga Pérez	Throughout
Javier Pérez Castro	----Fourth son of Gregorio and María	Throughout
Jesus Gallegos	----Husband of María Gallegos	Chs. 25,27
John Chisum	----Rancher in southern New Mexico	Chs. 15,16
John Slaughter	----Gunfighter, sheriff, and neighbor	Chs. 31,32
José and Salomé Adame	----Caretaker of the El Paso House	Ch. 11
José Gallego (Don José)	----Manager of Hacienda Oriental, Angélica's husband	Throughout
Joséph Baker Castro	----Mother's older brother	Chs. 18,19,32
Juan González	----Son of Pedro Gonzáles, playmate, manager of Estancia del Pérez de Colorado, and Dulce's husband	Throughout
Juanita Celaya	----Mother's friend and Olga's mother	Throughout
Juanita García	----Niñera (nanny) of María Castro and children	Throughout
Juh	----Chief of the Janeros group of the Ndendai band of the Chiricahua Apache	Throughout
Juliana Honeywell	----Macama (maid), wife of Edward	Throughout
Kit Carson	----Mountain man, explorer, and soldier	Prologue
Loco (Jlin-tay-i-tith)	----Chief of the Copper Mines Chihenne	Throughout

Lord William Baker	----Board member of the British Beef Producers and Shipping Corporation, Mother's cousin	Chs.32,33
Lozen	----Sister of Victorio, a skilled warrior, prophetess, Victorio's strategist	Throughout
Mahlon Pitney	----Classmate of Francisco at Princeton, lawyer for the Estancia, Supreme Court Justice	Chs. 11,14
Mangas Coloradas	----Principle chief of the Mimbreno	Prologue
Manuel Celaya	----Olga's father	Chs. 11,12,23
Manuel García	----Cook at Hacienda De Occidental	Chs. 7,8,9,23
María Aguilar Baker	----Wife of Joséph Baker	Ch. 32
María Gallegos	----Wife of Salvador Honeywell	Chs. 25,27,33
María Gallegos	----Mother-in-law to Salvador Honeywell, wife of Jesus Gallegos	Chs. 25,27
María Gómez	----Mother's personal maid	Chs. 6, 30
María Elizabeth Guzmán	----Daughter of Corporal and Saguaro Blossom	Ch. 29
María Hundhausen	----Classmate of Elizabeth, secretary, and office manager of Crossed Arrows Mining Corporation	Chs. 32,33
María White	----Daughter of Benjamin	Ch. 21
María Salomé Yanez	----Wife of Mario Cortez (called Salomé)	Chs. 30,34
Mario Cortez	----English-speaking vaquero, Corporal's assistant	Throughout
Martin Smith	----Foreman of Hacienda Colorado	Chs. 29,33
Mary Beth Machen	----Roberto's wife	Throughout
Mary (María) Elizabeth	----Wife of Gregorio, Mother of Francisco Pérez Prologue, Baker Castro	Throughout

Ramón Pérez Celaya	----Fourth son of Francisco and Olga Pérez	Ch. 35
Rosa Honeywell	----Youngest child of Edward and Juliana	Throughout
Running Bear	----Top foreman of Hacienda Oriental	Throughout
Salvador Honeywell	----Son of Edward, spy at Big Nose Kate's,	Throughout
Samuel Schutz	----Owner of the mercantile in El Paso	Chs. 11,16
Sargento Primero Guzmán	----Gregorio's Sergeant Major	Throughout
Saguaro Blossom	----Apache wife of Corporal	Throughout
Silas Leven	----Lawyer in Walsenburg, Colorado	Throughout
Singing Brook	----Apache wife of He Who Hunts	Throughout
Sir Percy Baker	----Same as Lord Baker	Chs. 32,33
Tall Runner	----A watcher and El Tigre's cousin	Throughout
Virgil Earp	----Marshall of Tombstone	Ch. 20
Victorio (Bibu-ya)	----Chief of the Warm Springs band of the Chihenne (Mimbreño) Apache	Throughout
Walter Vail	----Owner of the Empire Ranch	Throughout
Wyatt Earp	----Deputy Marshall of Tombstone and later a U. S. Marshall	Ch. 20
Woodrow Wilson (Woody)	----Classmate of Francisco Pérez, President of Princeton	Throughout